MH

M

"Prescott is a master at the thriller genre . . . unexpected twists that will leave the reader breathlessly turning pages well into the night. Make sure the door is locked and the curtains are drawn before you start reading. You won't want to put down this one."   —The Romance Readers Connection

"Stunning. . . . In Abby and Tess, Prescott has created two of the fiercest and most commanding heroines to come along in a while, especially Abby, whose borderline control is as compelling as it is convincing. And by putting these women on opposite sides of the law, he creates a daring dynamic that is simply fascinating . . . highly recommended."
                    —New Mystery Reader Magazine

Dangerous Games

"Seamless prose, gripping drama, and a blockbuster conclusion."   —*The Daily Oklahoman*

"[A] psychologically complex thriller. . . . Prescott's tightly wound plot keep[s] the reader hooked and guessing."
                    —*Publishers Weekly*

"Nobody ratchets up the suspense like Prescott." —SF Site

In Dark Places

"A fascinating suspense novel . . . gripping."
                    —*Cemetery Dance*

"Fans of psychological thrillers can never go wrong with . . . Prescott. He throws in a twist that knocks you sideways . . . thoroughly absorbing."   —Roundtable Reviews

"Those who prefer thrillers packed with psychological complexity, truly demented characters, and nonstop, unexpected plot twists will enjoy this terrifying treat. The suspense doesn't let up until the last page, and even then, readers will continue to speculate. . . . Without a doubt, this dark, compulsive read messes with your mind and makes you love it."
                    —*Publishers Weekly*

continued . . .

The Shadow Hunter

"So convincing . . . weave[s] brilliant elements of psychological horror into the standard hunter-and-hunted story."
—*Publishers Weekly*

"A thriller that gives new meaning to the word, *The Shadow Hunter* expands the parameters and adds a new dimension to the genre. . . . The fast-paced plot twists and turns like an out-of-control roller coaster, making the read irresistible, un-put-downable, and absolutely not a book you want to start late at night—not if you have to work the next morning. . . . A great protagonist . . . she certainly gained my admiration and inspired the hope that I will get to meet her again in another book."   —Crescent Blues

"Readers looking for a good scare should give Michael Prescott a try. . . . Horror on the dark realism side and it's definitely terrifying. Prescott knows what he is doing."
—SF Site

Comes the Dark

"Michael Prescott delivers a harrowing thriller of the first order. His characters are flesh-and-blood real, the atmosphere's intense, and the plot races along unceasingly."
—*New York Times* bestselling author Jeffery Deaver

"Prescott effectively captures the pain experienced by his characters and how it leads them to terrifying acts of desperation."   —*Publishers Weekly*

"A first-class thriller. . . . Prescott's smooth writing propels readers . . . first-rate."   —*Arizona Daily Star*

FINAL SINS

Michael Prescott

AN ONYX BOOK

ONYX
Published by New American Library, a division of
Penguin Group (USA) Inc., 375 Hudson Street,
New York, New York 10014, USA
Penguin Group (Canada), 90 Eglinton Avenue East, Suite 700, Toronto,
Ontario M4P 2Y3, Canada (a division of Pearson Penguin Canada Inc.)
Penguin Books Ltd., 80 Strand, London WC2R 0RL, England
Penguin Ireland, 25 St. Stephen's Green, Dublin 2,
Ireland (a division of Penguin Books Ltd.)
Penguin Group (Australia), 250 Camberwell Road, Camberwell, Victoria 3124,
Australia (a division of Pearson Australia Group Pty. Ltd.)
Penguin Books India Pvt. Ltd., 11 Community Centre, Panchsheel Park,
New Delhi - 110 017, India
Penguin Group (NZ), 67 Apollo Drive, Mairangi Bay,
Auckland 1311, New Zealand (a division of Pearson New Zealand Ltd.)
Penguin Books (South Africa) (Pty.) Ltd., 24 Sturdee Avenue,
Rosebank, Johannesburg 2196, South Africa

Penguin Books Ltd., Registered Offices:
80 Strand, London WC2R 0RL, England

First published by Onyx, an imprint of New American Library,
a division of Penguin Group (USA) Inc.

First Printing, April 2007
10 9 8 7 6 5 4 3 2 1

Copyright © Douglas Borton, 2007
All rights reserved

PUBLISHER'S NOTE
This is a work of fiction. Names, characters, places, and incidents either are
the product of the author's imagination or are used fictitiously, and any resemblance to actual persons, living or dead, business establishments, events, or
locales is entirely coincidental.
    The publisher does not have any control over and does not assume any
responsibility for author or third-party Web sites or their content.

Anyone who rises in a world that worships success should be suspect, for this is an age of psychopathy.

—James Hillman, *The Soul's Code*

There were times, later, when she wondered if she could have done things differently and saved his life. If she had been smarter or more cautious, if she had been more *aware* . . .

Probably it wouldn't have made any difference. Probably he would still be dead. And it would still be her fault. Ultimately and inescapably, her fault.

She was unaccustomed to recrimination. She didn't like it. Didn't believe in beating herself up, or looking back in the vain hope that somehow the past would change, like the shifting scenery in a rearview mirror.

It was done, and she had done it, and that was that.

But if it was really over, why did she spend every night awake, moving from bed to sofa to armchair, holding books she didn't read and playing music she didn't hear? Why did she never sleep until dawn? Was she so afraid of the dark?

She never had been afraid of it in the past. She had loved and embraced the night, the shadows. Nighttime was when she worked, when she lived.

But that was before.

Now she was a different person. She caught herself doing things she never would have done in her old life. Fretting about slight aches and twinges. Reading religious books. Crying a lot—so much that she was constantly surprised there were more tears left in her, when she'd been sure she had cried herself dry. Sometimes she tried bargaining with God like a small child.

Please make it so it didn't happen. Please make it all right again.

It would never be all right again. She knew it. God knew it.

The days of being all right were over. They had ended, though she didn't suspect it at the time, at eleven thirty in the morning on Wednesday, May 2, when she'd entered a coffee shop on Sunset Boulevard.

She had come early. But really she was already too late.

I

Abby Sinclair checked the special compartment of her purse where she kept her .38 Smith & Wesson, the snub-nosed model. In an emergency she knew she could get her hand on the gun in less than one second, firing through the purse if necessary.

It was doubtful she would need any firepower today, but nine years on the job had taught her the value of the Boy Scouts' motto: Be prepared.

Not that she was paranoid or anything. Well, maybe a little. The thing was, the dumb old joke was true: Sometimes they really were out to get you.

Take this situation: meeting a stranger in an unfamiliar café in Hollywood. All she knew about him was that he was a prospective client, he'd asked her to meet him here at noon, and he had a foreign accent. Over the phone she hadn't been able to identify it. Something European. Swiss or German, maybe. Accents weren't exactly her area of expertise.

He'd given no name and no details. Caller ID said he had phoned from the 323 area code, which could mean Hollywood, West Hollywood, or nearby points. She'd tried looking up his address in an online reverse directory, but he wasn't listed.

He might be someone famous. He had sounded cultured, sophisticated. She almost thought she'd heard his voice somewhere.

Movie actor? Rutger Hauer could be hiring her. That would be cool.

Or maybe the accent was fake, a way to disguise his voice. She might have met him before. Not as a client, but as a target.

It was just possible that the caller was setting her up. She'd made enemies over the years. Many of them were still in jail, but some were out. Although she had covered her tracks as thoroughly as possible, there was always a chance that one of them had identified her and tracked her down.

The voice on the phone hadn't sounded like anyone she'd put away, but she'd worked enough cases that she could no longer remember them all. And it would take only one man with a grudge to put a serious crimp in her afternoon.

So, yeah, she was being paranoid. And she made no apologies for it. Keeping her head securely attached to her shoulders was priority number one. She would have a hard time earning a living if she were dead.

Her first precaution was to get to the café ahead of time. The caller had said noon, so she was here at eleven thirty. She wanted time to suss out the place, get her bearings, and choose an advantageous table.

Of course, he might have anticipated this ploy and arrived even earlier. He might already be inside, watching the entrance. She attended to that possibility by pretending to window-shop the boutique next door until a small crowd of teenagers entered the café. She followed them, using the group as cover. As they moved into the room in search of seats, she drifted away and faded into a dim alcove that led to a unisex bathroom.

The alcove gave her a clear view of the coffee shop. It was crowded, and some kind of ugly noise was banging over the big speakers scattered throughout the room. Thrash metal or black metal or death metal—one of the countless variants on heavy metal music, anyway. It all sounded like howls and growls to her. She liked soft jazz and light classical pieces. Somehow, inexplicably, she'd outgrown her taste for rock 'n' roll, despite having sworn that this would never happen.

The music, such as it was, should have made it harder for her to concentrate, but she was accustomed to noise and distraction. She'd spent a lot of time in nightclubs and other cacophonous dives where conversation was carried out via hand signals and lipreading. This place was almost sedate by comparison.

It didn't quite live up to its name, though: Café Eden. She didn't think Eden had been this noisy. And Adam and Eve sure hadn't looked anything like Eden's clientele. Most of them were young, but here and there she saw a few of those balding ponytailed men who were in perpetual denial of middle age. Males outnumbered females, though it was hard to tell because their clothing and hairstyles were mostly identical. Metal wasn't only in the air; it bedecked the customers in the form of nose rings, chin piercings, tongue studs, bracelets, anklets, and heavy chains. There was a lot of leather.

So what exactly was this, an S and M café? *Would you like a little bondage with your latte? A half-caf cappuccino and handcuffs?*

Abby wasn't easily creeped out, but she'd never related to the idea of torture as a sexual stimulus. It seemed to her that if two people needed to hurt each other to show their affection, maybe their relationship was in need of a professional tune-up. She knew a little about that, having taken a master's degree in psychology more years ago than she cared to acknowledge.

These folks, though, didn't look like hard-core bondage types. More like poseurs, wannabes—though why anyone would want to be mistaken for a shackles-and-whips enthusiast was beyond her. Then again, she didn't get why people dressed their dogs in sweaters or ate rice cakes or collected porcelain frogs. Some aspects of human nature were just plain mysterious.

She was quite sure the man who'd spoken to her on

the phone was no kid. If he was here, he would be one
of the few older men. None of them looked familiar.
Nor did any of them look dangerous, in spite of their
efforts to dress the part.

Abby took her time memorizing the layout of the
room, then found a corner table with a view of the front
door. She sat with her back to the wall. Her purse was
on her lap, her hand on the clasp.

A waitress wearing various steel doodads on her otherwise attractive face asked for her order. Abby requested
coffee—nothing fancy, not a triple-caf mocha-cherry cappuccino with extra foam and cinnamon sprinkles. Just coffee. Ordinarily she would have specified decaf, since
caffeine made her jittery, and jumpiness was not an asset
in her line of work. Today it didn't matter. She wasn't
going to drink the coffee anyway. It was a prop, an excuse to occupy the table.

The coffee arrived. She let it steam in front of her.
Through the steam, she watched the door. The time was
nearly noon. She wondered if her mystery man would
be punctual.

He was. The door opened, and a man walked in. Not
a boy, like most of the members of the male persuasion
already inhabiting the café. This was unmistakably and
unarguably a man—a dangerous man, dangerous in a
way that the poseurs in leather and chains could never
match.

He stood in the doorway, limned by daylight, his features difficult to make out.

He had said he would know her. *You have been described to me,* he said, *by a mutual acquaintance.* She
hadn't asked who the acquaintance was. She never did.
Most of her clients came to her via recommendations
from previous customers, whose names were not to be
mentioned.

If she had been described accurately, then he would
be looking for a woman of thirty-five, of medium height,
her dark brown hair cut in a pageboy. He did not move,

but somehow she knew that his eyes were tracking horizontally across his visual field, scanning the room with slow precision. He saw her and started forward.

As he advanced, a second figure took shape behind him. A woman. Slender, almost too thin. His spindly shadow.

Neither of them showed any weapons. Abby read no threat in their body language. But she didn't take her hand off her purse.

The man arrived at the table. He leaned forward, bending at the waist in a move so elegant it was nearly a bow. And she saw his face.

Just as he introduced himself, she knew.

"Good afternoon, Miss Sinclair. I am Peter Faust."

Abby pushed back her chair and stood. Her voice was toneless and firm.

"This interview is over."

She started to walk away. Faust's voice stopped her.

"Now, that seems hardly fair."

She looked back. Faust was regarding her with what she might almost describe as a merry twinkle in his eyes.

"What would have been fair," she said, "is if you'd told me your name right off the bat. Then you wouldn't have wasted my time."

"I am prepared to pay you handsomely for your services."

"I'm not working for you."

"And why, pray tell, is that?"

She stared at him. Did he really say *pray tell*?

She'd seen Peter Faust before, of course. Never in person, but in photographs and video clips. He was famous, a celebrity. It was a measure of the sickness of today's world that a man like him could qualify, in his own way, as a star.

"You know why," she said. "Just like you knew I would hang up on you if you identified yourself on the phone."

His eyelids dropped briefly in the equivalent of a nod,

hooding his pale blue eyes. "I did suspect as much. And yet perhaps you would have come anyway. If only to satisfy your curiosity."

"That's what sideshow tents are for."

"You are most amusing."

"You're not."

They stood facing each other. She was conscious of the adrenaline stiffening her body, the clenched-fist fury that threatened to lash out. Faust, by contrast, seemed utterly composed. He might have been posing for a portrait, striking the casual stance of a bon vivant. Behind him, the too-slender woman stood watching the scene, her face unreadable.

"It is your rigid attachment to your ethics that I find humorous," Faust said. "You dislike me because I am a criminal. But so are you."

Abby felt red heat in her face. "You don't know anything about me."

"I know that you routinely violate the law in order to serve your clients' interests. Deny it if you can."

She couldn't deny it, so she took a different tack. "Breaking the law is one thing. Murder is something else."

"Have you never used force against another human being?"

"In self-defense."

"Perhaps you have even killed a man, hmm?"

"Don't try to lower me to your level." But he already had, if only by goading her into a debate.

"I merely make the obvious point. What is the saying? Residents of glass houses should not throw stones?"

She turned away. "Go to hell."

"An uninspired riposte."

She fixed him with her stare. "Eat shit and die. Is that inspired enough?"

Without waiting for a response, she walked away, heading for the door. Her usual good humor had deserted her. She felt the urge to punish, to—

To kill, she half acknowledged, hating the admission because it seemed to confirm what he'd said.

She was pushing open the café door when she felt a hand on her arm.

"Abby?"

A woman's voice. Faust's companion. Black hair, doe eyes, skeletal arms with knobby joints. Abby thought of the Little Match Girl in the Hans Christian Andersen story.

She almost pulled free, but there was something so waiflike and helpless about the girl that she couldn't simply ignore her.

"What is it?" she said coldly.

"I can understand why you're upset. Why you don't want Peter as a client."

"If you really understood, you wouldn't be hanging with him."

"He's not what you think."

"Yes, he is. He's exactly what I think."

"People don't know him."

"Look, I'm as big a fan of self-delusion as the next person. A lot of times it's all that gets me through the day. But you've got to draw the line somewhere. Making excuses for a man like Faust—well, it's just not smart."

"Peter doesn't have anything to do with this."

"He's the one who called me."

"On my behalf."

"What are you, exactly? His girlfriend? Or just one of his groupies?"

The girl drew herself up, straining for dignity. She must have been all of twenty years old. Her rail-thin body made her look younger. "I've been with Peter for three years. It's very serious, what we have. Very special."

Very special. Abby closed her eyes. "You must have a death wish."

"I don't. That's why I need your help. Please. Just give us a chance to explain."

Abby looked past her and saw Faust watching from the corner table, a knowing smirk on his patrician features.

"You're crazy to be with him," she said slowly. "He's a killer."

The woman bit her lip, her eyes huge in her drawn face. "He's not the one I'm worried about right now."

2

Abby wasn't happy about it, but she returned to the table. Faust, she noted, had taken her seat. Apparently, like her, he preferred to have a clear view of the door.

She sat opposite him and pulled her coffee cup toward her. She still didn't intend to drink it, but she wanted something to hold, and she didn't need to keep her hand on her purse any longer.

"I'm gratified you elected to rejoin us," Faust said. Those ice blue eyes were twinkling again. She wondered how her eyes—light brown and coolly serious—looked to him.

"I haven't made any final decision." She wrapped her hands around the mug, needing its warmth to counteract the chill of his presence. "But I'm willing to listen."

"We ask nothing more."

The waitress came by, and Faust ordered elaborate coffees for himself and his girlfriend. It was obvious he was a regular. The waitress even showed him a smile, revealing braces on her teeth that seemed to complement the studs drilled into her face. Abby wondered how she ever got through a metal detector at the airport.

When she was gone, Faust leaned forward, resting one arm on the table in a pose that seemed, paradoxically, both calculated and casual.

Abby took a moment to study him, and he waited, aware of her scrutiny and unfazed by it. He was in his midforties. His dark close-shorn hair was gray at the temples, but his clean-shaven face was unlined. Even so, there was nothing boyish about him, no roundness or smoothness anywhere. His features were sharp, his mouth a bloodless line, razor thin and ruler straight. He wore a black turtleneck that emphasized his long neck and well-defined trapezius muscles. His hands were bony and long fingered, the hands of a pianist, deft, flexible, and strong.

As far as she knew, he did not play the piano. He preferred other instruments. The branding iron. The leather strap.

"Moments ago," Faust said, "you compared me to a freak in a sideshow. This comparison, I hope you will admit, was most unfair."

"Yeah. To the freaks."

Faust laughed, a surprisingly hearty sound.

Abby didn't care for that laugh. It had too much merriment in it.

"By the way," she added, "that's the second time you've brought up the issue of fairness. Not exactly playing to your strength, are you?"

"It is your strength I play to, not my own."

"You think you can get me to work for you by appealing to justice and fair play?"

"Something like that."

"Justice, in my book, would mean putting you away for life. Not in a nice, cozy mental hospital, either. In a prison with sexually adventurous cellmates and guards who look the other way."

Faust tilted his head back, allowing him to look down at her in an attitude of dominance, or perhaps simple arrogance. "And even this would not be justice, would it? A life for a life, that is justice. I should pay for my transgression with my very existence. I should die."

"I'm not arguing."

"You would perhaps be willing to administer the lethal injection yourself."

Her voice, always throaty, dropped to a huskier tone. "Gladly."

"You would punch the needle into my skin with a smile."

"That's right, Peter. I would." She showed him a smile to prove it.

He smiled back—white teeth, feral against thin, pale lips. "So you see, we are not so very different from each other."

Abby realized she had been led into a verbal trap. "There's a difference between taking an innocent life—"

"And do you decide who is innocent? Who lives and who dies?"

She wasn't used to being put on the defensive in a conversation. In this case there was no good answer. Say yes, and she had placed herself above the law. Say no, and she must bow to the law—and in the eyes of the law, Peter Faust was a free man.

"I decide who I'm going to work for," she said after a moment's hesitation, "and who I'm not. Right now, you and your main squeeze are in the second category."

"Main squeeze?" Faust was unfamiliar with the expression.

"Your honey, your Kewpie doll, your death groupie. 'Squeaky' Fromme over here."

It was the girl's turn to look puzzled. Lynette "Squeaky" Fromme, a member of the Manson clan, had been before her time.

Faust understood the reference. For the first time, he looked displeased. She saw his Adam's apple jerk, a common response to stress. The Adam's apple, its muscles mediated by the vagus nerve, often served as an indicator of emotional changes.

"You should not compare me with him," Faust said.

Manson, he must mean. "With Charlie? Why not? You two have loads in common. Admittedly, you're better dressed, and you do a better job of hiding your craziness—"

"There is nothing to hide. Mr. Manson is insane, just as you say. And his followers and admirers—there are some, even now—are sadly deluded. They have given over their lives to a madman. They are lost children."

"While *your* followers, on the other hand, are models of mental health."

"I have no followers."

"Your fans, then."

"Fans. I abhor the word."

"You're a celebrity, whether you like it or not."

"Fame means nothing to me. I have no need of it, no desire for it. I am indifferent to such things. I have never sought a following. Those who admire me are drawn to my truth."

"I don't think you and truth go together real well."

"There you are wrong. I do know truths, and I speak them. And others—a few enlightened souls—hear what I say."

"What do they hear?"

"That modern life is a lie. Our deepest, most primal instincts are denied. We are cut off, alienated, from our animal selves. For we are animals, you see, and little more. The Romans knew it when they crowded into the Circus Maximus to see weaklings torn limb from limb for an afternoon's amusement. They knew it when they pinned their vanquished foes to crosses that lined the Via Appia, each sacrificial victim squirming in exquisite pain like a bug on a pin. Think what a spectacle it must have made."

"Yeah," Abby said. "Good times."

"Indeed they were. The old pagan ways were incontestably superior to the thin gruel of love-thy-neighbor. The ancients were ahead of their time. They were Darwinists two thousand years in advance of the *Beagle*'s voyage. They understood nature, red in tooth and claw. They admired power. They did not flinch from inflicting pain. They did not avert their eyes from cruelty. They reveled in it."

"Like you."

He nodded. "I am a throwback, if you will. Or perhaps a bridge to the new age to come."

"You're looking more like Manson every minute."

"Only to one who cannot see. I am no madman. I am, perhaps, a visionary." His eyes narrowed. "An artist," he added in a lower voice.

His change of tone and expression made her wary. She wondered if he was serious or just shining her on.

"What is art," he continued softly, "but reassembling reality on our own terms? All creativity consists of the manipulation of things in the world to create new combinations, new arrangements."

"Things, not people."

"People, things . . ." He shrugged, and in his sublime indifference she knew she was facing a pure sociopath. "To take the elements around us and remodel them along the lines of our thought, our will. I took a living human being and made it a corpse." Abby noted the word *it*. "In so doing, I re-created the world."

"You didn't create anything. You destroyed—"

"Destruction and creation are the two faces of Janus. There is not one without the other."

"Tell that to Emily Wallace."

His nostrils flared, a sign of arousal. "I did—before I killed her."

"Tell it to her family."

"I have. They didn't listen."

"Neither will I." She started to get up.

His arousal had told her everything about him that she needed to know. He was a typical anger-excitation sadist. For all his superficial polish, he was really no better than any back-alley rapist.

"A man has been stalking Elise," Faust said, with a nod toward his companion. "I believe he means her harm."

Abby hesitated, then resumed her seat, knowing that Faust was playing her—and ordinarily she was not the type to be played.

"Give me the details," she said.

Faust complied. He and his girlfriend, Elise Vangarten, had first spotted the man at Café Eden ten days ago. They had assumed he was a fan, a "lookie-loo," as Elise put it. Abby thought the expression was appropriate. Lookie-loos were bystanders at crime scenes and accidents, drawn by morbid curiosity.

When the man began appearing at other locations, Faust pegged him as a stalker. Two nights ago he shadowed Elise through a Century City parking garage. The experience left her rattled.

"So call the cops," Abby said.

Faust frowned. "The police will not assist me. They seem to regard me with distaste."

"Imagine that."

"I am a legal resident of this country. I am entitled to certain rights. But the authorities see me only as the Werewolf. That was my nickname in the tabloid press, you know." He sounded faintly proud of it.

"I remember." Abby's nose wrinkled in disgust.

"They cannot look past such labels and superficialities."

"It's hard to look past the murder of an innocent woman. How old was she? Early twenties? About Elise's age?"

She hoped to draw a reaction from the girl, but there was none.

Faust waved off the question with an airy flutter of his hand. "You in this country are so provincial. You cling to the simplistic morality of small-town burghers. Good versus evil, right and wrong. You are children who will not grow up."

"Thanks for the sociology lesson. I assume it was after the parking garage incident that you decided to try a private operative?"

"Operative." Faust pronounced the word slowly as if tasting it. "Yes."

"It's not like I advertise in the Yellow Pages. How'd

you find out about me?" This was a question she normally wouldn't ask, but she couldn't imagine which of her former clients would travel in Faust's circle.

"That is best left unstated."

"Is it? Why?"

"I was sworn to secrecy."

"So?" She tried turning his own logic against him. "Right and wrong are only childish concepts. Violating an oath must be okay."

"I have my own code of conduct. It is not imposed on me by deities or traditions. It is my choice, my will."

Logic hadn't worked. She tried begging. "Give me a hint, at least."

A smile played briefly at the corners of Faust's mouth. "It was someone in the law-enforcement field," he said finally.

Law enforcement. That was weird. Abby couldn't recall ever having had a client with a job in that line.

Of course, Faust might be putting her on. He didn't strike her as a guy who had a lot of connections with officers of the law.

"That doesn't help me too much," she said.

"It was not meant to."

She dropped the subject. "I assume your friend gave you some idea of how I conduct business."

"Indeed. You are a stalker of stalkers. You make them your prey."

She wasn't sure she cared for the word *prey*. "Let's just say I identify a stalker, infiltrate his life—"

"Determine his whereabouts," Faust said.

"And assess his threat potential. That's really the most important part."

"Yes, certainly," he added as if it were an afterthought.

"Tell me about the guy. What he looks like, where else you've seen him. That kind of thing. It's what the folks in the writing game call exposition—boring but necessary."

"He looks like anyone else. He's just a man."

"That description is less helpful than you may think. Nobody is just a man. Everybody has something distinctive about him."

"Not this man."

"Try harder. Short, tall, fat, thin, young, old . . . ?"

"Average height, average build, nondescript appearance."

"You're trying to make this as hard as possible, aren't you? How about hair color?"

"Brown."

"More blond than brown," Elise said.

"I would say brownish," Faust amended.

"Great. Is he Caucasian?"

Faust nodded. "Yes, this much I can say with certainty. He is Anglo."

"Well, that helps a little. But not much, because most stalkers are Anglos. As a pastime, stalking hasn't caught on in the minority community in a big way. Sort of like serial killing. But then," she added with a nod toward Faust, "I guess you would know about that."

"I am not a serial killer. I killed just once."

"Once that we know about. Ever miss it?"

"I beg your pardon."

"The thrill of the hunt, the taste of blood? Ever start jonesing for it?"

"I could ask you the same question, could I not?"

"You're a smooth one, Peter. I'll give you that. Eyes?"

"What?"

"Your stalker. Presumably he has eyes. What color are they?"

"I have not the slightest idea. I have never been that close to him."

"Elise, little help here. If he's after you, maybe you've gotten a better look."

The girl seemed reluctant to join in the conversation. No surprise. Anyone who was attracted to a man like

Faust would have low self-esteem and probably poor social skills. Elise might be intelligent enough, even creative in her way, but she would be overloaded with
chronic anxiety and fear.

"I've only seen him from a distance," Elise said, her
voice very low, "usually in places that are pretty dark."

"Okay, well, that takes us to our next question. Where
have you seen him, exactly, besides the parking garage
and this café?"

"All over."

"Narrow it down."

"He seems to know where I'll be. It's like he's there
waiting for me."

"He's *where* waiting for you?"

"All the places I go. Clothing stores, nightclubs, ad
shoots . . ."

"Elise is a model," Faust put in.

It made sense. She had the anorexic look favored by
the purveyors of designer jeans and overpriced perfume.

"He's been present when you're working?" Abby
asked. "In a photography studio?"

"No, in public. Last week we did a shoot on the beach
in Santa Monica and another one on Mulholland Drive.
People will stand around and watch. Both times he was
there in the crowd."

"He might be following you from home. Do you two
live together?"

Elise shook her head. "I have my own place. Need
my space, you know. Sometimes I leave from Peter's
house, sometimes from my condo, sometimes from
someplace else entirely. How can he always know where
I am? Is he following me twenty-four hours a day?"

"I doubt it." It was almost impossible for one person
to maintain around-the-clock surveillance.

"Since this started, I've been checking my rearview all
the time. I've never seen anyone behind me."

Abby felt a tingle of interest in the case. It was a
challenge. They had no idea where the man would turn

up next. No description. No details. The challenge appealed to her, even if the clients did not.

"Okay," she said, "maybe I'm barking up the wrong tree here. When was the last time you saw him?"

"Yesterday," Elise answered. "I went to the Farmer's Market, and he was there."

"You were alone?"

"At first I was. Peter joined me."

"How did Peter know where to find you?"

"I text-messaged him to let him know where I was going. He messaged back and said he'd meet me there for lunch."

She looked at Faust. "Where were you when you got the message?"

"At home."

"You got the message on your cell phone?"

"That's right."

"You do that a lot? Exchange text messages via cell?"

"Quite often, yes. In Europe this technology has been popular for some years." His eyes narrowed. "Have you stumbled across something, Miss Sinclair?"

I wouldn't call it stumbling, she thought irritably. "Maybe. These other occasions when the man has shown up . . . did you text-message each other beforehand?"

"Probably," Elise said. "I like to let Peter know where I am."

Abby looked at Faust. "And were you always home when you received the messages?"

"I suppose I was. I am a bit of a homebody, you see."

"When you called me to set up this appointment, did you use a landline or a cell?"

"Landline?" He didn't know the term.

"Your regular home phone."

"Oh, I see. Yes, I used the landline, as you say."

"And when you got my name from your friend in law enforcement?"

"Also the landline." He seemed to enjoy saying the word, as if it were a new toy.

"Glad to hear it. Don't say anything about me over the cell phone, okay? And don't call me on your cell, either of you, unless it's an emergency. How about when you arranged to meet here today? Did you use your cell phones to work out the details?"

"No. We spoke in person."

"That's good. If you had, he might be here. Which I assume he isn't."

Faust's gaze traveled around the room, performing an efficient visual check. "He is not."

Elise leaned forward. "You really think this guy is intercepting our phone calls?"

"He could be." It wasn't easy, though. Digital signals were difficult to intercept, and they were normally encrypted to ensure privacy. "May I see your phones, please?"

They handed them over. As she expected, the phones were recent models, state-of-the-art. Both were E911-capable, meaning they were equipped with a GPS chip that allowed the cellular service provider to pinpoint the phone's position within as little as five feet. Abby herself used an older phone without GPS. She could still be tracked via cell-tower triangulation, but not as precisely. She didn't want anyone knowing exactly where she was.

Cell phone voyeurism had declined markedly since the systems had gone digital. Nowadays it would take some highly expensive—and highly illegal—equipment to pick up the signal and decode it. If their stalker was using that method to keep tabs on them, he was no ordinary wacko.

"You may be up against somebody who's a little more dangerous than the average starstruck celebrity hunter," she said carefully.

Faust smiled. "I am glad to hear you say this."

"You are?"

"Yes. It means you are intrigued. Your blood is up. You are on the scent."

"I'm not a hound dog, Mr. Faust."

"More like a jungle cat, I think. Sleek and stealthy, camouflaged by your environment, blending with the night."

"How poetic."

"It is accurate, is it not?"

"It's not the wildlife analogy I would use. I'm more like a pilot fish. You know those little fish that swim in a shark's wake?" The metaphor, she realized, was too complicated to convey to someone who spoke English as a second language. "Never mind."

Faust was watching her, his blue eyes glittering. "You will take the assignment, will you not, Miss Sinclair?"

Abby hesitated. She despised Faust and didn't care if he lived or died. But there was Elise. Probably just a naive kid mixed up in something ugly and stupid. She was dumb, sure. But Abby couldn't hate her for that. Dumbness was a prerogative of youth.

Besides, she did like a challenge.

"Not for your sake," she said at last. "For hers."

"I am most gratified."

"That is, assuming you can meet my price."

"I do not imagine that will be a problem."

"No. I wouldn't think so. Does it bother you at all to be living the good life after you took Emily Wallace's life away?"

"I see no connection between the two issues."

"You wouldn't."

Faust shrugged. "Oranges and apples."

"Apples and oranges is the circumlocution you're aiming for."

"Ah. I appreciate the correction." His manner was almost courtly. "My English is not always idiomatic, as you see."

"You still speak better than a lot of Americans do."

"A compliment. You are warming to me, Miss Sinclair."

She resisted this, but there was some truth in it. He had a strange charisma, his Old World courtliness and patrician bearing, his preternatural calmness, his air of wealth and worldly sophistication.

"I'm not a good judge of people," she said curtly.

"This cannot be true. You would not have survived so long in your profession if it were so."

"Maybe I've just been lucky."

"The panther stalking her prey does not rely on luck."

"I'm a pilot fish, remember?"

"You are a wild thing on the hunt."

"Takes one to know one," she said softly.

"Indeed," Faust said. "Indeed it does."

3

Abby felt vaguely dirty after her meeting in the café. She had to remind herself that she'd never shaken Faust's hand, never actually touched him at all. Even so, she couldn't shake the sense that she needed a hot shower or, preferably, a nice long bath.

Ablutions would have to wait. She had work to do. Her first priority was to determine how the stalker was reading his quarry's text messages.

Intercepting cellular phone calls wasn't easy. In the old days when mobile phones used analog technology, a Radio Shack police scanner could pull in the signal. It was no more difficult than listening in on walkie-talkie transmissions.

Today's digital cell phone signals were encrypted with cipher streams to prevent electronic eavesdropping. Even a thirty-thousand-dollar digital scanner would be unable to decode encrypted data. If it did intercept the signal, all it would get was an electronic squeal, like the irritating noise made when a modem or a fax machine connected.

But there was one way to tap a mobile phone—an IMSI catcher. The acronym stood for International Mobile Subscriber Identity, the unique fifteen-digit number stored in the SIM card of every cell phone.

The basic principle behind an IMSI catcher was simple enough. Cell phones were constantly seeking alternative signals in order to obtain the clearest reception. If the phone detected a cell tower with a stronger signal than the one it was currently using, it would instantly switch over.

An IMSI catcher simulated a cell tower. It sent out a strong signal that fooled the cell phone, tricking it into routing the transmission through the IMSI catcher itself. In this way it could pick up all cellular calls in its vicinity.

Even better, the IMSI catcher sent a command to the phone that turned off encryption. The intercepted message could be heard or read in real time.

After the IMSI catcher had snatched the call, it would route the signal to its intended destination—sort of an electronic catch-and-release policy. Neither the cell phone user nor the phone company would be aware of the deception.

The key, as in real estate, was location, location, location. The IMSI catcher had to be stationed in relatively close proximity to the targeted cell phone. That way its signal would be recognized as the strongest in the vicinity.

Elise had typically been away from home when she text-messaged Faust. But Faust had consistently been at his house when he received the messages. Abby was betting the stalker lived in Faust's neighborhood.

Of course, there was a chance that the IMSI catcher was installed near Faust's house, while the stalker himself lived elsewhere, receiving the signal remotely. Abby doubted it, though. The equipment would have to be installed indoors, hardwired into the main current. If the stalker had gone to all the trouble to find a home for his gear, he was likely to be living there himself.

A transponder of that type typically had a range of three hundred yards. That meant the eavesdropper was situated within a nine-hundred-foot radius of Faust's home. Closer was better, naturally.

If he were a longtime neighbor, Faust probably would have seen him at some point. Angelenos, like most urbanites, weren't the chummiest people when it came to making friends with the folks next door, but it was nearly impossible not to notice your neighbor at all. Abby figured the stalker was a recent arrival.

Before she left the café, Faust had given her his address. He lived in one of the few fashionable neighborhoods of Hollywood, the Los Feliz district in the foothills just south of Griffith Park. She knew the territory. Mostly houses, few apartments. Any rentals that might be available would be either single-family homes or guest cottages. The limited supply of rentals made her next step obvious. She stopped at the library.

A month's worth of the Sunday *L.A. Times* had collected in the periodicals room. She started with the edition from three weeks ago, scanning the classifieds for real estate rentals. At that time, not long before the first stalking incident, there were five listings of interest in Faust's neighborhood.

By the next weekend, only four properties were listed. The fifth had disappeared. Someone had rented it. The time frame fit the start of Faust's surveillance.

No address was given, but there was a phone number, of course. With any luck it would be the number of the homeowner and not a management company. Abby used one of the library's computer terminals to access an online reverse directory she subscribed to. The service gave her an address on Glendower Avenue, only a few doors from Faust's place.

Now she just needed to confirm that the property had actually been rented and not taken off the market for some other reason. She called the number and inquired about the guest cottage, only to be told that it had been rented more than two weeks ago.

She rechecked the classified ad. The property was described as a guest cottage with its own kitchen. Fully furnished, featuring a wide-screen TV. Two thousand dollars a month.

The price would not have been a deterrent. Anyone with the funds to acquire an IMSI catcher could afford to live in the high-rent district. Electronic surveillance technology of that quality did not come cheap, and it wasn't sold on the open market. If Faust's stalker had gotten hold of it, he had money and connections.

Most stalkers were neither rich nor well connected. They were underachievers, drawn into their obsession as a way of compensating for failures and disappointments in the rest of their lives. This was particularly true of stalkers who fixated on celebrities. They seemed to hope that some of the glamour would rub off on them—that they could become one of the beautiful people, if only by proxy.

A well-heeled stalker, renting a luxury guesthouse and using elaborate eavesdropping gear, was something new. She liked it. Stuff like this made her job interesting. She was grateful to God for supplying her with a wide variety of crazies. It kept her from getting into a rut.

Then again, this guy might not be crazy at all.

She could think of reasons for stalking Peter Faust and Elise Vangarten that had nothing to do with an irrational fantasy life. Faust had killed a woman and had never been properly punished. Some people, like the victim's relatives, might resent him for that. It was conceivable that they had hired an assassin to take him out. Or maybe Elise's family, if she had any, wasn't too thrilled at her choice of life partner. They might have contracted with someone to put him away. Or suppose somebody had decided to kidnap Elise for ransom. Faust was wealthy, and as he himself had observed, he did not enjoy good relations with the local police. That made him an excellent target for an extortion plot.

Lots of possibilities, but few facts. What she needed was a refresher course in Faust's life story. If someone from his past was after him, it would help to know exactly what he had done to deserve it. She remembered the broad outline but not the details.

Ordinarily she would use the Internet to track down that info. Since she was already at the library, she decided to try it the old-fashioned way. It took her only a few minutes to locate the true-crime shelf. Naturally there were books on Faust, including one he'd written himself. In addition to his other accomplishments, he was an author—an internationally best-selling author, according to the cover of the paperback.

She didn't start with his memoirs, though. First she flipped through a hefty volume providing an overview of notorious criminals from A to Z. Under F, she got the gist of Faust's biography.

He was born in Bonn, Germany, in 1962, an only child, the son of upper-middle-class parents. His father was an economics professor, his mother a high-ranking bureaucrat in social services. He had an uneventful childhood and adolescence, marked only by pronounced unsociability and a single arrest, at age thirteen, for animal abuse. He had been caught using a hot fireplace poker on a neighbor's cat.

During his young adulthood he worked a variety of jobs, never holding any of them for more than a few months. He seemed to have artistic aspirations but was not known to have sold any artwork. He attracted a small band of followers who considered him a neglected genius. He had several affairs, all short-lived. One of his girlfriends went on to commit suicide; another was confined to a psychiatric hospital.

At age thirty-five, still drifting from one employment opportunity to another, he found himself in Hamburg, known as the Venice of Germany for its intricate system of canals and its bohemian cafés. It was there that he met, kidnapped, and killed Emily Wallace, an American civilian working at the U.S. military base in Wiesbaden, who was visiting Hamburg on leave, sightseeing with a friend.

Faust held Emily captive for three days in his apartment before killing her. He said later that he enjoyed postponing the actual "execution," as he called it. "I wanted to be sure the victim suffered well," he said.

Although he made efforts to dispose of the body and

cover his tracks, he was quickly arrested by the local
police after Emily's traveling companion reported her
disappearance. Someone had spotted him in the vicinity
of the salvage yard where the body, sans head and
hands, had been dumped. His description was circulated.
He was identified. What the police found in his apartment erased any possible doubt as to his guilt.

Faust never denied the crime. His parents obtained
expensive legal counsel who insisted that their client was
"psychologically abnormal" and suffering from "diminished responsibility." Astonishingly, the prosecution
agreed, merely requesting a slightly longer period of in-
stitutionalization. The trial lasted four days and ended
with a sentence of six years in a "secure psychiatric facility." Within three years he was released. There were
rumors that his parents, politically well connected, had
put pressure on the government to spring their son
from confinement.

The murder had taken place a decade ago. Faust had
been a free man for the past seven years, and had capitalized on his notoriety with the publication of his memoir even before his release. Once free, he had been
interviewed on many TV shows, had done book readings
and book signings in dozens of cities, and had been the
subject of two documentary films. A big-budget feature
film based on his life story had been in development
for some time, though the project had stalled for lack
of financing.

Emily Wallace's family had attempted to sue for dam-
ages, only to find that Faust's growing pile of money was
salted away in Swiss bank accounts, untouchable.

Faust now divided his time between Europe and
America. He had homes in Berlin and Los Angeles. He
went skiing in Saint Moritz and Aspen. He was dis-
turbingly popular in Europe, with a smaller but no less
loyal following in the U.S. Prominent death-metal bands
had written songs in his honor. The Goths, a major cul-
tural force in Germany, had adopted him as their unof-

ficial standard-bearer. Faust himself was cool to the Goths, saying of the movement, "It is a mélange of vulgar Nietzscheism and Dungeons & Dragons, dressed up in jackboots—a game for frightened children." These comments only endeared him further to his fans.

She turned to Faust's memoir. In chapter one, she found a firsthand description of the crime that had made him famous.

> *I would like to say that the murder itself was a fever dream, that I lived it in a haze of dazzled frenzy, that I knew not what I did. Then perhaps you would forgive me, and I could rejoin your most civilized company and dine in your elegant restaurants without drawing stares. I must, however, be honest. It is my one vice, honesty. I cannot bear deception. Or in saying this, am I only guilty of yet another deceit?*
>
> *No matter. This is the truth. Killing Emily Wallace was my great accomplishment, and I have no wish to report it inaccurately.*
>
> *I knew precisely what I did. I was in complete control of myself throughout. Indeed, I have never been so utterly sure of myself.*
>
> *I killed her with a leather noose. The world knows this. It was the subject of much discussion in the press, and even gifted me with an alliterative sobriquet, the Hangman of Hamburg. In the end, this name fell out of favor, as it should have—for I did not hang Emily. I eased the noose around her neck while she lay half-conscious, shackled to the radiator. I then began to draw it tight, slowly, my fingers electric with the texture of the leather, its suppleness and softness. Leather is tanned flesh— and how it rubbed against the downy skin of her neck, how it caressed her, gently at first, while she moaned, her eyelids fluttering, her body quivering.*
>
> *The bluenoses among you will never understand. They have allowed their natural bloodlust to ebb.*

They have smothered instinct under a blanket of homilies. They are eunuchs. Like all castrati, they will not be satisfied until the rest of humanity shares their affliction. Impotent themselves, they make their flaccidity a virtue, and paint virility as a vice.

Some of you are different. It is for you that I write. For you—and to you.

Can you feel it, the leather in your hands? The strap was thirty millimeters wide and one meter long. I pulled it tight enough to choke off breath. She came fully awake then. She tried to raise her hands, but they were fastened to the radiator. I let her struggle for air. Then I loosened the loop. She could breathe again. I heard the delicious gasp of her intake of air, a wet and hungry sound. When she had recovered her strength, I tightened the noose again.

There is a game some people play in which they bring themselves almost to asphyxiation in order to heighten the pleasurable intensity of orgasm. I have not played this game. But I had designed my own variation on it, as you see. In bringing Emily to the edge of death again and again, I was heightening my pleasure.

Please do not misunderstand me. I am not speaking of mere physical enjoyment. Some oaf, in the aftermath of my arrest, editorialized that I had taken a life for only a few seconds of gratification. In truth, sexual gratification was not my motive. These moldy Freudian fairy stories should be laid to rest. There is more to a man than genitalia. Was I erect when I drew the noose taut? Doubtless, I was, but I scarcely noticed. Erections are not so precious to me, or so rare. My attention was focused on higher things. In those final minutes, as I played out the endgame, I experienced what I can only call transcendence. I was lifted up, possibly to the third heaven of which Saint Paul writes. I was trans-

*ported, liberated. Sex is a mere flicker of sensation
in comparison to what I felt and knew. I was more
than a man, or perhaps I should say that I was the
only true man, the sole man on earth who was at
one with his deepest needs and highest passions.
Killing Emily Wallace was a religious experience in
the truest sense.*

*I cannot say how long our liaison lasted. Time
had stopped, or, more precisely, it ran on but I had
stepped out of its stream, had ceased to be conducted by its flow.*

*Some have speculated that I did not mean to kill
Emily, that I misjudged, made the noose too tight
for too long, broke my toy by playing with it too
lustily. This is incorrect. As I have already written,
I was in control throughout the exercise.*

*I drew the noose tight for the last time, grasping
her chin and raising her head to face me. She saw
my smile—it must have been radiant—and she knew
that there would be no coming back. She did not
resist or pull away, but I saw a tear, pearlescent and
perfect, expand in the corner of her left eye.*

*I knew the exact instant when she died. It was
when the teardrop shimmered and broke free of the
eye that cupped it, tracking down her cheek. The
tear moved, but she did not.*

Abby put down the book slowly. This was the man
she was working for.

Well, at least she hadn't shaken his hand.

4

Peter Faust sat limply in his chair at Café Eden, his every muscle relaxed. It was a trick he had mastered long ago, the art of complete ease.

"That went well," he said with satisfaction.

Elise shifted restlessly. She was always moving about, incapable of relaxation. Like most Americans, she had never been schooled in leisure.

"I don't know," she said, biting her lip. "There's something about her I don't like. She scares me."

"Everything scares you."

Elise shot him a darting look, half-timid, half-sly. "*You* don't."

"And yet I am the one thing you ought to fear."

"Do you think *she's* scared of you?"

Faust considered the question. "Yes," he decided. "But she enjoys the sensation. She thrives on fear. It is mother's milk to her."

"She looked at me like I was . . . I don't know."

"Like you were what?"

"A stupid kid. Like I was ten years old. She feels sorry for me. That's why she took the job. Out of pity."

"And if this is true, what of it?"

"I just don't think she should have looked at me that way."

"It is of no importance how she feels. If you can use her feelings to your advantage, do so."

"Easy for you to say. You don't give a shit what other people think."

He patted her hand sedately. "I am not convinced that other people *do* think."

Not for the first time, Faust asked himself if he loved Elise Vangarten. He could not say. Love, to him, was only a word, like *God* or *virtue,* a sound ritually repeated and apparently invested with meaning by his fellow humans, but denoting nothing to him. Still, he had grown attached to her.

Three years ago they had met at a cocktail party hosted by a rising young movie director known for his outré tastes. Faust had provided some uncredited but handsomely remunerated technical assistance on the director's last film, a study in serial murder. For the most part, Faust generally got along famously with Hollywood people—they were so refreshingly amoral—and so he had accepted an invitation to the soiree.

Elise, then nineteen and new to L.A., had come on the arm of an independent producer who was endeavoring to conceal his homosexuality. Faust met her at the buffet table. She did not know who he was. Even when he introduced himself, she failed to recognize his name. He found her ignorance beguiling. And he was intrigued by her gauntness, the bony outlines of her undernourished figure, the hollows of her cheeks. She might have been a concentration camp survivor.

At the buffet table she snacked on celery, a food that consumed more calories in digestion than it supplied. A person who dined exclusively on celery would starve to death. Faust was fascinated by her iron self-denial. Wasting away and confronted with heaping platters of cold meats and frosted pastries, she nevertheless chose the celery. It was as if she had no will to live.

He easily coaxed her away from her faux boyfriend. That very night they made love in his house. Her body was as lean and sinewy and flat-chested as a boy's. It delighted him. And she was so young. He had always appreciated youth. He himself had felt old even in

childhood—*an old soul,* his teachers had called him. He
had missed out on the pleasures of youth, but he could
enjoy them vicariously.

Faust knew the exact moment when Elise became his
soul mate. It was when he showed her a documentary
film about his life. When it was over, she asked only,
"Did you look into her eyes when you were killing her?"
She was unafraid. She simply wanted to know. She had
the earnest, uncomplicated curiosity of a child.

They rarely spoke of Emily Wallace. He was not sure
if Elise believed that the murder was a singular episode,
some breakdown in his normal habits of control, or if
she believed him to be capable of repeating the performance at any time. The remarkable thing was that she
did not seem to care. She accepted him completely. Perhaps this was love. Whatever it might be, he had found
he needed her, and he would not lose her. He would
not allow her to be endangered. No human life mattered
to him, save hers.

Familiar voices broke into his thoughts. At the café,
he and Elise were always running into people they knew.
This time it was Edward and Dieter, both of whom
worked in the fashion industry—Edward as a hairstylist,
Dieter in set design. They had met Faust through Elise
and had quickly become attached to him. Perhaps overly
attached. Faust found their adoration tiresome. But Elise
liked them, and he tolerated their company for her sake.

They sat at the table, Dieter garrulous and voluble
as always, Edward characteristically reserved. Both were
Americans; Dieter's name was an affectation no less artificial than his bleached blond hair. Since meeting Faust,
they had both somehow managed to acquire traces of his
accent, as if they were remaking themselves in his image.

Dieter joked that they simply must stop meeting like
this. It was like that awful American sitcom where sex-
crazed, aimless young people sat around at a coffee bar.

"Only we're not like that," Edward added.

"No," Faust observed, "we are not young."

This observation was greeted with laughter. Faust was much admired for his wit.

Dieter had picked up a religious booklet somewhere and was having fun with it. He was amused by anything he considered mundane and common—religion, television, sports, fast food, backyard barbecues, holidays, the obituary pages. Edward shared his contempt but not his humor. Elise encouraged them in their talk, while Faust leaned back, taking his ease in aloof splendor. He did not speak for a long time, but when he did, the others fell silent immediately. There was a magnetism he exuded that drew them closer, as if he were a fire and they sought to huddle around his heat.

"We had a companion at our table before you arrived. A business associate. She does not approve of me."

"Who does?" Dieter ventured, earning a laugh from Elise and a disapproving shake of Edward's head.

"She was appalled by my criminal past. The taking of an innocent life."

"No one is innocent," Edward said soberly.

"Quite true, in which case it follows that no one is guilty, either."

"There is no guilt or innocence. There is only this." Edward rapped the table with his fist. "What is real, what is immediate. Nothing else."

"I declined to engage her in such metaphysical speculations." Faust smiled. "You know these Americans— they have no head for philosophy."

"What *did* you tell this cunt?" Dieter asked.

"That I am an artist."

Smiles bloomed around the table.

"An artist?" Dieter arched an eyebrow. "I don't remember hearing that one before."

"I am sure I made reference to it somewhere in my book."

"Who remembers your book?" Dieter laughed, but no

one joined him. A line had been crossed. "Only joking, of course," he amended hastily.

Faust showed him a cold smile. "Of course. There are times when it is helpful to portray myself in an artistic light. I have taken this approach in some of my interviews with the media."

"But you don't suffer for your art," Elise teased.

"He makes others suffer!" Dieter said, to be rewarded by a warmer smile from Faust.

"You see," Faust said, "it can be inconvenient to have people regard me as an enigma. People need explanations. Explanations comfort them."

"Was this bitch comforted when you said you were an artist?" Edward asked.

"I think so, yes. She feels now that she understands me, at least to a certain degree. What she understands, she can tolerate. It is only an insoluble mystery that is unbearable."

"You *could* have been an artist," Elise said.

"I could have been anything. Instead I am . . . everything." Faust sipped his coffee while the others pondered this statement.

"Hitler was an artist," Edward said finally.

Faust frowned. "Herr Schicklgruber," he said, using Hitler's family name, "was a gauche little man with a loud voice. Nothing is so annoying as a tiny man who commands a big spotlight."

"And he was a shitty artist, anyway," Dieter observed.

"Even if he were a genius," Faust said, "do you think anyone in today's world would be fearless enough to admit it?"

Elise patted his arm. "*You* would."

"Yes, I am the man without fear." The others could not tell if this was a joke. Smiles flickered uncertainly on their faces. "As a child, I did feel fear at times, and I hated it. Hated myself for that weakness. Then one night I learned never to feel fear again."

"One can't just talk oneself out of fear." Edward spoke with the certainty of a man to whom fear was an intimate and constant companion.

"It was much more than talk," Faust said slowly. He shifted into what he thought of as his storytelling voice, languid and rhythmic, almost hypnotizing. "When I was ten years old, I vacationed with my parents in the Black Forest."

All of them had heard the tale in one of his numerous interviews, or read it in his book, but they listened anyway, attentive as schoolchildren.

"We rented a cabin in the woods. One evening when my parents were asleep, I crept outside, alone, to see the night sky. There was a full moon. In the moonlight I saw a silver shadow among the trees, creeping nearer. It was a wolf, wild and solitary.

"When I recognized it for what it was, I felt a rush of fear. My childish head was filled with stories of evil wolves, like the one who devoured Red Riding Hood's grandmother. I was sure I would be eaten alive. My one hope was to race for the cabin. But I could not move. I was frozen in place, a statue of a boy.

"The wolf moved closer. His eyes gleamed. I gazed into those eyes. And suddenly I was unafraid.

"All concern for my safety vanished. I was certain that the wolf would not harm me. I knew this—because he and I were one. At some deep, unfathomable level we shared the same spirit. We were of a single will, a single heart. We were, both of us, wolves. Wild things of the night. And neither of us knew fear. Fear is not the predator's way. And that is what I am, a predator. I knew it then, for the first time. I watched the wolf until he turned and prowled away. Then I crept back to my bed. But I was not the same child I had been. And I have never felt fear again."

"That must be something," Dieter said wistfully.

"It is a state of mind available to any of you. All that is necessary is to realize that fear and ecstasy are the same emotion, the same chemical broth. It is only our lying conscious mind that stigmatizes the one and celebrates the other. Fear is a ruse, like guilt or shame, a manufactured feeling. In its pure state, fear is exhilaration. One must make up one's mind never to be tricked into regarding any emotion as negative. There are no negative states of mind, except those arbitrarily defined as such by social convention."

"Defined—for what purpose?" Edward asked.

"Control. What else? Fear keeps them in line—the little people, the burghers and hausfraus, the common ones. Fear and guilt, shame and pity are the levers of social control. I let no one pull my levers."

"You should have said as much to that bitch," Dieter muttered, "rather than feeding her some bullshit about art."

"She would not have understood. And even if she had, I would not care for her to know me so well. One's soul need not be bared before strangers."

The word *soul* startled them, though he had intended it only figuratively.

"I didn't know you were religious," Dieter said with a grin.

"Now you have insulted me," Faust replied with mock indignation. "God, you know, is the root of fear and guilt and shame. The root cause of all weakness and vice."

"And this is why you don't worship God?" Dieter asked.

"That—and pride." He tasted his coffee, taking pleasure in its bitterness. "If there were a God, I would require *him* to worship *me*."

"He really would," Elise seconded.

"I would, indeed," Faust agreed. "And why not? *He* may be the creator of the universe, but *I* am the destroyer of worlds."

"That's Shiva," Edward said, pedantic as always.

"It is I. I ended Emily Wallace's world, did I not?"

He received uncomfortable assents. Putting a name to his victim had abruptly made her too concrete, too real—not a symbol, but a person.

The human mind, Faust reflected, was a peculiar thing. It could countenance endless varieties of cruelty as long as they remained safely abstract. But show it cruelty in action, inflicted on flesh and blood, and—in some cases—the mind rebelled. The same person who calmly accepted a thousand earthquake fatalities in China would recoil at the sight of a kitten in pain. The dead Chinese were statistics. The kitten was real.

Within another hour the little group had run out of conversation. When Faust suggested it was time to part company, Edward and Dieter quickly assented. They left first, sticking Faust with the tab, as usual. Faust didn't mind. He rather enjoyed paying for them. It cemented his position of superiority and underlined their utter dependence.

He and Elise left together. He escorted her to her cherry red Infiniti coupe, which he had paid for. As she took out her keys, she said, "He never showed up."

"Your stalker? I noticed this, as well. Perhaps Miss Sinclair is correct in her cell phone hypothesis."

"It's a good thing, too. If he'd seen her with us . . ."

"Then her cover would have been blown, and we would have to find a new security consultant. Which would be a pity, as Miss Sinclair seems so ideally suited to the task."

"You really think she can find him?"

Like a child, she was perpetually in need of reassurance. "Of course she can," Faust said, "and she will. She may have no grasp of metaphysical truths, but she is reputed to be eminently competent in her narrow field of expertise. In this, she is like most Americans—practical in small things, ignorant of what matters most. She will get the job done."

"I hope so. But once she finds him—"

"She will deal with him."

"And if she doesn't?"

"Then I shall handle it. I shall arrange matters so your unwanted admirer never troubles you again."

"She may not let you do what . . . what needs to be done. She may, you know, get in the way."

Faust smiled, assisting her into her car. "If it should come to that, my darling, I shall handle her, as well."

5

Abby guided her Miata through the neighborhood of Los Feliz, around winding streets that climbed the foothills. Pricey part of town—not that any L.A. real estate was cheap these days. Her little Westwood condo, all one thousand square feet of it, punched a gaping hole in her checkbook every month.

At Faust's address she paused, idling outside. His house was largely concealed behind high walls. Through the iron gate she had a glimpse of a sprawling stucco pile landscaped with palms and yuccas. Nice place—much too nice for the man who had tightened a leather noose around Emily Wallace's neck. But then, nobody ever said life was fair.

The rented guest cottage was a few doors down and across the street, at the rear of a smaller but no less elegant estate. Abby saw the roofline of the cottage through a scrim of oleander. A black sport-utility vehicle was parked in a nearby carport. Her quarry's transportation, probably. If so, he was home.

She could lure him out at any time, but she preferred to wait until after dark. As much as she hated to admit it, Faust might have had a point when he compared her to a jungle animal. Most of them hunted at night, amid the shadows.

Nighttime is my time, she thought, *like the song says.*

It was two thirty now. The sun wouldn't set for another five hours. In the meantime, she needed to work off some of the nervous energy that always developed when she was on a case.

Not to put too fine a point on it, she needed to get laid. She wondered how Faust would work that detail into his jungle-predator metaphor.

Vic Wyatt lived in a one-bedroom Culver City apartment with thin walls and noisy neighbors. Abby knew he could have afforded better on a cop's salary, especially after his promotion to lieutenant, but he was the kind of guy who barely noticed his surroundings. For him, the apartment was only a place to crash. His quality time was spent working on the rebuilt engine of his latest acquisition, a classic Mustang.

Well, most of his quality time, anyway. Abby liked to think that her visits would also rate inclusion in that category.

She ascended the stairwell—*Never ride the elevator when you can walk,* that was her motto—and made her way down the corridor to his door. Two or three prolonged buzzes got his attention.

The door opened, and Wyatt was there, his sandy hair slightly tousled, the way it got when he'd been sleeping.

Abby grinned. "Hope I'm not interrupting anything."

"Just a nap."

"It's nearly three o'clock. Not feeling very industrious, are we?"

"One of the occupational hazards of working the night watch."

"If you need your beauty rest, I can always come back later."

"I'm wide-awake now."

He ushered her in. She looked around, frowning. "You know, this place is starting to have kind of a funny smell."

"Maybe I should get a maid."

"You sure you don't already have one?" She patted

a heap of unsorted laundry on the sofa. "She might be under here somewhere."

"I would've heard her screams for help. Something to drink?"

"No, thanks. I wet my whistle at a coffee bar earlier today."

"I never thought of you as the Starbucks type."

"This wasn't Starbucks. Not a place where the elite go to meet and greet. More like a caffeinated watering hole for the young and the clueless."

His arms encircled her waist. "Then what were *you* doing there?"

"Does that question imply that I'm not clueless, or not young? Wait, don't answer that. I was meeting a client. A pretty unusual guy, actually."

"You can tell me all about him—later."

"Come to think of it, maybe you can tell *me* a little about him."

His face changed almost imperceptibly. "Here we go," he said in a quiet voice.

"What do you mean, 'here we go'? Where are we going? Did I miss something?"

"No. I did." His arms weren't around her waist anymore. "I assumed you were here for some . . . intimate companionship. When in fact you're here to pick my brain."

Abby made a face. "Don't say 'pick my brain'. It's gross. Makes me think of a George Romero movie."

"To pump me for information, then."

"I *am* planning to pump you." She teased him with a smile. "But not for information."

"Then why are we having this conversation?"

"We don't have to be. We can proceed wordlessly to your boudoir."

"I don't have a boudoir." He turned away. "And I think it's funny how this question of yours just happened to come up as soon as you arrived."

She took a moment to process this. "Are you saying I'm using you?"

"No way. That would be like saying the sky is blue or two plus two equals four."

"Math has never been my strong point, but I'm pretty sure that two plus two *does* equal four. And when it's not too smoggy out, the sky *is* blue. So you do think I'm using you?"

"Come on, Abby." He sounded tired. "We both know how you operate."

"I seem to be in need of a refresher course. Enlighten me."

"You use me. You use everybody. It's just how you are. Nothing gets between you and your objectives."

"Nothing gets between me and my Calvins. As far as my objectives are concerned, I'm not so sure."

"You live for what you do. And every person in your life serves a purpose in helping you do your job. That's how you got to know me in the first place. You never would have talked to me if I hadn't been in a position to assist you."

"That's how it started, I admit. But things have progressed considerably beyond that point, Vic. I mean, we've been together for . . . what is it, nine years?" She was surprised to realize that it had been that long. She wasn't the type who kept track of such things. But it was true. Wyatt had been thirty-one years old when they'd met. He was turning forty this year.

"Nine years we've known each other," he said. "Eight years we've been more than just friends."

"Okay, eight years. That has to count for something."

"You'd think so." He rested on the arm of the sofa, brushing laundry out of his way. "So what is it this time? How may I be of service?"

"Never mind. Forget it."

"Go ahead and ask. I'm easy. But you already knew that."

She sat on the pile of clothes and took his hand. "It's not why I came over. I just had some free time. Got something going tonight, but I'd rather be Audrey Hepburn, as usual."

"Audrey Hepburn?"

"Wait Until Dark. Get it?"

"I'm embarrassed to admit that I do. So you've got a couple of hours to kill. Naturally, you came here."

"You're putting the most negative possible spin on this."

"I'm a cop. Cynicism comes with the territory."

She released his hand and stood. "Maybe this wasn't such a good idea."

"Maybe not."

"Guess I'll be going, then."

He let her get as far as the door before he said, "Not without asking me what you need to know."

"No, thanks. I wouldn't want to *use* you."

"Drop the attitude and ask."

She almost refused, then decided she was being childish. "Peter Faust," she said simply.

"What about him?"

"I need to know if he's done anything to get the LAPD's attention."

"You mean, besides get away with murder?"

"That was ten years ago, in Germany. I'm talking about since then."

Wyatt shrugged. "Faust doesn't live in my division. He's in Los Feliz. That's part of Northeast."

Abby knew this, but Wyatt had worked out of Hollywood for the past decade, and Hollywood was directly adjacent to Northeast.

"So you can't answer my question?" she said a little peevishly.

"Oh, I can answer it. If anything was going on with Peter Faust, I'm sure I'd hear about it."

"And nothing is?"

"Nothing recent. Of course, there was that whole mess three years ago."

"What mess?"

"You haven't heard? Then you haven't done your homework. He was the focus of an investigation. It didn't lead anywhere."

She wasn't too thrilled with the homework crack, but she let it pass. "I'm surprised I didn't hear about it in the news."

"You may have been out of town. You do that a lot."

"Excuse me for having a life."

"A young woman went missing and turned up dead, dumped in Griffith Park. Roberta Kessler, nineteen. Last seen in a bar on Sunset Strip, chatting up a man who could have been Faust. LAPD got a warrant, searched his house. Didn't come up with anything." He shook his head. "Whole thing was kind of an embarrassment, actually."

"What's so embarrassing about suspecting a murderer of another crime?"

"He's a celebrity, in a way. We wanted to keep a lid on the investigation, but it leaked. You know how the damn department is. Can't keep a secret, at least where the rich and famous are concerned. The tabloids were all over us. You sure you never heard about this?"

"I don't read the tabloids. Well, except for the *Weekly World News.* I love that. Did you hear about the Venusians' secret plan to clone JFK?"

"Fascinating."

"Seriously, the Faust story never came across my radar screen. I was probably working a case at the time. You know how I am when I'm on the job. I get kind of a narrow focus."

"You get downright obsessive. Even more so than usual."

Another shot. She tried to ignore it, but she was starting to get seriously pissed off. "Griffith Park is fairly close to Faust's home."

"True, but that didn't prove anything. A lot of bodies get dumped there."

"Was the MO consistent with Faust's history?"

"The body had been decapitated, and the hands had been severed at the wrists. It's the same way Faust's victim in Germany was found. That's what got investigators thinking about Faust. But of course, it's not the first time a body has turned up without a head or hands. That kind of postmortem mutilation is standard procedure if you're trying to prevent the victim from being identified."

"Yeah, I guess dental records and fingerprint comparisons were pretty much out of the question. How *did* you identify her? DNA?"

"Anatomical abnormality. She was born without a uterus. Coroner compared the body's reproductive system with Roberta's MRI. Obviously, it's something Faust didn't know about."

"So you do think Faust did it?"

"Faust—or whoever. As I said, there was nothing to tie him to the crime."

"There was the eyewitness at the bar."

"Her testimony wasn't too helpful. Sure, the man she saw could have been Faust. Could've been a thousand other guys, too."

"Still, I'm surprised LAPD didn't pursue it further."

"Faust is a wealthy man. He has a certain amount of influence. I guess when you're a star, you have clout, no matter what you're famous for. His lawyers let it be known that if their client was subjected to any more harassment, there would be legal consequences."

"And since then?"

"Since then, he's never been a suspect."

"How about a person of interest?"

"That's a term we only use on TV when we're trying to be cute."

"So he's clean, you think?"

"I would hardly say *clean.*"

"I mean as far as his recent activities are concerned."

"I have no evidence to the contrary."

"That's really all I had to ask. Wasn't so difficult, was it?"

She was sorry she'd brought it up. The information would have been readily available on the Internet, without all the Sturm und Drang. Whatever the hell Sturm and Drang were; she'd never been quite sure.

Wyatt was looking at her with a worried expression. "This client you met with—is he saying Faust is after him?"

"No, it's nothing like that."

"Look, if you've met someone who thinks Faust is a threat—"

"I haven't."

"Then why would this subject even come up?"

She didn't want to tell him, but she had to. And to be honest, part of her actually did want to, if only because she knew it would make him mad.

"The client I met wasn't worried about Faust. The client I met with *was* Faust."

He got up slowly and stood very still, like a man posing for a picture. "Say that again."

"Peter Faust hired me. He and his girlfriend are being stalked."

"And you took the job?"

"Yeah. That's what I do, you know. I stalk the stalkers. I'd have it printed on my business cards—if I had business cards."

She said this with a smile, but Wyatt wasn't in the mood.

"Faust"—his voice was unnaturally low—"is a goddamned killer."

"I know very well what he is."

"He murdered one woman that we know of. He may have murdered others. How can you possibly offer him your services?"

"What he did in his past is not the issue."

"And what he may be doing right now?"

"You just told me you have no evidence of any recent crimes."

"I still wouldn't exactly give him the benefit of the doubt."

"I don't have to give the benefit of the doubt. I just have to protect him, the same way you would. If he placed a nine-one-one call, are you telling me LAPD wouldn't dispatch a squad car?"

"That's different. We're a public service. We can't deny help to anyone. You pick and choose your clients. You could have turned him down."

"Why should I?"

"If you don't know the answer to that question, I doubt I can explain it to you."

"You know, I'd appreciate it if you didn't tell me how to do my job. I've been doing it long enough to make my own decisions."

"I'm disappointed in you, Abby."

"Oh, come on. You're not trying to guilt-trip me about this?"

"There was a time when you would never have had anything to do with a man like Faust. You would have spit in his face before you worked for him."

"Maybe I've evolved to a higher level of awareness. Maybe I'm more tolerant and accepting."

He took a moment to answer. When he did, his voice was low, almost mournful. "Or maybe it's not about good and evil anymore."

"What does that mean?"

"Lately you seem to be less concerned about the moral issues."

He was really pushing her buttons now. "Then what *am* I concerned about?"

"The professional challenge. It used to be about justice for you. Street justice—but justice. Now I think it's more of a sport. A game. You enjoy playing, and I'm not sure you care which side you're playing on."

"Bullshit."

"Nice comeback."

"That's the second time today someone said that to me. I must be losing my gift for repartee."

"Who was the first to say it? Faust?"

"Actually he used the term *riposte,* but the meaning was the same." She crossed her arms over her chest, aware that this was defensive body language, but feeling the need to protect herself. "Not that I have to justify my actions to you, but I took the case because Faust's girlfriend is the probable target. She must be pretty messed up to be hanging with a creep like him, but as far as I know, she's not a criminal, and she doesn't deserve to die just because she's become the focus of some deviant's obsession."

"Not so long ago you would have said that any grown woman stupid and self-destructive enough to hook up with Peter Faust deserved whatever she got."

"If I'd said that, I would've been wrong. And if that's what you think, then you're wrong, Vic. Speaking of judgments—maybe I've misjudged *you.*"

She left, retaining enough presence of mind not to slam his door. It was a rule of hers never to let anyone see how badly she'd been wounded.

People could hurt her. Over the years, she'd learned there was nothing she could do about that. But she could at least deny them the satisfaction of ever seeing her pain.

6

It took Abby a good half hour to cool off after her encounter with Wyatt. Probably he did have a legitimate beef about her casual attitude toward their relationship. On the other hand, she'd never promised him a rose garden, in the immortal words of Lynn Anderson. He'd known what he was getting into.

And his reaction to Faust—it had been over the top. At least, she thought so. Unless he was right, and her judgment was faulty. More likely he was just itching for a fight, and Faust was a convenient excuse. That was how Wyatt had been lately—edgy, moody, resentful. A man preoccupied. A man with something on his mind.

She was still agitated when she parked the Miata in the underground garage beneath the Wilshire Royal, the condominium high-rise in Westwood where she'd lived for the past ten years.

Near her reserved parking space was a second slot where she kept a beat-up old Hyundai Excel, the latest in a series of used cars she'd bought for undercover work. The Miata was too flashy to be a good surveillance vehicle, and its registration was in her real name, making it a poor choice of wheels when she was on assignment. The Hyundai was junky enough to pass unnoticed in most environments, and it was registered to a dummy corporation with the safely meaningless name of Consolidated Commercial Exchange.

From the Miata, she removed her purse and Faust's memoir, which she'd checked out of the library after discovering, to her surprise, that she actually had a library card that was still valid. It wasn't exactly the sort of book she liked to curl up with at bedtime, but she found herself wanting to know more about her latest client. No particular reason, just that Boy Scout motto again: Be prepared.

In the lobby, she waved hello to Vince and Gerry, the two guards who had manned the big mahogany desk roughly since the La Brea Tar Pits had been sucking down saber-toothed tigers. The doorman, Alec, was chatting with them. Unlike the guards, he was a new arrival, on the job for only three months. Abby hadn't warmed up to him. She didn't like the way he looked at her whenever she passed by. There was a reptilian quality to his gaze, a kind of cold, patient hunger, which wasn't masked by his artificial smile and cheerful bonhomie.

That smile and that stare were both on display as he turned to her.

"Hey, Ms. Sinclair. Got some reading matter, I see."

This was embarrassingly close to the winner of the World's Lamest Pickup Line Contest: *Whatcha readin'?* She wedged the book more tightly under her arm. The cover was hidden from anyone's view—a precaution she'd taken without conscious thought.

"Alec," she said coolly. She greeted Vince and Gerry in a warmer voice. "How are you guys doing?"

"Hanging in there," Vince said.

"Not that we have a choice," Gerry added.

Variations on this exchange had been played out almost daily over the last decade. The rote predictability of it pleased Abby. She liked to have some things in her life that were utterly dependable. There would always be traffic on the 405, there would always be *Law & Order* reruns on cable, and Vince and Gerry would always be stationed at their desk.

And Wyatt would always be there for her when she needed him—and *only* when she needed him.

Damn. That subject again. Her frown returned as she
rode the elevator to the tenth floor and unlocked the
door to unit 1015, the extravagantly overpriced one-
bedroom cubbyhole she called home.

She opened the curtain over the glass door to the balcony, exposing her view of Wilshire Boulevard and letting in a cascade of afternoon sun. Then she sat in her
overstuffed armchair and took another look at Faust's
memoirs. The slim hardcover volume had Faust's face
on the cover, below the title in jagged red italics: *Tasting
Blood.* As far as she knew, Faust had not actually tasted
Emily Wallace's blood; the title no doubt had been chosen to reinforce his image as the Werewolf, the nickname bestowed on him after his arrest.

According to the cover, *Tasting Blood* had been
"Newly Updated, with a New Chapter by the Author."
She glanced at the copyright page and found that the
updated edition had been issued just last year.

Idly she flipped through the book and came across a
photo section in the middle. Black-and-white photos—
apparently the publisher hadn't wanted to spring for
color. Or maybe the somber monochrome was more appropriate to Faust's subject matter.

The first photos were of Peter Faust as a baby, looking
as innocent as any infant, then as a young boy and a
teenager. By the time his picture had been snapped on
the streets of Hamburg, he was playing the role of an
itinerant artist, dressed for the part in a joyless black
ensemble. His face, no longer boyish, had hardened into
a cold mask. That face aged slightly in subsequent photos, taken during his arrest, at his trial, and upon his
release from the psychiatric hospital, but in its fundamental quality of icy ruthlessness, it had not changed.

There was a photo of Emily Wallace, too, lifted from
her high school yearbook when she was a graduating
senior. That would have been only one year before Faust
killed her. She was blond and pretty and looked impossibly young. Juxtaposed with the yearbook picture was a

shot of Wiesbaden Army Airfield, where she had
worked as a civilian employee. Abby didn't know how
or why the girl had ended up in Germany, and she
doubted Faust would explain it in his book. To him,
Emily Wallace was not a person, but only an item to be
used and disposed of.

She turned the page, and the next photo, shocking in
its abruptness, was Emily's dead body on an autopsy
table. No head, no hands—but those items had been
found in Faust's apartment and were displayed on the
facing page. Emily's eyes were open, her face purplish
and bloated. The back of her left hand bore the mark
of Faust's branding iron—a backward Z with a short
horizontal line slashed through the middle. A caption
identified the symbol as a *wolfsangel,* meaning "wolf's
hook."

Abby put down the book, switched her desktop PC
out of suspend mode, and Googled *wolfsangel.* The
mark, she discovered, was sometimes said to be an ancient rune, though actually it had first been described in
1902 by a German mystic who'd seen it in a vision. The
basic design was similar to that of a medieval snare used
against wolves. The iron snare's top hook, corresponding
to the upper arm of the backward Z, was pounded into
a tree trunk, and a hunk of meat was pinned on the
lower hook. Any wolf that leaped up to take the bait
would be impaled.

The Nazis adopted the symbol as part of their arsenal
of neopagan lore. Members of certain SS units wore it
on their collars. It was also associated with Hitler's
"werewolves," a guerrilla force assembled in the closing
days of the war.

She returned to her armchair and Faust's book. At
least now she understood his nickname.

Police evidence photos showed the leather strap that
had strangled Emily, and the branding iron that had
seared the back of her left hand. Abby wondered where
Faust had obtained a brand like that, or if he'd made it

himself, perhaps in a metalworking shop. The book might tell her. It was the kind of detail he would be happy to relate.

After photos of Faust's trial came a shot of the hospital in Berlin where he had been institutionalized for less than three years. The sentence seemed preposterously short, but the German penal system was notorious for its lenience. The man who'd stabbed Monica Seles on a German tennis court had received only a two-year suspended sentence. More recently a German cannibal who had killed and eaten a houseguest was convicted only of manslaughter. With good behavior he would serve no more time than Faust had.

Faust had been a celebrity ever since his arrest, and his fame had only increased as a result of his flamboyant behavior at his trial. He had been defiant and unapologetic, and on the witness stand he had delivered contemptuous, haranguing monologues in response to the simplest questions. He styled himself as a rebel, a man who despised and flouted all social rules, who cared nothing for morality, who refused even to distinguish between good and evil—"those twin chimeras, those modern myths," as one caption quoted him.

For all this he won a following. A wide-angle photo of one of his public appearances gave a fair idea of what kind of following it was. Almost all his fans were young. Males outnumbered females, but not by as large a margin as Abby might have expected. Roughly half the crowd wore the black outfits and heavy mascara typical of the Goth movement. Many of the rest had chosen Nazi-like garb—knee-high boots, pseudomilitary jackets, runic symbols worn like insignia of rank. It was a merging of Goths and skinheads, and it gave Abby a cold feeling in her gut.

In the background of the shot, spotlighted before the crowd, stood Peter Faust.

The photo section ended. She flipped to the back of the book and found the newly included chapter, which recounted Faust's more recent accomplishments. Skimming the paragraphs, she saw no mention of Elise, even though the girl said she'd been with Faust for three years. Apparently she didn't qualify as a major development in his life.

Then she stopped, her attention caught by a name she knew.

Tess McCallum.

What the hell was *Tess* doing in Faust's book?

She backtracked to an earlier page and located the start of the story. It was the case Wyatt had told her about—the murdered girl, Roberta Kessler. Three years ago. Abby hadn't known Tess back then, so even if she'd seen her name in connection with the story, it wouldn't have stuck with her.

Faust reported that he had become a suspect, "for no good reason, but simply by virtue of who I am, or perhaps I should say, what I am."

A search of his home, he wrote, had yielded no evidence—"although I was briefly concerned that the authorities, in their zeal to convict an innocent man, might plant evidence against me." Even after the search, the authorities weren't finished with him. They wanted him to be interrogated by someone from the FBI.

"By this point, I had acquired a certain leverage," he wrote, "inasmuch as I had been the victim of their harassment and abuse. My attorneys advised me to refuse the invitation. Being of a generous nature, however, I permitted the indignity of an interview, on the condition that it be conducted by Special Agent Tess McCallum."

He had wanted to meet her because of her highly publicized role in the Mobius case a short time earlier. "I was fascinated by the media accounts. She sounded like a gunslinger out of the Wild West, and her final showdown with mad Mobius was worthy of a Sergio Leone epic. She had killed a killer. I very much wanted to meet a woman capable of such a feat."

The FBI complied. Faust flew, at his own expense, to Denver, where Tess headed the field office, and on a breezy September day he met her in an interview room.

He didn't say much about his encounter with Agent McCallum, except that she had disappointed him with the plodding obviousness of her questions. Abby doubted this was true. Tess might be many things, but plodding and obvious were not among them.

Whatever the truth might be, Faust conceded a grudging respect for "the shootist," as he called her. "Like most Americans, she was fundamentally unimaginative and uncultured, but I could discern flashes of mental acuity and stubborn grit. I admired her for this, if for nothing else. I even sent a gift basket to her office as a token of my appreciation for her time. No doubt the basket and its contents were subjected to the minutest analysis by overzealous security personnel. Quite possibly no part of it reached her. I would like to believe so, as otherwise I am at a loss to explain her failure to send a thank-you note."

That was all he wrote about Tess McCallum, but for Abby, it was enough.

Abby closed the book. She thought of what Faust had said to her. That she had been recommended by a friend. By someone in law enforcement.

Now she knew who.

7

Tess was between classes, enjoying the warm May evening and the first glimmer of stars over the pin oaks. Late springtime in Virginia. She liked it, though the scene might have been more peaceful without the distant, incessant sound of gunfire from the firing ranges.

Still, she was content to be here—almost contented enough to wish she didn't have to go back inside for the evening session of the seminar. She was scheduled to lead a roomful of agents in a discussion on the protocol surrounding a chemical weapons threat. Her work on the Mobius case had rendered her an unofficial expert on that scenario.

Law-enforcement seminars were commonplace at the marine corps base in Quantico, where the FBI Academy trained new recruits and retrained experienced agents as well as law officers from other agencies and even from foreign countries. To the public, however, Quantico was probably best known as the home of the FBI's Behavioral Analysis Unit, the profiling squad that had received so much attention in movies and TV shows—though as a matter of mundane fact, the unit was no longer headquartered on the base but a short distance down the road.

At the moment she didn't want to think about profiling, training, or WMD scenarios. She wanted only to watch the false nettle and blunt brown sedge as it rippled in the cool breeze off the Potomac. Denver was far away, and she didn't mind. As much as she loved the mountains, she was glad to find some respite from the daily bureaucratic battles and the pile of paper crowding her in-box. It would be nice to just sit here in the stillness and silence and watch the night descend.

Her cell phone rang.

Probably it was someone from Denver, calling about some new crisis. As special agent in charge, she was responsible for all major managerial decisions. She plucked the phone from her jacket and pressed the keypad. "McCallum."

"Hey, what's up?"

She was pleased to hear Josh Green on the other end of the line. Josh was the assistant special agent in charge of the Denver office, her immediate subordinate. He was also—quite contrary to FBI policy—her lover, and had been for the last two years.

"Not much," she said, relaxing in his presence, even if he was two thousand miles away. "How are things in Denver?"

"Lonely."

"Glad to hear it. It means you miss me."

"I do miss you. I also miss my bolo tie, the black one. I think I left it at your place."

"I hope I mean more to you than a necktie."

"Don't be too sure. I really like that tie."

"You'd better be glad there's a continent between us."

"I'm not, though," he said. "Not glad, I mean."

She smiled. When she had first started seeing Josh, she hadn't thought the relationship would go anywhere. For a long time she had been convinced she could never fall in love again. And certainly not with another agent of the Bureau. Not after Paul Voorhees. Not after she'd found him murdered in the bed they shared, a victim of the serial killer Mobius.

She'd told herself she couldn't risk that kind of loss again. Her fear was irrational, of course. The mortality rate for FBI agents wasn't high. And Josh, like herself, was a supervisory agent who rarely did fieldwork. He wasn't going to get killed in the line of duty. He wasn't going to get killed at all.

Still, she had worked hard to talk herself out of loving Josh. The echoes of her relationship with Paul made her uncomfortable, and she didn't like keeping secrets about her personal life. She had told herself that whatever she and Josh had together wouldn't last. It was only a fling, fun and games, nothing serious, a way to get back into the dating scene without the hassle of blind dates or singles bars. Convenient, that's what it was.

She had maintained this fiction for the better part of a year before gradually allowing herself to know that she and Josh were a couple. A real couple with a real commitment to each other, a commitment that went beyond the bedroom.

She still didn't know where it would lead. She was almost afraid to think about it and risk blowing it. But there would come a point when decisions would have to be made. Before long, Josh was likely to be promoted to an SAC position at another field office. Then there might be a continent between them all the time. Unless one of them decided it was time to quit the Bureau. And which one of them would that be? That was a question for which neither of them had an answer.

Josh was speaking again. "You're still on schedule to come back tomorrow, right?"

"Taking a seven P.M. flight. The afternoon session tomorrow had better not run long."

"If it does, just duck out and say you're going to the ladies' room. Then don't come back."

"Very professional."

"It's stealthy. The Bureau appreciates stealth."

"You're just trying to get me fired so our relationship can be out in the open."

"No, I like the secrecy. The lure of the forbidden."

"You don't think that part of it is getting old?"

"Well . . . maybe just a little."

"What are we going to do about this, Mr. Green?"

"Our options are limited. Of course, the Bureau's mandatory retirement age is fifty-seven. That's only nineteen years away for me."

And seventeen years for me, Tess thought. Josh was too diplomatic to mention the fact that she was two years his senior. Not that she was touchy about her age—even if the big four-oh, in July, was rapidly closing in.

She knew she looked good, even for a gal pushing forty. She was of vigorous Scottish Highlands stock, from a long line of McCallums who had trod the windy heaths and braved the winter cold. Her smooth complexion showed little evidence of time's passage, and a thick fall of strawberry blond hair still framed her face attractively. Only on TV shows did all female FBI agents wear their hair short. Real life was more forgiving.

"Nineteen years," she said with mock seriousness. "I don't think we can maintain our relationship in secret for quite that long. Besides, what if we want kids?"

"You can tell people you're putting on weight."

"And how do I explain the sudden appearance of a child on the scene?"

"Stork brought him. That's what my parents told me about my baby brother."

"They didn't."

"They did. Very reserved people, my parents. I didn't get the lecture on sex from my father until my senior year."

"You were a senior in high school?"

"Worse. College."

She laughed. "Every day I learn something new about you."

"I'm endlessly fascinating. Um, someone's knocking on my door. Guess I'd better go. I'll see you at the airport. *Ciao.*"

He was gone, the line dead. She wished they could have talked longer.

Apparently she wasn't the only one who wanted the conversation to continue. Already her phone was ringing again. She touched the keypad.

"Forget something?" she asked.

"Are you screwing with me?"

The voice she heard didn't belong to Josh. It was a woman's voice, stiff and angry, not immediately recognizable.

Tess frowned. "Who is this?"

"Is it your idea of a joke? Because it's not funny."

She shut her eyes, placing a name with the voice. A voice she hadn't heard in nine months. "Oh, God. Is this Abby?"

"You know damn well who it is. I've just been doing some research on Peter Faust. You may have heard of him."

"Of course I've heard of him. I interviewed—"

"Tell me something I *don't* know."

Conversations with Abby were often confusing, but this one, so far, was incomprehensible.

"I literally have no idea what you're talking about," Tess said.

"Then let me make it simple for you. I don't know exactly what's going on here, whether you're messing with my head or you think that by helping me, you can get back on my good side—"

"Abby—"

"Whatever it is, I don't care. We're not friends anymore. I told you so the last time I saw you. I meant it."

"I know you did."

"So I don't need you to scare up business for me. Okay? And where Faust is concerned, *scare up* is the appropriate phrase."

It took Tess a moment to sort this out. "You mean to say you're *working* for Faust? And you think *I* hooked you up?"

"Yeah. I know, you're just shocked, *shocked,* to find gambling going on here."

"Gambling? What gambling?"

Abby blew out an exasperated sigh. "I forgot you're not a movie fan. Let's just say I don't take your protestations of innocence too seriously."

"I haven't talked to Faust since the interview. It's not as if he's on my Christmas card list."

"Nice try. But I know what I know."

"You're *wrong*. And whoever did hook you up isn't doing you any favors. Faust is a sociopath."

"Gee, ya think?"

"He can't be trusted."

"I figured that out on my own."

Tess tightened her grip on the phone. "You should steer clear of him, Abby."

"Too late. I've signed on. And I'm still convinced you had something to do with it. I don't know why, but then I've never cared to explore all the emotionally repressed corners of your Catholic-schoolgirl mind."

"The way you're talking, you're the last one to be making any psychological diagnoses right now."

"Yeah, I got it. I'm nutty as a squirrel. But you're the only link between Faust and me. So whether you were trying to help or trying to hurt, just knock it off. I don't want you in my life again, Tess—ever. Have you got that?"

"I've got it."

"Well . . . good." She sounded surprised Tess hadn't put up a fight. "I guess that's all I had to say."

Click, and the call was over.

Tess stared at the phone. The pin oaks and the false nettles were forgotten. The breeze from the river barely registered in her thoughts. Even the crackle of reports from the ranges had faded away. Her mind had room only for Peter Faust.

It had been three years since she'd interviewed him, but the memory hadn't faded. The memory of his cultured speech, his lashless ice blue eyes, his long-fingered hands.

He had been kind to her—no, not kind; that was the wrong word. Courteous. He had conducted himself with impeccable charm. But beneath the facade there was nothing charming about him. He was a snake, cold-blooded and deadly.

Why the hell would Abby be mixed up with him?

Abby could take care of herself, of course. She had dealt with all sorts of psychopaths. Even so, Tess wondered if Abby knew, really *knew*, what she was getting into.

"Not my problem," she reminded herself. "She said it. We're not friends."

Tess slipped the phone into her pocket and headed inside to talk about chemicals and death.

8

Abby felt a little better after her phone call to Tess. It had been a way for her to blow off steam. And no matter how roundly Tess denied it, there was no doubt she had been Faust's contact. Why Faust would call her, Abby had no idea. But he had, and Tess had given him Abby's name. Doing her a favor, conceivably.

Well, that was a mistake she wouldn't make again.

There was a time when Abby had genuinely liked Tess. Even though the two of them were opposites in most respects, she thought she had felt a connection. That was ancient history now. Funny how a relationship could change completely over the littlest things. Like, in this instance, Tess having arrested her and held her in FBI custody for the better part of a day, facing the prospect of life in prison for a crime she hadn't committed.

On second thought, it wasn't *such* a little thing.

The last time they had seen each other was in Abby's condo last August. Tess had come to apologize or make amends or something. Abby wasn't buying.

She'd told Tess they weren't friends.

What are we, then? Tess asked. *Enemies?*

Not yet. But if you ever come back to my town and get mixed up in my business again—we will be.

Recommending her to Faust was not exactly the same thing as getting mixed up in Abby's business, but it was close enough to get her hackles up. Whatever hackles were. She didn't know, but they were up, for sure.

She was all frazzled and needed to calm down. Anger

was a distraction, and she could not afford to be distracted when she was on the job. She willed herself to stop the chatter of her thoughts. There was a meditative technique she used, which involved the repetition of a simple mantra: *Mind like water.*

That was what she needed. Her mind as clear and calm as still water. A reflecting pool, a liquid mirror. No worries, no anger, no ego. Only stillness and depth.

Mind like water . . .

She allowed herself to relax into the cushioned softness of her armchair. After a few more repetitions of the mantra, she was calm. The left hemisphere of her brain, with its linear logic and obsessive verbalizing, had been silenced. The other half of her brain, the side that functioned wordlessly and holistically, had been activated. She could observe without judging, could act without doubt.

She called Faust, using her landline and reaching him on his. This seemed to be the safest means of communication between them. There was no evidence his landline had been tapped.

"It's me," she said when he answered.

"My hired predator."

"Not really how I like to think of myself. Look, I think I've tracked down your mystery man—"

"So soon? Miss Sinclair, you exceed even your considerable reputation."

Just what she wanted, compliments from a homicidal maniac. "I aim to please. Now I need to initiate contact."

"Where is he located?"

"Huh?"

"You said you had tracked him to his lair."

"I didn't say *lair*." And she was *not* giving Faust his address.

"I would be most curious to know where it is he operates from."

"That's not the way it works."

"I am paying your fee, am I not?"

"Yeah—and I'm calling the shots. I don't give out that kind of info to clients. I wouldn't want any of them to take matters into their own hands."

"You believe I would do this?"

"In a word, yes."

"You distrust me."

"Thought I'd made that clear. Try to keep up, okay?"

"Well"—he sounded nettled—"if you will not oblige me in my small request, then what is it I can do for you?"

"You can text-message Elise from your cell. Tell her to meet you someplace at eight o'clock." That would be after dark. According to the *Los Angeles Times,* delivered to her door daily, sunset was at seven thirty P.M. "Where's a spot you might go at night?"

"There are many. We frequent alternative bookstores, underground clubs, experimental theater, poetry recitals—"

"I get it. The classic bohemian lifestyle. Pick one. Not the poetry thing. Something less . . . boring."

"Do art galleries bore you?"

"Yeah, but I can handle it. What gallery?"

"The Unblinking I, on Melrose. Tonight they're showing the works of Piers Hoagland. Do you know him?"

"Didn't he play Screech on *Saved by the Bell*?"

Faust seemed to take the inquiry seriously. "I do not believe so."

"Then no."

"He is a native of my country. A holographic artist who specializes in images of death."

"Sounds peachy."

"Tonight is the opening of the exhibit. Elise and I had considered going."

"Don't. I don't want you there. I need to get to know this guy, and that won't work if he's tailing you. Just send the text message, stay put, and hope he takes the bait."

"You are the boss. Is there anything else you require of me?"

Abby hesitated. "Where'd you get the branding iron?"

"Why should this concern you?"

"I've been reading your book. There's a picture of the branding iron. I just wondered how a person acquires an item like that."

"Perhaps you are interested in making such an acquisition for yourself?"

"No, I'm not really into pain, self-inflicted or otherwise. So where'd you get it?"

"An antiquities shop in Berlin. I do not think the proprietor even recognized the symbol. It has been prohibited in Germany, you know, along with the swastika and other insignias of the National Socialists."

"You just found it lying around?"

"Indeed. It was most—what is the term?—serendipitous. I took it as an omen. A harbinger of my destiny."

"You're a superstitious guy."

"I am a believer in fate. In what the Greeks called *Moira,* necessity. We are all players in a game, the outcome of which is predetermined. We can do no more than act out our parts."

"And Emily Wallace's part was to be branded by you?"

"Yes."

"And to die at your hands?"

"Yes. Are there further questions?"

"Did you brand her before or after she was dead?"

"Before. It was the penultimate act. I seared my totem onto the back of her hand, and then I brought out the strap and with it I encircled her slender neck. Your neck, also, is most slender and well shaped."

"That's not what I'd call a compliment. More like grounds for a restraining order."

"You, of all people, must know how useless a restraining order can be."

"Are you trying to scare me, Mr. Faust? Because you need to know, I don't scare that easily."

"I am merely indulging in some harmless conversational byplay. Why should I threaten you? We are on the same side."

Abby didn't like that thought. "Yeah. I guess we are. So do your part and make the call. Remember, eight P.M."

"There is never a need to tell me anything twice."

She believed him. She heard the click as the call ended.

On the same side. She really wished he hadn't put it that way. Still, it was true. She was working for a man who had branded a young woman before killing her, a man called the Werewolf.

And tonight—also according to the *L.A. Times*—was the first night of a full moon.

9

Raven wasn't scared.

She was past all that. Fear had been a constant presence in the room with her for so many days. Yet now it was gone, just gone, and she felt nothing.

She had seen an old-fashioned device in her parents' attic once. Her grandmother had used it. You put wet clothes between two wooden dowels and turned a crank, and the dowels squeezed the water out of the clothing as it rolled through. A wringer, it was called. That's where the expression came from—*put through the wringer*.

And now she knew how it felt to be *put through the wringer*. Because she had been wrung out, wrung dry, every living feeling squeezed from her body until she was limp and numb.

Not all of her was numb, though. Her teeth ached from biting down on the linen gag knotted around her head, the gag that had made her want to retch when it was first tied on. God, he had tied it tight, with the knot at the back of her head, digging into the base of her skull.

And her wrists—they weren't numb, either. They stung like crazy. The steel manacles had chafed her skin raw and left bleeding sores that were starting to ulcerate. The sores stood out against her pale skin, as did the large purple bruise on her thigh where he had punched her after she tried to kick him. The bruise was high up on her leg and normally would have been concealed by her shorts, but she wasn't wearing anything. She had no idea what he had done with her clothes.

The bruise had hurt at first, but she no longer felt it. Her wrists were the focal point of her pain now. Of course, she wouldn't have abraded them so badly if she hadn't spent hour after hour tugging on the manacles, trying pointlessly to free herself. Even as she'd done it, she had known it was no use. She lacked the strength to pull free, and even if she did somehow get loose, she would still be trapped in the room.

The room was windowless and uncarpeted. It contained only two items of furniture. One was the bed on which she lay, a bare mattress with a steel frame and a brass headboard. Her wrists were cuffed to the headboard, impossible to work free. She was unable to get off the bed, and though she kicked and thrashed on the mattress, she had not succeeded in moving it or in making any significant amount of noise.

The other item in the room was a tall cabinet that stood against the far wall. The cabinet had never been opened in her presence, and she had no idea what secrets it held. She didn't think she wanted to know.

On one wall there was a strange buzzer thing—she didn't know what it was—some kind of intercom, maybe, though she had never heard any voices on it, just an occasional buzz, prolonged and insistent, like an angry bee. She thought it might be a signal to indicate that the doorbell had been rung, but she wasn't sure. It was hard to imagine visitors ever coming to this place.

There was nothing else in the room, only four walls and a ceiling with a single bare lightbulb. And the door. The locked door. She knew it was locked, even though she couldn't reach it, because she heard the jingle of keys whenever her captor came to visit.

Each time he entered, she tried to see beyond the doorway and the figure of the man silhouetted in it. Tried to see something, anything, even if it was only a sliver of daylight or a corridor that led nowhere—some proof that there was a world outside, that she was not alone in a universe that had shrunk to the dimensions of this room.

But she had seen nothing. Only darkness.

So perhaps there was no world beyond this one. Perhaps all the rest of her life had been only a dream, or a series of vivid hallucinations, and there was no sky or green grass or lilacs blooming in the spring, and she had no mother who looked the other way while her father crept into her bedroom at night, no home she had abandoned for life on the street, no friends who congregated beneath an underpass to exchange smokes and lies, no cubbyhole in a deserted building where she slept at night, shivering under a thin blanket.

All of that might have been only imagination. For all she knew, she had been born in this room and she would die here, if she ever died, if her captivity did not continue for all eternity.

Or maybe she was already dead, and this was purgatory or hell, where she had been condemned to suffer for her small sins, endlessly. If that was true, then the man who came through the doorway must be the devil himself.

She had never believed in such things in her former life. But if that life had been purely imaginary, then perhaps everything she had dismissed as illusion was real.

She didn't know. She didn't care, much. She was past caring, too. She was past pretty much everything— hunger and thirst and exhaustion and hope. She only wanted it to be over. She wanted it to stop.

Life and death—those were just words. Here in this room there was no life, and there was no death. There was only the waiting and the visits, and it was hard to say which was worse.

No, not hard to say. The visits were worse. His hand in her hair. His hand that stroked and caressed, so gently, as if he were petting a tremulous animal. His hand and his closeness and the hatred she felt for him, the hot, helpless hatred that made her want to leap up and lash out, all the while knowing she couldn't, because her wrists were chained.

Blinking, she raised her head. She realized she'd been wrong. She was not past everything, not yet. She still felt one thing.

She still felt rage.

Maybe it was her rage that was keeping her alive. If so, she ought to find a way to lose it, cast it off and be done with it, so she could finally die.

But in her heart she knew she didn't want to die . . . unless *he* died first.

IO

Abby didn't like to be slowed down by a heavy meal before a job. She fixed herself a small salad of mango, pineapple, and banana, and ate while standing on her balcony overlooking rush hour on Wilshire. She found the sight oddly soothing. The endless tide of traffic reminded her of the procession of waves to the shore.

She showered and changed into an outfit that, she hoped, combined a certain art-house sophistication with more than a hint of sexual availability. It also matched her purse, the one with the special compartment for her .38. She checked the gun: fully loaded.

Her purse held other secrets, among them a tiny vial of white pills—Rohypnol, the date-rape drug. It was illegal in the U.S., but she never let little things like criminal statutes get in her way. The newer version of Rohypnol had been designed to turn blue when it dissolved, tipping off a potential victim. Luckily for her, the older kind was still available on the black market. It dissolved clear.

She selected her fake ID for the evening from among several possibilities. The wallet, complete with driver's license and credit cards, went into her purse also.

She felt the itchiness that usually came over her at the start of an assignment. She was glad to feel it. After so many jobs, she sometimes worried she was losing her edge. A slight case of the jitters reassured her that her head was still in the game.

Tonight she might have more reason than usual to be nervous. It was rare for a stalker to intercept his quarry's

phone calls. If this guy was doing so, he was a cut above
the average in terms of smarts and resources. She would
have to watch herself.

But then, she always did.

At seven thirty she left the condo and descended to
the garage, where she got into the Hyundai, her undercover car. She joined the ocean of traffic, which seemed
hardly diminished, and drove east, with the dying sunset
in her rearview mirror.

Her route took her to the junction of Wilshire and
Santa Monica Boulevard. She turned onto Santa Monica,
then hooked east on Melrose. The cobalt blue immensity
of the Pacific Design Center, known to locals as the Blue
Whale, passed on her left. The building, crowded with
the showrooms of interior designers, was a fun place to
go for a stroll. There were lots of neat getaways in West
Hollywood—WeHo to residents—a chic community that
blended the upscale lifestyle of West L.A. with the funk-
iness of Hollywood proper. Its largely gay population
had earned it the nickname Boys' Town. She smiled,
thinking of a onetime WeHo gym called the Sports Connection, which had been so popular with gay cruisers
that it had become known as the Sports Erection. Although Bally had bought the establishment a few years
ago and changed the name, the tag still stuck, at least
for folks with long memories.

To an outsider, L.A. was a shapeless sprawl, but to
those in the know it was a complicated mosaic of neighborhoods, each one distinctive in its special shops or
eateries or back streets. There were specialty bookstores
and revival movie houses, sidewalk cafés and mom-and-
pop diners, and assorted other treasures—but only for
those who knew where to look. After more than a decade in this town, she knew it as well as any cabdriver.
At times the city felt almost like an extension of herself,
its landscaped gardens and graffiti-scarred walls mirror-
ing her changing moods.

She arrived at the art gallery just after eight P.M. It

was doubtful that Faust's stalker would be here quite so
early, but, as was the case in the coffee shop, she wanted
to be first to arrive so she could scope out the territory.

By now the sun was gone, and the promised full moon
had yet to emerge. She parked at the curb and walked
to the gallery, her purse slung over her shoulder.

The Unblinking I was exactly the sort of place its
name suggested, a self-consciously chic storefront operation selling overpriced objets d'art to self-consciously
chic customers. Tonight's opening had drawn a decent-
size crowd comprised equally of men and women. The
men could be neatly divided into two categories, the
shaggy and the bald, with the shaggy holding a slight
numerical advantage. The women were mostly clones of
Elise Vangarten—too thin, too pale, too waiflike. Some
of the waifs were pushing sixty, but they still had that
anorexic, concentration-camp look.

At the door each customer was offered a booklet on
"creative holography" and a tiny plastic cup of red wine.
Abby was no connoisseur, but even she knew the stuff
was cheap. It tasted like grape juice that had been left
out on the counter too long.

Out of habit she noted the gallery's layout. She was
like a seasoned traveler who always checked for the exit
nearest her hotel room. The gallery was built in the
shape of the letter L, with the long arm running parallel
to the street and the short arm extending behind the
building as an alcove. There was just one story, although
a door marked BASEMENT indicated some sort of room
belowground. A couple of security guards observed the
customers unobtrusively. There were no visible cameras,
but she did see motion detectors, which would be used
only when the gallery was closed.

As Faust had told her, tonight's exhibit featured the
works of Piers Hoagland, who had evidently received
glowing write-ups in a variety of publications, including
the *L.A. Times*. Having read the *Times*'s art critics,
Abby knew there was no manifestation of psychopathy

masquerading as creativity that they would not endorse. She expected no less from Hoagland, and he did not disappoint.

The long arm of the L was broken up by movable partitions into several inner rooms, each exhibiting a dozen or more of Hoagland's artworks. People who hadn't seen holograms usually pictured them like the three-dimensional images in science-fiction movies— animated, multicolored figures in the round, floating in space. The reality was slightly more prosaic. Hoagland's holograms were somewhat flatter than the Hollywood version. Like the picture on a liquid crystal display, they could be seen only from certain viewing angles. Images snapped into view out of nowhere as she got within range. One moment there was nothing to see; the next, a seemingly tangible object was projecting into the air before her face. Parts of the images did seem to extend a few inches—even a foot or more—into space, but even the protruding parts were tethered to the vertical plane of the holographic plate.

And the colors were mostly limited to one or two primary hues. There was something unappealing, almost sickly, about the vivid boxes of pure red and pure green, standing out like the square panels of a comic strip.

Lighting in the exhibit rooms was low, and all windows had been blacked out. The holograms showed up clearly once they came into the viewer's range. The largest plates, measuring three by four feet, were suspended from the ceiling. Smaller plates were mounted on black pylons that stood around the room at irregular intervals, or on small black pedestals. Above each installation was a ceiling minispotlight, the fifty-watt halogen bulb adjusted at a forty-five-degree angle to light the plate from the front and properly diffract the image.

All that Abby knew about holograms was that they were created by projecting a laser beam over the subject, and displayed by shining another ray of light on—or through—the resulting photographic plate. By some alchemy known only to physics buffs, the original object was reconstructed as a three-dimensional image, hauntingly real, encouraging the viewer to reach out and touch, but mocking these efforts with its insubstantiality.

According to the booklet, these were reflection holograms, viewable in ordinary incandescent light from a small light source. They were more practical for exhibition purposes than the older transmission holograms, which could be viewed only with the aid of a laser. They were suitable for home display, and were available for sale.

Abby wasn't going to be making any purchases tonight. She had no idea who would see Piers Hoagland's artwork as a decorative touch.

Hoagland's principal motif was decay. He liked images of things that had been alive and now were not. Some of his subjects were harmless enough—fallen leaves rotting in a pile, fruit moldering in a cobwebbed bowl.

When he turned his attention to more advanced lifeforms, things took a disturbing turn. A series of holograms addressed the subject of roadkill. Mangled and flattened squirrels, chipmunks, and possums hung in the air like ghosts. In one case the hologram had been artfully layered so that as the viewer moved past it, the dead animal dissolved through stages of putrescence, ending as a scatter of bones.

As she passed an artfully composed image of a garbage dump, a skeletal hand blinked in and out of sight. She had to shift back and forth until she saw it clearly. It was a single image embedded in the hologram, visible from just one angle. A subliminal effect.

The bone fingers seemed to be rising from the mound of refuse, clawing for the light.

Then there were the skulls. Abby found them in the alcove that constituted the base of the L—a long series of human skulls receding down both sides of the room like images in a hall of mirrors. Here the lighting was especially dim, the effect far more hallucinatory.

These images—if they *were* images—did not appear to be bound to the plane of any holographic plate. They did not merely extend into space from a flat background. They hung in space, connected to nothing, life-size, glowing in different shades of red, blue, and green.

She moved through the room. As she got closer to the nearest display, she understood what she was seeing. Each skull hovered inside a clear cylinder, and the cylinder was mounted on a black table that blended with the darkness. A low-wattage bulb shone down upon the cylinder from the ceiling.

The booklet, readable in the glow of her penlight, explained that these were cylinder-format holograms. The holographic plate, instead of being laminated onto a flat surface, was attached to a transparent cylinder. When illuminated from above, the plate focused an image in the center of the cylinder, an image that could be viewed from any angle.

She walked around the nearest skull, which, like the rest, floated at eye level. She could see it from front, sides, and back—even the crown of the head, if she stood on tiptoe.

The other skulls passed by as she made a circuit of the room. She'd assumed Hoagland had used the same skull over and over, but no, each was different, with its own peculiarities of wear and structure. Only the eyes were the same—or the eye sockets, rather. Dark ovoid holes that seemed to stare back at her as if taking her measure.

She was glad to get out of the skull room. She retraced her steps, holding her little cup of cheap wine and pretending to inspect the exhibited masterpieces, but actually looking for Faust's stalker. Of course, she had never seen him, and her clients had provided a description that was only marginally more helpful than a Rorschach inkblot. Even so, she would know him when she saw him.

He would be the other person in the gallery who was

pretending to look at the so-called art, while actually scanning the crowd.

Finally she stopped in the exhibition room nearest the foyer, where Piers Hoagland himself was holding court before a rapt throng of culturati.

"Holography," he was saying in a voice clipped with a German accent, "is a metaphor for reality. The hologram is an image, but possessing the three-dimensional properties of the tangible. An illusion, yet seemingly real. Just as reality, in turn, is only a shared illusion, or perhaps I should say a shared *delusion*. An image collectively agreed on, ostensibly authentic, yet receding into mists and vapors when we approach too near."

Abby surveyed the audience and saw one person who didn't belong. A man alone, who was only pretending to listen, while actually watching the entrance.

Her man, of course.

Faust and Elise were right. He *was* nondescript. Average height, average build, hair neither dark nor light, no distinguishing facial marks. And he had none of the squirrelly energy she usually saw in these guys. He was calm and controlled, even as he awaited his quarry's arrival.

He wore a charcoal blazer and an open-collared shirt. Though she saw no bulge of a firearm beneath the jacket, it was a safe bet he was armed. He might be wearing an ankle holster.

She estimated his age as mid- to late forties. A little old for a stalker. Most of them developed their obsession earlier in life.

Abby joined the group, standing near the man. She waited for an opportunity to initiate contact.

"The world," Hoagland was saying, "is a projection, a false front, what your writer Melville called a pasteboard mask. 'If man will strike,' he wrote, 'strike through the mask.' "

Abby tuned him out and studied Faust's stalker on

the periphery of her vision. The guy was edging closer to her. She forced herself to look away. She couldn't risk letting him sense her scrutiny.

The vibe she got from him was slightly worrisome. She couldn't put her finger on it, but she was now certain, with no room for doubt, that this was no ordinary nutcase. This was a man with experience, with skills. A pro, maybe. Could be a PI, a bounty hunter, a hit man . . .

"You look skeptical." A voice in her ear. His voice. He had come up alongside her so stealthily that she hadn't noticed his proximity.

She glanced at him, taken aback and trying not to show it. She was always the one to initiate contact. Most stalkers were so antisocial, so introverted, they wouldn't dare make the first move.

"Do I?" she whispered. "I guess I'm old-fashioned enough to think that reality is something hard and tangible."

"So you're a realist."

She smiled. "Been called worse."

"I'm a realist, too. If you can't see it, touch it, smell it, then what good is it?"

He wasn't quite so nondescript up close. She remembered asking Elise for the color of his eyes. They were cobalt blue, like the glass walls of the design center she'd passed on her way over. And also like those glass walls, they reflected the ambient light but afforded no glimpse of what lay inside.

He showed her a slightly crooked smile. The mechanics of smiling were of considerable interest to her. A smile, she knew, was produced mainly by the zygomaticus major muscle, which could be activated at will. But in a true smile, the muscles of the lower eyelids were also engaged, and most people could not control those muscles.

To distinguish a true smile from a polite smile, always look at the eyes.

The smile he was showing her was false. A gambler's smile.

He was not what he appeared to be. His friendly persona was just another hologram in the gallery, an image masquerading as reality.

Of course, she was no better. The woman she appeared to be tonight was only a projected persona, no more real than his.

"That being the case," she said, "why are you here?"

He made a vague gesture. "Friend of a friend invited me."

"Where is he? Or she?"

He looked again at the entrance, then shook his head. "Doesn't look like he's going to show."

"Some friend."

Something was very wrong. He had given up on spotting Faust too quickly. As if, perhaps, he knew—or guessed—that Faust would not be making an appearance.

He might be onto her. He might know that she had come here to intercept him.

How he could know, she wasn't sure. Maybe Faust had been more careless in his cell phone conversations than he'd admitted. Or maybe this man was tapping Faust's landline also, or bugging his house. Maybe he had followed Faust to the café and observed their meeting.

Or she could just be paranoid. He might not have caught on to her at all.

She didn't think it was paranoia, though. She'd lived by her instincts long enough to establish a healthy trust in them.

"How about you?" he asked. "How'd you get dragged here?"

"Came of my own free will. Although I guess free will isn't something you can see, touch, or smell. So maybe it's not real, either."

"This is getting too philosophical for me. I don't ask deep questions. I just take what comes."

"Not a bad way to live."

"It's worked for me so far. You had dinner?"

He wasn't playing hard to get, wasn't being coy or standoffish. He had made the first move. He was making *every* move.

"Only a bite," she said.

"There's a Cambodian place down the street that's not too bad."

"They don't serve dog meat, do they?"

His crooked smile flashed again. "If they do, it's not identified as such."

"What I don't know can't hurt me."

He took her by the arm—another unexpected development—and steered her away from the group. "That's where you're wrong. It's what you don't know that can cause the worst kind of hurt."

"I thought you weren't philosophical."

"I have my moments. You bring a coat?"

"It's May."

"Gets chilly at night."

"I'm impervious to cold."

"Me, too. Cold is good. It toughens you up. You know what Nietzsche said. What doesn't kill us makes us stronger."

He studied her with his opaque blue eyes. Enjoying himself. And letting her see his enjoyment. It wasn't enough that he was playing her. He wanted her to know she was being played.

That scared her. It suggested reserves of self-confidence that ran frighteningly deep.

"Who's being philosophical now?" she said lightly.

"I suppose quoting Nietzsche *was* a little over the top. You have a name, by the way?"

"Abby. Abby Robinson."

"Mark Brody."

As he escorted her to the door, she understood what

kind of vibe he gave off, and why she had almost recognized it. It was her vibe, her energy.

Faust had called her a jungle animal on the hunt. So she was.

And so was Mark Brody.

II

The restaurant was dim and quiet, with photos of the ruined temple complex of Angkor decorating the walls. Abby ordered sautéed boneless chicken in lemongrass, a dish identified on the menu as *moarn char kroeurng*. Brody tried the *nhorm yihoeur,* which turned out to be boiled calamari. He seemed more knowledgeable about Cambodian cuisine than she was—not that this was saying much.

"So, Mark Brody," she said between bites, "what do you do for a living?"

"Nothing interesting."

"You one of the umpteen million Angelenos looking for that big break in showbiz?"

"I don't think I'm exactly Hollywood material."

He might be right about that. He had none of the boyish affability that characterized most movie stars today. In another era, things might have been different. He could have held his own against Robert Ryan or Lee Marvin—men, not boys. Dangerous men.

She couldn't stop focusing on his eyes. Sanpaku eyes, in the terminology of Eastern medicine. Eyes that showed the whites of the eyeballs on three sides. An unusual trait. Tradition held that if you stared into sanpaku eyes, your life energy would be weakened.

She didn't know if she believed that. Those eyes, though—they mesmerized her. They were the hooded eyes of a reptile.

"Where are you from, originally?" she asked.

"How do you know I wasn't born and raised in L.A.?"

"Nobody is actually *from* L.A. It's a city of new arrivals."

"People grow up here. They must."

"Do you know any native Angelenos?"

"No. But I'm sure I've seen them." He waved his hand vaguely. "On the streets. You know. Children."

"It's true," she said gravely. "There *are* children here. But when they grow up, they move away."

"All of them?"

"Every one. I think it may be a law. Or just some sort of migratory instinct. Anyway, they leave, and their place is taken by someone just getting off the bus from Kansas City or Detroit."

"What bus did Abby Robinson arrive on?"

"The one from Phoenix." She really had grown up in Phoenix, or just south of there, on a ranch near the Superstition Mountains. It was always safer and easier to tell the truth about things that didn't matter.

"Why'd you come here?"

"Job opportunity."

"There are jobs in Phoenix."

"There was also . . . a man." This also was true. She was on a roll.

"Isn't there always?" Brody smiled. "He's not in the picture anymore, though, is he?"

"He hasn't been in the picture for years." She didn't want to talk about this. "You haven't told me where you hail from."

"Baltimore."

"Good crab cakes there." That was the one and only thing she knew about Maryland.

"I don't miss them. I don't miss anything about it."

"Was it so bad?"

"Not bad at all. I just don't believe in looking back. I'm a realist, remember? What's real is the here and now. The present moment. This table." He reached across and clasped her fingers. "Your hand."

His grip was dry and cool. If he was nervous, he wasn't showing it.

"You putting the moves on me, Mark Brody?"

"You make it sound so calculating."

"I'm a realist, too—remember?"

He nodded. "We have a lot in common."

But he already knew that, Abby thought. Didn't he?

Dinner was over, and they had ordered coffee, which Abby didn't touch. Brody was telling a good story, inspired by the Cambodian decor, about a trip to Phnom Penh that had almost ended badly. He and a friend had come close to being arrested for disturbing the peace after a drunken romp.

"And from everything I hear," he said, "a Cambodian prison is not a place you want to be."

Abby wondered what sort of work had taken him to that part of the world. "How'd you avoid the hoosegow?"

"Paid off the cops. American dollars speak a universal language."

"The experience taught you not to overindulge when abroad, I guess."

"Believe me, we were stone sober after that. My life was almost a sequel to *Midnight Express*."

"That was Turkey."

"*Brokedown Palace,* then."

"That was Thailand."

He regarded her with amusement. "So you're a movie fan."

"Seen 'em all."

"Nobody's seen them *all*."

She folded her arms across her chest. "Test me."

He thought for a moment. *"Plan Nine from Outer Space."*

"Too easy. It's the worst movie ever made, and therefore a must-see for the serious film fan. To save you time, I've also seen *Glen or Glenda, Bride of the Monster*—in fact, the entire Ed Wood oeuvre."

"Impressive. *The Rocketeer*."

"Jennifer Connelly in her ingenue days. Retro Disney jetpack-versus-blimp movie. Seen it."

"*Under the Rainbow*."

"Chevy Chase and a cast of midgets. How could I *not* see something with a logline like that? You aren't even challenging me yet."

"*The Incredible Mr. Limpet*."

"Cartoon fish fights the Nazis. Seen it."

"*Call Me Bwana*."

"Bob Hope in Africa. Seen it."

"*Showgirls*."

"The film that made Elizabeth Berkley a star. Seen it."

"*Abbott and Costello Meet the Abominable Snow-man*."

She wagged a finger at him. "No fair making up movies. Abbott and Costello met Frankenstein, the Invisible Man, Dr. Jekyll and Mr. Hyde, and the Mummy. But never a yeti."

"Damn, you're good. *The Scarlet Letter*."

"Demi Moore does Hawthorne. You think I'd miss that? It's like Britney Spears doing Molière. Which she hasn't yet, but when she does, I will be first in line. By the way, have you seen the magazine with the headline 'Britney Spears Speaks Her Mind'? Now, honestly, how long can that really take?"

He would not be distracted. He was playing the game in deadly earnest. "I've got one. *The Alien from L.A.*"

Abby had to think about that one. "Supermodel falls down rabbit hole, discovers underground civilization. Seen it."

He shook his head, by all appearances genuinely frustrated. "There is *no* way you could have seen that movie. *Nobody* has seen that movie."

"Hey, it was late at night, and my only options were the subterranean supermodel or an infomercial. I went with the supermodel. In retrospect, the infomercial would have been a better choice. As I recall, it was for the Total Gym and featured a different supermodel."

He took a long pull on his coffee, then set the cup down with a confident air. "I have you now."

"Don't count on it."

"*Steel Magnolias.*"

She was about to say she'd seen it, then realized she hadn't. "You're right," she admitted. "I took a pass on that one. But how could you possibly know?"

"It's not your kind of thing. Too sentimental. Too . . . I don't know . . . girly."

"I *am* a girl, you know."

"You're not a girl who would sit through *Steel Magnolias.* Probably not *Terms of Endearment,* either. Or *Sweet Home Alabama,* or *Hope Floats,* or *Pay It Forward* . . ."

"Okay, okay, I give. You've found my Achilles' heel. I don't go for soapy, sappy cinema. I'm still amazed you guessed, though."

"Everybody has a weakness. It was just a matter of time until I found yours."

"Congratulations," she said sourly.

"Thanks." He finished his coffee. "You put up a good fight. But I knew you would be mine eventually."

There were several ways in which this remark could be interpreted. She wondered how many levels of subtext she was meant to find.

"I guess I haven't seen literally *every* movie," she said lightly, "but I've seen a bunch. It's an addiction, like cocaine, only without the improved work efficiency and nasal bleeding."

"Why do you think they appeal to us so much?"

"Movies? Escapism, I suppose."

"Brings us back to the art gallery, doesn't it? Illusions projected into space. They seem real. We can even get lost in them. But at the end of the day they're just images."

"You're more philosophical than you let on."

"Maybe I've just had too much to drink."

But he had hardly touched his cocktail. She'd avoided hers, as well. Each of them was staying sober and alert, pretending to be jokey and casual, but actually sizing up the other. She thought of some other movies he might have brought up in his impromptu quiz. *Mask,* maybe. *F Is for Fake. Shadow of a Doubt. Masquerade* . . .

"That's the best feature of the place where I'm staying now," he added.

She didn't follow. "What? Holograms?"

"A wide-screen TV. High-def. Forty inches."

"You must've shelled out big bucks for that one."

"It's not mine. Came with the place. I rented it furnished."

"What kind of rental comes with a forty-inch TV?"

"Why don't I show you?"

No, he was definitely not playing hard to get.

She assessed the risk of being alone with this man in his rented guesthouse. If he was onto her, he might get nasty when not in public. But she doubted it. They had been seen together at the gallery and the restaurant. If she were to disappear tonight, he would be implicated.

Besides, she could take care of herself. In a world of uncertainties, this was the one conviction on which she never wavered.

"Well, gee," she said with a teasing smile, "I don't know. Is there anything good on TV?"

"We can make our own entertainment."

"How bold of you."

"So I'm coming on too strong?"

"Nope. You're coming on just about right."

The thing was, she wasn't kidding. He hadn't made a single misstep all evening. He was even a movie fan.

Yes, he was dangerous, but that little detail only contributed to his allure. She had no objection to getting it on with a bad boy. Hell, she was a bad girl herself, most of the time.

Not that she would actually *do* anything. This was a job, not a date. Nothing would happen.

Of course it wouldn't.

12

Leaving the restaurant, Abby made a point of joking around with the maître d', asking about take-out and delivery services, and acting—as they said on the late-night TV sex-chat ads—"fun 'n' flirty." She managed to drag Brody into the conversation and even mentioned his name. She wanted to be sure the maître d' remembered them both. More important, she wanted Brody to *know* that the man would remember.

On Brody's face she saw the same calculating expression he'd worn earlier at the gallery. It was an expression that said he knew what she was up to and he found it amusing. It said she could not outthink him and she shouldn't try. It said she might put up a good fight, but he would win in the end.

They drove to the guest cottage in separate cars, Abby using the excuse that her car would be towed if it was parked at the curb all night. This was true, but she also needed the car handy so she could make a getaway. Her plan was to slip Brody a Rohypnol tablet, wait for him to conk out, then search his place and see what turned up. Standard operating procedure.

Somehow she wasn't quite comfortable with it, though. Maybe because Brody hadn't had much to drink, so there was little chance he would chalk up his loss of consciousness to overindulgence. He would know he'd been drugged. This would preclude her from seeing him again. Without further contact, she might find it difficult to assess his intentions.

Still, she had to dope him. Otherwise, she wouldn't have the chance to search the premises. Besides, she wasn't going to give the guy a roll in the hay. Right?

"Right," she assured herself as she followed his black SUV into the Los Feliz district.

They parked near the guest cottage, which sat well away from the main house, screened off by eucalyptus trees and oleander hedges. The lights of the cottage glowed dimly behind drawn curtains.

When Brody opened the front door, an alarm began to beep in a quiet, insistent monotone. He had a security system with a front-entry delay. The delay gave him time to punch a four-digit code into a keypad by the door, silencing the beeps. Abby knew that if he hadn't entered the code in time, the alarm would have gone off, and the police would have been summoned.

She also knew what the code was. She had clearly seen him input the numbers. Sloppy of him not to block her view. It was the first mistake he'd made.

He led her through the foyer into the living room.

"Home, sweet home," he announced.

If anything, the classified ad had undersold the place. It was spacious, clean, and furnished in exquisite taste.

"Pretty swank," she said.

"Think so?"

"If it were any more swank, it would be Hilary Swank." She frowned. "I don't know what that means."

"It was a valiant effort."

"Sometimes the quips work; sometimes they don't. That's one you can edit out."

"So you *do* have an edit button?"

"If I do, I haven't found it yet. Then again, I've never looked."

He led her into the kitchen and poured a reprise of the drinks they'd ordered at their table.

"What prompted you to relocate yourself in this pricey neck of the woods?" she asked, while she placed one hand in her purse and found the vial of pills.

"I have expensive taste."

"You never did tell me what you do for a living."

"It's not exactly a nine-to-five job."

She just bet it wasn't. "Secret agent? International man of mystery?"

"Nothing that exotic."

"You're not living off a trust fund, I hope."

"My folks never had any money. Never had any hopes for me, either."

"Ouch."

"Sorry. Didn't mean to get sentimental."

"It's okay. I don't mind a good moment of shit."

"A what?"

"That's what TV writers call it when the characters have to stop being funny or scary or whatever, and open up with some heartfelt emotion. Usually near the end of the episode. The moment of shit."

"Is that what this is?"

"It can be. I don't mind."

He finished making the drinks and turned to replace the two bottles in the cabinet. This was her opportunity. It would take only a second to spike his cocktail while his back was turned.

Inexplicably she hesitated. Then he was facing her again, handing her a Scotch and soda. She took a sip, wondering what the hell was wrong with her.

"Why didn't your parents have hopes?" she asked, trying to maintain the conversational flow.

"Probably because I gave them no grounds for any." He walked with her into the living room. "I wasn't exactly a good kid. More like a bad seed."

"You seem okay to me, seed-wise." She sat next to him on the sofa.

"Don't let appearances deceive you. I did all the usual juvie stuff. Cut classes, ran around with the wrong kids, got pulled in by the cops for penny-ante bullshit."

"Ever do time?"

"Came close."

"What saved you?"

"I signed up for the ROTC. Got a four-year college scholarship in exchange for a commitment to serve."

"The military's a pretty tough gig. Jail might've been easier."

"I wasn't looking for an easy way out. I wanted some direction. When you can't discipline yourself, you find people who can do it for you."

"That's either an inspiring piece of self-help wisdom or the slogan of a less-than-reputable massage parlor."

He looked away, and she realized this was something he didn't joke about. "It worked for me. I got turned around. I learned who I really am."

Abby wondered just exactly who that was. "After college you went into the service?"

He nodded. "Army."

"You were a grunt, huh?"

"I was Special Forces."

"Rangers?"

He shook his head. "Green Berets."

The elite of the elites. "Wow."

She had a feeling he was telling the truth. Anybody could claim to be a Green Beret, but that kind of training and experience would go a long way toward explaining his self-confidence, his almost uncanny coolness. Someone who'd done HALO jumps into enemy territory—high altitude parachute drops—wasn't likely to get rattled by anything.

"How long were you in the army?"

"Twenty years."

"Guess you saw some action."

That crooked smile was back. "Desert Storm, for one thing. Though that hardly qualified as combat. More like extermination. The Iraqis were so outmatched, I almost felt sorry for the poor sons of bitches."

"Anywhere else?"

"Bosnia."

"I thought we fought that war from the air."

"Not all of it," he said darkly.

She knew Special Forces teams could be deployed to direct bombers to their targets, gather intel on the ground, or raid enemy compounds. She wondered which of the above he'd been involved in.

"Afghanistan?" she asked.

"We made some noise there, yeah."

"Iraq? The second time, I mean."

"For a while. I got out in 2003, after I'd seen a little action."

"Were you wounded?"

"No, but they were going to reassign me. Bring me back to the States, kick me upstairs to a staff position. It wasn't what I wanted. So I got out."

"Was this before or after your adventure in Phnom Penh?"

"After. I'd been to Cambodia while I was on leave. A little R 'n' R."

"You must've seen a lot more of the world than just combat zones."

"I have. And you know what? It's all pretty much the same. You can find a McDonald's in every big city, and American TV shows running night and day."

"How about if you get out into the countryside?"

"That's all the same, too. Chicken coops and thatch-roofed huts and dirt roads. And people wearing T-shirts with pictures of Bruce Springsteen and Madonna."

"America is everywhere."

"We're the new Rome."

Abby smiled. "I guess that's better than being the new Carthage."

"I'm impressed. You know your history."

"Mostly from movies. Did you know Julius Caesar bore a striking resemblance to Rex Harrison?"

"And Genghis Khan looked a lot like John Wayne."

He took a generous swallow of his drink. She was glad

to see it. Maybe he would be getting drunk, after all. Then the effects of the drug would be ascribed to alcohol.

But it wouldn't matter unless she got the damn pill into his drink. She had missed one chance. She needed to give herself another.

"You have anything to eat in the fridge?" she asked. "Some crackers, maybe?"

"Still feeling peckish?"

"I could use a little something to settle my tummy."

He got up. "I'll see what's there. Can't promise much."

She watched him disappear into the kitchen. He had left his drink behind. She would never have a better opportunity.

She removed a tablet from the vial, reached for his drink. And then she knew why she had hesitated in the kitchen, and why she wouldn't use the pill now.

She didn't want him drugged and unconscious. That wasn't where this evening was headed. Some part of her had known it all along, ever since he'd made the first move at the Unblinking I.

So what was this? Revenge on Wyatt for insulting her? She was still pretty damn mad at him, she had to admit. Maybe retribution did play a role. But there was more to it than that.

Brody intrigued her. He was something different in her world. He was a challenge, an enigma. And he was a pro, like her.

A predator—like her.

She replaced the pill in the bottle, which vanished into the crowded abyss of her purse. She was lounging on the sofa when he returned with two small plates.

"Cheese, crackers, and olives. That okay?"

"Very Mediterranean."

She fixed herself a small cracker sandwich.

"In Italy," he said, "when the workers brown-bag their lunch, they take some bread and olive oil. Tear off hunks of bread and dip it in the oil, wash it down with a little wine."

"It makes you wonder how McDonald's ever caught on over there."

"Or anywhere else, for that matter. That's one way people *are* different. Americans want to get things done. The rest of the world is more interested in just letting things happen."

"How so?"

"There's a fatalism in most cultures. People accept life for what it is. A piece of bread and some olive oil can be savored for its own sake. In America, we fight with our environment. We want to change it. We want progress, and we're in a hurry to get it. So we wolf down our Quarter Pounder with cheese, because we're impatient to get to the next meeting or the next sales call. With us, it's all about results. With other people, it's about the process."

"You're saying we can't just enjoy the moment?"

"Not even if it's a moment of shit." He winced. "Which I guess this one is."

Abby studied him. "Doesn't feel so shitty to me."

13

She had no idea what to expect from him in the bedroom. Vaguely she thought he would be quick and efficient, giving her a good ten minutes—what she thought of as a speed hump.

She was wrong.

He took his time undressing her, stripping away each article of her clothing and running his hands over her skin, feeling the taut contours of her musculature and smelling the soft golden down on her arms and the nape of her neck.

Most men acted as if there were only three erogenous zones, maybe four on a good day, but he knew the secret of real lovemaking—that every part of her body could be caressed and stimulated, that his mouth on her neck or his hands kneading the small of her back could send a thrill of pleasure through her, a needle shot of pure hedonistic gratification that left her limp.

By the time he explored her breasts, she was already shivering with the afterburn of a succession of inner explosions, so exhausted she almost feared she couldn't take any more. He would have to stop, she must tell him to stop, but she didn't, because it was so good to feel the slow circles of his palms against her breasts, the friction of skin on skin, her impossible sensitivity heightened more and still more, until just the touch of his lips was enough to release a bloom of warmth that suffused her body.

She wasn't sure what happened after that, what he did

or how he did it, only that it kept on going as he explored the rest of her, moving with expert precision from her wrists to her thighs, from her earlobes to the insides of her knees, until there was nothing but his breath on her skin, his tongue, his touch, the scent of her wetness on his fingers as he brushed them across her lips, her own hand between her thighs as he placed it inside her and then drew her moistened fingers into his mouth.

The end, too, was not what she expected. She found herself on top, straddling his hips, impaled on him, while his hands on her waist pressed her gently downward, then released, then pressed down again, each time driving him in deeper, penetrating her by slow degrees but with escalating urgency, then a final release, and with it a wail rising out of her own throat, emptying her.

When it was over and he was asleep, she pulled on her underwear and blouse and began to search.

The place was too big to be thoroughly tossed while he slept. There was too great a risk that he would wake up and catch her in the act. All she could do was check a few obvious things and make preparations for a return visit.

She started with the clothes he'd discarded on the floor. She'd heard a soft thump as his belt dropped off. Fitted to the belt was a black leather Yaqui slide holster holding a subcompact semiautomatic, a Beretta Mini Cougar 9mm with a 3.6 inch barrel and a truncated grip. The short grip made the weapon easy to carry concealed; it wouldn't print against the clothing and give itself away. She smelled the gun—freshly oiled.

She'd been pretty sure he was carrying, but before he'd disrobed she would have bet on an ankle holster. The little Beretta had been invisible beneath his jacket.

In the back pocket of his trousers she found his wallet, which contained a California driver's license in the name of Mark Andrew Brody. She memorized his date of birth, his address—an apartment in Reseda—and his DL number. He carried credit cards under that name also.

It proved nothing. Her wallet was full of items establishing her identity as Abby Robinson.

She checked the bed. He was still asleep.

To properly inspect the cottage, she would need to be here alone. All she could do now was make it easier to reenter the premises.

She went down the hall and unlatched the rear window but didn't open it. In a hall closet she found the security box, nerve center of the alarm system. She pulled out some wires, cutting the communication link. Now if the alarm went off, the police wouldn't be called.

She took note of the system's layout. Sensors on the front and side doors, motion detectors in the hall and bedroom. The windows weren't armed, but anyone entering via a window would be picked up by one of the motion sensors before getting very far.

From the bedroom came sounds of movement. He was getting up. She busied herself in the kitchen. When he came in, wearing boxer shorts and an untied robe, she was spooning pancake mix into a measuring cup.

"I guess I worked up an appetite," she said. "Hope I didn't wake you."

"Even if you did, I wouldn't complain. But you didn't. You're as quiet as a mouse."

He said it as if he knew she'd been sneaking around. She only smiled. "I'm light on my feet. Want some pancakes?"

"I wouldn't turn 'em down."

She added more of the dry mix to the cup. "Not quite as elegant as our first meal tonight."

"Looks good to me. Remember, I've subsisted on MREs for extended time periods."

"Then this has got to be an improvement. So tell me about the Green Berets."

"What do you want to know?"

She poured oil on the griddle. "They operate in teams, don't they?"

"Twelve-man units, typically. Each man has a specific function."

"What was yours?"

"Chief warrant officer. Second in command."

"A lot of responsibility."

"Especially when the commander gets blipped."

She looked at him. "Did that happen?"

"Once."

"How?"

"We were on a special reconnaissance mission in Iraq. Scouting the territory south of Baghdad while the infantry guys—the 'big army,' we called them—raced north across the desert on their initial push. There's a bottleneck in a mountain pass, name of Karbala Gap. Obvious place for an ambush, so we had to stake it out, report what we saw."

"Couldn't the military have used satellite imagery to find out?"

"Eyes on the ground beat eyes in the sky. That's the whole idea behind recon missions. Anyway, it should've gone smoothly enough. It didn't."

"What happened?"

"We got spotted. Pinned down by enemy fire from the high cliffs. We were maneuvering for cover when our captain—young guy, pretty raw, had hardly been tested—well, he took a round in the head. You know how head wounds bleed. Or maybe you don't."

She did, but she couldn't say so.

"He died right next to me. Leaning on me. Crying. Then I was in charge."

She began spooning the liquefied mix onto the griddle. "You had to get your people out."

"Like Xenophon," he said cryptically.

"Who?"

"Soldier in ancient Greece. He and his men got trapped behind enemy lines, had to fight their way home. He made it—and wrote a book about it."

"I'll bet you got your guys out, too."

"Eventually. First I led the team to a wadi, a dry river-bed, which afforded some decent concealment. Radioed for a chopper. Took a long time to get there. We kept scrambling from place to place along the riverbed so they couldn't pick us off. We'd ditched our packs for greater mobility. We ran out of water and ammo. We were pretty much down and out when we saw our ride. Big Chinook bird, beautiful sight. But it couldn't land too close to the wadi or it would be in range of the enemy guns. We had to sprint for the pickup zone, dodging mortar fire. But we made it. Even the captain—we got his body out. We weren't going to leave it there in the field for those fuckers to . . ." He took a breath. "Sorry."

"It's okay."

"We all came home. Eleven of us alive."

She started flipping the pancakes. "And not long afterward, you got out of the military and out of Iraq."

"I didn't leave Iraq."

"You stayed on as a civilian?"

"For a while."

"Why? What was there for you?"

"Nothing. Not a goddamned thing." He looked tired as he said it. Tired and older than he'd looked before. "You know what I remember most about Iraq? How bad the place smelled. They've got raw sewage running down the streets. They burn their garbage. They cook their meals on open fires. All those smells—food and trash and shit—they all blend together, and you think, Christ, what am I doing here?"

"What *were* you doing there?"

"I was looking for something. Looking for . . . Never mind."

Redemption, she thought. Atonement for letting his captain die. "You can't blame yourself for anything that happened," she said quietly.

"I don't. I'm a realist, like I told you. What's done is done."

"Anyway, you're out of the war zone now."

"You're never out of the war zone, Abby. Never."

It was the first time he'd used her name.

She served the pancakes. He got out some syrup and gave his a generous coating, then began to eat with gusto.

"Looks like you worked up an appetite, too," she said.

"Not yet." He gave her a knowing smile. "But I intend to."

She caught his meaning. "After your first performance, I wouldn't think you'd have the energy for an encore."

"Then you'll be pleasantly surprised."

As it turned out, she was.

At dawn she left, saying she had to get ready for work.

"I guess you do, too," she added.

"I work at home."

"Doing what?"

Another crooked grin. "Getting myself into trouble."

He still wouldn't tell her. Weird that he didn't just deliver a cover story. It was almost as if he felt it would be an insult to their mutual intelligence to indulge in such an obvious lie.

She got into her Hyundai and drove off the premises. As she passed the main house, she saw a woman watching her, the flower-print curtains pulled back from the window. A woman in her fifties, hair set in a bun.

Abby waved to her, one gal to another. The woman didn't wave back. There was a disapproving downward curve at the corners of her mouth.

"*Some*body didn't get any last night," Abby said to herself. "Well, we can't all be lucky."

Her smile faded when she realized that before long she might have to contrive a way to put Mark Brody in jail.

When she thought about that, she didn't feel so lucky, after all.

14

It was crazy, but Tess couldn't get it out of her head.

Peter Faust. Ever since that phone call yesterday evening, she'd been reliving her interview with him from three years ago. This was all Abby's fault, of course. It was never good news when that woman called.

Last night she'd lain awake trying to reconstruct the interview, trying to remember every detail of Faust's body language and facial expressions, trying to put herself back in the moment. She didn't know why it was important. She only knew she had to remember.

Her obsession had not gone away in daylight. Even though she was scheduled to fly back to Denver this evening, she was almost tempted to have a copy of the interview transcript faxed or e-mailed to her. Then she realized there was an easier solution. The Behavioral Analysis Unit was located close to the Quantico base. They would have the interview on file.

She dropped by on her lunch break, parking her rental car at the North Stafford office building that housed CIRG, the Critical Incident Response Group—more than three hundred operatives whose purview included operations support, tactical support, crime analysis, and criminal profiling. The latter was where BAU came in.

The unit had gone through several name changes. It was best-known as the Behavioral Science Section, but it had been the Behavioral Analysis Unit for some time. The art of profiling was now known as criminal investigative analysis. The semantic changes were perhaps a tacit recognition that profiling was less a science than an art. More likely, they were just a reflection of the FBI's bottomless appetite for new terminology. Since the first adoption of profiling techniques by the Bureau in 1972, the profiling section, or elements of it, had been variously known as the Behavioral Science Investigative Support Unit, the Profiling and Behavioral Assessment Unit, and the Child Abduction and Serial Killer Unit.

For a while the profilers' duties had been divided along geographical lines, with one unit working cases east of the Mississippi and another unit working the western end of the country. After September 11, the profilers had been split into three units handling counterterrorism, crimes against children, and crimes against adults, with a fourth unit running the old VICAP program. In addition, the FBI's Training Division maintained its own profiling section for educational purposes—a section known, confusingly enough, as the Behavioral Science Unit, the very name that had started it all.

Profiling had generated a lot of publicity, but Tess remained skeptical of it. She had seen too many cases where some perfectly ordinary, perfectly innocent civilian was subjected to law enforcement harassment because he happened to meet somebody's idea of what the suspect ought to look like. Profiling was a matter of playing the percentages. Most serial offenders could be divided into fairly distinct categories and ascribed reasonably predictable behaviors. But not all of them. Some stood outside any established category or managed to confound the analysts by combining qualities that were supposed to be mutually exclusive.

Novelists and filmmakers had jazzed up the work of FBI profilers considerably. In works of fiction, the profilers were always flying off to the scene of a grisly crime to make a personal inspection of the evidence. They attended autopsies. They interviewed victims, witnesses, and suspects. Sometimes they got into shoot-outs with the bad guys.

Real life was less dramatic. The profilers weren't Sherlock Holmes. They were more like Mycroft Holmes, the great detective's smarter brother, who rarely left the comfort of his armchair. The BAU analysts worked at their desks. Law-enforcement agencies requesting their help had to fill out tedious questionnaires. The answers were then entered into the profilers' computers. Most of the analysis was done automatically by matching up these answers with standard profiles. Agents reviewed the work to ensure accuracy and add personal touches.

They almost never went to a crime scene. They certainly never attended any autopsies. They did not interview persons of interest in the case. Most of them probably neglected to carry their firearms, and it was doubtful that any of them, at least in their capacity as behavioral analysts, had ever used one. If there was a less glamorous job in the Bureau, Tess didn't know about it.

Even their offices lacked allure. Drab and utilitarian, they had all the ambience of a third-rate accounting firm. There could at least have been some paintings on the walls, but evidently art wasn't in the budget.

Tess identified herself to the duty agent and requested a transcript of the interview, giving the date and other particulars.

"I can do better than a transcript," he said after checking the files. "We've got that one on DVD. Would that be preferable?"

She almost said no, then remembered that her laptop had a DVD drive. She waited while he disappeared into another room to burn the disk.

It would be strange to see the interview on video—to watch herself in dialogue with Faust. She wondered if his personality would come across on her laptop screen—no, not his personality, but his essence, the dark heart of his being, which she had glimpsed. The evil inside him.

Evil. There was a word that wasn't spoken very often in these offices. Behavioral analysis was all about patterns of activity, family history, psychological triggers, psychosexual needs. In these surroundings it would be a serious faux pas to bring up any moral considerations. Which was not to say that the good people at the Behavioral Analysis Unit weren't concerned with matters of right and wrong. But they had learned to compartmentalize. Right and wrong, good and evil—these were things that might occupy their minds while raising their children or sitting in church, but not at their desks. Here they had to be objective—and objectivity, at least as it was commonly construed, meant that moral judgments must be put on hold.

It was funny, in a way. The same people who so assiduously divided their subjects into categories, who routinely distinguished between the organized and the disorganized offender or between the antisocial and the asocial personality type, could not bring themselves to make the simplest distinction of all, one that any child could make—the distinction between good and bad.

Tess had no such qualms. She believed in evil. Maybe it was her Catholic upbringing, or maybe it was the way she had lost Paul to Mobius's knife.

Or maybe her belief stemmed from a night early in her career, when she was stationed in Miami. She'd just gone off duty when a Hispanic agent who'd grown up locally invited her to witness an exorcism. It was the kind of opportunity she couldn't pass up.

The exorcism took place in the Little Havana apartment of a Santeria priest, a *babalawo*. The tiny one-bedroom unit was crammed with icons of the saints and makeshift altars, and suffused with smoke from a *sahumerio,* ritual incense. Candles burned everywhere, all of them white—the sacred color, she was told, of the god who would be invoked tonight.

In the bedroom she found the *babalawo* and his patient, a nine-year-old boy whose parents were convinced he was possessed by evil spirits. The boy lay quivering and twitching on the bed, his eyes rolling madly. The smell of the incense was strongest here, and the candles seemed to burn with extra brightness.

The ceremony began with an invocation of the king of the spirits. All-powerful, he must be mentioned for safety's sake. But the real focus of the ritual was the lesser god who could expel evil spirits from their unwilling host.

A basin of water lay on the floor. The exorcised spirits would be driven into the water and thereby cleansed.

When the second god was summoned, the boy began to shake violently. The *babalawo* called on the god for deliverance. The boy writhed on the bedsheets. Sweat popped out on his face. Shouts and moans issued from his mouth. His lips were stretched wide, his teeth bared.

There was a squawking hen in a cage by the bed. The *babalawo* pulled it out and cut its throat, then dribbled its blood over a heap of stones sacred to the god. His voice rose, becoming a wild, keening wail.

And then something happened, or seemed to happen, something that Tess could not explain. Suddenly it was as if the boy were sinking into the bed—sinking *through* the bed. As if he were being dragged down through the physical reality of the bed itself, into some lower dimension.

It had to have been an optical illusion, or a hallucination brought on by the eye-watering smoke and the *babalawo*'s chants. But she could swear she saw it.

And she was equally sure she saw a dark, miasmic cloud rise from the boy and hover in the candlelit room, a fog of chittering evil, blacker than the *sahumerio* smoke. It lingered for a moment, then vanished into the basin.

On the bed, the boy lay quiet, his breathing normal, his flushed face quickly resuming its natural color. After a minute or two he awoke from his trance. He seemed composed and happy. His parents thanked the *baba-lawo* effusively.

Tess left the apartment, shaken. She wasn't sure what she had witnessed. But of one thing she was certain: In the instant before the black miasma had disappeared into the water, she had felt a *presence* in the bedroom. A presence of pure malice, of unadulterated evil. In a rush the sermons she'd endured at Catholic services had come back to her—Satan the evil one, devils and the outer darkness, the wailing and gnashing of teeth. It had been a long time since she'd taken such stories literally. Yet in the bedroom, in that moment, they had felt real. Not metaphors, not myths. Real.

It would have been easy to forget what she'd seen and felt, chalk it up to an overactive imagination or the power of suggestion. She was not naive enough to be so skeptical. She could no more forget what she had perceived than she could doubt the reality of her own body. *Something* had taken control of that boy and had been forced out. *Something* had been overmastered and tamed in that barrio bedroom.

There was evil in the world, and it was real and tangible.

She hadn't thought of the Santeria exorcism very often over the years, but she did think of it when she met Peter Faust. Because if there was an immutable evil that moved through this earth like a silent plague, then Peter Faust was its host. And unlike the boy in Little Havana, Faust was a willing host. He had spread out a welcome mat for evil and embraced it with open arms.

The duty agent interrupted her thoughts. He had finished making the copy.

"Here's the disk. It contains the complete interview, plus a little bonus at the end—the LAPD video of their search of Faust's home. They gave us a copy for our files."

"Thanks," she said. "I appreciate it."

"I thought you might want to see where he lives. You know," he added almost shyly, "you have a lot of fans here, Agent McCallum."

"Do I?" Now she felt guilty about having criticized the BAU, even if only in her thoughts. "Well, thank you. I need all the support I can get."

She took the disk from him. It felt oddly warm in her hand, as if it held some concentrated heat, like the fires of hell. As if it were not a video disk but a lump of brimstone.

Crazy. Faust wasn't the devil, no matter what the demonic connotations of his name. He was a man; that was all.

Only a man.

15

Faust spent the night with Elise, departing in midmorning to drive home. As always, he took a certain sensual pleasure in operating his BMW sedan. The hum of the engine was a throaty, leonine growl, the sound of a hungry animal. And he relished the feel of the leather upholstery, soft and yielding. Leather had very positive associations for him. Caressing the seat cushions, he remembered the strap as it tightened around Emily Wallace's neck.

As he neared his house, he was pleasantly tingling with what Americans called a buzz. In his case it was not a buzz of alcohol, narcotics, or even caffeine—he did not indulge in the first two at all, and never overindulged in the third. It was merely a slight thrill of anticipation, similar perhaps to what small children felt on Christmas morning as they prepared to see what gifts Santa had left.

He had never known that particular thrill. He had never believed in Santa. Nor had he believed in God. The devil, however, was another matter. He had always been sure the devil was real.

He wondered if Elise believed in evil. No doubt she would swear she did not. She was too sophisticated for such empty moralism. But could he trust her? She was as innocent of her own innermost depths and subconscious motives as any child.

Faust had often told Elise that Americans were naive

and easily fooled. Yet it never seemed to occur to her that she herself was an American.

She saw herself as cosmopolitan and worldly-wise. She was in the fashion industry, was she not? She traveled the globe, hobnobbed with intellectuals, and pretended to understand their chatter. She disdained ethics, mocked religion. She even spoke a smattering of French.

With these accomplishments to her credit, she thought she had earned entry into the elite. She could feel superior to all the unenlightened ones, the hoi polloi with their potbellies and bumper stickers and hometown sports teams. She was not among them, or so she thought.

She was wrong. She might have forgotten her origins, but Faust had not. She had been raised in a suburb of Detroit by parents who ran a sandwich shop. Imagine that—*a sandwich shop.* They sold hoagies or heroes or subs, whatever those repellent foot-long sandwiches were called in that part of the country. They took vacations to Disneyland and Sea World. They watched situation comedies while eating dinner on plastic trays.

She might be a world traveler now, but she could never escape her beginnings.

And so he could not trust her, not fully. There was no way to ensure that she would not revert to the girl she had been, whose mommy and daddy had taught her so earnestly about right and wrong.

No way to be certain that she would not betray him.

She *might* rise to the challenge. Or she might not. He could not take the risk. And so there were things he had not told her.

Raven, for instance.

Elise knew nothing about her.

He reached his house and pulled into the curving driveway, leaving the BMW parked by the front door.

His home stood on a half acre, a spacious lot by local standards. It was high enough in the Los Feliz foothills

to command what the real estate agent had described as
"jetliner views"—the sweep of the city from the downtown to the sea, framed in steel casement windows and
French doors. The estate was surrounded by high walls
topped with metal spikes; entry was afforded by a
wrought-iron gate, operated by a key card.

The house, in southern California's trademark Mediterranean style, had been built in 1926 by an insanely
imaginative architect. It had seven bedrooms, five full
baths and two half baths, a vast kitchen, a step-down
living room under a barreled ceiling, a study, a media
room, and a covered veranda featuring one of the
home's four fireplaces. And a maid's room, de rigueur
in the twenties. But Faust had no live-in help. He enjoyed privacy.

The maid's room was on the ground floor near the
back door. It was windowless and small.

Six years ago, when Faust purchased the house, he
made alterations to the room. The work was done quietly and without the inconvenience of government per-
mits or union contractors. He stripped the faded
wallpaper and had the room soundproofed. He had the
flimsy door replaced with one of solid oak. He tore out
the carpet, exposing the hardwood floor.

To carry out his final alterations, he hired day laborers
who spoke little English and had no idea who he was.
At his instruction they built a new paneled wall in front
of the door to the room. The wall had a hinged section
that could be swung forward to permit access to the door
behind it. When the hinged section was closed, it
blended seamlessly with the rest of the wall.

The maid's room had effectively ceased to exist. No
visitor to his home—or almost none—ever imagined that
there was a room behind the paneled wall. Although
Elise had spent many nights in the house, had roamed
it freely, even she did not know.

But Raven knew.

Faust had kept Raven in the hidden, soundproofed

room for ten days now, subsisting on soda crackers and bottled water. He was most impressed with her. She had held out so bravely during her captivity.

But all her courage would not save her from the same fate as the others. The many others whose lives he had taken, all the pretty young things killed by his hands.

I am not a serial killer, he had told Abby Sinclair. *I killed just once.*

He had delivered the same lie to Elise. She believed him. Sinclair had been skeptical. Yet in the end she had taken the job anyway. For Elise's sake. To protect the innocent. That was the sales pitch, and it had worked. He had turned her own morality against her.

Now Sinclair was working as his agent, while convinced she was on the side of good. He wondered what Raven would think of that.

Faust almost asked her, after he unlocked the door and entered the room and untied the linen gag from around her head. But he forgot. He was struck again by her beautiful innocence, her absolute helplessness.

She lay before him, naked, bruised, manacled to the headboard, coughing weakly after biting down on the gag for many hours. He never left her unmuzzled. Although the room was soundproofed, he took no chances. For the same reason he had positioned the bed well away from the walls, so she could not stamp her feet and create reverberations that would travel through the house.

Her hair was long and black, and might be silky when clean. He wouldn't know. She had been dirty when he met her, one of countless urchins living in the streets or in condemned buildings, turning tricks for a little pocket money. She was a runaway from somewhere. The appellation Raven was only a nickname, presumably a tribute to her jet-black hair; he had no notion of what her real name might be. She would doubtless tell him, but he had never thought to ask.

Although she had been dirty enough on their first encounter, she was positively filthy now. The sealed, airless room was hot, and she was scared, a combination that had left her ripe with body odor. He did not mind. He liked the smell of unadorned human flesh. Americans masked their scent with perfumes, colognes, and deodorants. He preferred nature's uncomplicated musk.

Although he was indifferent to her true name, he had inquired after her age. She was fifteen, she had said. That was good. He still liked them young.

She had concluded her coughing fit. He unscrewed a bottle of mineral water and tipped it to her mouth. It was a gesture not of kindness but of necessity. Deprived of water she would expire of thirst, and he did not want her to die that way.

She swallowed half the bottle, choking on it at the end. He pulled it free and wiped her chin.

With rheumy eyes she peered up at him. She asked the question she always asked.

"Why?" Her voice was a sad, toneless croak.

She had asked him this question many times over the past ten days, sometimes tearfully, sometimes angrily, and sometimes—as she did now—in exhausted futility. Always he gave her the same answer, the only answer there was, but one she did not want to hear.

"There is no why," he said. "There is no reason for anything, ever. You distract yourself in seeking what cannot be found."

She only stared at him. The words had not reached her. They never did. She was a creature of her ethos, her mythos. She believed in reasons, in purpose. She could not accept, could not grasp, the ultimate pointlessness of it all.

After a long moment she asked a new question, one she had not voiced before.

"When?"

In the deflated pessimism of her tone, he caught her meaning. When would it be over? When would *she* be over?

"Soon," he said, almost kindly. He could afford to be kind to one who was utterly under his power.

He never could predict his exact timetable. There came a point, invariably, when the victim ceased to interest him. When the last glimmer of life and hope had drained away, and there was only a shell, staring and mindless. He took no enjoyment in maintaining the victim's life after that. Once she had been thoroughly broken, reduced to something less than human—then it was time to put her down.

He thought of it as a mercy killing. The termination of a life no longer worth living.

Raven was nearly at that point. He had charted her descent with scientific exactitude. In the beginning, she had tried to kick him whenever he approached; her legs were not chained. When ungagged, she had screamed for help, the cries echoing through the empty house.

He had not punished her for these actions. They were a natural response, a manifestation of the will to survive. She was no better than an animal, after all, and like an animal she acted on instinct.

Now she neither fought back nor called out. She was spent. Or nearly spent. But not quite there. A day longer, perhaps two, and she would be done. When the last faint spark faded from her eyes.

"Soon," he said again, brushing her matted hair. "Soon now."

He was so very pleased with her.

16

At eleven A.M. Abby called Faust on his landline. He answered on the second ring, sounding unusually cheery. "And how may I be of service?"

"We need to work out your plans for tonight."

"I am afraid I already have plans. I am making a public appearance at a bookshop in Santa Monica. The event is long scheduled and cannot be changed."

"That's okay. What time are you supposed to be there?"

"Seven o'clock."

"Is Elise going, too?"

"Why, of course," he said, as if his girlfriend's presence was inevitable at any of his events.

"What I need you to do is text-message Elise, reminding her of when to be there and where to go. Be sure you mention the name of the store."

"All this is for my stalker's benefit, I presume?"

"Exactly."

"And you still will not share his name or address with me?"

"I'm funny that way. Get used to it."

"It appears I have no choice. Your assumption is that the man will be present at the bookshop?"

"He'll show."

There was an uncomfortable pause as Abby realized she had run out of things to say. To fill the silence, she asked if he expected a big turnout.

"A select crowd. Those of refined sensibilities. Those who embrace the full implications of the postmodern."

"Terrific. What are you going to do, read from your book?"

"That would serve no purpose. Everyone in attendance will have read it already. No, I will deliver some extemporaneous remarks and answer questions. Perhaps," he added, "*you* have some questions you wish to have answered."

"Why would I?"

"In our last conversation you seemed most interested in my modus operandi."

"I don't have any questions."

"Pity. I do enjoy talking about myself. I am quite shameless in that respect. Most people, of course, are too courteous—or too intimidated—to ask about Emily Wallace. Ordinarily they select some safer topic. Geschwur, for instance."

"Geschwur?"

"Surely you've heard of them. They are one of the most commercially successful musical groups in Germany. They have been awarded two Echoes, the German equivalent of your Grammy Awards. Not to mention the Comet, another prestigious prize."

"The Comet, huh? How about the Ajax? Or the Formula 409?"

"You make light of them. You should not. Their most recent album sold more than four million copies. It was titled *Flammen.*"

"Meaning?"

"Flames. The fires of hell, perhaps."

"Lovely. Why would anybody be asking you about this band?"

"Because I toured with them. Oh, yes. For more than four months."

"You don't strike me as a rocker."

"I have no musical talent. I spoke to the audience from the spotlight while the band played and appropriate images were projected on the screen above the stage."

"Appropriate images. Such as Emily Wallace's morgue photos?"

"Among other things. The audience adored my performance. I made many new fans."

"Well, I'm not interested in Gesundheit."

"Geschwur," he corrected. "The word means *ulcer*."

"Somehow I don't think they'd appeal to me."

"I believe they would. They speak to the jungle animal within us all. Some listeners are too civilized to hear their siren call. But not you, I think."

"You're not one to be passing judgment on who's civilized."

"No judgment. Merely an observation. I know you, Miss Sinclair. Perhaps better than you know yourself."

Abby wasn't too happy with that thought. She did her best to get it out of her mind when the call was over, throwing herself into the task of researching Mark Brody.

She accessed several online databases and ran the name and address on his driver's license. The address—an apartment in Reseda—was legitimate, but out-of-date. He had moved out six months ago, having lived there for less than a year. Before that time, there was no record of his whereabouts. She searched news stories on the Iraq War. There was a Mark Brody who was involved in action at Karbala Gap that took the life of his CO. Without a photo she couldn't be sure that it was the same man; conceivably her Mark Brody had stolen the other guy's identity. Still, she thought he probably had been telling the truth.

He said he'd left the military after the incident, which meant he had become a civilian sometime in the late spring of 2003. From that time forward, until he established residence in Reseda, his history was a blank. Well, he'd told her that he had remained in Iraq. Whatever he'd been up to over there, he'd stayed off the grid.

She checked other databases. He had a few credit cards, but they were all registered to the defunct address. Presumably his mail was being forwarded, but to where?

She returned to the news articles on the Iraq incident. One of Brody's fellow A-team members was quoted. His name was Carter Holloway, and according to the story he hailed from the small town of Creston, Idaho. If he'd left the service by now, he might have gone back there. She looked him up in a database of Creston residents and found his name and number. She called. When a man answered, she asked to speak to Carter Holloway.

"That's me."

"Sir, did you serve in the army with Mark Brody?"

His wary pause told her the answer. "Who's asking, if I may?"

"Oh. Sorry. My name is Sally Mayhew. I knew Mark in Iraq, but I've kind of lost touch with him, and I'm trying to track him down."

"I was with him in Iraq. I don't recall meeting you."

"This was after he left the military. As I guess you know—or maybe you don't—he stayed on in Iraq for some time afterward."

"I don't know anything about that," Holloway said, but his guarded tone made her pretty sure he was lying. Whatever Brody had been up to in Iraq, it hadn't been the sort of thing his friends wanted to discuss with strangers.

"I was just wondering if you had a way for me to reach him. Telephone number or address, e-mail, anything at all."

He thought it over. "I can give you his number. Hold on."

She waited while he got it, then wrote down a number with an 818 area code. That made it a San Fernando Valley location, but it didn't match the number associated with his old apartment.

She thanked Holloway and was about to hang up

when he asked, "How exactly did you know Brody, anyway?"

"Well, you know . . ." She was good at sounding shy and flustered when she had to.

"Yeah, I think I get it. Look, miss, don't go messing things up for him, will you?"

She wasn't sure what this meant. "I just want to say hi to him, that's all."

A grunt of skepticism. "I hope that *is* all. He's been through a lot. He doesn't need any more . . . complications in his life."

"I'll remember that," Abby promised.

She had a feeling Mark Brody's life was already a good deal more complicated than Holloway knew.

At the computer again, she ran the number on a reverse directory. The address that came up was in Van Nuys. No unit number, so it was apparently not an apartment but a house.

She took the Miata, speeding north on the 405 into the Valley. His place was a modest ranch-style house on a tree-lined street. The lawn and hedges were neatly trimmed. She parked at the curb a few doors down, wondering if she should risk a little B and E. The house might contain secrets she couldn't learn anywhere else. But breaking in was chancy, especially in broad daylight. Even so, she just might go for it.

First she rang the doorbell, simply to confirm that the place was empty. If Mark Brody happened to be here, she would have a lot of explaining to do. But she was sure he would still be staking out Faust in Los Feliz. He had to be there to pick up the cell phone messages. He—

The door opened. She missed a couple of heartbeats before realizing that the figure standing before her was not Brody, but a woman in a blue housecoat. A pregnant woman, who appeared to be in her third trimester. If Abby could judge from the nonstop yelling of a tyke in another room, it wasn't her first child.

Abby was good at a lot of things, and one of them was improvising when circumstances took her by surprise.

"Why, hello," she said smoothly in a Southern accent that had come from nowhere. "I'm looking for a Mr. Mark Brody."

The woman frowned, unaccustomed to visitors. "I'm afraid he's not at home right now."

"That's too bad. I wanted to see him, and I won't be in town long."

"I can leave a message. Who should I say dropped by?"

"Sarah Joiner." Instinctively she used a different name from the one she'd given Holloway. "I knew Mark when he was in the army. Friend of mine told me his address."

"You knew him from the military?"

"From Fort Bragg." This was where the Green Berets trained. All of a sudden she understood the reason for her Southern accent. Fort Bragg was in North Carolina. "I was on the civilian support staff."

"You an old girlfriend of his?" the woman asked, pretending to smile.

"No," Abby reassured her with a dismissive flutter of her hand, "no, it was nothing like that."

"I'm glad to hear it. Don't really want the competition."

"I take it you're . . . with him now?"

"I'm his wife," she said coolly. "Patricia."

Wife. Hell. And she had one kid, and another in the oven. This was not what Abby had expected from Mark Brody. Suddenly their close encounter between the sheets was looking a lot less romantic. But at least now she knew what Holloway had meant about not making Brody's life more complicated.

"Nice to meet you," Abby said, turning on the Southern charm. "Well, if you could just tell him I came calling. Like I said, I'm in town for only a couple days. I can give you my number at the hotel—"

Patricia cut her off. "Mark won't be back that soon. He's away on business."

"Still the traveling man, huh? He always wanted to see the world. Action and adventure, that was his thing. I guess it still is."

"Seems so," Patricia said curtly. Her smile had frozen in place.

"What part of the planet is he off to this time?"

"South America. Now if you don't mind, I was just in the middle of something."

"Sorry, didn't mean to be standing here running my mouth off. My apologies for intruding. You say hi to Mark for me when he gets back."

"Will do." That smile never wavered, even as the door slowly closed.

Abby walked back to her car. So Mark Brody had a house and a pregnant wife and a kid. The wife might be covering for her husband with the South America story, or maybe she just hadn't felt too sociable with someone who, despite her denials, could be one of his old flames.

But Abby suspected that Patricia really believed her hubby was south of the border. It seemed doubtful that Brody would have told her what he was actually up to. Special Forces guys, like cops, tended to be reticent with their family members, even their wives. Brody, of course, wasn't Special Forces anymore, but old habits died hard.

The bottom line was that she wasn't going to learn anything in Van Nuys. The guest cottage was the place to look. Seven o'clock couldn't come soon enough.

17

On her way home Abby stopped at a music shop in Westwood Village and hunted down a copy of *Flammen* in the International section. Geschwur's four band members glowered up at her from the CD package, youngish men in severe black ensembles, their hair close-cropped, their faces clean shaven. The color scheme was red, black, and white—the colors of the Nazi flag. The photo looked like a recruiting poster for the Hitler Youth.

The clerk ringing up the sale looked at her with a hint of interest. "You into these guys?"

"Someone recommended them."

"They're great," he said, the words sounding less like an endorsement than like a dare.

She played the CD when she got home.

The first track opened with a rush of electric guitar chords and the shrieks of a soprano choir, which gave way to loud, pounding drums. The music abruptly dropped in volume as the lead singer began growling into the microphone. He had a harsh, raspy voice that reminded her of the devil in *The Exorcist*, only deeper and more seductive. Seductive but sickening—he spit some of the words with such amplified force that he sounded like a man retching. His every utterance was laced with contempt, the guttural quality of his German intentionally exaggerated to suggest the grunts and barks of an animal. It was the voice of a psychopath.

Abby liked good headbanging, balls-to-the-wall music as much as the next person, but there was something unmistakably creepy about this stuff. It was the audio equivalent of weird old German movies like *The Cabinet of Dr. Caligari*—the vocals distorted, the sounds grating and unpleasant, the tone unremittingly dark. And all of it was dominated by the lead singer, rasping in her ear like a pervert making an obscene phone call, his voice conveying the message that life is ugly, bleak, dark, and meaningless, and there is no escape, no hope except surrender to violence and craziness. She wasn't sure that a nation with Germany's history was doing itself any favors by listening to that voice. Four million copies sold, Faust had said. . . .

The first track ended with the wails of the choir, sighing and moaning like lamenting ghosts. She sat through two more tracks, mostly indistinguishable from the first, before shutting off the CD player. She'd heard enough.

She wasn't in touch with pop music very much anymore, certainly not with metal bands, and obviously not with European metal bands. It was music for the alienated, the outcasts. She had ascribed Faust's celebrity status to his charisma, but she began to think it was something more. He had killed for pleasure and gotten away with it. He had lived out the fantasy of all those angry adolescents, those sulking narcissists, those budding sociopaths. He was their spokesman, their role model.

She wondered just how much influence he had, and how far it extended. She thought of the clerk in the music store—

The intercom buzzed, interrupting her thoughts. "Yes?"

Gerry's voice came over the speaker. "Mr. Bryce is here."

She frowned. Bryce was the name Wyatt used when he visited. She wished he hadn't come now. She wasn't in the mood for another confrontation. But she could hardly send him away.

"Miss Sinclair?" Gerry asked.

"Okay, let him come up."

She was still ticked off at him. And though she hated to admit it, she was also feeling guilty. She could still feel Brody's touch on her skin.

After a few minutes there was a rap on her door. She opened it and wordlessly let him in.

"I won't stay long," he said. "I imagine you're working."

"Gotta pay my bills." She was straining for a light tone but missing it.

"Right. I just wanted to talk to you about something."

"Okay."

"First of all—I'm sorry. I mean, for the things I said. I was unfair. It wasn't the right way to say it, or the right time, or anything."

"We were both a little worked up. I'm sorry, too."

"Thanks." He stood there awkwardly. "That's not all I came here to say."

"All right."

"I still want us to be friends, Abby. I'll help you out when I can. You can come to me for info. I won't complain. But . . ."

Suddenly she knew where this was headed. The part about still being friends was the tip-off. There was only one place he could go after that. But she couldn't quite believe it, had to hear him say it.

"But," he went on, "I don't think we can be more than friends anymore."

She took a breath. "You're saying . . . the party's over?"

"I'm saying *we're* over. Us. Our relationship, or whatever the hell this has been."

There was no way he could mean it. No way. He had been part of her life for so long that she couldn't imagine him just going away. It wasn't possible.

She reached out her hand to him. "Vic, I know you're upset. . . ."

He ignored the gesture. "I'm not upset. I've been

thinking about this for a long time. Months. I guess most guys would say I'm crazy. They'd tell me I have it all— sex without commitment. Who would give that up, right? But I want something else, Abby. I want a future. A family. I want . . . more."

Of course he wanted more. He'd been telling her as much for months, maybe for years. She hadn't listened.

"Maybe I can give you those things," she said, but the words sounded false even as she heard them.

"You can't. You know it. It's not in your game plan. You won't settle down. At least not anytime soon. And I can't wait any longer."

His last words pricked her. She felt she was being accused of something.

"It's not like I kept you waiting," she said. "I never made any promises."

"I know that. I'm not blaming . . . anyone. It's just one of those things. We want different lives."

She extended her hand again, and this time he took it. "We can work it out, Vic."

"I don't think so. What we had"—she noted the past tense—"it worked for you, I guess. But not for me."

"I didn't hear any complaints for most of the time we were together," she said softly.

He looked away. "At first it was great. It was perfect. But you know, things change. I'm almost forty. I want . . . I want a wife."

She said nothing.

"Kids," he added. "The whole suburban deal."

Just like Brody, she thought irrelevantly.

"I don't even know if I'll be a cop much longer," he said. "Another few years and I'll have put in my twenty. Maybe I'll leave L.A., move someplace that's not so insane."

Her throat was dry. "You . . . and your wife and kids."

"In a minivan, probably." He tried to smile.

"You have anyone in mind for this wife position that's just opened up?"

"Nope."

"But you're sure she's out there?"

"I won't know unless I look."

She couldn't argue with that. It was funny, though. She would have preferred it if he'd had another woman lined up, even if he'd been boffing her on the side. That way would have been less humiliating. To be thrown over for a rival was one thing. To be dumped for nobody, just the hope that someone better might come along—that was worse.

"So this is really it?" she whispered. "End of the road?"

"I said I want us to stay friends. I wasn't kidding. You can come to me anytime. For anything. Except . . ."

"Yeah. Except."

The hell of it was, they probably *would* remain friends. And she *would* come to him for inside info. She wasn't proud.

"If you think about it," he said gently, "you'll see it makes sense. For both of us."

This pained her. "Since when are relationships supposed to make sense?"

She wanted him to argue, to fight. If they fought, there would be a connection. But he only smiled.

"You got me there. I'd better be going. You've got work to do."

"Work. Right."

"Take care, Abby."

He didn't kiss her. She watched him leave.

18

Tess leaned back in her window seat with the notebook computer on her lap. The disk from Behavioral Analysis was in the DVD drive. Noise-canceling headphones, purchased at an airport gift shop, sat on her head. Her seatmate, an obese man with a ZZ Top beard, had drifted off to sleep. There was no food service on this flight. No more excuses for delay.

She had thought she wanted to see the interview, but strangely she found herself hesitating. It had been years since she had heard Peter Faust's coolly urbane elocution or had seen the malicious merriment in his pale blue eyes. She wasn't sure she wanted to open this particular door into her past.

But her past had many doors she preferred not to open. She couldn't avoid them all.

She activated the disk and switched off the reading light above her seat, allowing the screen to glow in the darkness. Legalese prohibiting the distribution of this recording to non-FBI personnel appeared and vanished. A menu came up. The two items on the disk were the interview and the LAPD search of Faust's home. Procrastinating, she clicked on the search video.

Handheld camera footage fed the screen. She watched as the video cam followed the search team, traveling into one room after another. The sunken living room with its high, barreled ceiling and casement windows letting in a flood of sunlight. The dining room, one wall lined with French doors that opened onto a columned terrace. The spacious kitchen and adjacent breakfast room, overlooking a garden. The library, the family room, the paneled foyer, the guest bathroom, the walk-in closets, the master suite with its elaborate baths.

Nothing had been found. At the end, the camera caught a glimpse of Faust, arms folded across his chest in a pose of satisfaction, a cool smile on his lips. Tess wished desperately that there were a way to erase that smile.

The menu returned. She could put it off no longer. She selected the interview.

This time there was no shaky handheld footage. The video had been taken by a stationary camera mounted in an upper corner of a windowless interrogation room in the Denver field office. Faust was seated alone at the table, his hands steepled before him. Tess remembered watching this very image on the monitor in the observation room.

"An interview with the vampire."

That's what the tech officer had called it as he adjusted picture and sound. He was a wispy, bright-eyed guy, almost too short to meet the Bureau's height requirement, and he talked constantly.

Tess had just looked at him, not getting the reference.

"He's Lestat, you know?" the technician said. "That's the way I think of him, anyhow. But not Tom Cruise. Tom Cruise was all wrong."

She wondered if everyone in the world was movie-crazy except her. "Tom Cruise?"

"He played Lestat in the movie. But that's not the right look for Lestat. They should've gotten Faust. He would've been perfect."

"When did the movie come out?"

"Maybe ten, fifteen years ago."

"Fifteen years ago Peter Faust was still unknown. Ten years ago he was in a mental hospital."

"So he wasn't a viable casting choice—is that what you're saying?"

Was that what she was saying? Surprisingly enough, it actually was.

The man's chatter died down when Tess ostentatiously began reviewing her notes. She had researched Faust's history after being informed that he would speak only to her. She had offered to fly to Los Angeles, but Faust had proved remarkably accommodating, jetting to Denver for the interview. He'd explained that he planned to get in a little skiing in Aspen later in the week.

She had expected him to arrive at the field office with a phalanx of lawyers, but as it turned out he had no legal counsel present for the occasion. "I have nothing to hide," he'd told the ASAC with a smile.

Tess knew that wasn't true. Everybody had something to hide.

Having been briefed by the profiler assigned to this office, having studied Faust's crime and his psychological analysis, and having watched him on the monitor for the last ten minutes, Tess was ready. She entered the interrogation room and calmly shook Faust's hand, then seated herself across from him. Her first question was why he had insisted on speaking only to her.

"I have wished to meet you," he said, "since reading of the Mobius affair."

"Why?"

"Because I am a killer. And you are a killer of killers."

"I killed Mobius in self-defense."

"Of course. And that man in Miami, the drug merchant—that was self-defense as well?"

"If you know about that, then you already know the answer." And Miami, she thought to herself, was a long time ago.

"Still," he said, "it is rare. Few federal agents ever so much as discharge their sidearms in the line of duty. Fewer still have killed a man. You have killed two."

"I'm not proud of it."

"But you should be. You are a successful combatant

on the battleground of life. You have exhibited a flair for survival that is positively Darwinian."

"I did what I had to do."

"As do we all," he said with another charming smile.

She expected to see dark depths in his eyes, like wells of shadow, but instead they were open and clear. Somehow this bothered her more. The man was a snake, and he should have a serpent's eyes, hooded and cold.

She asked him about Roberta Kessler, the dead girl in L.A. He gave all the predictable answers. He'd never heard of her until the police came calling. They had searched his home thoroughly and found nothing. The authorities' continued interest in him was beginning to constitute harassment.

"My attorneys have advised me that I may decline to cooperate in this investigation. They have suggested that I give you the—what is the idiom?—the cold shoulder."

"Why don't you?"

"I have given my reason already. I wished to meet the great Tess McCallum, the fastest gun in the West."

"Only the luckiest."

"False modesty is most unbecoming. A woman of your skills should not adhere to such trite conventions."

She disliked receiving compliments from him. "A patron of the bar where Roberta Kessler was last seen—"

"I was not at the bar."

"—says she saw you—"

"She is mistaken."

"—talking to Roberta."

"It was another man. I do not go clubbing. It is a childish pastime. At any rate, your witness cannot say for certain that I am the one she saw."

"What makes you think that?"

"Because if it were otherwise, I would have been arrested by now."

This was true. The witness had provided a description so vague as to be almost useless as evidence. The fact that she had been doing bourbon shots and Ecstasy for a good part of the night added nothing to her credibility.

"Why do we not desist from these games?" Faust went on. "They bore me. This murdered female, Roberta Keller—"

"Kessler."

"*She* bores me. Every aspect of this situation is tedious to me except one. You, Special Agent McCallum. You intrigue me."

"We're not having this meeting to satisfy your curiosity."

"Oh, yes, we are. That is the one and only reason I am speaking to you. I called for you and only for you. I wanted to take your measure."

Tess met his gaze. "And I wanted to take yours."

"Have I measured up?"

"You're exactly what I expected."

"I do not think so. You expected a monster."

"That's just what I found."

She could not read his expression, could not tell if her response pleased or displeased him.

The interview continued for more than two hours. At one point Faust took a scrap of fabric from his pocket and began toying with it. She asked what it was. His good-luck charm, he said, his talisman. She asked to see it, and he courteously obliged.

It was a collar tab, black, with the *wolfsangel* symbol sewn on in white thread.

"This was worn, circa 1944, by an SS officer in the Landstorm Nederland, the Nazis' Dutch grenadier division," Faust said. "I purchased it at an auction in Santa Barbara. Smell it. Inhale its aroma. It still carries the scent of the battlefield, the scent of death."

"It's just a piece of old cloth."

"To the undiscriminating eye. But to the connoisseur it is so much more. A fragment of history."

"I guess I shouldn't be surprised that you'd be nostalgic about the SS."

His expression soured. "Please. I have no interest in such things. I am entirely nonpolitical. What fascinates me about this artifact is that it is a mere symbol, and yet it had the power to spur men to kill and die. Think of it. These Dutchmen volunteered to fight for the Nazis. This was after Hitler's armies had overrun Holland and turned it into an occupied territory. What would make a man side with his own oppressors, his conquerors? Why would he fight for them and not against them?"

"Maybe he wanted to be on what he thought was the winning side."

"Yes, certainly. But why was it the winning side? Not simply because the Netherlands had fallen after a mere five days' resistance. It was because the Nazis were larger than life, invincible, indestructible. A force of nature, an irresistible tide. This was the general belief—and it was grounded in symbolism. Symbolism like this."

His finger stabbed at the cloth in her hand.

"Men must believe, you see. It is in their nature to believe. And this SS rune, this totem worn as a symbol of power, fed that belief. The man who wore this insignia on his collar *believed* he had assumed the cunning and ferocity of the wolf. He *believed* he was undefeatable in battle. He *believed* he was part of a superhuman tribe, at the vanguard of a new world order. All this power and meaning he invested in what you call a mere piece of cloth."

"And he was wrong. The Nazis lost the war."

Faust sighed. "How prosaic your mind is. It is of no importance which side wins or loses. This is not a game in which one keeps score. What matters is only what this man felt. His raw experience. For those hours of combat he was truly alive. He was afire with reckless courage. He blazed like the sun. He *lived*."

"Like you did, when you murdered Emily?"

"Yes."

"And Roberta?"

He shook his head, disappointed in her obviousness.

"You insult my intelligence, Agent McCallum. I cannot be ensnared by such a threadbare net."

He retrieved the collar tab and put it back into his pocket.

She continued to spar with him, getting nowhere. Finally he grew bored with the sport.

"You are afraid of me, Tess McCallum," he said, as if this explained why she had drawn no blood in her attacks.

"Don't overestimate yourself."

"I never do."

"Oh, yes, you do. That's the besetting flaw of sociopaths, isn't it? Grandiosity. Megalomania."

He didn't answer, merely watched her, his pellucid stare registering indifference.

"Or should I call it what it really is?" she went on. "Narcissism. You're a classic narcissist, you know."

"Oh, is this a therapy session now?" He yawned.

"You're familiar with the myth of Narcissus, I assume."

"Refresh my memory."

"Narcissus was a beautiful boy who fell in love with his own reflection in a pond. He couldn't turn away. He just sat and stared at himself. In some versions of the story, he leaned so close to his reflection that he fell into the pond and drowned."

"How sad for him. And in other versions?"

"He forgot to eat or drink and wasted away and died."

"It seems unlikely in either case. Your boy sounds like a halfwit."

"All narcissists are halfwits, Peter." She noted his reaction to the use of his first name—a transient look of disapproval and, perhaps, discomfort. "You should know."

"I have been accused of many vices, Agent McCallum. Stupidity is not among them."

"But you *are* stupid. After all, you got caught."

"What if I did?"

"A smart criminal would have covered his tracks better than you did, don't you think? The way you disposed of Emily's body, for instance. Very amateurish."

"Do not presume to lecture me."

"You must have thought you were clever, dumping her body in a salvage yard. But really it was the worst location you could have chosen. People came there all the time to hunt for scrap metal and usable parts. That's why it's called a salvage yard. Because people salvage things from it."

"Yes. I understand the etymology."

"Apparently you don't. You were seen by one of the scrap hunters."

His face had gone rigid. He did not like to be instructed in his errors. "Hamburg is a crowded city. My options for the victim's disposal were limited."

"It's only your imagination that was limited. You could have dumped her in a waterway. There's a lot of water running through Hamburg, right? I've never been there—"

"Of course you have not." He tried to reassert control. "You Americans never leave the comforting familiarity of your provincial world. Most of you do not even own a passport."

"I've never been there," she repeated, "but I know there's a system of canals. A canal makes a good hiding place. Weigh her down with chains, dump her in the water, and let the fish do the rest. By the time she surfaces, if she ever does, she'll be unidentifiable." She paused. "That's how an intelligent killer would have handled it."

"I could not risk being seen with her remains—dumping them in the water—there are too many buildings, all with windows—"

For the first time, his self-control was breaking down. She pressed him.

"That's all bullshit, Peter. You risked being seen with her when you took her to the salvage yard. You didn't put her in the water because you never thought of it. It would have been the smart play, but you're not smart. And so you got caught."

"You understand nothing."

"I understand that you were apprehended by the municipal police in Hamburg. Local authorities. They're not exactly Interpol. They spend most of their time handing out traffic tickets and citing drunks for public urination. But they got you. In record time, too."

"Perhaps . . . perhaps I intended to be caught."

"Then why'd you remove her head and hands, if not to make identification more difficult? Why'd you hide her at all?"

He had no answer. His silence was the most satisfying sound Tess could have heard.

"You never meant to be caught. But you were stupid. You screwed up. You're a loser, Peter. You think of yourself as a superior human being, but all you really are is another failed criminal."

"Perhaps I failed that time—" he began, then stopped.

"Yes?"

"Nothing."

"You failed then, but not other times?"

"How clumsily you put words in my mouth."

"Maybe with Roberta you did better?"

He expelled a slow breath, and abruptly his features were smooth again, an unflinching mask. "I have never met the woman, Special Agent. I have already told you this."

Tess sighed. She'd gotten under his skin, put him on the defensive. But in the end it had gained her nothing.

In truth, he was *not* stupid. He would not be goaded into incriminating himself. He could be pushed just so far, but no further. He would never fold, never give her anything she could use.

She stood up without a word and left the interrogation room. In the hall she conferred with the case agent who'd flown in from L.A.

"This is a waste of time," she said. "He won't crack. He's not the type."

The case agent agreed. "Hell," he said, "maybe the son of a bitch is even innocent."

Tess knew he was wrong about that. Whether or not Peter Faust was involved in Roberta's murder was an open question.

But he was not innocent.

He was the least innocent man on earth.

19

Pulp Friction was a radical bookshop in Santa Monica, on the southern end of the outdoor mall called Third Street Promenade. Its inventory was a haphazard mix of new and used books, though the used ones went for full retail price, or more in the case of rare editions. Among the stacks were primitive carvings, faded Flower Power posters, erotic figurines, and other oddball ornaments picked up at garage sales.

Kitsch, Faust thought. A word in his native language that had made its way into American idiom.

There was also a cat, plump and glossy, lurking like a witch's familiar. The cat was afraid of him. It kept its distance.

About fifty people had shown up for the book signing and his accompanying talk. The event had been mentioned in the newspaper and advertised at the store. He had expected a turnout of roughly this size. In Europe he would have had three times this many attendees. In parts of eastern Germany, the former Communist areas, he might have had five hundred people.

His admirers sat before him, arrayed in folding chairs. Most were young. Some of their faces he recognized from Café Eden. They were people he knew, at least in passing. Edward and Dieter were there, and Elise, of course. There was one girl who had pressed pages of poetry into his hand from time to time, her eyes yearning. She couldn't have been more than nineteen— another Raven, but too closely linked to him for safety.

It would be interesting, though, to have a *willing* captive. A prisoner in the hidden room who wanted to be there, who savored the experience—all of it, even the final killing pressure of the strap around her neck.

The others were typical "fans," mere dabblers. No one was well dressed except Faust and Elise. Even the shop's proprietor had not dressed up. Faust frowned. The sloppiness of people today was a form of decadence.

He noted how many copies of his book the store had ordered—a nice stack. But it was the paperback. This annoyed him; the hardcover was still in print, and he earned higher royalties from its sales.

The proprietor glanced at the clock on the wall, which read 7:15. She asked Faust if he would "say a few words."

He nodded courteously, acknowledging his audience. He spoke without notes, having made no preparations. His tone was cordial, conversational. His sentences were perfectly parsed. Subordinate clauses did not confuse him; agreement of subject and verb never slipped him up. He could speak better than most politicians— certainly better than most American politicians. But his calling was a higher one than public service. He culled the herd. He taught cruelty. He was the harbinger of a new world.

"Good evening, all," he began. "I thank you very much for coming. I may say that while I am flattered by your attention, I do not merit it. There is nothing exceptional about me. I am not the world-historical hero of Hegel's fantasies. I am neither the way, nor the truth, nor the life, and no one comes to the Father through me. Not that I believe in the Father, of course. I believe in nothing except myself. In this I am the opposite of most men, who believe in everything except themselves."

He saw smiles around him.

"My only noteworthy quality is unflinching honesty. I do not shrink from truths. I do not comfort myself with lies. I do not prattle about virtue. Good and evil do not exist. Good is what works. Evil is what fails. That is all. The rest is mere rationalization. Were we living in biblical times I might put it another way. Having come down from the mountain, I would say to my flock, 'This is the whole of the law: Do what thou wilt.' Or to paraphrase the words of a later prophet, 'If a man smites thee on the right cheek—smash him on his left.' "

The audience tittered, and the poetry girl applauded briefly but with fierce intensity.

"Please do not misunderstand me. I am far from comparing myself to Christ. This would be an insult—to my dignity, at least, if not to his." The line, one of his standard tropes, got a laugh, as it always did. "It has been said that the antipodes of history are Caesar and Christ. If this is so, permit me to ally myself unreservedly with Caesar. Caesar was a *man*. It is to him that we should pay homage, not to some prattling carpenter with a Jehovah complex."

More laughter, flowing easily now.

"Old Pilate was correct to crown that fool with thorns. He has been a thorn in the side of real men, men like Pilate himself, and Caesar, ever since. We are told that Christ influenced history more than any other figure, and perhaps this is so. But was his influence benign or malignant? This is the question. You know my answer. I do not stand here blushing delicately and reciting homilies about the blessedness of the meek and the weak. Indeed the modern outlook has been a blessing for only the meek. They have inherited the earth, as prophesied, and look what they have made of it. The milk of human kindness is poor nourishment. Give me blood. Blood is life, and our hearts know it, even if our priests do not.

"Unlike Job—and Handel—I know that no redeemer liveth. I do not grovel before deities. I demand that deities pay obeisance to me. I do not suffer guilt or shame. I practice all sins, and I revel in them. I do not want a world of love. I want hatred. Hatred is something pure and powerful, intoxicating, exhilarating. I worship nothing but myself, and I issue no commandments except one: Hate thy neighbor. Taste his blood."

He went on, letting the words bubble up from some deep well of eloquence. His talent at moving a crowd was one that had surprised him when he finally discovered it. Despite his childhood encounter with the wolf, it had taken him years to realize his calling.

He had never seriously entertained the prospect of a career. To work at a desk would be torture, worse than incarceration. He would quite literally have preferred to be buried alive. At least in a grave he would suffer no one's company but his own.

His solution was to become an artist. As an artist he could be free. He need answer to no one. He need only follow his creative impulses wherever they led. To his chagrin he learned that they did not lead very far. People looked at his paintings and felt nothing. This was no great mystery. He felt nothing when he rendered them.

Occasionally he fell into a way of getting money. For a time he had been a kept man, the favorite pet of a lonely older woman. He had cared nothing for her, and she had cared nothing for him; their relationship was one of mutual convenience, an exchange of bodily fluids and gifts. This arrangement suited him to perfection. It ended only when the lady became bored.

On other occasions, he relied upon handouts from his coterie of admirers, the lost youths who gravitated toward him, drawn by his fundamental indifference. They were sad creatures who fretted endlessly over other people's opinions of them. They had grown up seeking to please parents, teachers, pastors. In Faust they found a man who simply did not care about others. He was a god to them. They crowded around him, scrapping for his affection like puppies squabbling over teats. Some had money. He accepted many loans, none of which he repaid.

His life might have continued indefinitely in this vein,

had he not been arrested, at the age of thirty-five, for the murder of Emily Wallace. His subsequent notoriety had ensured an endless stream of income.

Not that his celebrity was in any sense mainstream. He would never be pictured on a box of Wheaties or hired to tout American Express cards. His following was of a more select nature. He had more admirers in Europe than in the States. But then, the U.S. was still so puritanical, encumbered by religious traditions that refused to die. He was encouraged, however, by the predominance of young people among his fans. The newer generation, or the more sophisticated among them, had taken him to heart. These young people had rediscovered the ancient pagan wisdom that prized power over mercy. They were little Neros, young Caligulas, untouched by what the modern world called morality. They were both a throwback and a leap forward. The world had taken a long and circuitous detour these past two thousand years, but now it was again finding its way. And its way was death.

"My critics," he was saying, "are forever trying to pigeonhole me, to classify me like some exotic species of protozoan, to tag and label me. But you see, I resist categorization. I am sui generis. I am rara avis. And as I am speaking Latin, let me add: *Ecce homo*. Behold the man. Behold me.

"Of course they have labeled me the Werewolf. It is the one tag that has stuck. People inquire if I take offense at this nickname. I do not. The wolf is a most estimable creature. For centuries he terrorized the collective imagination of the European continent. He gave rise to lurid fairy stories and grotesque superstitions. He was often confounded with the devil—another unfairly maligned figure, I may add.

"The wolf embodies cunning, boldness, stealth, rapacity. He is an archetype of sexual aggression. What do *you* think he had in mind for Little Red Riding Hood? It was not only his ears and teeth that were noteworthy for their size, one may be sure. I like to think that in the unexpurgated version of the story, Little Red found out exactly how big the wolf was in *all* his parts.

"The wolf indeed represents lust, sexual hunger—hunger of all varieties, even the hunger for money that we call greed. He is always contrasted with the weak and the soft—those potbellied, pork-bellied Three Little Pigs, for instance. Who among us has not wished to hear those pigs squeal as the wolf's jaws snap shut? I myself was always most disappointed in that fable's outcome.

"The ancient Greeks had a word, *lussa,* meaning wolfish rage, the insane ferocity that takes possession of a man fighting for his life—a man on the battlefield, perhaps. The wolf has always been the favorite totem of warriors, the symbol of all the restless and reckless men who seek blood and conquest, men who will not be bound by society's dictates. The wild men among us, the killers in our midst.

"And I am one of them. I am the wolf, and he is I. Although I did not choose the name, I could not have selected one better."

They applauded him. Dieter, Edward, and the poetry girl rose to give him a standing ovation. Many others followed suit.

Faust accepted their adoration calmly. He was accustomed to it by now. He had more admirers all the time. The trend of history was turning in his favor. How many serial murderers had practiced their trade before, say, 1960? A bare handful in all of history. Yet since 1960 their numbers had swollen in a rising tide of mayhem. For a time the media could tell them apart only by assigning lurid nicknames—the Night Stalker, the Hillside Strangler, the Werewolf. Now even nicknames were passé, all the good ones having been taken. There were too many killers to keep track of. And more of them all the time. Sociopaths everywhere. Conscience had become increasingly irrelevant. It was akin to the vermiform appendix: still in place, but no longer functional.

Men without conscience occupied corporate board-rooms, ran for high public office. Some wore uniforms and badges. Some were doctors, attorneys, respected members of the community. Not all were killers, but all were capable of killing without remorse, should the need arise.

More of them every day. Most would not recognize him as one of their own. But their children would, and did. Their children, here in this room.

His children, really. The future as he was shaping it.

He smiled on them—his progeny, the work of his hands.

20

Shortly after seven o'clock Abby parked her Hyundai on a side street two blocks from Brody's guesthouse. She approached the property, carrying her purse. The estate was not gated, merely surrounded by a low brick wall, which she easily scaled. Brody's SUV was gone. He must be at the bookstore by now.

Before entering the cottage, she ventured close to the main house. She heard no voices, music, or TV noise from inside, and saw no movement in the windows. As far as she could tell, the owners weren't home.

She returned to the cottage and inspected the front door. She had a tension wrench and a set of lockpicks in her purse, but as she'd suspected, they would be of no use against the cottage's high-quality dead bolt. She would have to do it the hard way.

She went around to the guesthouse's rear wall, hoping Brody hadn't noticed the unlatched window and locked it. Of course, she could always break the window to gain entry, but she preferred to leave no sign of trespass.

She was in luck. The window opened easily. She slipped through, into the dark rear hall.

The motion detector would pick her up as soon as she moved away from the window. Unlike the front door, there would be no time delay; the alarm would sound instantly.

She shut the window so the noise would be contained within the cottage. The other windows, she'd noted, were already closed, and the air-conditioning was on. Since no one was in the main house, and the neighbors weren't close, there was a good chance no one would hear the alarm. Having cut the communications wires, she could be sure the signal wouldn't be transmitted to the alarm monitoring station.

She took off down the hall at a sprint. At once the cottage was filled with a high-pitched keening and an amplified electronic voice that repeated, *"Intruder alert, intruder alert . . ."*

The distance to the control panel in the foyer was short. She made it there in less than five seconds and tapped in the four-digit code.

Silence fell.

She peered out the front window, checking for any indication of activity in the main house. There was none.

It looked like she'd gotten away with it. Before she left, she would reattach the wires in the security box, leaving no sign of any damage. She would reset the alarm and exit via the front door during the time delay.

But first she had work to do. Last night she'd seen no eavesdropping gear. If he had some, it had to be hidden. She looked through the living room and kitchen, finding nothing.

She retreated to the rear of the cottage and stepped into the bedroom. It was dark. Her hand found a light switch on the wall by the doorway, but she chose not to turn it on. As she recalled, there was an overhead light, and she was pretty sure it was controlled by the switch. She didn't want a bright light coming on and perhaps attracting attention.

Instead she made her way to the bed and switched on the bedside lamp on the nightstand. The three-way bulb glowed feebly at its lowest setting. It was the only light in the rear of the house, but it was enough.

She scanned the room, noted a TV set opposite the bed. A smallish, older model. It looked incongruous in a guesthouse with a forty-inch high-definition TV in the living room. Although the cottage had come furnished, Brody might have brought this TV with him.

More interesting was the absence of a cable or satellite box. A power cord trailed from the rear of the TV, out of sight behind a bookcase. She tugged gently on it and felt resistance. The cord was plugged in. But when she switched on the set, nothing happened.

She rapped the side of the TV. It made a hollow sound.

In less than a minute she found the concealed hinges that allowed the front of the console to swing open. The set had been gutted, its circuitry and other electronic parts removed, leaving a sizable cavity. In this hiding space were three black boxes, neatly stacked. The bottom box was featureless. The box in the middle had a large monitor, currently dark, and a few buttons and slots; it looked something like an old DOS computer. The third box was slimmer and more stylish, resembling a DVD player. Next to this setup were two cordless phones, antennae extended, and a laptop computer, hooked to a port in the rear of the stack. Multiple cords ran from the devices, all plugged into a power strip. It was the power strip's cord that had been fed out the back of the TV to the wall socket.

She knew what she was looking at, of course. It was an IMSI catcher. Specifically, a Rohde & Schwarz model, which had once been offered for sale on the open market but had been withdrawn after concerns about privacy violations. The item still turned up on the black market, but it wasn't cheap. It probably retailed for a cool two hundred thousand. A lot of money for an ex–Special Forces guy to shell out on a piece of hardware.

On the closed lid of the laptop lay a spiral notebook. She flipped through it. Most of the pages were blank, but the first few sheets recorded Faust's movements in minute detail. Everything was there, up to Faust's no-show at the art gallery last night, and his scheduled appearance at the bookstore right now.

The phone in her purse rang.

She wanted to ignore it. Let her voice mail get it.

But inside the hollowed-out TV, the IMSI catcher was registering activity on its monitor. It had picked up the call.

That was odd. Brody would have programmed the machine to intercept only the calls he wanted to catch—those made by Faust and Elise.

She set down her purse and took out the phone. Caller ID displayed Elise's number. Abby answered. "Yes?"

"Abby? It's Elise."

"I'm kind of busy here."

"I realize that. I just thought you should know—I'm at the book signing with Peter. . . ."

"Right. And?"

"My stalker—he hasn't shown."

"He's not there?" She checked the time. It was after eight o'clock. "You sure? He may have hidden himself in the crowd."

"There aren't *that* many people."

"Faust sent you the text message, didn't he?" Abby asked, knowing the question was pointless, because she had seen the bookshop event listed in Brody's notebook.

"Yes. I sent back a reply, said I'd meet him here."

It didn't make sense, and Abby was suddenly very worried. "Okay, thanks for the heads-up."

"Maybe you scared him off."

"Yeah. Maybe."

She hadn't, though. Brody was not a man to be easily scared.

Abby closed the phone and bent forward, reaching for her purse on the floor—then stopped.

She had once seen a professional skeptic on TV arguing that nobody actually could sense being watched. This was only an old wives' tale, the skeptic had main-

tained. Abby had known he was wrong. She'd often had
an awareness of someone else's gaze—someone staring
at her from behind, or through a window. Her subliminal
perception of such things was nearly always accurate. It
could not be coincidence, as the skeptic had claimed.

She had another proof of this now. Even before she
straightened up, even before she turned to face the bedroom doorway, she felt his gaze on her. She knew he
was there.

When she pivoted slowly and saw Brody with the Beretta Mini Cougar in his hand, she wasn't the least bit
surprised.

21

"Hands up, Abby," Brody said quietly. "Up high. There you go. That's a good girl."

She stood with arms lifted, watching him. She was in a tight spot, no doubt about it, but the situation wasn't entirely hopeless. There might be an opening. He had already broken the first rule of gun violence: He had hesitated to shoot.

"I see you found my equipment." He nodded toward the TV. "Took you long enough."

"You don't seem surprised to find me snooping in your house."

"Why should I be? You left the window unlocked, disconnected the comm link for the security system. And of course you know the alarm code. I made sure to give you a good look at it last night."

"You wanted me to break in?"

"Hell, I even arranged for Mr. and Mrs. Hunter in the main house to be out tonight. Told them I'd lucked into a couple of theater tickets I couldn't use. They're enjoying a road-show production of *Les Mis* right now."

"You went to a lot of trouble to get me here. Might've been easier just to invite me to look around."

"That's not how the game is played. Besides, it's not that I wanted you pawing through my stuff. I just wanted you here. Alone."

"I was here last night."

"Yeah, but you played a good hand. That crap you pulled at the restaurant, making sure the maître d' would remember you. That was clever. You saved your life by doing that." The gun steadied, aiming at her heart. "But it was only a stay of execution."

"At least," Abby said softly, "you got a pretty good roll in the hay out of it."

He shrugged. "I've had better."

"Nice."

"Just telling it like it is. Besides, I would've gotten a turn in the sack anyhow. Only instead of smoking a cigarette afterward, I would've smoked *you.*"

He flashed his crooked smile. She wondered how she could ever have seen anything appealing in it.

"I could have drugged you last night," she said. "Knocked you out."

"You could've tried. But it wouldn't have worked. I popped a flumazenil while I was on my way home from the restaurant. You know about flumazenil, right?"

"Benzodiazepine antagonist. Counteracts the sedating effects of—" She stopped, not wanting to say too much.

"Of Rohypnol," he finished for her. "That's right. I dosed myself with five milligrams and was prepared to take more if I felt drowsy."

"Countermeasures and everything." Her throat was dry, and her upraised arms were starting to ache. "But how'd you know I might try using Rohypnol in the first place?"

"It's what Abby Sinclair always uses."

She needed a moment to register the significance of this statement.

He knew her name, her *real* name.

"Yeah," he said, reading her reaction. "I'm surprisingly well-informed. Now you're going to take these."

In his left hand he held up a pair of flex handcuffs, plastic restraints sometimes used in lieu of the more traditional steel cuffs. Once they were put on, they could be removed only if they were cut off. Twisting your hands was useless; it only made the plastic loop cinch tighter.

"I don't think so," she said.

He shook his head slowly, an adult amused by a child's bravado. "Oh, yes, you are, Abby. And I'm going to have fun watching you do it."

"Are you?"

"Enjoy the moment; that's my philosophy."

"I thought you weren't philosophical."

"That's one of several things I lied about." He took a step forward, out of the doorway. "Extend your hands."

She didn't move. "If you're going to shoot me, you may as well do it now."

"Who said anything about shooting? I'm just going to have you secure your wrists. Then we'll have a long talk. Not about movies this time. This is real life."

"I don't think I like you quite as much as I thought I did."

"Funny. I don't think I give a shit. Put out your hands."

A dozen self-defense scenarios flashed through her mind. She was trained in Krav Maga, the Israeli street-fighting technique. She had dropped bigger guys than Brody. But none of those guys had been pointing a loaded semiautomatic at her chest. And none of them had been trained as a Special Forces operative. Whatever moves she knew, Brody could anticipate them.

"Do it," he said, his voice harder.

Her one hope was that he was making her cuff herself. That meant she would have to keep her hands in front of her, not behind her back. She would still have some limited options.

Her purse was on the floor where she'd set it down. Her purse, with the gun inside.

She accepted the cuffs. They were a single plastic strip, like a cable tie, twenty-two inches long. She inserted the pointed end of the tie into the locking mechanism and wound the loop loosely around her wrists. "How am I supposed to tighten them?"

"With your teeth."

"Not very ladylike."

The Beretta remained steady in his hand. "Just do it."

She snagged the end of the loop in her teeth and drew it through the ratchets until it was tight enough to almost cut off the circulation in her wrists.

"Good job," Brody said.

He was too much in control. She wanted to knock him back on his heels, at least a little. "Don't you want to know why I didn't drug you?" she asked.

"The answer's pretty obvious." He chuckled. "You were warm for my form."

What stung was that this was basically true. "Someone thinks highly of himself, doesn't he? I had a better reason than that."

"Such as?"

"If you were out cold, you wouldn't have been talking. And you were telling me too much to let that happen."

"I didn't tell you a fucking thing."

"Iraq? The Green Berets? That was some quality background info. It checked out, too. I tracked down the news reports on that Karbala Gap shoot-out."

"Good for you."

"I also found your home address."

"No, you didn't. The address on my driver's license is out-of-date. My current address is unlisted."

"Even unlisted addresses are available, if you know where to look. I found your sweet little ranch house in Van Nuys."

He glanced sharply at her. She nodded.

"That's right, Brody. I paid a visit to your wife."

He stood very still for a moment. Then savagely he shoved her backward onto the bed.

"What the *fuck* did you say to her?"

She twisted herself to a sitting position, her bound wrists in her lap, and regarded him coolly. "I guess that's one of those things you'll have to get me to talk about."

"I will. I guarantee it. You're going to tell me everything you said to my wife, and everything you've learned about me."

"And when I've given you all the details, I suppose you'll let me go."

He expelled a slow breath. "When you've given me all the details, I'll kill you."

"You're not giving me much incentive to cooperate."

"It's not a question of cooperation. I know how to get information out of people."

"Torture? Is that what's on the menu?" She got no answer. "So what are you, Brody? A psychopath?"

"A professional."

"Professional what? Bounty hunter, kidnapper, assassin?"

"A little of all three, I guess."

"You must have one hell of a résumé."

"You want more background info? What the hell, it just might loosen your tongue."

He stepped away from her, toward the doorway. The gun never wavered.

"Things shook out in Iraq just the way I said. I quit the service, but hung on in Baghdad. It's where a lot of ex-military types were hanging out. We'd get together at the local watering holes, and we'd trade bullshit and lies. One day somebody approached me for a serious conversation. He made me an offer. I could get back in the field, this time with no supervision and no chain of command to worry about. And no Geneva Convention, either."

She pulled herself to a sitting position on the bed, resting against the headboard. "Pretty attractive opportunity."

"Sure was. I organized a team, and we gathered intel about subversives—some of the old Fedayeen militiamen or the newer foreign recruits. Everybody was informing on everybody else. Brother against brother, father against son. We'd get a hot tip on where some of the bastards might be holed up, and we'd go round them up. Garbage collecting, we called it."

"You ran snatch-and-grab missions."

"Good for you. You know the lingo. Yeah, we'd roll out to some walled compound, kick doors, take names."

The bedside lamp was directly beside her. On the margin of her field of vision she saw the electrical cord slinking behind the nightstand.

"That explains bounty hunter and kidnapper. How about assassin?"

"We didn't always take them alive. Even when we did . . . sometimes they had a way of expiring after they'd been in our custody for a while."

"Which is where the torture comes in."

"We preferred to call it harsh interrogation."

"You were Special Forces. You weren't trained to lower yourself to the terrorists' level. You're better than that."

"Maybe I used to be. But now . . . well, I am what I am. And I never lost any sleep over it. I'm a realist, remember?"

The cord was bunched up on the floor in the narrow space between the bed and the night table. "So why aren't you still over there?"

"Things got a little too hot. The Iraqis started thinking they didn't need us to solve their problems for them. They started threatening us with arrest. If we'd gone to prison we would've ended up in a cell with some of the same guys I'd been hunting. I don't think we would've lasted very long. We had to get out."

"And now you're here, intercepting Peter Faust's phone calls." Casually she swung her legs over the edge of the bed and leaned forward. "How'd you manage that career transition?"

"That's not important. It's a whole other thing. What matters is that you understand who you're dealing with. I've broken men who were willing to strap bombs around their waists for the sake of their cause. Men who didn't fear death—or pain. I want you to think about that. I want you to ask yourself how long you're going to hold out, if those men couldn't."

"You know, as second dates go, this one kind of sucks."

"You had a good time last night, though, didn't you? I could tell you were into me. It made it so goddamned simple to manipulate you."

She eased her foot over the electrical cord, snagging it. "It's not nice to gloat."

"I'm just surprised you made it so easy. I was led to believe you'd pose more of a challenge."

She pulled the cord toward her, slowly taking out the slack. "Who gave you that idea?"

He shook his head. "It's not important. We've spent enough time on preliminaries."

The cord was stretched taut now. "Someone told you my real name. And briefed you on the Rohypnol, among other things. Who was it?"

"I'm the one asking questions tonight. And I guarantee I'll get answers."

"Right. Because you're a professional. But you forgot one thing, Mark." She tensed her body. "I'm a pro, too."

She yanked out the lamp cord with her foot.

The room went dark.

Brody fired.

She had expected him to be quick, but the speed of his reaction still took her by surprise. He snapped off a round less than a second after the light went out. But he aimed at the spot where she'd been seated, and she'd already thrown herself to the foot of the bed. A kick of her legs propelled her onto the floor. She landed hard, slamming into the carpet. Probably she made a thud, but she couldn't hear it and knew he couldn't, either. The gunshot had left both of them with ears ringing.

She swept the floor in front of her with her manacled hands and found her purse. A thousand times she'd practiced opening the gun compartment in the dark, or blindfolded. She unsnapped the clasp and thrust her hands inside, her index finger curling around the .38's trigger as she raised the purse—

Brightness.

He'd found the wall switch.

The ceiling light had come on.

She knew where the switch was, and she twisted onto her side and squeezed the trigger, firing through the purse, blowing a hole in it, and she had time to see Brody swinging his gun in her direction and to know she'd missed.

But she hadn't missed.

A red rose of blood bloomed in his throat where his Adam's apple had been.

The gun fell from his hand. He slumped against the wall and his knees folded slowly and he slid down to a sitting position, his head sagging sideways, eyes open.

His mouth moved. He might have been trying to speak. Deafened by the gunshots, she couldn't tell.

Then his mouth wasn't moving anymore, no part of him was moving, and although his eyes were still open, she knew he was dead.

Whether her shot had been luck or skill she didn't know. A little of both, maybe. She'd known where the wall switch was. He hadn't known her position. That fact had given her a split-second advantage that had made the difference.

She stood up slowly. Her mind was working calmly, logically. Had anyone in the neighborhood heard the shots? Doubtful. The main house was unoccupied, and the other homes weren't close. All the windows of the guest cottage were shut. The neighbors probably had their windows closed, as well, and their air-conditioning on.

She approached Brody. His gun lay near the slack fingers of his right hand. She kicked it away, out of his reach, even though she knew he was dead and would never reach for it again. She bent down and pressed her fingers to the carotid artery at the side of his neck, getting blood on her hands and not caring. There was, of course, no pulse. She just had to be sure.

His staring eyes should have unnerved her. They were still that peculiar shade of blue. Cobalt blue, she thought. Before too long they would lose some of their color. The eyes of the dead became gray and lusterless. But that would take time. For the moment it was as if those eyes were alive and watching her. Somehow she didn't care about that, either. She was past feeling anything. She had never been so much at peace.

In a kitchen drawer she found a pair of heavy kitchen shears and cut off the plastic cuffs. She put the cuffs in her pocket and replaced the scissors in the drawer after wiping the handles.

There was cleaning up to do. Operating without emotion, she quickly put the place in order. She wiped her prints off all surfaces she had touched. She reconnected the wires in the security box so there would be no indication of a premeditated break-in. She left the TV console open, the IMSI catcher in plain sight for the police to find. It would link Brody to Faust, and Faust would be questioned, but he had an alibi. He was at the book signing. And he wouldn't mention hiring her. She was serenely certain of that. He was not the type to assist the authorities. That was one advantage of having a homicidal sociopath as a client.

When she was finished cleaning house, she exited through the front door, not bothering to reset the alarm, since it didn't matter anymore. She left the grounds, climbing over the perimeter wall, and walked to her Hyundai. As she slipped behind the wheel, she noticed that her fingers were tacky with drying blood. She should've washed up before leaving the cottage. Hadn't thought of it. Well, she would do it at home.

Home. Yes, everything would be fine once she got home.

She keyed the ignition and drove away, heading toward Westwood. Two miles from the cottage, she pulled onto the shoulder, got out of the car, and threw up into a storm drain.

It had hit her suddenly, the full impact of what had happened and what she'd done. She shook all over with fever chills. She knelt by the side of the idling car and hugged herself.

She had killed before. Once before. It didn't get any easier the second time.

She thought of his blue eyes staring. The wet blood on his neck. His body pressed against hers amid the bedsheets. A dead body now.

She was sick again. As she raised her head, she saw a couple walking their dog across the street. They steered well clear of her. Her ears weren't ringing so much anymore, and she could hear one of them say the word *drunk*.

Probably she did look like a drunk in the gutter. That was good. It meant they wouldn't associate her with the crime, once it was reported. She was far enough from the murder scene that there would be no obvious connection, anyway.

Crime . . . murder . . .

Her crime. *Her* murder.

But it wasn't. It was self-defense. She'd had to save herself. Kill or be killed. Law of the jungle.

So maybe she *was* only a jungle predator, as Faust had said. A wild animal, a killer in the night.

All these years she'd used the analogy of a pilot fish to explain her job. A pilot fish swam with sharks but wasn't a shark itself. But she'd been lying. Masking who she really was. She was only another shark prowling the deep. Sharks had to keep moving or they would die. She was like that. She was a killer, and she always had to be on the hunt.

She got back into the car and drove on. At a red light in Beverly Hills she had a bad thought. She'd blown open the secret compartment of her purse when she fired. Was she sure the gun was still in there?

She grabbed the purse, felt for the gun, didn't find it. Could she have let it fall out, left it at the scene?

No—there it was, not in its special compartment but shoved into the main cavity of the purse. Thrown in there unthinkingly at some point after the shooting.

A horn bleated behind her. The stoplight was green. She motored through the intersection. Distantly she observed that she wasn't headed for Westwood anymore. She was going south. She must have some destination in mind, but she had no idea what it was.

The main thing was that she hadn't lost the gun. She hadn't screwed up that way. Hadn't screwed up at all. She was alive. That was the proof.

So why didn't she feel like celebrating? Why did she feel so sick and so scared?

Because it didn't make sense, that was why. None of it. What Brody was doing with Faust, with her. She couldn't understand what he'd been up to. The whole thing was wrong.

Just wrong.

22

Wyatt clocked out of the Hollywood station house at two A.M. and drove home, wearing the same frown he'd worn throughout the night watch.

He hated the way he and Abby had parted. She had been hurt and angry. And he never liked it when they parted angry, because if she got killed on the job, then things would remain forever unresolved between them.

Long ago he had accepted her lifestyle, but—he had to admit—he couldn't quite deal with it. He was jealous of the fact that her work came first. And pissed off that she wouldn't commit, or at least open up more.

Yet he loved her. That was still true. It would always be true.

It just didn't matter anymore.

He'd been right to break it off with her. He had no doubts about that. Abby would never settle down, would never be satisfied with the day-to-day routine of a normal job and a normal life. For her there would never be marriage or kids. She just wasn't the type, even though she would be great with kids; he was sure of it.

Sometimes he felt it was unmanly of him to worry about these things. That was what his friends would have said, if any of them had known about Abby. They would have told him to stop thinking so damn much.

But that wasn't his way. He had been in this relationship for a lot of years, and for him it had only become

more serious. But for Abby? The only thing she was
serious about was her job. Deadly serious about that.

As for the rest of it, she was just enjoying the ride.
He knew he could no longer enjoy it with her. He'd had
to end it.

Still, he wasn't so sure about the timing. She was in
the middle of a case. She didn't need to be distracted,
didn't need any emotional complications. Maybe he
should have waited till she was through with this particular job. Having made up his mind, he'd felt the need
to tell her, and he'd justified it by saying she deserved
to know.

But maybe he'd only been making excuses. He was
the one who wanted to get it over with, make a clean
break. It was like popping a dislocated shoulder back
into place, something he'd experienced after a nasty fall
in his rookie year. He'd known it would be bad, so he'd
gotten it over with. A few moments of pain, then relief.

So why wasn't he relieved?

"Shit," he muttered as he pulled into the parking lot
of his apartment building and dumped his car in the
carport. With Abby, nothing was ever easy. And nothing
was ever over. Maybe it would always be that way.

He climbed the stairs to his floor, noting a new patch
of taggers' graffiti on the second-story landing. The name
Orlando was written in florid curving script. He knew
Orlando. Lived in number 213. He wasn't too surprised
the kid was tagging, but he'd expected him to have the
sense not to sign his real name.

He headed down the hallway to his apartment. When
he reached the door, he found it unlocked.

Not good.

He wore an off-duty gun in an ankle holster. He drew
it now, then slowly opened the door.

Abby was there, sitting in his armchair. She must have
let herself in. He'd given her a key to his place years
ago, but he'd never known her to use it.

He shut the door behind him, not knowing why she was here or what he was supposed to say. Then he saw the dried blood on her hands, the emptiness in her eyes.

"What happened?" he asked, moving toward her.

She looked up at him, unblinking.

"Just hold me," she whispered. "Please."

23

Tess was toweling herself dry after her morning shower, trying to shake off the residue of bad dreams.

From the kitchen she heard a TV newscaster on one of the cable channels. It meant that Josh was currently making breakfast, a task that consisted of pouring two bowls of cereal. This was the limit of his culinary skills, but she couldn't complain. It was her limit, too.

But she wasn't thinking about breakfast. She was thinking of her dreams. In them, she had been chased through a labyrinth of shadows by a blurred, misty figure with pale blue eyes. Then she was locked in a room with him, a captive, and though she wanted to fight back, she couldn't move. And in his hand, a branding iron, searing her flesh and leaving—not a *wolfsangel*—but a swastika.

She dressed in a gray suit with a bolo tie. By the time she stepped into the breakfast nook, she had—almost— put the dreams out of her mind.

Josh was on his cell phone, thanking someone for the heads-up. He ended the call and turned to her.

"That was Cary Palumbo in Detroit. We went through the academy together. He's pretty well connected in D.C., and when he gets a hot news item, he likes to pass it around."

Tess carried a bowl of raisin bran to the table and sat down. "Was it good news or bad?"

"Bad." Josh sat opposite her and met her gaze. "It's nobody you know . . . but we lost one of our own last night."

The words sucked some of the strength out of her. For a moment she was at Paul Voorhees's funeral again, her hand on the mahogany casket, her mind a bruise.

"Where?" she managed to ask.

"L.A. It was a UC agent." Undercover, he meant. "He was working a deep-cover op, apparently. When he didn't report in on schedule, his supervisor checked on him and found the body. Shot through the neck in his own bedroom."

Paul had died in a bedroom, the bedroom of a house in a Denver suburb.

"I know this is hard for you," Josh added, watching her.

"It's hard on all of us." The words came automatically.

He took her hand. "Tess . . ."

"Okay," she conceded. "Maybe it's especially hard on me. After . . . you know."

"After Paul." She felt the warm squeeze of his fingers. "You can say his name."

She looked intently at him. "Josh, you know I love you, right?"

"Yeah, I've figured that out. And I think you know it's mutual." He gave her hand another squeeze. "What I also think is that you're still in love with Paul Voorhees."

Her denial was reflexive. "No, really I'm not—"

"Of course you are. And you always will be. It's all right. I know that's part of the deal."

She shut her eyes against a sudden sting of tears. "Seems like a pretty rotten deal from your standpoint."

"I don't have any complaints." He smiled. "From everything I've heard about him, he was a really great guy."

"You're a great guy, too."

"It's not a competition."

They sat in silence, hand in hand, for a few ticks of the clock.

"Did Cary Palumbo pass on any other details?" Tess asked finally, needing to return to safer ground.

"Just one, but it's definitely interesting. The undercover op involved—get this—your old friend, Peter Faust."

Tess went cold. This was not safe ground, after all. This was the territory of her nightmares.

"Faust?" she breathed.

"I don't know what they think they have on him. Maybe they're still trying to nail him for that case from three years ago. The dead girl in L.A."

"Roberta Kessler," she said quietly. The name was fresh in her mind from having watched the interview just last night. Maybe she'd been watching it at the very moment when the undercover man was being murdered. Shot in the neck . . .

Paul's throat had been cut. In each case, a neck wound, a flow of blood from the carotid artery or the jugular vein . . .

Then she remembered why she'd obtained the video of the interview in the first place.

Abby. Abby was working for Faust.

She spoke carefully, her tone uninflected. "Do they think Faust killed our guy?"

"Cary didn't say, which means he doesn't know." Josh shrugged. "It would seem like a fair assumption, though."

"You'd think so." Tess was staring past Josh, staring far away. "But maybe not."

"Why? You have another suspect in mind?"

"I just might."

Tess declined Josh's offer to chauffeur her to the airport for her hastily scheduled ten A.M. flight to L.A. He'd already done his duty in that regard for her last trip. This time she could drive herself.

She wanted time alone in her car, anyway. Time to think.

She knew it was pointless to call Abby and ask what was going on. This was the kind of thing Abby would lie about. She'd proved as much in the past. Less than a year ago, in circumstances very much like these, when Abby had been a suspect in a homicide, she had lied. She'd lied even though she had, in fact, been innocent. She simply hadn't trusted Tess with the truth.

Besides, Tess couldn't tip her off, because there was a chance Abby didn't know. Cary Palumbo had said the murdered agent was under deep cover. Quite possibly Abby didn't even realize she had killed a federal law-enforcement officer.

If she *had* killed him. Of course, it could have been Faust. But Abby was involved somehow, even if she'd only led Faust to the victim.

Unless all her theorizing was wrong, and Abby had played no part in any of this.

It was possible. She didn't want to jump to conclusions. Once before she'd thought Abby was guilty of murder. She'd been wrong then. She could be wrong now.

She would like to believe she was wrong. She really would.

It would be helpful if she had some plan of action, some idea of what the hell she was going to do when she got to Los Angeles. Unfortunately, nothing had yet come to mind. She could go directly to the L.A. field office with her suspicions, or she could investigate on her own, or she could try some other approach that hadn't occurred to her yet. She might do just about anything. At the moment she had no game plan.

But one thing, at least, was certain. It had been a dead certainty from the moment Abby's connection to the case had entered her mind.

If Abby had *anything* to do with the death of a federal agent—anything at all—then she would pay.

24

In the morning, it should have felt like a dream.

That was how it always was in stories. A person would do something violent and awful, and then the next day it would seem unreal, a fantasy.

Not this time. Brody was dead. There was nothing dreamlike about that.

Abby thought about it as she lay in Wyatt's bed, watching the pink glow of dawn brighten the ceiling. It was one of those typical apartment ceilings that had been sprayed with acoustic foam, producing a pebbly texture. There were a couple of holes in the white, bumpy expanse, presumably drilled by a previous occupant. To hang plants, maybe, or a ceiling fan. Or maybe a mirror over the bed.

She didn't know why the ceiling and its holes interested her. Then she understood that she was willing to think about anything other than what she'd done last night.

Cowardly of her—trying to evade the facts. Okay, so she had killed a man. It wasn't the first time. And she'd done it to save her own life. It was a kill-or-be-killed situation. She had nothing to feel guilty about.

Brody had been a dangerous man. A stalker, a killer, an all-around bad guy. The world was better off without him.

She wondered what his wife would say about that. Or the children who would grow up without a father.

Beside her, Wyatt lay asleep. He didn't wake when she rose from the bed and collected her purse.

She had never undressed—there had been nothing physical between them last night—and so she only had to slip on her shoes before letting herself out.

In the Hyundai she switched on the radio and listened to the news while she drove home. There was nothing about a death in the Los Feliz district. But, of course, it was too early for the body to have been discovered. And with so many homicides in L.A., this one might not even make the news.

As she parked in the garage under the Wilshire Royal, she noticed the dried blood still on her fingertips. She saw some on the steering wheel, too. Funny that she hadn't cleaned up before leaving the guest cottage. And all the time she'd sat waiting for Wyatt in his apartment, she had never thought to wash the blood off her hands.

She rode the elevator to the tenth floor. Entered her condo. Thought about fixing something to eat, but she had no appetite. She was tired, very tired, but she knew she couldn't go back to sleep.

She did wash her hands, at least. She scrubbed them until the dried blood under her nails had been worked free. When she was done, she took a long shower. Then she washed her hands again. Lady Macbeth and all that.

For a long time she stood on her balcony watching the morning rush hour. People going to work, as they did every day. Tonight they would come home to spouses or lovers. Life would go on. But not for Mark Brody.

She flashed on a memory of a woman in a doorway: *I'm his wife.*

The memory shifted. Brody with her in the dark. The caress of his fingers. The brush of his lips.

She could almost feel his body heat.

But his body was cold now. Lips bloodless, fingers stiff with rigor mortis.

A shudder traveled through her. She closed her eyes.

No one could blame her for what she'd done. No one. So why did she blame herself?

Sometime around midday, Abby got angry.

The shock and guilt had worn off a little, and she was feeling pissed. She didn't like it when things went wrong on the job. She didn't like it when she nearly got killed.

And she especially didn't like it when the stalker she was hunting knew her *name*.

Her name—and her MO. Brody had known enough to take a benzodiazepine antagonist on their night together. He'd expected her to use Rohypnol. Only someone with very good connections could have come by that kind of information.

And then there was Faust. How did he fit in? She didn't know, couldn't put it together. Too many pieces were missing.

Well, Faust himself knew more than he told her. Now it was time for him to open up, whether he wanted to or not.

She almost called his cell number, then thought better of it. Someone might still be monitoring. Though Brody was dead, he could have had an accomplice. Last night she should have disabled the IMSI catcher, but she hadn't thought of it. This was uncharacteristically careless of her, but she supposed she couldn't blame herself. Post-traumatic shock had a way of impairing a person's thought processes.

She called Faust's landline. When he answered, she said immediately, "We need to talk."

"Why, Miss Sinclair, how pleasant to hear your voice."

"Yeah. Ditto. We need to talk."

"Now is as good a time as any."

"In person."

"I am available. Elise, I regret to say, is not. She is working today."

"That's fine. It's you I need to talk to."

"There have been developments, I take it?"

"There's béen a major development. Which reminds me—is there any action in your neighborhood?"

"Action? I am afraid you have lost me."

"Police cars, ambulances, media, anything like that? In the general vicinity?"

"I am aware of nothing. But what you say is most intriguing."

"How about we meet at the coffeehouse in a half hour?"

"Café Eden is more than a coffeehouse, Miss Sinclair. It is an oasis in the parched desert of southern Californian anomie, a refuge for the enlightened few—"

"I don't need a sales pitch. Will you be there or not?"

"You could not possibly stop me."

She ended the call and left her condo, but only after transferring the contents of her handbag to a new, undamaged purse. The gun, of course, was among them. The murder weapon. Really, she should have tossed it already. But she had a funny feeling she might be needing it again.

25

By the time the MD-80 touched down at LAX at twelve noon, Pacific time, Tess had decided on a course of action.

She knew that after the Medea case, Michaelson, the ADIC of the L.A. field office, would jump at any chance to get Abby behind bars. Once Tess shared her suspicions with him, Abby would be the target of an all-out manhunt.

Probably she shouldn't care about any of that. As Abby herself had reminded her, they weren't friends anymore. She'd said as much at the conclusion of Medea, and she'd reiterated the point on the phone just the other night. And she was working for Faust, a known killer.

On the other hand, Abby *had* saved her life once. That was the kind of thing that ought to buy her some benefit of the doubt. So Tess would pay her a visit. She owed Abby that much.

Yes, it was probably a mistake to tip her off and perhaps give her a chance to run. Yes, Abby was a proven liar in this type of situation, and whatever she said was unlikely to allay Tess's doubts and fears. Yes, yes, yes, that was all true. But she would do it anyway. She had to give Abby a chance. It was more than she'd done last time, and she would not make the same mistake again.

She rented a Toyota Camry and took the Santa Monica Freeway north, exiting at Wilshire Boulevard. There was a strange sense of freedom in driving a rented car in a city where she had established, as yet, no official presence. She almost felt like a civilian. But the SIG Sauer 9mm in the reinforced pocket of her trench coat was there to remind her of who she really was.

Traffic was bad, of course. It was always bad in L.A. She had almost forgotten how much she disliked this city, with its grungy corridors of strip malls and garden apartments, its sickly palm trees leaning against graffiti-sprayed walls, its atmosphere of laid-back menace. Illness festered here.

No wonder Faust had bought a home in L.A. This was his kind of place, soulless and narcissistic, a surface coating of charm concealing the emptiness within.

She shook her head. She didn't want to think about Faust. It had been a mistake to relive her interview with him. Watching the video had brought back old fears—and old obsessions.

Tess had never shared her deepest thoughts on Peter Faust with anyone. She had no friends outside the Bureau, and no one in the Bureau—not even Josh—would have understood. She wasn't sure that she herself understood.

It was the damn History Channel that was to blame. One night, alone and bored, she'd been flipping through the channels when she stopped on a documentary about Adolf Hitler. A detail of the narration had caught her attention. Hitler, said the voice-over, was known for his hypnotic gaze and ice blue lashless eyes.

She had seen eyes like those before.

She watched the program. Later she bought a biography of Hitler. She found herself constructing a profile of Adolf Hitler as if he were one of the BAU's neatly labeled psychopaths.

He had been born in Austria but had always considered himself a true German. He was incarcerated at age thirty-five and subsequently released, arrest and confinement having only magnified his celebrity status.

He frequented coffeehouses. He was charismatic. He

acquired a following among the young and rootless. He published his memoirs and was the subject of contemporary documentary films. He'd tried to establish himself as an artist, and had failed.

He was drawn to much younger women, often of a waifish appearance. He led some of them to destruction. Several of his girlfriends committed suicide, or tried to.

He was fascinated by wolves. He'd once gone by the alias Herr Wolf. In the last days of the war, he created a brigade of "werewolves," guerrilla fighters who were expected to carry on the fight during the Allied occupation.

In all these respects there were parallels with Faust. Of course, the similarities could be coincidental. Sociopaths typically exhibited a limited repertoire of behaviors. That was the whole concept behind criminal profiling. She could rationalize the issue that way.

But part of her wondered if there was a deeper explanation. Late at night, when sleep eluded her, she would remember the Santeria exorcism in Miami. She would think of evil—not a horned satyr, but a black, miasmic cloud. A force, a kind of bodiless will—one that could inhabit a boy and drive him insane.

And could inhabit other human hosts, as well.

There had been something demonic about Hitler. His good fortune was uncanny. He survived thirty-six major battles in World War I. At Ypres his entire section was wiped out, while he was not even grazed. On two occasions he took leave of a group of comrades only seconds before an artillery shell exploded among them. Once in power, he faced repeated assassination attempts without injury. His imperviousness to the dangers around him had given him an aura of supernatural invincibility. It was as if he were protected by some malevolent guardian angel. Perhaps he had been.

And if evil could possess a human host named Adolf Hitler, could it not do so again? If there could be one Hitler, why not another?

Why not Peter Faust?

*   *   *

At the Wilshire Royal she parked in the curving drive-way near the fountain, which had been turned off for repairs. She introduced herself to the two guards at the lobby desk, flashing her creds to get their attention, and asked if Abby Sinclair was in.

"Miss Sinclair just left," one of them said.

"How long ago?"

Shrug. "Fifteen, twenty minutes." That would have been about twelve thirty.

"Do you know when she'll be back?"

"She didn't say. It's not like she checks in with us."

The other guard asked, "Is she in some kind of trouble?"

Tess thought that was a good question. She didn't an-swer. "You guys are being straight with me, aren't you? I mean, if Miss Sinclair were here, you would tell me, right?"

"Why wouldn't we?"

"I don't know. You might think you're doing her some kind of favor. But you ought to know it's a federal crime to lie to an agent of the FBI."

"Nobody's lying."

"She still drive that red Miata?"

The guards nodded.

"Maybe I'll just take a look in the parking garage and see if it's there."

"It won't be. That's the car she took."

Tess started to walk away, then stopped. *That's the car she took.* Peculiar phrasing. What other car would she take? Then she remembered that Abby used a backup vehicle when she was on assignment.

She turned back to the desk. "Miss Sinclair keeps an-other car here, doesn't she?"

The two men shifted in their seats.

"Does she or doesn't she?" Tess pressed.

"She has a Hyundai Excel."

"Where's it parked?"

"Don't you need a search warrant or something?"

"I don't need a search warrant to see if the car is there or not. Tell me where it's parked."

Reluctantly one of the guards flipped through a book and found the number of the assigned space. "Sixty-nine."

In the garage she found the beat-up old Hyundai. The doors were locked. She took out a Mini Maglite flash and aimed the beam inside.

On the steering wheel, there was a rust-colored patch. Tess had seen enough dried blood to recognize it.

Though it had dried, it had to be recent. Blood wasn't the sort of thing a person would leave in her car for long.

She wished she could take a sample, but she didn't have the necessary equipment. For now she would have to leave the vehicle and hope Abby didn't return and wipe off the evidence before it could be collected.

So what did the blood prove, exactly? It didn't make Abby a murderer. There might be valid reasons for her to have blood in her car. She could have been injured— her job was certainly risky enough. Maybe the injury had no connection to the Peter Faust case whatsoever.

Or maybe the blood belonged to the dead FBI agent. Even so, there was conceivably a way to explain it. If Abby had been following him or watching his house, she might have come upon his body and checked for signs of life.

Tess frowned. She was reaching, obviously. Doing her best to deny the clear implications of what she'd found. She just didn't want it to be Abby. She didn't want to go down that road.

What she needed was more evidence. And she knew where to look for it.

She returned to the lobby and faced the two guards at the desk.

"I've found blood in her car. That means we have exigent circumstances. I don't need a warrant to enter the premises."

"You're saying there could be someone in danger in Miss Sinclair's unit?" one of the pair asked skeptically.

"It's possible," she lied. "That blood had to come from somewhere. Was Miss Sinclair injured or wounded when you saw her?"

Reluctantly they shook their heads.

"Then I have a reasonable basis for assuming another party has been injured. I need to see the interior of her apartment. If you won't cooperate, I can have additional agents here within minutes. They'll be all over the building. Your other tenants won't like that. So what do you say? Do we do this quietly or do we make a lot of noise?"

The men looked at each other. The older of the two reached a decision. "Vince, take her up."

Vince obeyed. He escorted Tess to the tenth floor and unlocked Abby's condo. Tess stepped in, surveying the place. The last time she had stood in Abby's living room, she had come to apologize, only to be told that if she ever reentered Abby's life, it would be as her enemy. It was a prediction that showed every sign of coming true.

She was no crime scene technician, but she knew the basics of inspecting a suspect's residence. First she found a package of Ziploc plastic bags in the kitchen and a black felt marker in a drawer. She took these with her as she explored the rest of the condo.

Her first stop was the bathroom. She noticed a scouring pad near the sink, the kind of thing used for scrubbing pots and pans. It seemed an odd item to have in a lavatory. Carefully she examined it, holding it close to the light, until she saw dark maroon flecks amid the bristles. Blood? Scoured off Abby's fingernails?

She bagged the item, marking the bag's label with the felt pen.

The shower was still wet and had been used sometime today, but there was no obvious sign of blood on the tiles. What might be found in the plumbing beneath the drain was a different story, but she lacked the tools and the expertise to look.

The small laundry room was adjacent to the bathroom. She found a wet load of clothes in the washer. Dark blouse, dark skirt. The kind of items Abby might use for snooping around at night. The blouse was spotted with faint stains of some kind, which the first run through the wash cycle had failed to eradicate. Blood-stains?

The blouse went into a large plastic bag.

In the bedroom she checked the closet, paying particular attention to Abby's shoes. Footwear often picked up telltale items from a crime scene, but in this case she saw nothing on the soles of the shoes that seemed incriminating. A microscopic analysis might yield a different conclusion, of course.

"Are you gonna be much longer?" Vince asked irritably from the living room.

Tess didn't answer. She was preoccupied with the bottom drawer of Abby's dresser. There, beneath some undergarments, was a black plastic trash bag, neatly folded, and inside the bag was a purse. It contained a special compartment that probably had held a gun. There was a hole in the side of the compartment, and the fabric of the interior was speckled with black soot around the edges of the hole.

As if the gun had been fired from inside the purse, blowing a hole in the fabric.

It went into a labeled bag.

In the trash bag with the gun was a long strip of plastic. It took Tess a moment to identify it as a pair of disposable handcuffs, which had been cut apart. They were the single-loop variety, white, brand name EZ Cuffs. The cuffs were sold in bulk, mainly to law-enforcement personnel.

A bad thought formed in her mind. She tried not to dwell on it as she bagged the cuffs.

On a table in the corner, she found a library book—

Faust's memoir. It helped establish a link between Abby and Faust. It was bagged, as well.

Then she set down the various bags on the bed and put together a story.

Abby had been hired to work for Faust. The job had somehow brought her into contact with the FBI man, who had caught her doing something illegal—some B and E, maybe, or planting surveillance gear. The agent had placed her under arrest; this explained the handcuffs. Abby had gotten hold of her gun inside her purse and shot the man, getting blood on her hands and clothes and transferring some of it to her car. She was now trying to cover up the crime by cleaning herself up and washing her clothes. She had hidden the cuffs and the purse in a trash bag and planned to dispose of them in a dump bin somewhere, probably after dark, when she was less likely to be seen.

The cover-up implied consciousness of guilt. Moreover, if this scenario was correct, then Abby knew the man she killed was a law officer. She had known it, in fact, as soon as he arrested her, if not before—which meant she knew it when she killed him. To save herself from jail, she had murdered a federal agent in cold blood.

Or maybe not. Maybe there was some other explanation. But whatever the truth, there could be no doubt that Abby was mixed up in something illicit and ugly. Last time there had been only suspicious circumstances. In this case there was physical evidence. And physical evidence did not lie.

"Oh, Abby," Tess whispered. "Damn it, Abby, you're in deep this time."

She no longer had any doubt about her next move. She had to go to the field office and tell what she knew. And she had to do it fast—because when Abby returned home, she would find out that her apartment had been searched, and she might take off.

Tess went back into the living room and told Vince

she was finished. "You taking those things?" he asked, looking at the plastic bags in her hand.

"I am."

"Miss Sinclair is in trouble, isn't she?"

"Vince . . . I'm afraid she is."

26

The federal building, also in Westwood, was only a few blocks away. Tess reached it in less than ten minutes, delayed only by the ever-present L.A. traffic. She left her rented Camry in the outdoor parking lot, because the underground garage was reserved for the agents stationed here and for official visitors. She became at least semiofficial after obtaining a security pass in the lobby.

With the ID tag pinned to her lapel, and her collection of evidence in her briefcase, she rode the elevator. She noticed that she was still wearing her bolo tie—fine in Denver, out of place in L.A. But she had bigger things to worry about than her fashion sense.

At suite 1700 she was buzzed in by the agent on duty. He was nonplussed when she said she had to see the ADIC right now. Nearly all other field offices were run by a special agent in charge, but the L.A. office, in recognition of its size and prominence, was run by an assistant director. At the moment, the ADIC was Richard Michaelson, a man adept at Bureau politics, if not at anything else.

"I'm not sure that's possible," the duty agent said.

"I have information pertaining to the death of an L.A. field operative last night."

"If you could brief me—"

"I'll brief the Nose."

The Nose was Michaelson's nickname, a tribute to his most prominent facial feature.

The agent on duty disliked hearing the nickname. He glanced around self-consciously, as if afraid the reception area was bugged. Hell, Michaelson was paranoid enough; maybe it was.

Eventually he relented and used his key card to admit her to the rest of the suite. She remembered the way to the director's office. When she entered the anteroom, Michaelson's secretary recognized her and frowned. The frown was nothing personal, merely an acknowledgment of her boss's antipathy to Tess.

"I need to see him," Tess said, nodding at the closed door to Michaelson's office.

"I'm afraid you don't have an appointment—"

"Skip the power play." Making her wait was one of those games that personal assistants indulged in when they could. "I'm in from Denver, I have a lead in an ongoing high-priority investigation, and I'm going to see him *now*."

The secretary didn't like it, but she announced the visitor on the intercom, then told Tess to go right in.

Michaelson looked up from behind his desk, doing his best to show no surprise. "Tess. What an unexpected pleasure."

"Pleasure is all mine, Richard."

For two people who detested each other, they sure knew how to make nice.

"What brings you to L.A.?" he asked, straining for an idle conversational tone.

"Peter Faust." She sat in an armchair. "I understand you lost an agent last night."

Michaelson's false smile faltered. "There's no way you could possibly know about that."

"And yet I do."

"How?"

"Even in Denver, I'm not entirely out of the loop. I hear things."

"All right. What does that have to do with you?"

"It has nothing to do with me." She drew a breath, hating what she had to say next. "It may, however, have something to do with Abby Sinclair."

Michaelson sat very still for a moment. Then he rose, his hands locked together in front of him. Tess noticed that his fingertips were squeezed red with pressure.

"Sinclair is mixed up in this?" he said softly.

"She may be. Let me tell you what I've found out."

"Hold on. The case agent needs to be here for this." He buzzed his assistant. "Have Agent Hauser get in here now."

"Hauser is in charge?" Tess asked.

Michaelson caught the sour undertone of her question. "You don't like him?"

"*He* doesn't like *me*. Last time I was here, he told me I'd betrayed the Bureau by secretly working with Abby."

Michaelson leveled his gaze on her. "He was right."

"You don't believe in forgive-and-forget, do you, Richard?"

"That's never been my style. You showed your true colors when you hooked up with Sinclair. The media may think you're a hero, and you may have your partisans in D.C. But I know you, McCallum. I know you for what you are."

Tess sighed. "It's so good to be back in L.A."

The door opened, and Ron Hauser stepped in, his crew cut a little grayer than Tess remembered, his face more sallow and lined. He must be pushing the Bureau's mandatory retirement age of fifty-seven, but he was one of those guys who would hold on to the end.

Tess had liked him when they met nine months ago. She still did. But the feeling was no longer mutual, as demonstrated by the frown that crossed his face as soon as he saw her in the room.

"McCallum. What the hell are *you* doing here?"

Tess managed a smile. "Hello to you, too, Ron."

Hauser ignored her, looking at Michaelson. "What's going on?"

"Tess thinks she has some information on the Faust case. It involves her friend Abby."

Hauser sat down slowly in the armchair beside hers. "I'm listening."

"We both are," Michaelson said.

Tess told them about Abby's phone call, her visit to the condo building, the blood in the car. She opened her briefcase and passed around the bagged items of evidence, explaining each one. When she was finished, there was a moment of pained silence.

"Shit," Hauser said finally. It seemed as good an assessment as any.

Michaelson rubbed his forehead as if a headache were coming on. "So Sinclair killed Brody. . . ."

Brody—the undercover agent. Tess hadn't known his name.

"We don't know anything for sure," she said. "There may be some reasonable explanation."

"Reasonable, my ass." Hauser was fuming. "We need to pick up Sinclair and grill her hard. We need to find out what she did and what she knows."

"We do," Tess agreed. "And I'd like to be part of it." *Like* was, of course, the wrong word. She *needed* to be part of it.

She expected opposition from the two men, neither of whom was exactly a charter member of her fan club. But the Nose surprised her.

"You know her better than anyone. You should be involved. You can work with Agent Hauser."

This was unusually magnanimous of him. Naturally Tess suspected a double-cross. The Nose was always playing the angles.

"I'll need more information," she said. "I don't know what kind of operation Brody was conducting. Actually, I don't know anything at all, other than what I've told you."

"Hauser can brief you. Tell her everything, Ron."

"Are you sure that's a good idea? She hasn't exactly proven herself trustworthy." Charming, the way he was speaking of her as if she weren't even there.

Michaelson waved off this concern. "She brought us this lead, didn't she? So play nice. I don't want personal animosities interfering in this investigation. We're talking about an agent who lost his life. And," he added as if personally affronted, "it happened on *my* watch."

Now Tess got it. Brody's death made Michaelson look bad. He needed to wrap up the investigation as soon as possible to salvage his reputation. And he was willing to work with anyone, even her, in order to do it.

"Understood," Hauser said curtly. He said nothing more until he and Tess were out in the hallway. "What do you say we pay Sinclair a visit?"

"She wasn't home an hour ago. I doubt she'll be there now. I'd advise sending evidence technicians with a warrant for the Hyundai and the apartment. While they're getting started, I'd like to see the crime scene."

"That's a half-hour drive."

"You can fill me in on the way. Oh, and we'll need a photo of Abby from the files."

"I'm surprised you don't keep one in a locket around your neck. I mean, seeing how close the two of you are."

"That's it, Ron. Just keep baiting me. Very professional."

He gave her a cold stare. "You're the last person who's going to talk to me about professionalism."

"I'm sensing a certain hostility."

"Damn right you are. I gave you wide leeway in the Medea case, and the thanks I got was having you go behind my back to work with Sinclair. As you may have noticed, the ADIC isn't your biggest fan. I took a risk trusting you, and I ended up getting screwed."

"That was never my intention."

"I don't give a *damn* about your intention. You betrayed me, and you betrayed the Bureau. Michaelson was none too pleased with me, I can tell you. You, he couldn't touch. You're golden. Since he couldn't take it out on you, he went after me."

"I'm sorry to hear that."

"Well, then, that makes everything okay. You know I was hoping for a transfer to D.C., a move up? Not going to happen now. I'm stuck at this post, and at my age I'll be ending my career here, as a middle manager with a permanent black mark on my record. And a permanent enemy in Richard Michaelson."

"Michaelson must trust you somewhat. He made you the case agent on the Faust investigation."

"Only because I begged him for it. And I don't like to beg, McCallum. It pisses me off. I've given everything I have to the Bureau. Never had time for a wife and kids. It was all work, twenty hours a day. Now I'm going out as an object lesson in how *not* to supervise a field agent. Maybe they'll teach a class about me at the Academy. They can call it 'Don't Let This Happen to You.' "

"There's nothing I can say, Ron."

"Why should you *say* anything? It worked out for you. You're a goddamn hero."

"A hero who's posted in Denver for the foreseeable future, because I'm considered too unreliable for further advancement."

"Denver is exactly where you want to be. You and I both know it. If you ever got transferred, what would happen to your love life?"

She froze. "What's that supposed to mean?"

"It means you're not as good at keeping secrets as you think."

He walked off. She followed, shaken.

She wondered how much he knew. He might have heard only rumors. She hoped so, but . . . but she hadn't thought there *were* rumors. Hadn't thought anyone suspected. Hadn't heard anything.

But then, how would she know? She and Josh would be the last ones to hear any gossip at their expense.

And Hauser, a man who blamed her for his career meltdown, was in on the secret. Was holding it over her head.

Oh, yeah, this trip was working out just great.

27

Café Eden hadn't changed. It seemed to Abby that the exact same clientele were occupying the exact same tables as last time.

For this meeting Faust had arrived first. He, too, was ensconced at the table they'd used before. A cup of coffee rested near his hands, which lay flat on the table, manicured nails gleaming.

She slid into the chair opposite him without a word.

"I hope," Faust said, "we may dispense with introductory chitchat. My curiosity, Miss Sinclair, has been piqued."

"I'm so glad I could make your life more interesting."

"Tell me, please, why you should ask if there are police or reporters in my neighborhood."

"Because the man who was stalking you lived only a block away."

"So close? How bold of him. And yet I never noticed him in the area."

A waitress—the girl with metal doohickeys in her face—drifted by to ask Abby if she wanted anything. Abby shook her head. When the girl had left, Abby said, "He was a recent arrival. Renting a guesthouse."

"You use the past tense. He is gone now?"

"He's dead now."

"Is he?" He lifted his coffee cup and took a complacent sip. "Well, then, it appears our problem has been solved."

"That's it? That's all you have to say?"

"And what am I expected to do? Express my condolences? Bewail our common mortality? Launch into Hamlet's soliloquy about the undiscovered country from which no traveler ever returns?" He set down the cup, smiling. "Incidentally, Shakespeare got it wrong. Someone did return. Hamlet's own father had come back in the form of a ghost. Odd that Hamlet should forget a thing like that."

"You don't seem too interested in how he died."

"Hamlet's father? As I recall, he was poisoned by Claudius. Some nonsense about poison poured into his ear."

"Your stalker. You haven't asked about the circumstances of his death."

Faust stared into his coffee cup as if seeing visions there. "He is greatly overrated, Shakespeare. But then, all genius is overrated. Genius is merely a deviation from the statistical norm. As is perversion, for that matter. Or great goodness. Or great evil."

Abby leaned forward. "You seem to want to talk about anything except what happened to the man who was stalking you."

"I assumed that you would prefer to keep such incriminating details to yourself." He looked up, his gaze frank. "You *did* kill him, did you not?"

She'd known this question would come, and how she would answer it. "I'm not a killer."

"Quoth the jungle cat."

"I didn't kill him. I found him dead in the guest cottage last night."

Faust seemed to see through her pose. "It must have been difficult for him to let you in, given his condition."

"I let myself in. I thought the cottage was empty. It was dark inside, no sign of activity. I found him there. He'd been shot."

"Tragic."

"The fact that there are no police or media in your

neighborhood probably means the body hasn't been discovered yet."

"I imagine his landlord will find it soon enough. When does the rent come due?"

"This is a joke to you, isn't it?"

Faust sighed. "Life is a joke to me. Life—and death also, of course. There can scarcely be one without the other."

Abby watched him. It seemed to be as good a time as any for her to try her bluff. "It's crossed my mind that you killed him."

He barely reacted. "Has it?"

"Unlike me, you *are* a killer. And you had motive. You wanted to protect Elise."

"Motive perhaps, but not opportunity. I did not know the man's whereabouts. As I recall, you stubbornly and rather unsociably declined to share that information."

"You could have found him by following me the first night. You knew I was going to meet him at the art gallery. You could have followed us back to his place."

He pressed his lips together, making a *tsk-tsk* sound. "You went back to his cottage with him on that very night? Miss Sinclair, I am beginning to think that you are not the sort of girl one brings home to Mother."

"Yeah, I know. I put the *pro* in promiscuity. Stick to the subject. You *could* have followed me. You could have found out his address, then sneaked in during the day—"

"And shot him? Had you troubled yourself to do even the most rudimentary research, you would know that guns are not my style."

"Not when you're killing a woman who's half your age and half your size. Against a guy like Brody, it could be a different story."

His eyebrows lifted. "Brody? Was that the gentleman's name? How very American. Like a GI in one of your World War Two movies. Stalwart Sergeant Brody leading his platoon ashore on Omaha Beach."

"So far you haven't exactly denied killing him."

"I deny it. There. Are you satisfied?"

"Hardly."

"What more can I do?" He spread his hands in a charming gesture of helplessness.

"You can tell me what's really going on."

"I fail to comprehend your meaning."

"Brody was no ordinary stalker. And I don't think he was hassling Elise. He was after *you.* I want you to tell me why."

Faust sounded bored. "I am sure I do not know."

Abby got up. "Okay, nice gabbing with you. If you'll excuse me, I need to see a man with a badge."

He leaned back in his seat, luxuriating in his private amusement. "You, go to the police? A most incredible supposition. You operate strictly outside the law."

"I have contacts in law enforcement. I can pass on some info without getting myself directly involved."

"What sort of 'info'?" He placed a slight, sardonic emphasis on the term.

"The fact that you had a problem with Brody, to begin with. And now he's dead, just a few doors down from your house. And you're a murderer. You know, that kind of thing."

"Such an accusation would be as unwise as it is baseless." He didn't sound quite so bored anymore.

"It's no accusation. Just a statement of fact, or actually several facts. I'll let my friends in blue connect the dots. You know they will. They've been wanting to get you for a long time."

He shifted in his chair. "They can prove nothing."

"Only that Brody was harassing you, and he got killed. Are you alibied for yesterday, Petey?"

"I was at a book signing, as you well know."

"All day? Every hour, every minute? I got to the cottage after your book signing started. Brody was already dead by then. He'd been dead for some time."

"This is absurd."

"Don't worry. You've got the dough for a legal dream team. Too bad Johnnie Cochran's not around these days. Maybe you can hire Robert Blake's lawyer. That guy's a miracle worker. And a miracle may be just what you'll need."

She took a step away, sure he would stop her.

He did. "Sit down."

"Sorry. Got a date with a cop."

"Sit."

She relented. Now she was the one wearing a smile. "Feeling more cooperative?"

Faust regarded her coldly. There was no merriment in his eyes any longer, merely infinite disdain.

"I had thought I would like you, Miss Sinclair, at least insofar as it is possible for me to like anyone. But I was mistaken. I detest you."

"I'm crushed."

"You are . . . common."

"And you're sweating just a little. Which is *un*common—for you. Tell me about Brody."

"There is nothing to tell. I know no more about him than what I told you on our first meeting."

"That's your story, and you're sticking to it?"

"It is the truth."

She was pretty good at reading people. She didn't think he was lying. "So you never meant to kill him?"

He hesitated. "Had you given me his address . . ." His shoulders lifted. "I will not mislead you. The man was frightening Elise. And I do feel rather protective of her. Killing him would have disturbed me not in the least. But I never had the chance. Someone else, it appears, did my work for me."

He spoke the last words while looking right at her, leaving no doubt whom he took to be the culprit.

Abby tried a new tack. "Who recommended my services?"

Faust shook his head, confused by the switch of topics. "How can that datum possibly be relevant?"

"Let me worry about the datums—I mean data. Just give me the name."

"I prefer not to."

"Why not?"

"It is a matter of honor."

"You don't have any honor. You'll have to come up with a better excuse."

"I was pledged to secrecy. I will not betray a confidence."

"I can still go to the cops, Petey."

"Do you imagine you are intimidating me? You are merely a distraction."

"Yeah, you're looking fairly distracted, all right."

"You bait me, goad me. You seek to exploit my perceived weaknesses. You remind me— It is no matter."

"Who do I remind you of?"

He waved a long-fingered hand, as if swatting a fly in slow motion. "An FBI agent who interviewed me a few years ago. She also tried to—how do you say it?—get under my skin. She failed, just as you have failed."

"Tess McCallum."

"Why, yes." He looked pleased. "It appears you have done your homework on me, after all."

"Funny you should bring up her name right now."

"Is it? Why?"

"Because *she's* the law-enforcement contact you mentioned. *She's* the one who told you about me."

Faust laughed, a hearty, robust sound that instantly deflated her suspicions. "Agent McCallum? That is scarcely plausible. We did not exactly, shall I say, hit it off. There was no kismet, I am afraid. And how ever would she know of you, anyway?"

Abby ignored the question. So it hadn't been Tess. "If not her—who?"

"I will not say." He folded his arms across his chest, a classic signal of defiance. "This is what happens, Miss Sinclair, when the irresistible force meets the immovable object."

"All right then." She stood up again.

Faust managed a theatrical yawn. "Off to see your friends in the police department?"

"Not exactly. You going home after this?"

"I expect to, yes."

"Good. Stay there."

"Why should I do this?"

"You'll see."

She left the café, climbed into her Miata, and drove to another coffee shop in the neighborhood, one that wasn't so weird. She didn't want coffee. The place was a Wi-Fi hot spot. She booted up her laptop and jumped online, tracing the name Elise Vangarten. It took only a couple of minutes to track down the modeling agency that employed her.

Faust had said Elise was at work. The question was: Where?

Abby called the agency and represented herself as Elise's roommate, who needed to get in touch with her because someone in Elise's family had taken ill. "She must have turned off her cell, or the battery's dead. I can't get through. Can you tell me where she's working today?"

The receptionist probably wouldn't have given the information to a man, no matter what his cover story. But a woman seemed safe. There were advantages to being a member of the fairer sex.

Elise was doing a photo shoot at an address in the Valley. Abby knew the neighborhood—a less-than-upscale corner of Sylmar. It seemed like a funny place for a photography studio. She said as much.

"Oh, it's not a studio," the receptionist explained. "They're shooting in a graveyard."

Of course they were.

28

"All right," Hauser said as he steered the Bureau LTD out of the federal building's underground garage, "here's the story. Try to keep up."

Tess, in the passenger seat, judiciously ignored the advice. She focused on stowing her laptop, nestled in its carrying case, on the floor of the car. It was the only item she'd removed from her Camry in the parking lot. Unlike the underground garage, the outdoor lot wasn't secured, and there would be hell to pay if a Bureau computer was stolen.

"We've wanted to get Faust for a long time, as you know. He was a serious suspect in the murder of Roberta Kessler three years ago. But we could never tie him to that crime or to any of the others."

She looked sharply at him. "Others?"

"Over the years there have been at least a dozen homicides that match Faust's MO. I'm talking about young women—sometimes teenage girls—who turn up dead, dumped in a park or landfill, with the head and hands removed. In all cases there are signs that the victim was held captive for some period of time. Minimal food product in the digestive tract, evidence of dehydration, things like that."

"Were all these victims local?"

"They're all over the map, or at least the western states. L.A., Frisco, Santa Fe, Seattle. If they're the work of one guy, he's mobile."

Tess nodded. Multiple jurisdictions across state lines

would provide a legitimate basis for FBI involvement. "Mobility wouldn't be a problem for Faust," she said.

"No, it wouldn't. And as I said, the victimology and MO are his. But without something more definite, we can't prove anything. Faust published all the details of his crime, so we can't rule out a copycat. Or it could be a coincidence. There are practical reasons, after all, for leaving a body without identifiable features. And with the sheer number of homicides every decade, you're going to get some apparent similarities that don't mean anything."

"But you don't believe that."

"No, I don't. I think Faust is our man. I think sometimes he works close to home, like with Roberta Kessler, and other times he takes a trip." Hauser tightened his grip on the steering wheel. "The thing is, a man like him doesn't just stop killing. He doesn't wake up one morning and decide he's not a homicidal maniac anymore. You know what these guys are like. If they've committed one sexually motivated, ritualistic murder, they'll commit others. They'll keep on honing their craft until they're caught."

Tess thought about it. "There ought to be something we can do. Match his travel records to the dates of the victims' disappearances, for instance."

"Tried that. No luck. Either he drives everywhere and pays cash for his hotel rooms, or he has some other way of getting around."

"Private plane?"

"He doesn't own one. If he's borrowing someone else's, they've both kept quiet about it." Hauser shook his head, dismissing this line of thought. "Anyway, we got frustrated with the lack of progress regarding Faust, so recently we decided to turn up the heat."

"Who decided?"

"It was my idea. Took some lobbying before Michaelson approved it. He doesn't necessarily share my concern about Faust. He thinks it's possible the guy was a one-shot killer. I know he's not. And I always said I'd get that coldhearted bastard if it was the last thing I ever did."

He looked away, perhaps embarrassed by his vehemence. So the operation was his brainchild, his baby. Perhaps his one last chance for redemption after the dressing-down he received for Medea.

And now Abby had entered the picture—again. And spoiled everything for him—again.

"Anyway," he went on, " I got the green light. I initiated WEREWOLF."

"Say again?"

"It's the code name for the operation."

"I'll bet you came up with it."

"We had to call it something." There was a touch of asperity in his tone.

"I assume this is where Brody comes in."

"That's right. He was assigned a deep-cover role. Before joining the Bureau he was a Special Forces operative. Those guys know how to improvise under pressure. How to adapt to changing circumstances. Brody was one of the best."

"How well did you know him?"

"Well enough. He did some security work in Iraq after he left the service. Developed quite a reputation."

"Security work? For who, the CIA?"

"For us. We have counterterror operatives in Iraq, Afghanistan—all over the Middle East."

"He was contracted to the Bureau?"

"Yes. But not officially."

"I don't understand."

"He needed the leeway to do things his way. No questions asked."

"So he was a private operative drawing a Bureau paycheck?"

"Drawing a paycheck that could never be traced to the Bureau. It's all about deniability. We couldn't know too much."

"*You* seem to know a great deal."

"That's because I was supervising him."

"You were in Iraq, too?"

"Among other places. Until a year ago I was stationed overseas. I came out of military intelligence—which is not an oxymoron, no matter what anyone says. I joined the Bureau in 1987 and worked stateside for years. But after nine-eleven, when we made counterterror a top priority, I was reassigned to the Middle East. With my background, it only made sense."

"But you're home now."

"Got rotated out."

"And Brody? How long had he been back?"

"More than a year. Long enough to obtain official Bureau status, buy a house in the Valley, and get his wife knocked up for the second time."

"He had a wife." Tess closed her eyes.

"And a baby boy. He met Patricia in Turkey. She was working in an embassy there, staff position. The kid was born here in the U.S., while Brody was still in Baghdad. He was looking forward to being there when his second child was born. I guess it wasn't meant to be."

"He was your friend," Tess said quietly.

"He was a good man. His loss . . . well, it's a big deal."

"Losing any agent is a big deal." Tess was thinking again of Paul.

"Obviously. But Brody was something special. I would have bet he could handle anything. Apparently I was wrong."

They were silent for a moment, listening to the hum of the sedan's tires on the road surface. Tess asked, "What exactly was Brody up to?"

"He rented a guesthouse in Faust's neighborhood. His job was to stalk Faust—basically go wherever Faust was planning to be."

"That's all? Just stalk him?"

"No, the stalking was only part of it, the least important part. It was meant to rattle Faust—assuming the cold-blooded son of a bitch *can* be rattled. The main thing was blackmail."

Tess wasn't sure she'd heard correctly. "Blackmail?"

"Brody was planning to make contact with Faust and claim to have evidence linking him to Roberta Kessler. He would threaten to go to the police unless he was paid off. The idea was to intimidate Faust into making the payment. That would constitute an admission of guilt. Then we'd bring him in and put pressure on him to confess."

"Why bother with the stalking? Why not just approach Faust right away with the blackmail demand?"

"Our behavioral analysis guys said it would work better like this. Faust is the ultimate hard target, psychologically speaking. Brody's job was to soften him up. That's why he was working so hard to get in Faust's face as often as possible. He wanted to keep the pressure on. He even shadowed Faust's girlfriend. We wanted him to be a man of mystery, a guy who's always there, always one step ahead, but who fades back into the crowd if you try to get near him. It was all psy-op stuff. It could have worked. It *should* have worked."

"How long was Brody going to play with Faust's head before making his move?"

"Originally, at least a month, but we learned something yesterday that would have accelerated our timetable. LAPD forwarded a report on the disappearance of a street kid known as Raven, real name Jennifer Gaitlin. One of her street friends last saw her going with a guy who drives a gray or silver BMW sedan. Faust drives a gray BMW 550i."

"How long ago did she disappear?"

"Ten days. Unfortunately, her friend didn't make the report immediately. He finally told a social worker at a shelter. The report was passed on to us as a possible kidnapping."

"If Faust has Jennifer . . ." Tess said.

"Then her time is limited. Faust kept Emily Wallace

alive for just two or three days. Our behavioral guys
think he may be extending the period of captivity, trying
to get more and more out of it. So there's a slim chance
Jennifer Gaitlin could still be alive. Brody was going to
move against Faust today or tomorrow. If Abby Sinclair
killed him, then she may have cost Jennifer her life."

"You could still get a search warrant for Faust's residence—"

"After the LAPD fiasco last time? I don't think so.
And the witness's story isn't good enough for a warrant.
There are a lot of gray or silver BMWs in this town."

"You could get a warrant based on Brody's homicide.
Faust has to be a primary suspect."

"Until you showed up, he was the only suspect. But
your info has given us a whole new investigative thrust.
Now I guess maybe Faust didn't pull the trigger, after
all. Maybe he doesn't even know Brody's dead. It looks
like your girlfriend did it all."

"She's not my girlfriend. And we don't have to tell a
judge about Abby. We can get the warrant based on
reasonable suspicion—"

"It's not going to happen."

"Why not?"

"It just isn't."

Tess began to understand. "What role are the police
playing in all this?" she asked slowly.

Hauser hesitated, then seemed to decide it was too
much trouble to evade the question. "Zero," he said.

"How is that possible?"

"The last time the LAPD got involved in an investigation of Faust, it was leaked to the media and became a
major embarrassment. This time we're keeping it
under wraps."

She couldn't believe the local authorities hadn't been
informed. "Do they know about Brody's murder? About
the dead body in the guesthouse?"

"They don't know a damn thing. The Bureau is handling it."

"Yes, you seem to be handling it real well."

"Maybe you think you could have done a better job. I might remind you that the operation was proceeding as planned until our undercover man got killed. And it may very well be your friend who killed him."

"How many times do I have to tell you she's not my friend?"

Hauser turned to her. His face was hard. "Say it as often as you want. You're the one who worked with her on two previous investigations, without authorization and against protocol. You're the one who sold out the Bureau—and your integrity."

She met his gaze. "Michaelson told us not to let personal animosities get in our way."

"Michaelson's not here right now. Is he?"

29

The key in the lock.

The door, opening.

Raven barely raised her head to see him enter. She had no strength, no will. She was past caring what happened to her, past caring about anything. Let death come. It didn't matter.

Then he was standing over her, staring down at the bed where she lay. His face was different than she had seen it before. He had always looked so composed, so unflappable. Now he was angry.

Angry at her? She couldn't imagine why. But if she had made him mad somehow, maybe he would finally kill her and get it over with.

"There you are," he said in a curiously hushed voice. "Waiting for me, as I knew you would be. I am so pleased to see you."

He wasn't mad at her, then. That was too bad. It meant she might have to live a little longer.

He reached down, stroked her hair. She didn't shudder or pull away. His touch no longer repulsed her. She felt nothing.

"You respect me, Raven, I know. Or you fear me, and this is far better. Sinclair neither respects nor fears."

Raven didn't know who Sinclair was, but evidently this was the person he had come here to forget.

His hand strayed to the gag around her mouth. He fingered it lightly, making no effort to remove it. "I am afraid, my dear, that I cannot permit the use of your voice during today's visit. The reason shall become plain. There is a certain ritual, a rite of passage, that we must perform."

Ritual. The word ought to have frightened her, but like everything else it was distant and unimportant.

He moved away from her, crossing the room to the cabinet against the far wall. He opened one of the two doors, leaving the other closed. From inside the cabinet he brought out a tool of some kind, with a rubber-coated handle and a long power cord. He plugged the cord into a wall socket.

"You should not look on this as punishment," he said. "It is an honor to be marked with the *wolfsangel.* It is the sign of the wolf, that most noble animal, the beast that is my totem. The sign of the werewolf, as well. You are perhaps familiar with this creature only through your vulgar horror films. But the real werewolf is not a B-movie actor in greasepaint and crepe hair. It is the synthesis of man and animal, which produces the most perfect predator."

There was a metal rod extending from the handle, with another metal piece attached perpendicular to the end. She had no idea what it was for. But she could see it slowly turning red as it heated up.

"Now, here is the part that will interest you. It is said that whoever bears the mark of the *wolfsangel* is invested with the life force, the very power of the wolf. Would you not relish such power? With the strength and savagery of the wolf, you could break your bonds and tear out my throat. You would like that, would you not?"

There had been a time when she would have liked it very much, but she no longer cared. Saving herself, killing him—it was of no consequence. She only wanted to go away, and make everything else go away, too—this room and this man and her own body, all of it.

"Well, then," he said, "let us see how it works."

He carried the instrument to her. She could see it clearly now. The flat metal piece, red-hot, looked like the letter Z with a crossbar through the center.

The *wolfsangel,* he had said. This must be what he meant.

It is an honor to be marked with the wolfsangel.

Marked . . .

She understood. The tool was a branding iron, and it would sear her flesh.

She hadn't thought there was any fight left in her. She'd been wrong. Abruptly she was twisting on the bed, shaking her hands against the manacles, averting her face as her legs kicked wildly, and the sounds that came from behind the gag were stifled screams.

He seized her left hand and flattened it, palm down, against the headboard.

And then there was pain.

It began as a shock of sudden numbness on the back of her hand, like the kiss of an ice pack, and she had time to think this wasn't so bad, not too bad at all. But the numbness lasted less than a second, and it was followed by a savage bite of pain, like fangs closing over her hand, peeling away skin and tendons, seeking bone.

She shrieked through the gag, producing only a hoarse, strangled cry.

"All done now," he was saying.

Past a cloud of tears she saw that he had withdrawn the branding iron. But the pain in her hand was undiminished. It roared through her body, ringing in her ears.

"Now you see why I could not undo your gag," he said calmly. "Although this room is soundproofed, I could not allow such a scream. It would be too painful for my delicate ears."

He took her hand and studied it almost lovingly, then wrenched her arm toward her and forced her to look.

"Observe how lovely you are."

The back of her hand was one huge purple welt in

the shape of a backward, crosshatched Z. The ugly design crawled over her knuckles and blue veins like some misshapen spider.

"You are now forever mine," he said with satisfaction. "Like all my others."

He returned to the cabinet and opened a second door to reveal rows of shelving, and on the shelves there were jars of greenish fluid, and in the jars . . . in the jars . . .

She turned away, crying.

In the jars were hands, scarred with the same mark. Severed hands, branded, preserved for display.

When she looked up again, the branding iron had been put away, the cabinet was closed, and he was once more standing over her.

"So *do* you feel it, Raven? The magical power of your talisman? The power of the wolf? Sadly, I think not. But there is another tradition associated with the *wolfsangel* that I earlier neglected to recount. It is said that anyone bearing this sign is marked for death at the claws of the wolf. Or the werewolf, as the case may be. This is your fate, Raven. But not yet. Not quite yet."

Oh, God, she wanted him to kill her. She wanted to die, wanted it so badly, more than anything she'd ever hoped for. But the terrible thing was that he *knew* what she wanted, and he would not give it to her. He was too cruel for that, and too patient.

He left, closing the door, and she heard the turn of the key in the lock.

30

At three P.M., Tess and Hauser arrived at the house in the Los Feliz district where Brody had rented a guest cottage. Hauser parked the Bureau LTD around back, where it wouldn't be spotted from the street.

"Who are the homeowners?" Tess asked.

"Mr. and Mrs. William Hunter. He's a big wheel in real estate."

"Do they know . . . ?"

"They know. But we've asked them to stay quiet about it for now. Don't want the neighbors talking, especially since one of them is Faust."

"And the body? Is it still in the cottage?"

"Long gone. It was taken out before sunrise in an unmarked van. The evidence techs have been all over the guesthouse. They're gone, too."

"The neighbors didn't notice any of this activity?"

"The crime scene guys arrived in an undercover van with a carpet cleaning company's logo on the side. They were shampooing the rugs, as far as anybody knows. Let's see what kind of job they did."

"Wait a minute. Are the homeowners around?"

"The wife is, I think. Husband works. They've already been interviewed."

"But not about Abby."

Hauser knocked on the back door. A woman in her fifties, smartly dressed, answered at once. She must have seen the car drive up to the cottage.

She let them in and escorted them to a parlor, where

she sat facing them. Her face, lit by a shaft of sun through a bay window, was narrow, her skin too tight against her skull; she'd had more than one face-lift. Tess thought there was something to be said for growing old gracefully, but maybe not in California.

"This is a lovely house," Tess said, simply to establish a rapport. "Have you lived here long?"

"Twenty years now."

"Have you rented out the guest cottage all that time?"

"Only for the last five years or so. It's not for the money, really." She seemed a little defensive. "It's that the cottage was just going to waste."

"I guess you don't exactly need the extra space."

"That's for sure. There are so many rooms in this house, a person can get lost in here. You practically need a map to find your way around."

Tess shifted into her professional mode. "Mrs. Hunter, we have an interest in talking to a woman who may have been acquainted with Mr. Brody. I wondered if you've seen her with him."

"I don't keep track of my tenants' social lives."

"Even so, we'd like you to look at this photo and just tell me if you've ever seen this woman."

Before leaving the field office, Hauser had pulled a photo from Abby's file. He handed it to Mrs. Hunter, who stared at it for nearly a minute.

"Oh . . . yes," she said finally.

"You have?"

"I'd forgotten all about it. But I *did* see her early yesterday morning. She was leaving the cottage. Driving away in her car."

"Do you remember what kind of car it was?"

"Not really. I don't know much about these things. It was old, beat-up. Looked pretty awful. That's what got my attention—the car. I was looking out the window— it was about six o'clock in the morning, and I'd just gotten up and was fixing myself a cup of coffee. I looked out, and I saw the car and this woman in it."

"Are you sure it was the same woman? She must have been some distance away."

"Oh, it was definitely her. She saw me looking at her. She waved to me."

"Did she?"

"Yes, a rather impertinent little wave. I remember thinking she must have spent the night. Did she have something to do with Mr. Brody's death?"

"She's just somebody we want to talk to."

"You people always say that. You always say it's someone you want to talk to when really they're the suspect. Is she a suspect?"

Tess took back the photo. "Thank you, Mrs. Hunter. Thank you for your time."

"So we know she spent the night," Hauser said as he walked with Tess to the guest cottage. "Is sleeping with the enemy part of her job description?"

"I don't think so. But . . . there aren't any hard-and-fast rules."

Hauser unlocked the door to the guesthouse and led Tess inside. The cottage was much nicer than she'd expected. Lavish, even.

"The rent on this place couldn't have been cheap," she said.

"Nothing in this neighborhood is cheap."

"Mrs. Hunter seemed a little too insistent about not needing the money."

"I'm betting they can use the extra dough, no matter what she says. A lot of folks in this town are house-poor. They've got all their cash tied up in their house, and none of it to spend." Hauser smiled. "One thing I've learned in this job. When they say it's not about the money, it's *always* about the money."

Tess explored the cottage. All the lights were on. Brightly colored fingerprint powder had been left on most smooth surfaces. There was no indication of a struggle in the living room or kitchen.

The bedroom was a different story. Blood had splashed the wall near the doorway in an arterial spray. More blood had soaked into the carpet in the same spot. Brody must have been hit while standing. He had slumped to the floor and expired in a spreading red pool.

The bedside lamp had been knocked over, the plug pulled out of a wall socket. The bedsheets had been disarranged.

"Evidence techs dug a nine-millimeter round out of the headboard," Hauser said, pointing to a white circle drawn around a deep pockmark where the bullet had hit. "Haven't done a ballistics match yet, but from the angle of fire they're betting it's from Brody's gun. He carried a Beretta Mini Cougar."

Tess glanced at him and caught a pained expression on his face. It puzzled her for a moment, and she wondered if he was falling ill. Then she remembered that Brody had been his friend, and Hauser had found him here in this room only a few hours earlier.

"What about the round that killed him?" she asked quietly.

"It didn't exit. Lodged in his neck, blew out his larynx, then probably tumbled into the base of his skull." Tumbling was a term for the multiple ricochets of a bullet inside the human body as it bounced off bone. "That's guesswork on my part. Autopsy hasn't been done yet."

Circling the bedroom, Tess saw how it probably had gone down. Abby had been on or near the bed with her hands in restraints. Her wrists must have been cuffed in front of her, affording her some mobility. She had distracted Brody by unplugging the lamp, and he had fired, missing her. She'd killed him with a shot fired through the purse.

It would have happened in a second or less. There might be room for Abby to plead self-defense. Once Brody fired on her, she would have felt no compunction about shooting back.

Of course, if she hadn't resisted arrest in the first

place . . . if she had gone along quietly . . . then Brody would be alive and there would be no homicide charges in the offing. And a plea of self-defense wouldn't work very well in circumstances involving an escape from FBI custody.

As Tess finished her circuit of the room, she saw a small table, dusty around the edges but with a rectangular dust-free space in the middle.

"What used to be here?" she asked.

"TV set."

"Why is it gone?"

"Because it wasn't a real TV. Brody had hollowed it out and put some electronic gear inside."

"What kind of gear?"

He hesitated. "Elsur equipment." Electronic surveillance, he meant. "For intercepting cellular transmissions."

"Did he have a warrant?"

"No."

She looked at Hauser, silently pressing for elaboration. After a moment, he obliged.

"I told you he was under deep cover. I gave him free rein. Didn't try to micromanage. Apparently he decided he could shadow Faust more efficiently by picking up his cell phone chatter. That way he could anticipate Faust's movements, show up wherever Faust was going without the risk of tailing him. It made sense."

"It was illegal."

"Like I said, I didn't know about it."

"Is the surveillance team monitoring Faust's phone calls now?"

"No. We still don't have a warrant."

"That didn't stop Brody."

"I'm not Brody." Hauser's tone was sharp.

"But you're stuck cleaning up his mess." Tess frowned, glancing at the blood on the wall. "Sorry. That didn't come out the way I intended. What I mean is, you can't get a warrant to eavesdrop on Faust for the same reason you can't get a warrant to search his house. Because in either case you'd have to tell a judge about Brody's murder. And the judge might talk to someone at LAPD. And when LAPD finds out you've been running a murder investigation without their input, all hell will break loose. Right?"

"We're handling it," he said irritably.

"This is a disaster, Ron, and you know it. You allowed Brody to cut corners, and now you're trapped into cutting corners yourself."

He glared at her. "I don't need a lecture from you on that subject."

"No, I guess you don't. But Brody sure as hell did. For someone who's such a stickler for the rules, you let him write his own ticket on this case."

"It's the way he worked. I guess maybe . . . maybe I should have supervised him more closely. But I thought he'd . . ." He let his words trail off.

"Thought he'd what?" No answer. "What is it you're not telling me?"

"He had a . . . reputation," Hauser said slowly. "In Iraq."

"Not a good rep, I'm guessing?"

Hauser sighed. "Not after a certain point, no. See, the thing is—"

He would have said more, but the chirp of his cell phone intervened. Hauser took the call, communicating mainly in grunts. When he was finished, he snapped the phone shut and looked at Tess with something like triumph in his gaze.

"Just got word from the surveillance team. They followed Faust to a café he frequents. He met a woman there. Guess who."

Tess turned away. "I don't have to guess."

"No, you don't. It was Sinclair."

"If they were in the café, Abby may have spotted them. She's pretty good at countersurveillance."

"They weren't inside. They knew they would stand

out in the crowd, so they watched from a parked car across the street. Had a view through a window. They saw Sinclair enter the café and sit with Faust. She left first. They didn't follow her because they didn't have a heads-up on her at the time."

"We have to bring her in," Tess said quietly.

"Damn straight we do. Michaelson's already given the orders. And the evidence guys are working her car and her condo. It was blood on the steering wheel, all right. You want to bet it's *not* Brody's?"

"No." Tess sighed. "We'd better get over to her condo. Maybe she's headed there herself. Maybe she'll come home."

"Or maybe she's racing for the border," Hauser said. "But wherever she is, we'll get her. This time Sinclair is going down."

31

Pioneer Cemetery lay under an incongruously blue California sky. Traffic zipped past on the 210 Freeway, immediately northeast of the graveyard. The sprawling complex of the Olive View UCLA Medical Center lay just across the freeway, looking shiny and new.

There was nothing either shiny or new about Pioneer Cemetery. A sign identified it as the second-oldest burial place in the San Fernando Valley, dating to the 1800s and abandoned in 1960. Maintenance was problematic. Headstones had been toppled and smashed. Weeds had sprung up copiously amid tufts of dead grass. Gopher holes dotted the grounds.

Abby knew the technical term for an ecosystem like this: *prairie meadow.* To her, it seemed like a nice way of saying *vacant lot.*

She watched from a distance as the photo shoot unfolded. To enhance the graveyard's desolation, the art director had strewn withered flowers around the marble obelisk where Elise was posing. She modeled a chic black ensemble that would have seemed more appropriate for a cocktail party. On the other hand, her rail-thin figure did not appear out of place in an abode of skeletons.

The photographer snapped pictures at an incredible rate while maintaining a running commentary like infield chatter. "That's it, that's beautiful, just a little more attitude, darling, tilt your chin up just a tad, little more, perfect, no, don't smile, you're angry, I want to see rage, scare me, darling, glare at me, burn right through me with those beautiful angry eyes. . . ."

Abby couldn't detect much anger or any other emotion in the girl's vacuous gaze. Maybe the photography studio could add some expression to her face after the fact. Photoshop it or something.

She had to admit, though, that Elise did have a certain distinctive look. With her angular limbs and sharp-planed face and windblown hair—tossed in elegant disarray by an off-camera electric fan—she captured the plaintive allure of a lost soul. Possibly that was exactly what she was.

A small crowd of bystanders observed the shoot. Abby, standing among them, knew it was only a matter of time until Elise noticed her. When the girl turned her head in Abby's direction in response to the photographer's command, their eyes briefly locked.

"Come on, darling, give me more, we were in the zone but we're losing it now, come back to me, be in the moment, focus, focus. . . ."

No use. Elise was distracted. Seeing Abby had broken her concentration.

The photographer could not have known the reason, but he did perceive the results. He stopped clicking the shutter and suggested a ten-minute break.

Abby waited for Elise to approach her. It took a while for the photographer, the art director, and a bevy of assistants and makeup and hair people and assorted go-fers to leave the area, retreating to a staging ground in the parking lot where three trailers were arrayed in a tight formation. Then Elise was alone, except for a set dresser busily rearranging the dead foliage.

She walked up to Abby, who had remained behind as the rest of the onlookers, losing interest, drifted away.

Up close Elise didn't look quite like herself. She wore pancake makeup, heavy eye shadow, and pale lipstick. "Hey, Abby. He's not here today."

Abby almost asked who, then realized Elise was refer-

ring to Brody. He had shown up at her other outdoor
shoots. "No," she said, "I guess not."

"That's good, right? Maybe he's given up, gone
away."

He had gone away, all right. "It's possible. But we
can't make any assumptions. In fact, I need your help."

"Okay, sure. I'll do anything."

She was so guileless and helpless, Abby almost regretted what she was about to do. But the girl had hooked
up with Peter Faust. She wasn't entirely innocent.

"I think the man who's been tailing you has a partner," Abby said, reciting the words she'd rehearsed on
her way over. "I'm not a hundred percent certain of it,
though. I snapped some digital pics of the guy, and I've
got them on my laptop. I need you to look at them and
tell me if you've seen him around."

"No problem."

"The computer's in my car."

Abby led her toward a far corner of the parking lot,
where the Miata sat well away from the trailers. She
would have preferred to have the Hyundai, which was
less distinctive and harder to trace back to her, but she
hadn't wanted to take the time to go back to Westwood
and switch vehicles.

"Did Peter tell you I'd be here?" Elise asked.

"That's right."

"I'm surprised he even remembered. Half the time
when I tell him where I'll be shooting, I don't think he
even listens."

"Maybe he listens more than you realize." They
reached the car. Abby opened the passenger door.
"Slide in," she said casually.

"I don't know if I should. My clothes are kind of dirty.
And this darn body makeup gets all over everything.
Can't you just show me the pictures from here?"

"There aren't any pictures."

"What? You said—"

Even after Elise turned to face Abby, it still took her a moment to register the gun in Abby's hand.

"Hey," she breathed, sounding more offended than afraid.

"I want you to stay very calm, Elise. Don't make any noise. Just slowly get in the car."

Her nose wrinkled. "What the *hell* are you doing?"

"I need to take you somewhere. Not very far. I'll have you back here in no time."

"I can't *leave* the *shoot.*" She said it as if the very possibility were unthinkable.

"Yes, you can. You have to."

"Or else what?" She drew herself up, chin raised. "You'll shoot me?"

"That's it exactly. I will shoot you."

Elise blinked, taking this in. "But . . ." she said finally. "But you *work* for us!"

"I'm freelance. I don't work for anybody. Now get in the car."

Elise took another long look at the gun. Reluctantly she complied.

"Stay in the passenger seat," Abby ordered. "I'm going around to the driver's side. If you yell or try to get away . . ."

"You'll shoot me. I got it." She was trying to sound defiant, but the quaver in her voice betrayed her.

Abby slid behind the wheel, keyed the ignition, and pulled off. As the car headed for the exit, the photographer caught sight of Elise inside. He shouted something and waved his arms.

"You're getting me in a lot of trouble," Elise said.

Abby didn't answer, just kept driving. As they headed south on Foothill Boulevard, Elise said quietly, "You're going to kill me, aren't you?"

"I'm not going to kill you. Unless I have to," she added for effect.

"Great." Elise shivered and hugged herself. "We never should have hired you."

"Yeah, I get that a lot."

"I told Peter not to. I said we should just get a regular bodyguard. Or one of the security guys at the gallery."

Abby turned west on Hubbard Avenue. "The gallery?"

"The Unblinking I. You were there, right? They have security guards."

"Why would Peter hire one of them?"

"He knows them. He hired them in the first place. For the gallery."

This was news. "You're saying he helps run the place?"

"Why not? He's one of the owners." She put a hand to her mouth like a little girl who'd just said a bad word. "Oh, I guess I wasn't supposed to tell you that."

"Why not?"

"It's a secret. He doesn't, you know, publicize his involvement. Some people might have a problem with it because of his background and all."

Glenoaks Boulevard was coming up. Abby eased into the left-turn lane. "The fact that he's a cold-blooded killer, you mean?"

Elise nodded, oblivious to sarcasm. "It's an issue for some people. So he's got to keep some of his business activities quiet."

"He keeps a lot of secrets, I guess."

"Probably."

"He even keeps secrets from you."

"I'm sure he does."

"That doesn't bother you?"

"He has his reasons."

Abby shook her head. "Everybody has reasons, Elise. It doesn't mean what they're doing is right."

"You should talk. You're holding a gun on me and kidnapping me."

Well, she had a point there. Anyway, there was no time to pursue the issue. The gas station was coming up.

She had noted the Texaco station on the drive over.

It had gone out of business, which meant it was conveniently empty, and its rear lot was nicely screened from view by the windowless walls of a large brick building next door.

She pulled into the lot behind the station and emerged from the car, then escorted Elise to a pay phone in a kiosk. The phone worked; Abby had checked for a dial tone when she scoped out the place.

"Call Peter," Abby ordered. "Not his cell. His landline."

"I don't have any change."

Abby popped some coins into the slot. "Dial."

Elise obeyed. Abby hoped Faust hadn't changed his mind about going straight home.

"Hello, Peter? Something's happened. I think Sinclair's gone crazy—"

Abby grabbed the phone. "You hear that, Faust? I have your girlfriend. Right now I'm holding a gun on her. Tell him, Elise. Tell him I'm holding a gun."

She held out the phone, and Elise started babbling that it was true, she was, she really *was*.

"When I met her," Abby added, "she told me she didn't have a death wish. It looks like she was telling the truth, because she's plenty scared right now."

Faust's breathing, low and fast, was audible in her ear. "What the hell do you mean to accomplish by this?"

"I want to know who gave you my name. Your friend in law enforcement."

"Or you will what? Kill an innocent woman?"

"Maybe not kill. I might just settle for taking out her kneecaps."

Elise moaned.

"You're a poor bluffer, Miss Sinclair." Faust was breathing harder. "You will not harm her."

"You want to take that chance? Let's ask Elise what she thinks."

She again extended the phone, and Elise, crying now, began to beg. "Tell her, Peter, tell her whatever she wants, please tell her, she's crazy, she's got a gun and she kidnapped me right out of a shoot with all these people watching, and we're alone, and she's crazy, crazy, *crazy*—"

Abby took back the phone. "You get the drift. Now talk."

"Very well, God damn it. The man in question is—or was—a U.S. Marine."

"The Marines aren't in law enforcement."

"Actually, he was working for the Defense Intelligence Agency at the time. Or perhaps some similar operation; I have forgotten the details. I met him in Germany."

"How?"

"After I was arrested for Emily Wallace's murder, the American government was briefly concerned that there might be national security implications to the crime. Emily worked on a U.S. military base, you see. This rather earnest buzz-cut marine was sent to interrogate me in my cell. He quickly determined that I was not part of any terrorist cabal."

"You got my name from a marine you met in Germany more than ten years ago?"

"He is a marine no longer. Once I had settled in Los Angeles, he rang me up. Wanted to keep tabs on me, it seems. He was friendly enough, and I had no objection to his occasional calls. I knew the game he was playing, and he knew I knew."

Abby was lost. "What game? I don't get it."

"Oh, I did forget a rather crucial piece of exposition, did I not? Upon leaving the marines, he joined the FBI. He is stationed in Los Angeles and has no doubt been tasked by his superiors with maintaining contact with me. Given our previous encounter, he would be the logical man for the job."

"And he gave you my name?"

"He did. I called him to ask if he could suggest a

private operative who could assist in a stalking case, and
he supplied your name and your cell phone number."

"I'll have to thank him for the business. Which would
be a lot easier if I knew who he was."

"Have I not mentioned that? His name is Hauser.
Ronald Hauser of the Los Angeles field office of the
FBI."

Abby shut her eyes. "Okay."

"You are now satisfied?"

"Yes."

"Then kindly release the lady."

"She won't be hurt. She never would have been hurt."

"It was all a bluff, then?"

"Of course."

"I did suspect as much, although I wonder, Miss Sinclair, how far you might have carried your so-called
bluff, had I proved more intractable."

The dial tone buzzed in her ear.

Abby hung up. She stood for a long moment with her
hand on the phone before remembering Elise.

"Sorry about all this," she said lamely. "But I had to
know. I'll drive you back to the shoot."

"Uh-uh, no way, I don't *think* so." Elise was shaking
her head wildly like a panicked mare. "I'm not getting
in the car with you again."

"Fair enough. Here's some more change. You can call
someone at the shoot and have them pick you up."

Elise clutched the coins in a tight fist. "I'll call the
goddamned police; that's who I'll call."

"Probably not a good idea. Peter won't want the police brought in. Call him and see."

"You mean I'm just supposed to *forget* about you *kidnapping* me? How am I supposed to explain leaving
the shoot?"

"Tell them I'm your crazy roommate, and I drove you
off and left you here as a gag. Embellish it any way you
want. Maybe I was all coked up or something. Be creative."

"I hate you." She pronounced the verdict with a child's righteous scorn.

"Sticks 'n' stones," Abby said, getting back into the car. She was tired of Elise. Tired of Peter Faust. Tired of the whole business.

"Oh, yeah? Well . . ." Elise searched for a comeback. "Well, we're not paying you, that's for damn sure! And you won't be getting any recommendations from us, either."

"Right. I get it. I'll never eat lunch in this town again."

Elise's rage switched to bafflement. "Who said anything about lunch?"

It didn't seem like a question worth answering. Abby drove off. She watched Elise shrink in her rearview mirror, a small, angry figure, arms akimbo, hair flying in the breeze.

Abby couldn't feel good about what she'd done. But it had worked. She'd gotten the info she needed. She knew who'd set her up.

Hauser.

32

Tess hated this. Hated participating in Abby's takedown. Hated the thought that Abby would, very probably, end up in a federal prison for many years.

She sat beside Hauser as he drove back to Westwood. She was grateful for his silence, and unhappy when he broke it.

"You know, if Michaelson hadn't worked out a deal with Sinclair last time, she'd be in the pen right now, and Brody would still be alive."

"Abby didn't do anything wrong last time."

"Interfering with a federal investigation, withholding evidence, leaving a crime scene, using phony ID . . ." Hauser ticked off the charges on his fingers.

"She had good reasons."

"Right, take her side. I forgot how close you are to her."

"Ron, you've been riding me about Abby ever since you walked into the Nose's office."

"Don't call him that," he said peevishly.

"Do I have to remind you that I came to L.A. voluntarily to give you this lead?"

"You came here because you knew Sinclair would be tied to the murder eventually, and then a check of her phone records would show she'd spoken to you a day earlier. You were in cover-your-ass mode, as usual."

"That's ridiculous."

"Save it for your fans in the media. And for whoever's dick you're stroking on Ninth Street. He must be pretty high up to have shielded you from any blowback on Medea."

"I used to respect you, Ron. I'm having my doubts now."

"I used to respect you, too, McCallum. These days I have no doubts about you whatsoever."

Silence again. Tess stared out the window and went over the crime scene in her mind, reviewing the layout of the guest cottage, scanning her memories for something she'd overlooked. The images cycled past like the rooms in the search video that had played on her computer last night.

So many rooms . . .

She blinked. "Do you have blueprints of Faust's home?" she asked Hauser.

"I don't think so. Why?"

"We need to look at them."

"What for?"

"Just an idea I have."

"I'm not wasting time hunting down blueprints. Sinclair is the priority, in case you've forgotten."

"Fine."

She pulled out her cell phone and called Michaelson's office, getting through to him after a brief showdown with his secretary. Hauser threw irritated glances her way. She ignored him.

"Richard, I need to get hold of the blueprints to Peter Faust's home. Hauser doesn't have them, but they may be on file with the city."

"Hauser's backing you up on this?" Michaelson asked.

"Yes," she lied.

"All right, all right"—he sounded harried—"I'll see what I can do."

She ended the call, hoping Michaelson would follow through.

"Want to tell me what this is all about?" Hauser asked.

Tess smiled. "No, Ron. Actually, I don't."

*   *   *

They arrived at the Wilshire Royal at four thirty. Hauser stashed the LTD in a remote corner of the parking garage so that if Abby came back, she wouldn't see it and run.

He took his time getting out of the car, and Tess wondered what was the matter with him. He caught her questioning gaze and frowned. "Knees," he said. "Played too much football in my younger days. Now it's catching up with me."

He was limping a little as they walked from the garage into the lobby. The guards behind the desk weren't any more cooperative than last time, but they didn't have to be. A team of Bureau criminalists, bearing a search warrant, had already recovered the blood from Abby's Hyundai and now were working in her apartment. More agents were watching the entrance to the building from an office across the street.

"What worries me is those damn rent-a-cops," Hauser said to Tess as they rode the elevator to the tenth floor. "They'll tip her off if they can."

"Maybe we should station an agent in the lobby, out of sight from outside."

"It's a thought. Of course, if she's smart, she's not coming back."

And she *was* smart, Tess thought. Survival was Abby's specialty. She almost said as much, but Hauser had turned away to dry-swallow a couple of pills. Arthritis meds, maybe. His knees must be worse than she'd thought.

The apartment was in disarray, as it had been when Tess had last seen Abby. Then, Tess had found her cleaning up the mess left by another evidence team. Now her collections of CDs and DVDs were once again scattered on the floor, her papers removed from the file cabinets, her kitchen cupboards standing open. A photographer clicked off exposures on a digital camera.

Hauser requested a rundown on what had turned up

so far. A computer technician had recovered a record of
a Web search for information on Brody. Although Abby
had erased her Internet cache, the files had been re-
stored with a software application.

Other criminalists had found traces of blood in the
plumbing under both the shower and the washing machine. In a closet, they'd discovered extra ammunition,
though Abby's gun itself was missing. They would try to
match the ammo to the round recovered from Brody
once the autopsy was performed.

"So," Hauser said with satisfaction, "we've got her
with Faust in the café and with Brody in the cottage.
She was reading Faust's book and researching Brody's
background. We've got blood in her car, on her clothes,
and in her plumbing pipes. We've got a bullet hole in
her purse and disposable handcuffs that were cut apart.
I'd say we have a case, Agent McCallum. Wouldn't
you?"

Tess shut her eyes. "It looks that way."

The phone rang.

The two evidence techs in the living room glanced up.
Tess and Hauser turned.

It was Abby's home phone, on an end table by her
armchair.

As they all stared stupidly at it, the phone rang again.

"Has anyone called here before now?" Tess asked.

One technician shook his head. "First time since
we've arrived."

The phone rang for a third time. "Let her voice mail
answer it," Hauser said. "We can play back the message
and—"

Tess cut him off. "It's her."

"How could you possibly know that?"

"I just do." She picked up the phone. "Hello."

"Hey, Tess." Abby's voice, of course. "How's it
hanging?"

33

It was a risk, calling her condo. There was a good chance no one would answer. Even if someone did, it might not be Tess—and Tess was the only one Abby could trust.

Even so, she had decided to chance it. Making contact with Tess might be her last shot at getting out of this mess relatively unscathed.

Tess would be in L.A. by now, obviously. That much was easy to predict. From the moment Faust had mentioned Hauser, a number of things had become clear. One of them was that Abby had gotten entangled in an undercover FBI operation, with Brody as the UC man. This one fact explained a lot of anomalies. As an ordinary stalker, Brody made no sense—not with his background, experience, and equipment. But he fit the bill of federal agent just fine.

Except for the part about trying to kill her. But she had that figured out, as well. Hauser must have arranged it. Presumably, Hauser was his supervisor, and he had some kind of buddy-buddy thing going on with Faust. When Faust called him for advice on the unwanted attention he and Elise were receiving from the new man in their lives, Hauser suggested the services of one Abby Sinclair, certified stalker stopper. Which she really ought to thank him for, word of mouth being the best advertising and all, except somehow she didn't think he'd had her best interests at heart.

She remembered Hauser from the Medea case. He'd assisted in her arrest. He'd been none too hospitable toward her. He had, in fact, been royally pissed off. She had compromised the integrity of his precious FBI. He hated her for it. And apparently he was the type who held a grudge.

Ever since, he must have been looking for an opportunity to get her off the street. She was a loose cannon, which in his world was probably even worse than a loose woman. Which she also was, but that was another story.

Of course, putting her behind bars was one thing. Putting her in the morgue was something else. She wasn't clear on his exact motivation, but somehow he'd let personal animosity overrule his judgment.

And if he had been Brody's supervisor, then it was likely that he was now in charge of the homicide investigation. And it was a sure bet that Tess was hip-deep in this mess, too. As soon as she'd learned of a killing in conjunction with Faust, she would have informed her superiors of Abby's possible involvement. She wasn't likely to stay in Denver when something like this was going down. Most likely she was in L.A. already, working with Hauser and never suspecting that he was the real bad guy.

There were lots of other angles to this thing, and Abby had been exploring them ever since leaving Elise at the Texaco station. The business of the Rohypnol, for instance. Hauser would have known about that. He'd searched the contents of her purse—what cops called "pocket litter"—after her arrest. He would have found the small bottle of pills and understood their purpose. And, of course, he would have warned Brody, who'd taken the appropriate countermeasures.

Now it was time to take some countermeasures of her own.

She had crossed over the Hollywood Hills into the L.A. basin, chucking her cell phone into one of the canyons on the way. A cell phone sent out a periodic signal check even when it wasn't in use, which meant it could be used to trace her whereabouts even if she didn't place or receive any calls. She could have just switched it off altogether, but it was easier to ditch it. Most likely she would never be using it again.

In Hollywood she stopped at a thrift store and purchased a Mexican shawl, a pillow, and an oversize jacket. Then she drove into Westwood, parking her Miata on a side street several blocks from her condo building.

With the pillow stuffed under the jacket and the shawl wrapped around her head and shoulders, she looked like a pregnant lady from south of the border—one of the innumerable maids, housekeepers, and nannies who rode the buses into this neighborhood from East L.A. every day.

She stationed herself on a bus stop bench across the street from the Wilshire Royal. And she waited.

It wasn't a long wait. At four thirty a Hoover blue Bureau sedan pulled into the Royal's parking garage. A few minutes later Tess was visible through the plate-glass lobby doors.

"So you are here," Abby whispered. "Welcome back."

The man with Tess could have been Hauser, but Abby couldn't distinguish his features well enough to be sure. Anyway, she had seen enough. She left the bus stop and walked back to her car, shed her costume, and drove to a pay phone. She punched in her home phone number and hoped Tess answered.

Distantly she was surprised at how much she wanted to talk to Tess. How much she needed an ally in this fight. Had it been only a couple of days ago when she'd coldly reminded Tess that they weren't friends anymore? Yet now she needed Tess as a friend. Otherwise there was nothing left for her but the nuclear option, as she thought of it. And she didn't want to go nuclear. When it came to her personal future, she was definitely antinuke.

"Hello?"

Tess's voice on the phone. Abby closed her eyes and did her best to sound casual.

"Hey, Tess. How's it hanging?"

She heard a muffled movement on the other end of the line, which had to be Tess alerting her fellow agents to the fact that Abby Sinclair, the wanted criminal, the class-A fugitive, was calling. Abby had to hope they hadn't thought to put a trace on the line. She was betting they hadn't; they would never have expected her to call her own number.

"If you know enough to call me on your home phone," Tess said evenly, "then I guess you know."

"Yeah, I'm in another pickle, it looks like." She was trying to find her old insouciance but not quite getting it. "You know, if you were coming to L.A., you could've given me a heads-up. We might have been able to get together, chat about old times."

"We still can."

"Maybe not right now. My schedule's a little tight."

"Abby, what the hell have you gotten yourself into?"

"I didn't *get myself* into anything. I was set up."

"Set up. Is that the best you can do?" There was no empathy in her tone, no willingness to listen.

"It's the truth."

"Yes, you know all about the truth, don't you? How to spin it, how to conceal it, how to turn it inside out and play mind games with it . . ."

"I have to admit, Tess, you're harshing my mellow."

"This isn't a joke. And it's not a game."

"I'm very much aware of that."

"If you are, then why are you calling me with some kind of lame self-justification when it's one of *our people* you killed?"

"In self-defense," Abby said.

"Then you're admitting you did kill him." All the inflection had gone out of Tess's voice.

"I repeat: *in self-defense.* Three little words that make all the difference. Or actually two little words, one of which is hyphenated." She was racing through the story, her words crowding together.

"He had you in handcuffs, Abby. We found them here in your apartment."

"Yeah, so?"

"He had placed you under arrest. He was taking you in. All you had to do was cooperate. Instead you decided to shoot your way out."

"He wasn't taking me in. If you'll just listen to me—"

"I'm not interested in your lies."

"That's a pretty closed-minded attitude, wouldn't you say?"

"I don't know. Maybe it is. Did I ever tell you about Paul Voorhees?"

"Who?"

"Another fed, like me. He died seven years ago. Murdered. I found him. And by the way, I was in love with him. Care to make any wisecracks about that?"

"No," Abby said softly.

"Maybe you'll understand why I'm not too eager to hear your explanations right now. If you have anything to say, just turn yourself in and you can talk all you want. And I'll listen."

"I want you to listen now."

"And I want you to surrender yourself to the authorities now. So it looks like we're at an impasse."

"Tess, Brody wasn't going to take me in. He was going to kill me. He intended to terminate me with extreme prejudice. And you know how I hate prejudice of any kind."

"That's ridiculous."

"He told me his plans for the evening. They consisted of a prolonged and, it's safe to say, painful interrogation, followed by the old lights-out. He was buying me a one-way ticket on the midnight train to Slab City. He wanted me toe-tagged and body-bagged."

"Mark Brody was a federal agent."

"A *rogue* agent."

"I have no evidence whatsoever to support that claim."

"You have my testimony."

"And how much is that worth, Abby? You've lied to me before, when your neck was on the line. Who's to say you're not lying again?"

"See, this is why you're off my Christmas card list."

"Damn it, you *know* I can't trust you. I can't trust a word you say."

"So you're just blowing me off, is that it?" Abby heard her own voice climbing toward hysteria and tried to settle down. She hadn't realized until this moment just how badly she needed Tess to listen, to believe.

"I'm willing to consider what you're saying," Tess said. "If you give yourself up—"

"Not gonna happen."

"Then arrange a place where we can meet."

"Yeah, right. Like you're not going to take me down the minute I show up. I don't like playing whack-a-mole, Tess, especially when I'm the mole. Look, I'm taking a risk by making contact. I have a lead in the case. It involves—"

"I don't care what it involves. I'm not interested in whatever red herring you want me to chase down. As far as I'm concerned, it's just a ploy to distract my attention and waste investigative resources."

"I would never waste resources, Tess. I'm a conservationist. I'm also not a murderer. You ought to know that."

"I don't know anything about you anymore, Abby. You took a job working for Peter Faust. You placed a crazy phone call to me, making some wild accusations—"

"That's just the thing. I was wrong about that, wrong about you. I admit it. But it gave me the lead I—"

"You don't get it, do you, Abby? I am not giving you the benefit of the doubt this time."

That stung. "Since when have you ever given me the benefit of the doubt, Tess?"

"Since I first agreed to work with you. Which I never should have. I think we both know that now."

It was over. No sale. "Yeah. I guess we both do. I take it this means I can't exactly count on your support."

"No. You can't."

"Then all that's left to say is good-bye. So good-bye, Tess . . . and fuck you."

She slammed down the pay phone, drawing a stare from a homeless guy working the intersection. She paid him no attention.

She was on her own, no friends, no allies.

So what else was new?

"Abby," Tess said into the dead phone.

Nothing. She was gone.

Tess slowly replaced in the handset in its cradle.

At the far end of the room, Hauser came in from the bedroom where he'd been listening on the extension. "You should have acted more cooperative," he said. "Given her more hope of persuading you. Then maybe you could have talked her into a meeting."

"There was never any chance of that. She would see right through that kind of ploy. You realize that if she knew I was here, she had to be watching the building?"

"I have our guys across the street out scouting the neighborhood."

"She's long gone by now. They didn't see anyone earlier?"

"Mailman, delivery boy, pregnant Hispanic woman waiting for a bus . . ."

"Pregnant Hispanic woman?" Tess almost smiled.

Hauser turned away. "Shit."

Together they returned to the lobby, where they stopped at the front desk to ask once more if the guards had any idea where Abby might have gone.

"We don't keep tabs on our residents," one of them said coolly.

Hauser gave the men a parting glare before accompanying Tess into the garage. Halfway to their car, they came face-to-face with the doorman in his red livery.

"You two need to talk to me," he announced with a sly, oddly discomfiting smile.

"Do we . . . Alec?" Hauser had read the man's name tag.

Tess stood back and let him handle it.

Alec nodded. "I told Vince and Gerry I was taking a bathroom break. That was just so we could talk without them seeing. I don't want them to know." He released a nervous chuckle. "It's kind of cool, anyway—meeting in the garage. Like I'm Deep Throat or something."

Hauser managed a friendly grin. "You going to tell us to follow the money?"

"I'm going to tell you how you might be able to track down Ms. Abby Sinclair."

"We're listening."

"There's a guy who comes to see her pretty often. Drives an old Ford Mustang. Calls himself Mr. Bryce."

"When you say *calls himself* . . ."

"It's not his real name. His name is Wyatt."

"How do you know that?"

"I saw him on the local news. He was being interviewed at a crime scene in Hollywood. See, he's a cop. Sergeant or lieutenant, I think. Someone on the patrol side, anyway. Wears a uniform. I mean, not when he comes here . . ."

"I understand. A cop named Wyatt, works patrol out of Hollywood."

"That's it."

"You know where to find him?"

"All I know is what I just told you. Sinclair might be with him, or he might know where to find her. If anyone would know, it's him. He's the only person who ever comes to visit. Maybe the only friend she has."

Hauser thanked him. The doorman was walking away when Tess asked, "May I ask you something? Why did you help us out?"

Alec turned to look at her, and his blandly affable face turned hard and unfeeling. "Because the bitch thinks she's too good for me."

He left the garage. Tess stared after him.

"A cop," Hauser said. "You know what that means? We have leverage."

"Yes. We probably do." But Tess wasn't thinking about that. She was remembering what Alec the doorman had said so casually.

Maybe the only friend she has.

34

Loud rapping roused Wyatt from sleep. He looked at his clock on the wall: 6:15 P.M.

He'd been awake for much of the day, but had taken a nap on his sofa around five o'clock. Irregular sleeping habits were one of the hazards of working the night watch.

He checked his peephole and saw a man and woman in official-looking suits in the hallway. Immediately he knew they were trouble.

He opened the door. "May I help you?"

"Victor Wyatt?" the man asked.

Nobody called him Victor. "Yes."

"We're from the FBI. We'd like to talk to you."

He could ask what this was about, but there was no point. They would tell him when they were ready. "Sure, no problem. Come on in." It had to involve Abby. He was sure of it.

He sat on his couch and gestured vaguely to the other seats available—a somewhat ratty armchair and an uncomfortable folding chair with a canvas seat. Perhaps wisely, the two agents chose to stand. Of course, this also gave them a psychological advantage over him, but he tried not to worry about that.

"You're acquainted with a woman named Abby Sinclair," the woman said. She was about forty, with reddish blond hair. Somehow he had the impression he'd seen her before.

"That's not a question."

"No, Mr. Wyatt. It's a statement of fact."

"Do I know you?"

"I don't believe so."

"Come to think of it," he said, "I never did get a look at your credentials."

This was an obvious play for time, but he knew they had to show him their ID upon request. They did. He studied the two leather-backed ID folders. The man was named Ronald Hauser, and the woman . . .

"Tess McCallum. Now I know why you look familiar."

"Your reputation precedes you," Hauser told her sardonically.

"You did a hell of a job on Mobius," Wyatt said, not trying to kiss up to her, just stating a fact. "And the Rain Man . . . Medea . . ."

Something crossed McCallum's face when the last two cases were mentioned. "Abby's never spoken to you about me, I take it?"

"Why would she? Does she know you?"

"She's . . . she's a friend of mine."

Wyatt found this hard to believe, and said so.

Hauser cut in. "Why is it so implausible? You're in law enforcement, and you're a friend of hers. A very close friend—aren't you, Mr. Wyatt?"

"It's Lieutenant Wyatt," he corrected. "LAPD." As an intimidation tactic, this was weak. The feds never allowed themselves to be impressed by local law officers.

"Yes. We're very much aware of your rank." Hauser's tone was cool. "Do you think it's appropriate for a lieutenant of the LAPD to be consorting with Abby Sinclair?"

"I don't know." He glanced at McCallum. "Is it appropriate for an agent of the FBI to *consort* with her?"

Hauser wouldn't be put off. "You've had a long-term, secret relationship with Miss Sinclair. You've visited her at the Wilshire Royal on numerous occasions. And you've used an assumed name."

He thought about denying it, but knew it was hopeless. "That's not a crime."

"Conspiring with a vigilante *is* a crime, Lieutenant

Wyatt." Hauser was bearing down, playing the bad cop. "Giving inside information to a civilian who routinely goes outside the law is a crime."

Wyatt shrugged, feigning indifference, though his heart was starting to race. "You're fishing. You don't know anything."

McCallum took over. Her voice was gentle. "Abby's in trouble, Victor."

So she was the good cop. Using his first name, making nice, showing sympathy. Oldest ploy in interrogation techniques, but damn if it didn't work.

"Call me Vic," he said reluctantly. "That's what everyone calls me."

"Okay, Vic."

"What kind of trouble?"

"She's implicated in the murder of a federal agent."

He shook his head, rejecting the idea out of hand. "That's not possible."

"She claims she was acting in self-defense."

"When is this supposed to have happened?" But he already knew.

"Last night."

Hauser broke in again. "Have you had any contact with Miss Sinclair in the past twenty-four hours?"

Lying to FBI agents was a federal crime. "Yes."

"When?"

"She showed up here last night. She was here when I returned from work. I was supervising the night watch."

"What time was this?"

"About three thirty A.M."

"What did she say to you?"

"Nothing much. She was a little . . . stressed out. Wanted to bunk with me. That's all."

"When did she leave?"

"Sometime before I woke up."

Hauser scowled, observing Wyatt's unruly hair. "Looks like you just woke up *now*."

"I was up earlier, about seven A.M. Abby was gone

by then. I'd only gotten three hours' sleep, so I took a nap about an hour ago."

"Abby showed up last night at three thirty in the morning," McCallum said, "and you didn't ask her what it was all about?"

"I asked. She didn't want to talk about it. She's not real big on sharing."

McCallum nodded. "Keeps her distance."

"Always has." He felt a moment of connection, of shared understanding with this woman, and fought it off. It was what she wanted him to feel.

"Look, Vic," she said in a disarmingly low voice. "Abby killed one of our people. There may be extenuating circumstances. But we're not going to know until we get her cooperation."

"What are you asking for?"

"We need to determine her whereabouts."

"So you can arrest her."

"So we can begin to sort things out. Now—as soon as possible—before the situation gets any more out of control."

"You mentioned the Wilshire Royal. Post some men there. She'll show up eventually."

"No, she won't. She's gone to ground."

"How can you know that?"

"Because I've spoken with her on the phone. She admitted pulling the trigger. She knows we're after her. She won't be going home."

Wyatt stood, unable to remain seated any longer. "Wait a minute. You're saying she confessed to the crime?"

"She did."

"And she *knows* it was a fed?"

"Yes."

"And still she won't give herself up?"

"That's right."

Wyatt turned away. He had to think about this. Think hard.

That Abby could kill a law officer was bad enough. That she could know what she'd done and still refuse to face the consequences . . . it was incomprehensible.

Did he even know her? Had he *ever* known her?

"I couldn't help you," he heard himself say, "even if I wanted to. I haven't talked to her since last night. I don't have a clue where she is now."

"We were thinking you'd have a way to reach her," McCallum said.

He turned to face them. "Cell phone. Landline in her condo."

"Those options won't help."

"They're all I've got."

McCallum stepped closer. "Possibly at some point she'll contact you."

"Why would she?"

"You're her friend. She needs a friend right now. Or maybe you know how to contact her."

"I already told you. I don't."

Hauser folded his arms. "Your cooperation would be advisable, Lieutenant Wyatt. That is, if you want to retain that rank."

McCallum added, "We're not trying to threaten you, Vic."

Like hell they weren't.

Wyatt noted how smoothly they switched from intimidation to empathy and back again. It was an act—yet they weren't bullshitting him. He knew that. They'd lost a colleague. They were feeling the loss.

"We're just telling you how it's going to be, Lieutenant," Hauser said. "Without your cooperation, we'll have to report to your superiors. Internal Affairs will get involved."

"We call them Professional Standards now," Wyatt commented for no reason.

"They'll be on the case," Hauser went on. "They'll want to know if you passed investigative details to Abby

Sinclair. If you compromised the department, abused your authority, by cooperating with a private vigilante."

"Abby's not a vigilante. And I never told her anything confidential."

"No, I suppose all you and Sinclair talked about was the weather."

Apparently she wasn't Miss Sinclair anymore. The bad cop was getting badder.

"Vic," McCallum said in a softer tone, "let's face it. It looks pretty serious for you. At the very least you'll face disciplinary action. You could be terminated altogether. How many years have you put in at the department?"

"Fourteen," he said quietly.

"And there could be legal action," Hauser said. "Criminal charges. If Sinclair is found guilty of murder, you could be charged as an accessory."

"That's bullshit." Bad cop was overplaying his hand.

"It's unlikely things would go that far," McCallum soothed. "The point is, you stand to lose a lot if you don't give us your full cooperation."

"I told you, I have no idea where she would go." Wyatt met her gaze. "If you really do know Abby, then you know she's not the type to confide in anybody. She plays it close to the vest."

"That she does." McCallum hesitated. "Did she tell you who her latest client is?"

They had to know already, so he answered. "Peter Faust."

"How did you feel about her working for Faust?"

"It's her business, not mine."

"So you had no opinion."

"Okay, it pissed me off, all right?"

"Took you by surprise?"

"Yeah."

McCallum nodded. "Me, too. But maybe we shouldn't have been surprised. Abby's changed, don't you think?"

"Haven't noticed."

"I think you have. I've noticed, and I don't know her nearly as well as you do. She's gotten more reckless. More dangerous."

"Abby isn't a danger to anybody—" He stopped himself.

"Tell that to Special Agent Mark Brody."

"That's the man she killed," Hauser said.

"Right before she came here to console herself in your arms." McCallum paused to let that sink in. "Vic, I want you to think about Agent Brody. He was a veteran, a Green Beret. After leaving the service, he joined the Bureau. On the Faust case he was under deep cover. He was taking big risks, dealing with a known murderer in a sting operation."

Wyatt was trying not to let her get to him. "Now you're going to tell me about his wife and kids."

"Yes, I am. His wife, Patricia, is seven months pregnant with their second child. She already has a little boy. Now those kids will grow up without a father."

He looked away. His throat was dry. "Because of Abby."

"How would you feel if it was a cop she'd gunned down?" Hauser asked. "One of your guys?"

"It might just as well have been," McCallum said. "You and Brody were on the same team. Whose team is Abby on?"

Wyatt shut his eyes. "Abby's not exactly a team player."

"No, she isn't."

He was silent. He didn't know if he could stand by Abby if she'd killed someone who worked his side of the street. Killing a federal agent . . . it really *was* no different from killing a cop.

But he couldn't give her up. Couldn't betray her. Not after all their years together.

He gathered himself. "You two are good," he said as nonchalantly as possible. "Been working together long?"

"We don't work together," McCallum said. "I'm from out of town."

"Right. Denver, isn't it?"

"Yes."

"You came to L.A. because of Abby?"

She nodded. "And because we lost one of our own. You know how that is. How many funerals have you attended? How many times have you had to put black tape over your badge?"

Too many times, was the answer. He tried not to think about that. "Working undercover," he said, "you assume certain risks. . . ." It sounded weak even to him.

McCallum's gaze drilled into him. "You accept the risk of being taken down by the bad guy. But Abby's not the bad guy."

"Or is she?" Hauser asked.

That was the big question. Abby played by her own rules—but maybe she'd lost the ability to set any rules.

"Look," he said slowly, "what the hell do you want me to say? I don't agree with all the choices she's made. I didn't like her working for a scumbag like Faust. I told her so."

"What did she say?" McCallum asked.

"Nothing. I don't know. We argued."

"I'll bet there have been a lot of arguments lately."

She was right, of course. "There are always arguments in any, you know, relationship."

"Is that what you have? A relationship?"

What we had, he thought. Past tense. But he wouldn't tell them that. "Yeah," he answered.

"Relationships are built on trust. Do you trust Abby?"

"Sure. Of course." He said it automatically, but the truth was, he didn't trust her, not completely, not anymore.

McCallum lowered her voice. "Do you know where she was on the night before last?"

"Not with me."

"No, not with you. She was with Brody. He was renting a guest cottage in Los Feliz. She had dinner with him and went back to his place." There was a pause. "She stayed the night."

Wyatt heard the words but couldn't process them at first. "You're shitting me."

"The homeowner saw Abby leave at dawn."

An unpleasant grin spread across Hauser's face. "What do you think she and Brody were up to all night, Lieutenant?"

Wyatt tried to come up with an answer. "For all I know, she knocked him out and searched the place. That would be her style."

"If she searched the place," McCallum said, "why did she go back the next night? We know she did."

Wyatt said nothing.

"Brody was a real ladies' man," Hauser said. "Combat veteran, smooth talker. I knew a woman in one of our overseas posts who dated him for a while. She said he was hung like a goddamn stallion—"

This was too much. Wyatt flared up. "Go to hell."

Hauser ignored him. "It doesn't bother you that your girlfriend was getting some on the side? From a guy she thought was a stalker, a psycho?"

"You're trying to push my buttons. I know how it works."

"I think Sinclair was the one getting her button pushed, if you know what I mean. And I doubt it was the first time. Who knows how often she's had to go all the way to avoid blowing her cover?"

Wyatt didn't want to hear it. Of course, he'd always known that this kind of liaison was occasionally part of Abby's job. But he'd thought it was rare, very rare.

Maybe he'd been wrong.

He blew out a shaky breath and sat on the arm of the couch. "This is a waste of time. Like I told you, I don't know where she is or how to contact her."

"I think you do." Hauser was relentless. "I think you've known Sinclair long enough to have some way to reach her when her standard lines of communication are down."

"You're wrong."

"Then we'll have to bring this up with your superiors. It seems to me, Lieutenant"—Hauser put a sardonic emphasis on the word—"you're giving up a hell of a lot for this woman. You might ask yourself if she deserves it, after she spent the night with Agent Brody behind your back."

"And then killed him," McCallum added.

"We can show you a picture if you'd like to see it."

"I don't need to see a picture. I've been to plenty of crime scenes."

"Of course you have," Hauser said. "Normally you're out to catch the killer. In this case, I guess you've decided to protect her."

McCallum looked sad. "I'm sorry, Vic. Abby's my friend, too. But she needs to answer for what she's done. I thought you'd be able to see that."

She and Hauser moved toward the door. Then McCallum turned. "There's one picture I think you need to see."

"I told you, I've handled plenty of crime scenes."

"This isn't a crime scene photo." She returned to him and slipped a picture out of a manila folder. She handed it to him.

"Jennifer Gaitlin," he said. "I work out of Hollywood. I know about her disappearance. What . . . what does she have to do with anything?" He almost didn't want to know the answer.

"Any leads in the case?" McCallum asked.

"Not that I know of. The missing persons squad is covering it."

"We have a lead. We think Faust took Jennifer. We think he's kept on killing, all these years. Brody had put himself in the position to possibly get Faust to incriminate himself in an earlier crime. The Roberta Kessler case, if you remember it."

"I remember," he said, his voice thick.

"If the sting had worked, Faust would be in custody right now, and if he does have Jennifer—and if she's still alive—we'd have a good shot at getting her back." Her eyes watched him. They were kind eyes, he thought. Knowing eyes. "We've lost that chance now. Which means Jennifer may have lost her chance, too."

He stared at the photo for a long minute, then handed it back without a word.

"All right, then," McCallum said softly. "I just thought you should know."

She returned to the door. No bluff. She and Hauser were leaving.

Wyatt looked down at the carpet. He thought about Mark Brody, the badge he'd carried, the family he'd left behind. He thought about Peter Faust, a sociopath, a killer—and still Abby had chosen to work for him. Maybe dooming this girl in the process.

For the past few years she had been more and more out of control. Now she was deceiving him. She'd been unfaithful to him—not just unfaithful in bed, but unfaithful on every level, in every way. She was a user, a manipulator . . . and now a killer. A cop killer, or close enough . . .

The door was closing when Wyatt raised his head.

"Wait," he said.

35

Abby kept a storage locker in a rental facility in Tarzana, a town in the Valley named after the most famous creation of its most famous former resident, Edgar Rice Burroughs. She had never needed the locker, and she had hoped she would never need it. It was her nuclear option, her last resource when everything had gone to hell.

She needed it now.

If Tess had been more open-minded, if she'd been willing to consider another side of the story . . .

But she hadn't. There was no point in playing what-if games. Now she was left with only one course of action. She would give up her old life—her condo, her cars, her network of contacts, even her name. And she would leave L.A. for good.

She reached the storage facility and punched in a six-digit code to open the front gate. At her unit she entered her combination into the padlock, then rolled up the big metal door. Inside she had a mess of stuff that would come in handy for a person on the run.

Cash—ten grand in large and small bills.

A gun and ammo. A first-aid kit. A spare laptop.

A backup cell phone with an instant charger that could power the phone in twenty seconds and give her two hours of talk time or eight hours of standby.

The cell phone was in the name of Angela Marcus, with the monthly bill paid automatically out of a bank account under the same name. Abby had ID in the Marcus name—Social Security card, driver's license, credit cards, bank checks, passport. Over the years she had established a paper trail for Angela Marcus so it wouldn't look as if the identity had been created from scratch.

Besides those items, she had stowed away the means to disguise her appearance—wig, cosmetics, grooming tools, tinted contact lenses. And a whole suitcase full of spare clothes, along with a coat for a chillier climate than L.A.

She had a definite destination in mind, someplace she had scouted and approved in advance. Of course, it had to be a city, since she was a city gal. She would rent an apartment, start over, build a new life.

In San Francisco.

It was a great town, but she had never seriously expected to end up there. She thought of all she was leaving—her books and CDs and movie collection, her artwork and her comfy overstuffed armchair, Vince and Gerry at the front desk, her favorite little bistros and places she liked to walk.

But she would come back someday. Not to reclaim her life—that was gone for good—but to exact vengeance. She would find a way to get to Hauser and make him pay for setting her up.

Anger was helpful. It pushed away fear and sorrow. It gave her energy. She was grateful to Hauser for being available to hate.

She hooked up the cell phone to its charger, mentally reviewing the next steps in her plan.

Her first priority was to get out of town—but not going north. She would take the Miata on I-15 in the direction of Las Vegas. In Barstow she would trade it in for a used car. If the feds were able to track her that far, they would assume she was headed for Vegas. Instead she would double back to I-5 and shoot straight up to Frisco. Once there she would ditch the used car and buy a fresh set of wheels. She had to cover her tracks thoroughly. In a little while all fifty-six resident agencies of the FBI would be alerted and looking for her. But she knew what she was doing. She could lose them all.

Having reinvented herself, she would begin her career all over again. It wouldn't be easy without contacts or word-of-mouth referrals, but she could manage it. She could always land on her feet. Like a cat, she thought—then remembered Faust calling her a jungle cat.

The phone had already finished charging. She switched it on and was about to stick it into her purse when it rang.

The noise startled her. No one knew this number. No one except . . .

She checked caller ID. It was Wyatt.

Years ago she'd given him this number in case she ever had to disappear. He was the only one she'd told.

She almost didn't answer, but she had to.

"Hey, Vic." She tried to keep her voice steady.

"Abby."

"So . . . how much do you know?"

"Guy was found dead in Faust's neighborhood. The feds are all over it."

"That still doesn't explain why you called this number."

"I think it does. You weren't answering at home or on your regular cell. And the way you acted last night . . . I can put two and two together. You're going away, aren't you?"

"I have to."

"For how long?"

"Forever. That ought to be long enough."

"And that's it? You're just going to leave? No good-byes?"

"I didn't want to"—*say good-bye,* she almost said—"drag you into this."

"Like I'm not in it already."

"You know what I mean. Vic, I'm radioactive. You can't be anywhere near me. It's not safe."

"Nothing about us has ever been safe, Abby."

"I can't talk. I have to go. Maybe when I get where I'm going, I'll find a way to get in touch."

"You won't. It wouldn't be *safe*. Right?"

She closed her eyes. "Right."

"It's hard to believe this is the last time I'll ever hear your voice."

"Me, too."

"I wish we hadn't ended things the way we did."

"I shouldn't have argued with you. You were right. Getting mixed up with Faust was a bad idea."

"Is that all I was right about?"

"I should have confided in you more. I should have opened up." She felt tears starting. "We . . . we could have had more than we did. It's my fault. I was . . . afraid. Afraid to get close."

"I never knew you were afraid of anything."

She smiled, blinking away the wetness in her eyes. "Only of you, I guess."

"I want to see you."

"No, that's not possible."

"One more time. We can't say good-bye over the phone."

"It's too late—I'm already on my way out of town—"

"Then why don't you sound like you're in a car? Come on, Abby, don't lie to me."

"All right, I'm still in L.A. But I'm leaving now. I can't hang around. You said it yourself—the FBI is doing some heavy breathing on this one."

"You're smart enough to steer clear of them for another hour or two. Unless you're just making excuses."

"That's not what I'm doing."

"Have it your way." His voice had turned cold. "Who knows? Maybe you'll drop me a postcard sometime. Be sure to use a remailing service so there's no traceable postmark. And don't say anything about the weather where you are. It might tip me off."

"Vic—"

"I thought I meant more to you, that's all."

She knew it was a mistake. Any deviation from her carefully arranged escape plan entailed unacceptable risk. But . . .

"There's a closed-down Texaco station in San Fernando, near the corner of Glenoaks Boulevard and Haver Street. Meet me in back, away from the street, in an hour. That'll be"—she checked her watch—"eight o'clock."

"I'll be there."

She clicked off. As she put away the phone, it occurred to her that he could be working with the feds, trying to trap her. But she wouldn't believe it. She'd never shown him the trust he deserved.

She was going to trust him now.

Wyatt rested the telephone handset in the cradle. He turned to face the two FBI agents.

"It's arranged," he said.

Tess McCallum reached out and touched his arm. "You did the right thing."

He thought Judas must have heard the same words.

36

Hauser spent a few minutes on his cell phone, while watching Wyatt get cleaned up. The two of them met McCallum in the parking lot.

"You drive Wyatt's car," he told her, tossing her the keys. "He'll ride with you. I know the streets better than you, so you'll follow me."

"Why take two cars?"

"We need Wyatt's vehicle there so Sinclair will see it." Besides, he needed some time to himself.

"How about backup?" she asked.

"I called the field office. Four agents will meet us at the scene. They're wearing vests and bringing two more."

McCallum glanced at Wyatt, standing a few yards away, and lowered her voice. "He needs a vest, too."

Hauser shook his head. "No go. If Sinclair sees body armor underneath his shirt, she'll book before we can take her in."

"I guess that's right. You know, six agents isn't a lot for a high-risk takedown."

"It'll be enough."

"This is a severe arrest, Ron."

"She's only one woman."

"You don't know her."

"Just keep your eye on Wyatt. His heart's not in this."

"There's no chance he's carrying?"

"I frisked him. Unless he's got a twenty-two up his

rectum, he's clean. Now let's move. We don't have much time."

He put the magnetic emergency light on the roof of the LTD, then waited as McCallum transferred her laptop to the cop's Mustang and got in. Wyatt joined her, riding shotgun. With the red light flashing, Hauser led them out of the lot and picked up speed, heading for the freeway.

For the first time in hours, he was alone. He could think. He could wonder how it had all gotten so fucked up, when it should have been so simple.

Brody was the problem. He saw that now, in retrospect. Of course, he had always known about Brody's record. His less than perfect background. He had liked to think of himself as a model officer, but that wasn't how his colleagues saw him, at least not toward the end of his tour. He'd shown bad judgment on too many occasions. He'd become reckless.

During the engagement at Karbala Gap, when he and his team came under enemy attack, Brody risked leaving cover to return fire. It was a stupid move, suicidal. His captain tried to pull him back and took a bullet in the head for his trouble. The man died. Everyone else on the team saw it as Brody's fault, even if Brody would never admit it.

Afterward, they refused to go into the field with him. Brody was offered a promotion to a staff job that would keep him out of combat. But he didn't want a staff job. He received an honorable discharge, but stayed in Iraq, hanging out at bars, waiting for a chance to show the army they'd been wrong.

Hauser gave him that chance. The same qualities that made Brody a liability to the service—a willingness to take crazy risks, break the rules—made him useful to the Bureau, as long as they could keep him at arm's length.

And Brody was effective. He and his small team of like-minded vets hunted down the Fedayeen militiamen and their allies. They prevented the assassination of at least one interim government leader. No one inquired too closely into Brody's methods. It was a goddamned war zone, after all.

But then things went bad. Brody got played by one of his own informants. Acting on a tip, he picked up a group of men he thought were terrorists, imprisoned them in his home, and subjected them to what might be euphemistically called extreme abuse. The prisoners were hung from the ceiling by their wrists, scalded with boiling water, beaten with sticks. They confessed to nothing. The fact was, they had nothing to confess to. They were innocent. Brody had been given faulty information.

His informant promptly contacted the Iraqi government with word that Brody was holding the men in custody. One of the prisoners just happened to be the nephew of a prominent Iraqi official. The house was raided. The prisoners were freed. Brody and his team would be charged with running a renegade military operation. The Bureau couldn't let that happen, so by means of a liberal dispersal of cash to the appropriate pockets, Hauser got the men out of the country. He himself was rotated stateside a few months later. By then, Brody had already been taken on as a full-fledged agent of the FBI.

Given their prior relationship, it only made sense for Brody to work under Hauser in L.A. When the sting operation was approved, Hauser put Brody in the field.

Then Faust called Hauser to ask if he knew anyone who could handle a stalker. Of course, there was no way Faust could have known that the stalker in question was an FBI operative under Hauser's direct supervision.

Hauser saw his opportunity immediately. *As a matter of fact,* he answered, keeping his voice casual, *I do know someone. Her name is Abby Sinclair.*

The whole plan had come to him in an instant, in the beat of silence between Faust's inquiry and his response.

He would have Faust sic Sinclair on Brody. Sinclair would get close to Brody; she would have to; that was her job. And once Brody had her alone and defenseless, he would kill her. .

Oh, not right away, naturally. First he would use his interrogation skills to find out how much she'd learned about the operation and whom she'd told. Only once he was satisfied that she had revealed all her secrets would he finish her off.

The next day Hauser would approach Michaelson and reveal that he had encouraged Faust to hire Sinclair. His rationale would be plausible enough. He had rehearsed the conversation numerous times.

If I hadn't given Faust a recommendation, he would have gone on looking until he found someone on his own. At least if it's Sinclair, it's somebody we can control. We can tell her to back off if she gets in the way and threatens the operation. She'll have to listen to us. She doesn't want to mess with the Bureau again.

Michaelson would have bought it, just as he would have bought the rest of Hauser's story: that he had tried to contact Sinclair, but she wasn't answering her phone and hadn't been to her apartment. She had vanished.

Not long afterward, the mystery of her disappearance would be solved, when her remains were found in Griffith Park, only a short distance from Peter Faust's home. It was the same locale where Roberta Kessler had been found. And Sinclair's body would be in the same condition: no head, no hands.

Brody would have taken care of all that, and left the body where it was sure to be discovered by some jogger or dog walker.

Given Faust's connection with Sinclair and the condition and location of the body, Faust would be the obvious suspect. Then, even if Brody's blackmail scam hadn't worked, Faust could still have been taken down for Sinclair's murder. Hauser had no qualms about framing the son of a bitch. Faust was guilty of multiple homicides—

Hauser was certain of it—and he deserved whatever he got.

It had been a good plan, an unbeatable plan. With one stroke he would eliminate Sinclair and incriminate Faust.

The only possible obstacle was Brody. He had to agree to play along. It was one thing to kill ragheads in Iraq, and another to blip an American citizen on U.S. soil. He might balk at Hauser's orders. But Hauser took care of that, too. He let Brody understand that if he chose not to comply, then certain documents— documents proving conclusively that Brody was guilty of a variety of unsavory crimes against Iraqi nationals— might find their way to the *L.A. Times.*

The ensuing uproar would expose Brody's misconduct to public view for the first time. The Iraqi government, unable to overlook this affront to its dignity, would insist that Brody and his associates be extradited for trial in Iraq. The outcome of that trial was a certainty. To make those documents public was to sign Brody's death sentence.

Hauser himself could not be touched. There was no proof that he had known Brody was engaged in illicit activities.

Brody understood the situation. He did not try to fight it. Perhaps he even appreciated the irony. His job in the sting operation was to blackmail Faust. Now he was the one being blackmailed. He accepted his orders without complaint. *I'm a realist,* he said with a cold shrug.

The assignment should not have been too difficult for him. He had killed warriors in Iraq. All he was required to do in this case was kill a woman who had gotten in the way.

Incredibly, he had failed. He had proven to be the weak link in the chain, the one variable Hauser could not control.

And now everything was going to shit. Hauser was caught in a bind. He couldn't admit to Michaelson that he'd put Sinclair on Faust's payroll. If he did, he would be confessing to a fuckup of monumental proportions, a fuckup that had gotten Brody killed. The blowback would kill him.

He had to resolve the situation on his own. Had to get Sinclair into custody so the investigation would focus exclusively on her, and no one would think to ask any dangerous questions.

But there remained one worry. Faust. Hauser had to be sure he continued to keep their secret. Had to know, for certain, that Faust would cover for him. He thought he was on relatively safe ground. Faust never gave away anything to the authorities, never cracked, never opened up. And since he was no longer a suspect in Brody's murder, he would be under no pressure.

The only risk was if Faust learned that Brody had been an FBI agent. Then he would know that Hauser had been using him, setting him up. If that happened, all bets were off. But it was unlikely he would ever find out. The Bureau wasn't going to advertise a failed sting op to anyone, and certainly not to the operation's intended target.

Anyway, Faust didn't have to stay silent forever. He had to stay silent only for now. The future . . . well, the future would take care of itself.

As he hit the 405 Freeway, he took out his cell phone and punched in Faust's home number from memory. The phone rang twice before a cool voice answered. "Faust."

"It's Ron Hauser."

"Ronald, my friend. How is life treating you?"

"I've been better. Look, something's come up, and I just need a little reassurance from you."

"How unusual. People seldom turn to me for reassurance or comfort of any kind."

"Yeah, well, this is a rare occasion. It's possible you'll be receiving a visit from my colleagues before long."

"And why is that?"

"Abby Sinclair killed a man last night. I'm betting he's your stalker."

"I see."

"We're closing in on her now. Should have her in custody within an hour. When she talks, she'll say you hired her. That'll bring you into the picture."

"So it will."

"The thing is, I need your assurance that you won't tell anyone how you got Sinclair's name and number."

"You do not wish to be involved." Faust chuckled.

"As I told you at the time, it'll be bad for me if I'm known to have recommended Sinclair. FBI employees aren't exactly encouraged to direct people to vigilantes for assistance."

"I recall the conversation. You were most emphatic."

"And now, of course, there's this other thing. . . ."

"The death of my stalker, you mean? And the fact that you are indirectly responsible?"

"I wouldn't put it that way."

"Perhaps not. The fact remains that you steered me to Sinclair, and Sinclair in turn has committed homicide. This cannot look good on your record."

"Right. Which is why I want your, uh, assurance"—he wished he could come up with another word for it—"that you won't bring me into this."

"And who shall I say mentioned Miss Sinclair to me? Your associates will insist on knowing."

"I can give you a name to use. Someone who can't be checked out. It'll be a dead end. Just give me a few hours to do a little research."

Faust's voice was very soft. "I am afraid those hours would be wasted, Ronald."

Hauser felt a chill move through him. "What does that mean?"

"There is an old adage to the effect that a secret can be kept only when it is held by two persons. Such was our arrangement. But now the mathematics have changed."

"Changed?"

"A third party has learned the secret. Which means, I suppose, that it is no longer a secret at all."

"What third party?"

"Our Miss Sinclair, of course. She has proven herself distressingly unpredictable, has she not? She is, I believe, emotionally unstable. Most unprofessional in all respects."

"You told Sinclair," Hauser said, his voice flat.

"She abducted Elise and threatened her with bodily harm. Elise was badly shaken. I did what was necessary to ensure her safe return."

"It was a bluff. She wouldn't have hurt your girlfriend."

"She killed my stalker, you said."

In self-defense, Hauser almost blurted out, but caught himself. "Yes. Right. But she wouldn't hurt an innocent party."

"I did not wish to take that chance."

"So you gave her my name."

"Yes. Ronald Hauser of the FBI. I believe she remembers you."

"I'll bet she does," he muttered.

"I have no idea why she was so insistent on obtaining that particular piece of information."

"I don't know, either," Hauser lied.

Obviously Sinclair had put it together. Which meant it was over. As soon as she was in custody, she would talk. Hell, she would have spilled everything to McCallum on the phone if she'd had the chance.

For a moment he considered the quickest, easiest way out. He was in a car, on a freeway. All he had to do was grind the gas pedal into the floor and accelerate to top speed, then steer straight into the abutment of the next overpass. Death would be immediate. He would feel nothing. He would know nothing. It would all be over.

But there might be another way.

"You would not be withholding something from me, I hope," Faust said quietly, noting Hauser's long silence.

"I'm not withholding anything. I don't know what she's after or what she wants."

"Mmm." A noncommittal sound. "So you see, it will do no good for me to mislead your colleagues, because Miss Sinclair has no reason to protect your secret. She will surely tell the truth."

Hauser tightened his grip on the phone. "What if she doesn't?"

"I hardly see what would stop her."

"Suppose I find a way."

"In that event I will be glad to relate any plausible falsehood you concoct."

"You'd better. You owe me."

"Do I?"

"We had an agreement. You made me a promise."

The voice on the other end of the line sounded darkly amused. "Perhaps this will teach you not to take the devil at his word."

Silence. The call was over.

Hauser pocketed the phone. The game plan had changed. He had thought Sinclair could be taken alive. Now he knew that her capture would be fatal to his future.

All right, then. He would handle it. McCallum herself had said this was a high-risk arrest. The kind of situation where things could go wrong.

Where somebody could get killed.

37

At seven thirty-five, as the sun was setting, Hauser met the four new agents at the intersection of Glenoaks Boulevard and Harding Avenue, a few blocks northwest of the Texaco station. They couldn't risk a closer staging area in case Sinclair was already in the neighborhood, scoping out the rendezvous site.

All four of the agents were from his squad. They had shed their telltale business suits and shrugged on windbreakers that concealed their duty weapons and body armor. Unfortunately, the vehicles they drove were Bucars—a Bureau-issue LTD and a Ford Crown Vic—and he wasn't too happy about that. A pro like Sinclair could spot an official car a mile away.

"I told you I wanted you undercover," he said.

Garcia, the most senior agent, answered. "The field office didn't have any UC cars for us. We would've had to go through SOG, and we didn't have time." SOG, Special Operations Group, was responsible for most undercover surveillance ops. The group was headquartered in a secret location away from the field office.

There was no time to worry about it now. "Okay, here's the situation," Hauser said crisply. "We're arresting a female civilian, Abigail Sinclair, who is the prime suspect in Agent Brody's murder. She will be alone but armed. Typically she carries a Smith thirty-eight in her handbag. She is a private security operative trained in self-defense, evasion, and escape."

He passed around a file photo of Sinclair. The men studied it with grim faces.

"Don't underestimate her just because she's slightly built. She's a killer. She already has the blood of one field agent on her hands. The rendezvous site is a closed-down Texaco station on the east side of Glenoaks, one door south of Haver Street. Sinclair will go to the rear of the station intending to meet a friend. That's where we'll take her down. I've already done a drive-by recon of the site. There are only two exits—the street out front and an alley in the rear.

"Your job is perimeter control. Baker and Sorenson will cover the entrance to the alley. Garcia and Kent will cover the street. You need to be as inconspicuous as possible. Sinclair may use either route to approach the gas station, and we can't risk spooking her."

"Who handles the actual arrest?" Sorenson asked.

"I will, assisted by Agent McCallum."

Kent frowned. "Do you think that's wise, considering—"

Hauser cut him off. "I'm taking her in. If she bolts, you are to pursue. Otherwise you remain off-site until the arrest has gone down. Is that clear?"

Heads nodded, though the men were clearly skeptical. Standard procedure, as taught in Hogan's Alley on the Academy training grounds, would be to swarm the suspect on Hauser's signal, a tactic that could effectively nullify any resistance. But Hauser was boss, and they knew enough not to question him when his mind was made up.

"Where is Agent McCallum?" Kent asked.

"She and a civilian who's assisting us are positioning themselves at the scene. I'm headed there now."

Before leaving, Hauser accepted two Second Chance tactical vests with a Kevlar weave and a pair of LASH II radio headsets—plastic ear-molded receivers and throat microphones on elastic straps. The microphone picked up throat vibrations, allowing the user to communicate without raising his voice. The whole assembly could be plugged into almost any portable radio, including the Handie-Talkies used by Bureau personnel.

"I want all units on channel blue three. Minimize chatter."

Garcia asked if they were to deploy the rifles in the Bucars' trunks.

"That shouldn't be necessary," Hauser said. "We want Sinclair alive."

"But if she books?" Garcia pressed.

"Then you're green-lighted to take her out."

He left them with that thought.

Tess waited with Wyatt at the rear of the gas station. She was nervous, edgy, as she always was before a take-down. Wyatt seemed impossibly calm. Or maybe *calm* was not the right word for it. He seemed detached, emotionally shut down, as if he had lost all interest in his surroundings.

"It'll be all right, Vic," she said, knowing that the reassurance was meaningless and stupid.

He nodded, but he didn't seem to hear. His face was pale and slack.

"If Abby has a good explanation for what happened," she added, "she can still walk away from this."

"Yeah."

"We just need to get all the facts. We'll be as fair to her as possible. I guarantee that."

He was far away. "She'll never forgive me," he said softly.

"It's for her own good."

"That's not how she'll see it."

"Maybe she will. In time."

He lowered his head. His voice was a whisper.

"Never."

There was nothing she could say to that.

Hauser drove past the gas station for a final recon, then parked in a supermarket lot down the street and walked to the rendezvous site. A strange phrase played in his mind: a downward spiral. It applied to lots of things, didn't it? To water running down a drain, to an airplane trapped in a nosedive. And to his life. His life since Medea. That was when the downward spiral had begun for him. That was when it all started going to hell.

Now, like the pilot of that spiraling plane, he was plummeting down, down, and there was nothing he could do but let events play out.

Behind the Texaco station he found McCallum and Wyatt standing together near Wyatt's Mustang. The sun was gone now, but the sky had not yet faded to the dusky orange of an urban night. In the dimming light he surveyed the layout. Sinclair had chosen a good place for a rendezvous. The area behind the station would be unseen from the street. A high cinderblock wall protected the north side of the lot. To the east there was a hurricane fence, densely overgrown with weeds and climbing plants, with an open gate that led to the alley. The alley afforded a second means of approach, as well as an escape route. A windowless, warehouselike building loomed on the south, affording further privacy.

Wordlessly he handed McCallum her vest and radio set, while donning his own.

A small plane buzzed past, coming in for a landing at a private airfield just three blocks south. He thought of the nosedive again, the plummet and crash.

"She could be here any minute," McCallum said, attaching the LASH II's skeleton ear mold and fitting the strap around her neck like a bow tie. A transparent tube ran from the neck-mounted speaker to her ear. "Where are the others?"

"Guarding the perimeter." Hauser embedded the radio's press-to-talk switch in the webbing of his Kevlar vest.

"We need more than the two of us to take her in, Ron."

"No, we don't. We have the element of surprise. We can get the jump on her. Now I want you"—he pointed at Wyatt—"to wait here in plain sight. And if you attempt to signal Sinclair or give her any warning . . ."

"I won't," Wyatt said in a voice that was low and defeated.

"I'll position myself between the gas station and the warehouse. There's a narrow space between the buildings at the gas station's three-four corner." In Bureauspeak, a building's front side was side one, with the other sides numbered clockwise. "McCallum, you are to take cover behind the Dumpster in the alley. Hold that position until my signal."

She looked down the alley at the large trash bin some distance away. "That's too far. I need to be closer."

"No, you don't."

"From behind the bin I won't have a clear line of sight."

"You won't need one. Just wait for my signal."

"I don't like it, Ron. You're trying to pull off the takedown singlehandedly. It isn't like you to be a cowboy."

"You're not in charge here. This is my turf and my case, and we'll do things my way."

She gave him a long, hard stare. "It's your call," she said finally. "But I want it on the record that I object to the deployment."

"Duly noted. Now move. Sinclair could get here at any time."

He watched McCallum retreat into the alley and duck down behind the bin. With a parting nod at Wyatt, Hauser slipped into the narrow space between the gas station and the warehouse. He pressed the transmit button.

"One-oh-one, on-site and in place." Agent names were never given over the radio. "Report, two-oh-one and three-oh-one."

In quick succession, the leaders of units two and

three—Baker and Garcia—confirmed that they were in position and standing by.

It had all worked out. Of course, he was violating procedure, and he would catch hell for it later. But he could weather that storm. What he needed was an opportunity to act without witnesses.

The other two teams were out of sight. McCallum was too far away to have a decent view, especially in the gathering darkness. Wyatt would see what went down, unless his back was turned, but if the claims of a bereaved boyfriend contradicted Hauser's account, the boyfriend would be ignored, even if he was a cop. The Bureau always favored one of its own over an outsider.

There were no witnesses who mattered. When Sinclair showed up, Hauser would simply emerge from hiding and draw a bead on her. He would shout, "Federal agents, you're under arrest!" And he would fire.

His story, later, would be that she had been drawing down on him. If possible, in the confusion that followed the shooting he would remove the gun from her purse and leave it near her hand. Even if he couldn't manage that detail, he could always claim that he'd seen her reach into her purse. He knew she carried a .38 in there; he'd found it when he examined the purse during her prior arrest.

He might receive a reprimand for poor judgment, but no one would cry too loudly over a civilian vigilante who'd murdered a special agent in the line of duty.

McCallum might suspect the truth, especially since Sinclair had opened up to her on the phone. But she could prove nothing, and Faust would say he'd obtained Sinclair's number from some other contact. There would be nothing to tie Hauser to the events that had led to Brody's death, and thus no way to establish a motive for him to kill Sinclair.

The thing was, he had to be sure he *did* kill her.

Wounding her would do no good if she recovered sufficiently to tell what she knew. He had to nail her cold.

A head shot would be best, but too tricky, under the circumstances. In the movies, cops and FBI agents were always snapping off bull's-eyes in the heat of action, but in real life, with adrenaline roaring and hands shaking, it just wasn't that easy. And he would have only one shot, or two at the most. He could hardly justify emptying his magazine into her body. No review board, however sympathetic, would buy it.

Sinclair wasn't expecting an ambush, and as far as he knew, she didn't own any body armor. So he would go for her midsection, her main body mass. Put a round in her heart, or near enough to do mortal damage. If there was any doubt, he might risk a second shot with better placement.

Wyatt was unarmed, so he would be unable to shoot back. He would probably be screaming in protest, but that was okay; the more emotional he was, the easier it would be to discount his testimony.

This was going to work. He could feel it. Despite all the setbacks, he would make it work.

He had been unable to hurt McCallum. Despite her abuse of regulations, her outright violation of law, she had come through the Medea case unscathed. She had wrecked his life, ruined his chance to finish out his career on the seventh floor—the power center of the Hoover Building, where the key players were found. She had screwed him over and gotten away with it. But Sinclair was equally responsible. And she was vulnerable. When Faust called asking for help, Hauser had seen a way to use Brody to destroy Sinclair.

Even now he had no regrets, no remorse. Killing Sinclair was a public service. She was a lawbreaker, a vigilante, which made her no better than a virus. She was a pathogen to be eliminated from the system.

And she had destroyed him. Without meaning to, but

what did that matter? She had taken everything from
him—his reputation, his career, his future. Now he was
going to take just one thing in return.

Her life.

He heard a car approaching from the front of the station. He risked a look and saw a Miata pull into view.
Sinclair's vehicle. The dark-haired woman at the wheel
was his target. She was right on time.

He unholstered his Beretta.

Wyatt stepped away from the Mustang and walked
toward the convertible just as Sinclair got out. She was
carrying her purse—perfect. He had been afraid she
might leave it in the car, weakening his justification for
the shooting.

Wyatt stopped a few feet from her.

Their placement was nearly perfect—the cop with his
back to Hauser, Sinclair facing this way. The only draw-
back was that they were farther from him than he would
have liked. He wondered if they might move a little
closer, away from Sinclair's car.

Their voices weren't loud, but in the silence they carried easily.

"Hi, Vic."

"Abby."

"Sorry I almost ran out on you. You deserve better
than that."

He averted his face, obviously uncomfortable. "I'm
not so sure I do."

"Of course you do. That's what I was trying to say on
the phone. I've never really treated you right. I've taken
you for granted, and I'm sorry about that."

Wyatt turned and moved a few steps away from her.
Sinclair followed. They were coming closer, narrowing
the range.

"You don't have to say that," Wyatt said.

"Yes, I do. I need to say it."

He pivoted to face her. "That's not what I meant. I

don't *want* you to say it. I don't want to hear it. It's too late."

She approached him. He retreated another step.

They were coming nearer all the time. Another yard or two, and he would strike.

38

Tess didn't like it. The way Hauser was playing this thing made no sense.

Either Hauser was mishandling the arrest out of sheer overconfidence, or . . .

Or what?

She didn't know. But on the phone Abby had called Brody a rogue agent. Was it possible?

And if there was one rogue agent—could there be two?

She shook her head. Hauser was a veteran of the Bureau. He wouldn't be involved in anything dirty.

Even so, she found herself slipping out from behind the trash bin and advancing slowly up the alley toward the gas station's rear lot.

She would stay low, in the shadows, and use what concealment was offered by the overgrown oleander bushes along the fence.

Abby's voice carried to her from a distance. "I just think we both need closure."

"I already have closure," Wyatt said. "I ended it, remember? I ended *us*."

Apparently he had already broken things off with Abby. Tess hadn't anticipated that. Somehow it made the whole situation more painful, more tragic and confused.

"Nothing's ever final between us, Vic."

"This time it is. Come on, you know it."

"I guess I do. I just don't want to admit it. Even if you hadn't made your decision, I'd still be leaving town. And I won't be coming back."

"Why did you do it? Why'd you kill that man?"

"I had no choice. It was him or me."

"Then why do you have to run?"

"Because no one will believe me. There was one person who I thought might listen to my side of the story. But it didn't work out."

Tess winced. She suddenly understood how much Abby had lost—her home, her career, her lover. And the one person she'd turned to, her last resort, had refused to hear her out.

She crept nearer. Hauser still hadn't executed the takedown. What was he waiting for?

Sinclair was close enough now, but Wyatt was standing in front of her, blocking Hauser's shot. If the cop would just move out of the way . . .

"Just because one person wouldn't listen," Wyatt was saying, "doesn't mean nobody will."

"You don't understand, Vic."

"So explain it to me."

"There's no time. And it doesn't matter. Remember last night? What I needed from you then?"

"You needed me to hold you."

"I still do."

They embraced.

Hauser gritted his teeth. No good going for a kill shot now. The two of them had to be apart in order to afford him a clear shot at Sinclair.

After a long moment they separated, but Wyatt, damn him, was still in the way.

"Abby," Wyatt said, "I hope you can forgive me."

Forgive him for what? Hauser had the bad feeling that the cop was going to say too much.

"There's nothing I have to forgive you for."

"Yes, there is. You shouldn't be here."

Hell. He was about to blow the whole thing. Hauser had to fire, but he still didn't have a decent shot.

And then Wyatt turned aside from Sinclair, and there she was, totally exposed.

Hauser propelled himself out of hiding, the Beretta leading him, his voice booming in the stillness.

"FBI, you're under arrest!"

His index finger drawing down on the trigger even as he spoke, the gun sighted on Sinclair's chest, Sinclair reacting but too late, Wyatt spinning toward him, his eyes on the gun—

Hauser fired. The pistol bucked in his hand, a spasm of recoil vibrating through his forearm, the crack of the gunshot deafening him, and in the same instant he saw a bright bloom of blood.

Direct hit. A body falling.

But not Sinclair.

Wyatt.

Tess had seen it all.

She had drawn close enough to the fence at the rear of the lot to see all three of them—Hauser, Abby, and Wyatt.

Now she knew why Hauser had delayed action. He'd wanted a clear shot at Abby—and he'd taken it. A single shot, discharged a split second after he'd shouted his announcement. Discharged before Abby could possibly have reacted, before she could surrender, flee, or fight.

Hauser hadn't wanted her to surrender. Hadn't wanted her to have time even to process what was happening. He'd wanted her dead.

Tess charged into the lot, where Wyatt lay on his side, Abby kneeling by him, Hauser with gun in hand. For just a moment Hauser straightened his right arm as if preparing to shoot again. Then he saw Tess, armed, her SIG Sauer aimed in his direction.

"Drop the gun, Ron," she said.

Something like panic flickered across his face. He hadn't expected her to be so close.

"You left your position," he said. "That's a direct violation of my orders."

"I don't give a shit about your orders. Drop the gun."

"You can't be serious."

She steadied her pistol. "Try me."

Slowly his hand opened, and the Beretta fell to the asphalt.

Abby had turned Wyatt on his back and was straddling him, performing CPR. She seemed oblivious to Hauser and Tess, to any possible danger. She had torn open Wyatt's shirt and now had her hand over the wound, applying steady pressure. Her hair had swung over her face, and Tess couldn't read her expression.

She pressed her radio's talk button, telling both teams to report to the rendezvous site, but only after they had called a rescue ambulance. "We have a man down, GSW to the chest."

Abby was still sealing Wyatt's wound with her hand. Her face remained invisible.

The sky to the west was darker now, the sunset fading to the color of old blood.

Tess stared at Hauser. "I saw it, Ron. I saw it all."

"I don't know what the hell you're—"

"Save it. You gave her no chance to submit to arrest. It was a hit, plain and simple. No more complicated than a gangland drive-by."

"That's bullshit."

"You aimed right at her chest. You were going for the kill. Would've worked—if Wyatt hadn't stepped into the line of fire and caught the round himself."

"She was reaching for her weapon," Hauser said. "In her purse."

"She didn't reach for anything, Ron. You didn't give her time to reach."

A Bureau car pulled up in the alley, braking at the

rear entrance to the lot. Two agents Tess didn't know got out.

"What the hell happened here?" one of them asked. His partner, with a first-aid kit in hand, knelt by Abby. Without speaking, she placed his hand on the wound to maintain pressure, then opened the kit and took out a large square bandage.

Tess didn't try to explain. "We have a situation. I'm going to have to ask you to take Agent Hauser into custody."

Abby applied the bandage to Wyatt's chest, leaving the bottom of the square unsealed to create a flutter valve.

"She's crazy," Hauser said. "Loyalty to Sinclair has warped her judgment."

"I'm not the one whose judgment is warped." But Tess knew there was no reason for Hauser's guys to take her word over his.

She was debating how to handle it when a second Bucar pulled into the rear lot. Another two men she didn't know. Hauser's men.

And in the middle of the scene, in the enveloping dark, Abby leaned over Wyatt, checking his respiration, taking his pulse, never looking up.

"Agent McCallum"—that was the man whose partner had supplied first aid—"maybe it would be better if you holstered your weapon."

She made no move to comply. Her gun was still trained on Hauser.

"Let me tell you what just went down," she said, keeping her voice unnaturally calm, aware that any sign of emotion would only weaken her case.

The agent kneeling by Abby interrupted. "Someone get us a blanket." Like Abby, he was oblivious to the confrontation in progress.

One of the new arrivals retrieved a blanket from the car and draped it over Wyatt, leaving his face uncovered. When he stepped back, Tess tried again.

"Agent Hauser wasn't interested in taking Abby Sinclair alive. He was trying to kill her. Instead he shot Lieutenant Wyatt, an off-duty officer of the LAPD who was assisting in the arrest."

"It was an accident," Hauser said. Tess was pleased to note the thin leading edge of hysteria in his voice. "Sinclair was reaching for her weapon. I had to fire in self-defense. Wyatt just got in the way."

"Lieutenant Wyatt"—Tess stressed his rank— "deliberately intercepted the bullet meant for Abby Sinclair. Look at her. Is there a gun in her hand? Is there a gun anywhere in evidence?"

"It's in her purse," Hauser said. "She carries a Smith thirty-eight."

"But she hadn't drawn it. I'll bet you'll find the purse hasn't even been opened."

The purse lay discarded on the ground. The man who'd produced the blanket picked it up.

"Still clasped," he said quietly.

"I had no way of knowing that." Hauser was trying to sound reasonable, but he couldn't quite pull it off. "I acted in my own defense."

"No, he didn't. Think about it. Why did he draw up the arrest scenario the way he did? Why did he position you guys so far from the scene? Did he tell you that he and I were going to take down Sinclair together?"

The man holding Abby's purse nodded.

"That's not how he arranged it with me. He positioned me down the alley, where I wouldn't have a clear view of the action. He claimed he was going to conduct the arrest by himself. Why would he do that?"

"It's a fair question," the other new arrival said slowly. His eyes were moving from Hauser to Wyatt and back again.

Abby must have heard something worrisome in Wyatt's breathing. She began to provide assisted ventilation, like a lifeguard trying to revive a drowning victim. In, out. In, out.

"You're letting her manipulate you, for Christ's sake." Hauser was shaking. "She doesn't even work out of L.A. She has no business here."

"Agent McCallum has been to L.A. before," the fourth man said. "She's got a pretty good rep in this town."

"Rep?" Hauser made a sound like laughter. "I'll tell you about her rep. On her last two cases she was in league with Sinclair. They worked together. An SAC and a goddamn vigilante. A vigilante who killed Mark Brody in cold blood."

The two agents who had helped Abby began to move away from Wyatt, approaching Hauser—whether to back him up or to make a move on him, Tess didn't know.

"We worked together," Tess acknowledged without raising her voice. "And when it looked like she'd gone bad, I helped bring her in. But I didn't think I was setting her up to be killed."

"This is ridiculous." Hauser stooped, reaching for his firearm on the asphalt. "I'm through with this crap—"

"Sir." It was the man who'd checked Abby's purse. The note of command in his tone stopped Hauser cold. "Leave your weapon where it is, please."

Hauser stared at him, then at the others. Slowly he straightened up, leaving the gun untouched.

"I'm disappointed," he said. "In all of you."

No one answered.

In the distance a siren wailed, growing louder. The ambulance.

And Abby, kneeling alone on the ground, continued to breathe for Wyatt. In. Out. In. Out.

39

Not long afterward, the paramedics arrived at the scene and took control of Wyatt's care, and Tess eased Abby away. For the first time she saw Abby's face, and it was like looking at a stranger. All expression had drained from her features; all light had vanished from her eyes. Her facial muscles were slack, and her gaze traveled everywhere without registering anything.

She had not said a word since the shooting, and she remained quiet as Tess assisted her into the passenger seat of one of the Bureau cars. Tess did not put her in handcuffs. She couldn't make herself do that.

"I'm following the ambulance to the hospital," she told the other agents as she stripped off her body armor and headset. "Abby will ride with me. She may need treatment for shock."

"We're supposed to take her to the field office," one of them objected.

"First she needs medical attention. I'll take responsibility. You hold on to her purse and her car. If there's a gun in her purse, we'll need a ballistics test to see if it matches the round that killed Agent Brody."

"What about Agent Hauser?"

"He's in your custody. Take him to the FO. I'll brief the AD on my way to the hospital."

She retrieved her laptop from Wyatt's car, acting automatically, unwilling to let the data fall into the porous hands of the LAPD. When the ambulance pulled away, she followed close behind. The cell phone was already

in her hand, though she hadn't been conscious of picking
it up. She hit redial, since the last number she had called
was Michaelson's office. This time the secretary put her
through without a hassle. No doubt the Nose had been
waiting to hear the outcome of the arrest.

"We have Abby in custody," Tess said without being
asked, "but there's a problem."

Michaelson sighed. "There always is when you're
involved."

She ignored the dig. "Hauser shot the police officer
who was assisting us. He was hit in the chest and
looks"—she remembered Abby, seated beside her—
"well, he doesn't look too great. He's en route to the
hospital now, and I'm following."

"Which hospital?"

"Paramedics said it was Olive View. It's north of the
Two-ten Freeway—"

"I know where it is. Who has custody of Sinclair?"

"I do. She's with me."

"Why? Is she hurt too?"

"She may be in shock. The cop was her friend."

"In shock." Michaelson snorted. "She's malingering.
Bring her to the field office."

"She's not malingering, and she's going to the hospital," Tess said firmly. "But that's not what I need to
discuss with you. Four members of Hauser's squad are
on their way to Westwood right now. They're bringing
in Hauser—in handcuffs."

"What the hell are you talking about?"

"Hauser shot the police officer. He was aiming for
Abby. The shooting was totally unjustified. I saw it, and
I will testify to that effect."

"I don't understand what you're saying."

"Hauser is dirty, Richard."

Silence buzzed on the other end of the line for a long
moment. "You'd better be able to back up an accusation
like that."

"He was supervising Brody, and Brody was breaking all the rules. An illegal wiretap, for starters. I thought Hauser was just being lax in his oversight, but after what I witnessed tonight, I think he knew exactly what was going on. And I think he authorized Brody to kill Abby."

"Kill her? He was placing her under arrest."

"That's not how Abby tells it. She says he intended to interrogate her and then kill her, and she had to shoot him in self-defense."

"That's . . . absurd."

"Is it? From what I've been able to gather, Brody didn't exactly follow the rule book when he was stationed in Iraq. He took shortcuts, and the Bureau looked the other way. Maybe he got used to the idea. Maybe Hauser thought he could count on Brody to take Abby out. When the plan failed, Hauser decided to get rid of her on his own."

She anticipated an indignant denial of the theory. Michaelson could be expected to protect his people. But when he spoke, his voice was soft and thoughtful. "I knew it was a mistake."

"Mistake?"

"Allowing Hauser and Brody to work together. You're right about the . . . extralegal operations in Iraq. And when a person gets in the habit of breaking the law, it becomes hard to stop. I suppose your friend Sinclair could tell us something about that."

Tess said quietly, "So you suspected something was wrong?"

"Not specifically. I had no evidence. I just worried about the ramifications of those two teaming up."

"Did you ever raise your concerns with either of them?"

"I couldn't. Not without some solid basis for suspicion. What I did was curtail Hauser's responsibilities. I gave him lower-priority cases. I told him it was because I was disappointed in his handling of Medea. That was partly true, but mainly I was worried about his influence on Brody, or vice versa."

She remembered Hauser's words in the corridor outside Michaelson's office. "By telling him he was paying for Medea, you gave him the impression his career had stalled out because of me—and Abby. He blamed us, Richard. And since he couldn't go after me, he tried to take it out on her."

"I had no way of anticipating that development," Michaelson said, shifting instantly into defensive mode. "Anyway, we have yet to establish that your version of events is true."

"But you *will* look into it?"

"Of course I'll look into it. You think I would tolerate this kind of behavior from a subordinate? You think I would look the other way?"

"No, Richard. I really don't. It's no secret that I don't like you. To be quite honest, I think you're an asshole."

"McCallum—"

"But," she pressed on, "I *don't* think you would tolerate corruption. In fact, I'm sure you wouldn't."

"Well . . . thanks for the vote of confidence." He said it with sarcasm, but she could tell he was secretly pleased. "Let me know how things work out at Olive View. And if Sinclair's story is true, she'll get a fair shake from me."

They reached the hospital, set in the dusty foothills north of the freeway. Tess followed the ambulance to the ER entrance. She parked at a red curb, trusting the FBI seal emblazoned on the doors to prevent the sedan from being towed.

She opened the door, and the overhead light came on. In its glow, Tess saw that Abby's face was streaked with silent tears.

"He'll be all right," she said gently. "He'll pull through. You'll see."

Abby said nothing at all.

40

Tess showed her credentials to get her gun through the metal detector and into the ER. She wasn't sure why she hadn't just left the gun in the car. Perhaps after seeing Wyatt shot, she felt the need to keep protection close at hand. She'd brought her laptop, too, though she was getting tired of lugging the damn thing around. She couldn't risk letting it be stolen.

"We have to find you a doctor," she said, steering Abby through a crowd of people, mostly indigent, filling every available seat in the cramped waiting room.

Abby's voice was low. "I don't need treatment for shock."

"I'm not so sure. Those are the first words you've spoken since . . . since it happened."

"I just needed time to . . . I just needed time. And I needed to be here, in the hospital. Don't even *think* I'm going to leave until Vic's . . . until he's okay."

"It may not be possible for me to hold off a trip to the field office too long."

Abby turned to face her. "If you try to take me out of here before I know Vic's condition," she said softly, "I'll kill you."

"I'm armed, Abby. You're not."

"Do you really think that matters?" Her eyes were colder than any Tess had ever seen—colder than a serial killer's eyes.

Wyatt had been taken into surgery. An orderly escorted them to a waiting room on another floor, outside the suite of operating rooms. This area was empty of people. A TV set, tuned to a cable news channel, babbled in a corner. They sat next to each other in two chairs with worn armrests.

"How soon until Wyatt's shooting hits the news?" Abby asked when the orderly had gone. "Once the word is out, his fellow officers will be all over this place."

"I doubt it's been released yet. The Nose—I mean, Assistant Director Michaelson—isn't going to want this going out until . . . until he knows how to handle it."

"How to spin it, you mean. How to cover it up."

"I didn't say that."

"You didn't have to." Abby stared at the wall for a long moment. "If Wyatt dies," she said finally, "you're next."

Tess straightened her shoulders. "That's the second time you've made a threat against my life. You *do* realize it's a crime to threaten a federal agent?"

"Just giving you fair warning."

"How seriously am I supposed to take these warnings?"

Her gaze was fixed in a thousand-yard stare. "Dead seriously. It's your fault. You wouldn't listen. I tried to tell you the whole story—about Brody and Hauser, all of it—and you blew me off."

"Abby, try to see things my way—"

What happened next was very fast. Abby spun in her chair and grabbed her with one hand, and there was a sudden killing pressure on her throat, five fingers clamping down like hot irons, while with the other hand Abby secured Tess's wrist so she couldn't draw her gun.

"No. *You* try to see things *my* way for a change. I asked you to trust me, and you wouldn't. And now Vic is in there with a bullet in his chest, and I don't think he's going to make it. Do you? *Do you?*"

"No," Tess whispered. She had seen mortal wounds before.

It occurred to her that this answer might be enough to push Abby entirely over the edge. All she had to do was tighten her grip by another pound or two of pressure and Tess's airway would close. She stared into Abby's brown eyes and waited.

"Right," Abby said. "I don't, either." She relaxed her grip on Tess's throat just a little. "So don't tell me about your motivations and your perspective and your good fucking intentions. *You got Vic killed.*"

Every instinct shouted at Tess to agree, play along, tell this woman what she wanted to hear. Somehow she couldn't do it. "No, I didn't," she heard herself say.

"You did."

"No, Abby. *You* did. You're the one who went to work for Faust, when you should have known better. You're the one who shot Brody after allowing him to put you in a vulnerable position. You've gotten reckless and sloppy, and that's why Vic Wyatt is in surgery right now."

She counted ten heartbeats while Abby took this in. Then slowly Abby released her throat and turned away.

"Maybe you're right," she said in a deflated tone. "I've been on the job a long time now. Maybe I've gotten too sure of myself. Too willing to take risks that don't make sense. Maybe I'm not making the right choices anymore."

Tess rubbed her throat and thought about drawing her weapon now that her hand was free. But she knew there was no point. She wasn't going to shoot Abby. And Abby could probably take the damn gun away from her anytime she wanted. "Nobody makes the right choices all the time."

"I'm supposed to. When I slip up, people die." She was silent for a long moment, and Tess knew she was thinking of Wyatt. "How did you get him to call me, anyway?"

"We appealed to him as a fellow law-enforcement officer."

"It had to be more than that. Did you tell him he'd be investigated for passing info to me?"

"Yes."

Abby nodded. "That's nice, Tess. Very nice."

"One of our own people got killed. We weren't interested in playing around."

"Why wasn't he wearing a vest? You and Hauser had Kevlar. So did the others."

"We knew you'd spot a vest under his shirt the minute you saw him."

"You could have given him a sweatshirt or a windbreaker to conceal it."

"And that wouldn't have raised your suspicions? Besides, we didn't expect it to work out like this."

"No. You just *expected* to put me in handcuffs and have me frog-marched to the nearest federal penitentiary."

"It wasn't something I wanted to do."

"But you would do it, anyway. Duty, honor, country. Right?"

"I suppose so."

"Loyalty, decency, friendship—those things don't factor in."

"You're the one who said we weren't friends anymore."

"So it's back to me again. Great."

Abby was quiet for a while. The TV chattered about domestic crimes and foreign intrigues, politics and weather. Tess hardly heard it. She was thinking of Paul Voorhees. Thinking that what she had gone through, when she found Paul dead in the bedroom, was very much like what Abby was going through now. And the worst of it was that this was only the beginning. The first pains of a hurt that would never die. It would fade a little, with time, but it would always be there, trailing her like a shadow, haunting her nights.

Abby's voice broke the silence between them. "You know, you wouldn't last a day in my job. Not a single day."

Tess bristled. "I wouldn't want your job."

"Because you couldn't handle it."

"Because I don't believe in sleeping with the enemy," she snapped, then regretted it.

"Brody, you mean? You knew about that, huh?" Abby frowned. "Let me guess. The woman in the main house, Brody's landlady—she told you."

"That's right."

"I had a bad feeling about her. I waved to her, and she didn't wave back. Mrs. Hunter, that was her name. Brody sent her and her husband out of the house so he could have me alone last night. He . . ." The words trailed off as a new expression crossed her face. A look of disappointment so deep it bordered on disgust. "You told Vic, didn't you?"

Tess said nothing.

"Of course you did. More gamesmanship to turn him against me. A nugget of info like that is just too juicy *not* to use."

"We told him."

"And that's what did the trick. He felt betrayed, so he decided to betray me right back."

"That isn't how I interpreted it."

"It's what happened. It's the human thing to do. And he wasn't wrong. I *did* betray him. And . . . and *he* ended up paying for it." The smooth flow of her speech was breaking up under a rising wave of feeling. "And the last thing . . . the last thing he was thinking about me . . . was how I'd spent the night with another man. That's what was on his mind. You shouldn't have told him, Tess."

"I wish it hadn't been necessary."

"It *wasn't* necessary!"

"It was a judgment call. In the same circumstances, you would have done—"

"Don't tell me what I would have done. You don't know me. You don't know anything about me. You never have." Tears stood in her eyes, reflecting the shine of the fluorescents overhead. "God *damn* you, how could you hurt him like that?"

"I'm not the one who slept with Brody."

"No, you're just the one who used it as a weapon. Even though you *had* to know how it would make him feel. Hell, you used it *because* of how it would make him feel."

"I used it because we needed to find you and take you into custody."

"And that worked out just great, didn't it?" She slumped in her chair, her voice low. "I could forgive you for everything else, but not this."

"Abby—"

"Shut up. Just shut the hell up. I don't want to know you. I don't want to see your face or hear your voice ever again."

There was no more talk after that.

41

Abby had no idea how long she sat in the waiting room. Time had stopped. A minute was an hour was a week was a year. In meditation exercises she had often tried to achieve the complete cessation of any awareness of time. She'd never quite managed it. Now she had. And all it took was for Wyatt to die.

She didn't want to think of it that way. She wanted to believe that he would pull through. The wound had been bad, a sucking chest wound that could easily progress to a tension pneumothorax—but miracles happened.

He was still in surgery. The doctors hadn't given up. She shouldn't, either. There was a chance he would recover. A chance she could make things right.

But she didn't believe it.

What she wanted more than anything was to talk to him again. To hold his hand, look into his eyes, and somehow make amends. She wanted him to know that it hadn't meant anything, what she'd done with Brody. It had been impulsive and meaningless and stupid and wrong. She wanted him to understand and forgive.

Even if he didn't make it—even if she had the opportunity for just one last talk—it would be enough, or almost enough. She needed to make things right. If he died now, with things forever unresolved between them, she wasn't sure she could go on.

Yet she felt guilty even thinking this way. Because really it wasn't about her. It was his life that mattered, not her feelings, her issues. She wasn't important. The moment she'd seen Wyatt fall, she had ceased to exist.

A few more people wandered into the waiting room, huddling in small groups, speaking a babble of foreign languages. The TV continued to prattle. As if anyone in this room cared about the news of the outside world. There was no outside world, not for her. There was nothing but blackness and heat and a pain in her gut that felt like bleeding. That was all, nothing else. Maybe there never would be anything else, ever again.

Over and over she relived the event—that split second when the gun discharged and Wyatt fell. She kept trying to reconstruct what had happened, to make some sense of it. Had she seen the gun before Hauser fired? Had she reached for her purse? If she had reacted faster, if she had stepped in front of Wyatt, could she have taken the bullet?

The mental review served no purpose. She had no clear idea of the timing or sequence of events. She was only torturing herself by replaying them in her thoughts. Every time she saw Wyatt fall, it was as if she were seeing it for the first time. She felt the same shock, the dizzying rush of blood from her face, the spiraling terror and helplessness.

Over and over again . . .

She recognized the symptoms of post-traumatic stress. But knowing all about them didn't make them go away.

Distantly she became aware of a new person entering the room. Her heart sped up with the momentary certainty that it was one of the surgeons, here to report the outcome of the operation.

Then she relaxed. It was no one important. Only Michaelson, the assistant director in charge of the FBI field office. She had met him during the Medea case. She hadn't liked him, and she had no interest in seeing him now.

Nevertheless, he appeared to have an interest in her. He set down his briefcase and extended his hand. "Ms. Sinclair, I'm very sorry for what's happened."

She barely glanced at him. "Great," she murmured. "Now get lost."

"I'm afraid I can't leave just yet. There are matters I need to discuss with you."

"We have nothing to talk about."

He sat next to her, on the opposite side from Tess. "Agent Hauser is in custody. He has made no admission of guilt. But we've run his LUD—his local usage details, in other words—"

"His phone records," Abby whispered. "I know the lingo."

"Yes. Of course. Anyway, he placed a call to Peter Faust less than one hour before the rendezvous at the gas station. He has no explanation for this call."

Abby knew its purpose. "He wanted to know if Faust told me who recommended me for the stalker job. He wanted to know what I would say when I was interrogated."

Michaelson frowned at her. "That may be correct. . . ."

"It *is* correct. When Faust admitted he'd spilled the beans, Hauser panicked and decided to kill me during the arrest. That's why he fired without provocation. He wanted to shut me up."

"The way Hauser deployed his team at the arrest site was against standard procedure," Michaelson conceded. "And there are other details that put him in an unfavorable light."

Tess spoke up. "What details?"

"We found Hauser's car parked a block or so from the gas station. In the glove compartment there were pain pills—a lot of them. Multiple prescriptions from different physicians, filled at different pharmacies. He'd been doctor shopping."

"I saw him swallow some pills today," Tess said. "He claimed they were for arthritis in his knees."

"He lied. He's been seriously ill for some time."

"How seriously?"

"About two months ago he confided in me that he'd

been diagnosed with pancreatic cancer. Inoperable, incurable."

"I thought he looked older," Tess whispered. "And . . . I caught him looking like he was in pain. I chalked it up to grief over Brody."

"Maybe that was part of it. But judging from the stash of pills he was carrying around, I'd say he's in a lot worse shape than I thought."

"If you knew he was sick, why did you let him run the sting operation?"

"It's only *because* he was sick that we even initiated the op. Hauser wanted to go out with a successful operation to his credit. Wanted to balance out the black mark on his record from Medea. He lobbied me for one last shot at bringing Faust down. I should have said no. But under the circumstances, I gave him the okay."

Abby had been listening from what seemed like a great distance. "And then he got the chance to take me down," she said half to herself. "He decided to go for it. Figured if he was checking out, he would take me with him."

Michaelson looked away. "It's possible. But he hasn't admitted a thing. Hasn't said a damn word. Maybe he never will. Maybe he'll hold his peace until . . . until it doesn't matter anymore."

"How much time does he have?" Tess asked.

"A few weeks at most. Actually, I half expected he would be gone by now. He held on, I think, just to see this operation through."

"Or to see Abby die. He hates both of us so much."

"His career fell apart after Medea. And for Hauser, his career is his life. He never got married, never took a vacation. The job is all he has. Then, on top of everything, he got the diagnosis. . . . Maybe in some way he blames you for that, too. For his illness. I'm not saying it makes sense, but . . ."

"He thinks we killed him. Abby and I. And he was trying to even the score."

There was silence as they took this in. Abby thought perhaps she should feel sorry for Hauser. She didn't. Had he been in this room right now, she would have killed him with a palm-heel strike to the larynx. Crush his windpipe, watch him asphyxiate. A bad way to die.

Michaelson turned to Abby. "Your purse is here with me, in my briefcase. Your gun, however, is not inside. Since you have no law-enforcement credentials, you couldn't carry it around the hospital, so it's been left in your car. You'll be glad to know I had your Miata driven here from the gas station. It's parked in the hospital garage, space C-seventy-one."

"Terrific," Abby murmured.

"I might also mention that the arrest team found some interesting documents in your vehicle. Items in the name of one Angela Marcus. They had every appearance of providing you with an illegal identity."

"That was the idea, all right. I suppose your guys confiscated them."

"Not at all. The papers are still in your car."

"Doesn't matter. Now that you know about Angela Marcus, I can't use that identity anyway."

"You have other ways to reinvent yourself, I'm sure."

"It's what I do. Reinvent myself. You know, if you reinvent yourself often enough, you may forget who you really are."

Tess was watching him. "I don't believe you came here just to drop off our stuff, Richard."

"Well, no. There are certain outstanding legal matters to be taken care of."

Abby regarded him warily. "What legal matters?"

Michaelson hesitated, looking around the room at the other people in the chairs. Obviously he was reluctant to speak in the presence of outsiders. After a moment he seemed to come to the conclusion that no one else within earshot could speak English.

"May I remind you that you are the prime suspect in the murder of Agent Brody?" he said in a low voice.

"You *know* that was self-defense," Tess cut in hotly. "That's got to be clear by now."

"Don't speak up for me," Abby said. "I don't need your help."

"I understand you're claiming you acted in self-defense." Michaelson's tone was neutral. "But there is no proof."

"Then get Hauser to confess."

"That may not be possible."

"So put him on trial."

"He won't live long enough. Of course, Ms. Sinclair, we could always put *you* on trial."

"I'd be acquitted."

"There's never any certainty about what a jury will do. They could look at someone like you—someone who routinely violates the law, who works under multiple bogus identities backed up by phony paper trails, who obtains evidence by patently illegal methods—well, they could look at you and decide it would be better to keep you off the streets. *If* there is a trial. There doesn't have to be."

Abby understood where this was going. She wasn't even surprised. She was past any astonishment at the workings of the human mind. "You want me to make a deal," she said softly.

"I would like us to come to an agreement, yes." He placed his briefcase on his knees and unsnapped the clasps. "I've brought some documents drawn up by our legal staff. Essentially they absolve you of any guilt in the death of Mark Brody. I am prepared to sign those documents in the presence of Agent McCallum as a witness."

"And in exchange?"

"You will sign a statement pertaining to Lieutenant Wyatt's injury."

"A statement," she said flatly.

"Yes. It will say—"

"I know what it will say." She was very tired. "The

shooting was an accident, and nobody can be held responsible, and the FBI conducted itself with integrity, competence, and professionalism throughout."

"Something like that."

"You want me to sell out Vic."

"It's not a question of selling anybody out—"

"Yes, it is. You want me to make it impossible for there ever to be justice in this case."

"Justice is not always attainable in the real world, Ms. Sinclair. You know that."

"Maybe you ought to put that on the FBI seal. Truth in advertising."

Michaelson tried a different approach. "Lieutenant Wyatt is the one who lured you into an ambush. You don't owe him anything."

"He took a bullet for me. That's got to be worth something, don't you think?"

"If you were to go on trial, your identity would be exposed. Your work would be hopelessly compromised."

"You really think I give a damn about that?"

"What about Wyatt's reputation? Do you care about how he's seen by the public? By his peers? If all the facts come out, it will be known that he, as an officer of the LAPD, maintained a longtime personal relationship with a . . . well, with a vigilante, for want of a better word. That he passed on information to a lawbreaker, and aided and abetted her efforts. Is that how you want him to be . . . to be thought of?"

She knew he had been about to say *to be remembered*, before realizing that the word was premature.

The thing was, Michaelson was right. A trial would bring Wyatt's relationship with her into the open. No one would understand. His memory would be hopelessly soiled.

"If you cooperate with us," Michaelson added, "Wyatt will be seen as a hero. One of L.A.'s finest. Otherwise . . ."

"Otherwise he'll be a bad cop who consorted with a shady lowlife," Abby whispered. "Namely me."

"I'm afraid so."

She lowered her head, stared at the floor. Cheap short-nap carpet, worn and stained, smelling of disinfectant. She wondered how many shoes had trodden down that carpet, how many people had paced this room awaiting word of a loved one's fate.

There was so much pain in the world. Everybody lost someone. Everybody was, finally, alone.

"Ms. Sinclair?" Michaelson pressed.

She lifted her head. When she spoke, her voice was almost steady. "Just show me where to sign."

42

Shortly before midnight, Faust decided he could wait no longer. The victim had marinated in the stew of fear and helplessness long enough.

He opened the secret panel in the wall, unlocked the hidden door, and found her manacled to the bed, a sad, exhausted thing.

"I believe, my dear, that the time has arrived for your suffering to end."

He opened the cabinet and took out the leather strap.

"Well, no," he amended, "this is not quite accurate. There is still a bit more suffering to come."

He stretched the strap in his hands. She did not even look at him. Her eyes were glazed, her face empty.

"No great thing is ever easy. And to die at my hands is to attain a greatness you scarcely deserve. Your petty life now shades into myth and archetype. You, who are no more than a ragged and filthy scrap of flotsam from the streets, shall become something much more. You are to be part of me, absorbed by me, subjugated to my will forever."

He was sure she did not understand. How could she? And yet it was so simple. He had to bind them, had to put his mark, his personal stamp on them, in order to assert his absolute ownership of their bodies, their lives. It was an act of almost religious significance to him— although he was a man without religion—an act of ritual and passion, the moment when he staked his claim on the victim and made her his own, forever.

He approached the bed. She did not turn her head in his direction, did not struggle or tremble. She scarcely breathed.

"It is good you show no fear. Your lower instincts have been scoured away, leaving you pure. Not chaste, perhaps—this is surely too much to hope for in any modern American girl. But you have achieved a purity of the soul. All that remains is to cast aside the worn-out apparatus of your body. There will be pain, but it will prove fleeting. And then there will be peace. Do you wish for peace, darling Raven?"

Still no reaction. She was the shell of a girl.

"You wish for nothing, I see. That is best."

He leaned over the bed, and carefully he applied the strap, winding it around her neck and brushing her dark, matted hair out of the way. Abruptly she twitched, and her head jerked, shoulders jumping in sudden reflexive opposition. He had expected as much. The body resisted to the last, even when the mind had long ago made its peace with death. The spirit was willing, but the flesh . . . ah, the flesh was weak.

"There, there," he soothed. "Only a little farther down this path, and you are free."

The strap was in place now, coiled around her neck like a long brown snake, twisted at the base of her skull to form a simple slipknot.

He took hold of both ends of the strap, watching her face, hearing the chuff of her breath from behind the gag. Her eyes remained empty. It was not her will that fought him, not anymore.

That was proper. She had lost the last spark of self-preservation. Like a fine wine, she had been aged to perfection, and now she was ready to be savored, and consumed down to the lees.

He pulled the strap taut—

In his pocket, his cell phone rang.

He almost did not answer. But when he checked the screen, caller ID told him Elise was on the line.

He released the strap and stepped away from the bed so Elise would not hear the girl's futile struggle.

"Yes?" he snapped.

"Peter, it's me." He heard an edge of hysteria in her voice.

"I am quite aware of your identity. The hour is late, and I am occupied."

"I want to come over."

He glanced at Raven. "Tonight is perhaps not the most convenient time."

"I don't care if it's *convenient*. I . . . I can't sleep. I'm all worked up."

"On account of your experience with Miss Sinclair?"

"*Of course* on account of that. She *kidnapped* me, Peter."

"She would not have harmed you. You were merely a pawn in a game she was playing."

"Well, it didn't *feel* like any fucking game. She had a gun to my head. I think she's fucking *crazy*."

"Merely rambunctious."

"Ram*bunc*tious? Every time I close my eyes, I feel her behind me. I could've been killed."

"And you were doing a photo shoot in a cemetery. There is a certain irony, do you not think?"

"No, I do *not* think. Damn it, Peter, I'm not sleeping alone tonight. I'll go out of my mind if I do."

He could not argue with her when she was in such a state. Reluctantly he gave in.

"Come over, then. I will see you shortly."

Irritated, he ended the call without further comment. He was not accustomed to having her, as the Americans said, call the shots. It placed him in a dilemma. He did not wish to rush Raven's finale, yet he could hardly stand to put it off now that he had begun. The feel of the leather had set his hands itching.

"That was my girlfriend," he explained with a sigh.

"She is a child sometimes. Scared to be alone. But you are not scared, are you, Raven? Not scared even of death. Of course not. There is my good girl."

He stroked her hair, and his hand moved down slowly to the strap around her neck. To tighten it—or remove it?

A quandary. He could choose either course—but he must choose soon.

43

Tess watched while Abby signed Michaelson's papers, carefully initialing each page and placing her signature on various lines marked with yellow Post-its. When the ritual was completed, she handed back the documents and said, "That's that. Now go away."

"First let me return something to you." Michaelson delved into his briefcase and retrieved Abby's purse. Abby accepted it without comment. Clearly she wanted nothing more to do with either of them.

Tess couldn't blame her. Even so, she lingered for a moment, picking up the computer carrying case after Michaelson had left his seat.

"I'm really not comfortable leaving you like this," she said.

Abby glared at her. "If I need a shoulder to cry on, it sure as hell won't be yours."

"I'm certain Ms. Sinclair can take care of herself," Michaelson observed, glancing at his wristwatch.

Abby looked down at the floor. "Yeah, I'm good at that. I'm not so hot at taking care of the people around me, though."

"You can't blame yourself," Tess said.

"I don't. I blame you."

Tess swallowed. "I'll pray for Vic."

"You do that," Abby whispered. "When you're done, try praying for yourself."

They left her there, clutching her purse and staring at nothing. When they were out of earshot Michaelson asked, "What did she mean by that? Was she threatening you?"

"She's distraught, Richard."

"Maybe I shouldn't have given her back the damn gun."

Tess touched her throat, remembering the grip of Abby's fingers. "She doesn't *need* a gun. Besides, she's not going to come after me."

"How can you be sure?"

"Because she already had her chance. She could have killed me in the waiting room if she'd wanted to."

"Are you saying you let her get you in a vulnerable position?"

Tess smiled. "I didn't exactly *let* her. You've always underestimated her because she's not official. Not licensed. But that's what makes her so dangerous. She's never had an organization to rely on, so she's had to fend for herself. She knows how to do it. Believe me, she's more than a match for most of our people."

"She was more than a match for Brody."

"Yes. She was."

They rode the elevator in uncomfortable silence. At the ground floor Tess started to get off.

"Aren't you parked in the garage?" Michaelson asked.

She shook her head. "Outside the ER."

"Oh. Well, you need to come to my car anyway. I've got those blueprints you wanted."

It took Tess a moment to remember. Blueprints. Faust's home.

"And for Christ's sake," he added, "don't tell me you don't need them anymore. My assistant gave me all kinds of hell for sending her downtown for them."

Tess stepped back onto the elevator. All of a sudden she was glad she had the laptop with her. "There's something we need to look at. A video on my computer."

"This is hardly the time for entertainment."

"It's not entertainment. It's a possible lead. Something we ought to check out."

"We? As in the two of us?"

"I need someone's help, Richard, and it looks like you just got elected."

"Whatever it is, can't you do it later?"

Tess thought of Jennifer Gaitlin, aka Raven, missing for one week. "No," she said, "we have to do it *now*."

By the time they reached Michaelson's sedan Tess had done her best to explain her theory in a few hurried sentences. She couldn't gauge the Nose's reaction.

The car was unoccupied. She had expected to see a driver behind the wheel, the usual perk for an assistant director.

"No chauffeur?" she inquired.

"I drove myself here. My driver's off the clock."

"All right. So I'll fire up my computer, you get out the blueprints, and we'll go to work."

Michaelson fished his remote out of his pants pocket and used it to turn off the vehicle's alarm system. Even after the echoes of the two chirps had died away, he didn't move.

"I don't think so," he said.

She sighed. He hadn't bought it. Naturally, she'd known he might prove recalcitrant. It was unusual—okay, it was unheard of—to ask an assistant director to do hands-on work of this sort. Still, she had to push him a little. "What do you mean, you don't think so?"

"McCallum, I have better things to do than follow up some alleged lead based on nothing more than woman's intuition."

"You didn't really say *woman's intuition,* did you?"

"What else should I call it? You're telling me there's some part of Faust's home that the LAPD didn't search?"

"I'm saying it's possible. That's why we need to compare the blueprints with the video."

"Looking for what?"

"A room that isn't there."

"You've lost me."

"A hidden room, Richard. A room that would show up on the blueprints but wouldn't be apparent to a visitor."

"What makes you think there's a hidden room? Have you ever been inside the house?"

"No. But I was inside another house in the same neighborhood just today. The owner made an offhand comment. She said her house had so many rooms, she needed a map to find her way around."

Michaelson averted his face. In profile his proboscis loomed like the beak of some prehistoric bird. "And you read some cosmic significance into this?"

"Faust's home dates to the same era. It's just as lavish, just as large. It has lots of rooms. And unless the LAPD got hold of the blueprints, they didn't have a map. Which means one of the rooms could have been missed."

"I'm sure the search was very thorough."

"But you can't find what you're not looking for. If one of the rooms was hidden, they could walk right past it."

He made a noise that was somewhere between a grunt and a sigh. "You have no actual, specific reason to think there *is* such a room, though, do you?"

"It's a hypothesis."

"It's a hunch. The Bureau doesn't play hunches."

She shrugged, conceding defeat. "Then I guess I'll just take the blueprints and go."

"There's an idea." Michaelson opened the trunk and produced a hefty roll of papers.

"I'll have to check into a hotel. Maybe they can recommend one."

"I'm sure they can." He began to hand over the blueprints, then paused. "Who are *they*?"

"The police. As I recall, it was Northwest Division that handled the search. You don't happen to know the address of the station house?"

"The address?"

"Never mind, I'll get it from directory assistance."

"Why the hell are you going to the police?"

"Well, *someone* has to follow up on my woman's intuition."

His eyes narrowed. "Don't test me, McCallum."

"I'm not testing anybody. I have blueprints and a video record of the search, and I intend to see if any part of that house was overlooked. If the Bureau won't help me, I'll find an agency that will."

She let her words hang between them for a long moment. She knew Michaelson was thinking that if anything came from her idea and it resulted in Faust's arrest, he would look bad for having dropped the ball. Coming on top of Brody's death and Wyatt's shooting, this would be the third strike against him. In the Bureau, as in baseball, three strikes and he was out.

"Perhaps," he said finally, "it wouldn't hurt to take a look at that video."

She opened the passenger door and got in. "We may need to push our seats back."

"You want to do it *here*? In my car?"

"There's no time to waste, Richard. Faust may be holding a runaway teenager as his prisoner right now."

"This procedure would be more convenient back at my office."

"But it'll be faster here."

Grumbling, he slid into the driver's side. At her request he unrolled the blueprints and adjusted the ceiling light so it would stay on with the car doors closed.

She had left her PC in suspend mode. It took only a few seconds to come back to life. The DVD software was still running, and it was easy for her to find the LAPD video. She fast-forwarded from room to room, identifying each one in turn while Michaelson ticked off the corresponding rooms on the blueprints.

"All right," Tess said. "Now they're leaving the utility

room. Going down the hall, past some bookshelves. Still going . . . Now they're entering the breakfast nook off the kitchen."

"Wait." She heard the first note of interest in his voice. "You said they went directly from the utility room to the kitchen area?"

"Yes."

"What about this room here?" He tapped the blueprint.

She ran the cursor over the DVD program's onscreen controls. "Let me backwind this thing."

"Backwind? I haven't heard that term since I was working a Super Eight projector in high school."

She smiled. "AV Club?"

"It's not as nerdy as it sounds," he said defensively. "We made our own version of *Night of the Living Dead.*"

"Nothing nerdy about that. Okay, here they are leaving the utility closet. Heading down the hall . . ."

"There should be a doorway within five or six feet of the utility room."

She ran the video backward and froze it on a wide-angle view of the hall. "Nothing but bookshelves. Let me see the blueprints again." She studied the small, smudged outline of the mystery room. "No windows. No other exits. Too big to be a closet."

"Could have been a butler's pantry," Michaelson suggested.

"Or a maid's room."

He stared at the blueprints for a long time. "There may, of course, be a perfectly legitimate reason for remodeling the hall. . . ."

"And concealing the door?"

He had no answer.

She sensed a growing excitement in him. He never got to do this kind of thing anymore. His life, like hers, consisted mostly of reports, paperwork, conference calls, in-baskets and out-baskets. To actually participate in breaking a case—to be there at ground zero—was not something that happened very often, if at all.

And Peter Faust was not just any case. Of course, that was the problem. Faust was a celebrity. He had money, lawyers, and connections in the media. If the lead proved to be a bust, he could make things very unpleasant for Michaelson. Tess herself wouldn't take the hit. It wasn't her case or her call.

She thought Michaelson might choose the safer course. Table the idea until he could discuss it with his own people. Spend a day or two thinking it through. But by then Jennifer Gaitlin could be dead—if she wasn't already.

She pressed him just a little. "What's behind those bookshelves, Richard?"

Michaelson pursed his lips. "I suppose," he said finally, "we had better find out."

44

"Are you waiting for word on Mr. Wyatt?"

Abby looked up slowly and saw a man in a clean set of scrubs standing over her. Somehow she knew he was a surgeon, even though he looked too young.

And he'd used the word *Mr.*, not *Lieutenant*. Even the surgical staff hadn't been told Wyatt was a cop.

"That's right," she said.

"What is your relationship to him, if I may ask?"

She was ready for this question. "I'm his wife." She kept her hands in her lap, hoping he wouldn't notice the absence of a wedding ring. The doctors wouldn't give out personal information to anyone who was not a family member.

"I see." He glanced around at the other occupied chairs in the waiting room. "I'd like to go somewhere more private, where we can talk."

This was when she knew the news was bad. "Just tell me," she whispered.

"It would really be preferable—"

"Tell me." She did not raise her voice, but her tone allowed no disagreement.

The doctor nodded and sat beside her. "I'm very sorry. We did everything possible for your husband, but his injuries were too severe. We weren't able to save him."

She spent a long moment processing these words. "He's gone?" she said finally.

"Yes."

"All right." There was nothing else to say.

She sat very still. She had expected this outcome. She was too much of a realist to hope for anything different. Even so, it was hard to take in. Hard to make it real.

"I'm very sorry," the doctor repeated.

"So am I."

"Would you like to spend some time with him?"

With his body. That was what he meant. She almost asked what was the point. That thing in there . . . it wasn't Vic anymore. Only a pile of flesh and bone. No mind, no spirit. If there was a spirit.

Still, she heard herself say, "Yes, please."

He led her out of the waiting room and down an antiseptic hallway. In a room near the OR, Wyatt lay on a table with a sheet draped neatly over his midsection—a clean sheet, clean like the surgeon's scrubs. No blood here, no pain and disfigurement and death, everything clean and sanitary.

She stared at him. It seemed impossible that he wasn't simply asleep. At any second he could open his eyes. In a movie he wouldn't have died without regaining consciousness. He would have come to, at least long enough for some last words, a tender good-bye.

What was the last thing she'd said to him, before the gunshot? She couldn't remember.

The doctor pulled up a chair on casters and let her sit down. She held Vic's hand. It was cool, too cool. No warmth in it.

"I'll leave you alone," the doctor said. She heard the squeaking of his rubber soles on the tiled floor as he left the room.

She wondered what she ought to do. Speak to Vic? She didn't think she could. But she found herself speaking anyway, in a low monotone.

"Usually I don't have any trouble talking to you. Maybe that's the problem. I talked too much, didn't do enough listening. Didn't take you seriously when you said what you wanted. Always figured it wasn't what *I* wanted, so *you* couldn't really want it, either. Which was stupid. And selfish. And just . . . just a waste. That's really what it comes down to, a waste. There's so much more we could have done, if I'd been there for you, the way you always were there for me. It's like I thought . . . I always thought there would be more time. And I don't know why I believed that. It's not like either of us had a job that was exactly risk-free. It's not like we could count on always being around. But that's just the thing— I *did* count on it. I did think you would always be around. I thought I could always come by your place and knock on your door, and you'd be there. Even after Brody—after he was dead—that's where I went. And now I've got no place to go. And the thing that really pisses me off is, you saved me. You died for me. And you did it even though you knew about Brody. Which is just too goddamned noble. Nobody should be that noble. I wouldn't be. I never did anything for you. I just used you and led you on and slept with Brody behind your back. But I loved you. Believe it or not, I loved you. And I don't think I ever said it. I don't think you knew. I don't think you'll ever know."

She didn't say anything more. She just sat there, holding his hand. From time to time she felt the doctor's gaze as he looked in on her.

And it occurred to her that in the doctor's eyes she was finally what Vic had always wanted her to be—his wife.

45

It didn't take Michaelson long to obtain a telephonic warrant to inspect Faust's premises. The document was in the hands of the backup agents who arrived from the field office. Eight of them, four of whom Tess recognized from the gas station. They drove up to an improvised staging ground near Griffith Park, where Michaelson briefed them on the details.

Tess was a little surprised that the AD was going to lead the arrest team. But on second thought, it was entirely in character for him. If the raid went badly, he would be blamed whether or not he was there. If it went well, his presence on the scene would earn him extra credit from the higher-ups.

"How soon do we move?" one of the agents asked as Michaelson wrapped the briefing.

"As soon as the LAPD gets here," he said. "I've brought them in on this. No sense starting a turf war."

He was handling things differently from Hauser, and Tess was glad about that.

Two LAPD black-and-whites pulled up a few minutes later, along with an unmarked car driven by a detective. The cops received an abridged version of Michaelson's overview. The detective looked dubious. "You're saying our guys missed an entire *room*? I don't buy it."

Michaelson was smart enough not to argue. He said only, "We'll find out one way or the other before long."

The three police cars and four Bureau sedans formed a convoy to Faust's home. Michaelson and Tess, in the lead, were first to arrive at the estate's gated entrance. Michaelson buzzed the intercom. After a short wait, he buzzed again.

"Give him time," Tess said. "It's three in the morning."

"The bastard can catch up on his sleep in jail." Michaelson was antsy, drumming the wheel, tapping his foot. He had a lot riding on this.

He was about to buzz again when a female voice spoke through the intercom. "Who is it?"

"We're from the FBI," Michaelson said. "We have a search warrant. Let us in."

"You . . . you want to search the house?"

"That's correct. Open up, please."

There was a pause, and Tess wondered if the woman might refuse them access. Then the gate swung wide, and Michaelson motored through, followed by the rest of the vehicles. The fleet of cars pulled to a stop along the wide, curving driveway.

A willowy young woman in a nightgown was standing at the open door of the house by the time the small army of cops and feds reached the front steps.

"What's going on?" she asked.

Michaelson ignored the question. "Is Mr. Faust at home?"

"I thought he was. I mean, we were in bed. Asleep. Then I heard the intercom buzz—it woke me up—and Peter wasn't there."

"What is your name, ma'am?"

"Elise Vangarten. I'm a fashion model." This item of information was offered gratuitously.

"May we come in?"

"I guess so. I mean, I have to let you in if you have a warrant, don't I?"

"I'm afraid you do."

She stepped aside, and her visitors began filing in. Tess looked around tensely, nervous at being inside Faust's home, occupying his space, breathing his air.

"At least you're polite," Elise was saying. "When the police came by last time, they weren't polite at all."

Tess looked at her. She was astonished that the girl had known Faust that long. "During the Roberta Kessler investigation?"

"I don't remember the girl's name. Peter had nothing to do with it, anyway. And he hasn't done anything wrong this time, either."

Tess fixed her with a stare. "You do realize your boyfriend is a convicted murderer?"

"That was years ago. People change."

"Not always."

Michaelson dispatched agents to check the garage and see if Faust's BMW was missing. "So you didn't hear Faust leave the residence?" he asked.

"I told you, I was asleep. Sound asleep. It's been kind of a rough day." Tell me about it, Tess thought. "Why are you here again, anyway? You didn't find anything last time."

"There's been a new development," Michaelson said.

"Miss Vangarten," Tess asked, "do you know anything about a hidden room in this house?"

She watched Elise's reaction carefully. The girl's bewilderment seemed genuine. "Hidden room? What are you *talking* about?"

"We have reason to believe Mr. Faust has concealed a room. It shows up in the blueprints. You're telling us you don't know anything about it?"

"That's crazy. Has everybody in the world gone *insane*?"

The agents returned with word that Faust's BMW and a red Infiniti coupe were both parked in the garage.

"The Infiniti is my car," Elise said.

Michaelson asked her if she or Faust had any other vehicles on the property. She said no.

"Then he must be around somewhere," Tess said, feeling still more uneasy.

"Maybe in that room," one of the cops suggested. "Holed up inside."

"We'll exercise all due caution when entering," Michaelson said.

"*What* room?" Elise was becoming hysterical. "You people aren't making any sense!"

Michaelson stationed an agent named Hanson in the front yard, then led the rest of the team into the rear of the house. They moved warily, alert for an ambush. Tess hadn't drawn her gun, but she kept her hand in the reinforced side pocket of her coat, where the SIG Sauer rested.

In the back hallway she saw the same scene she'd frozen on her computer screen—the door to the utility room, the wall of bookshelves.

"Along that wall," Michaelson said, "approximately six feet from the utility closet."

"There's nothing there," Elise protested. "Can't you see? It's just a bunch of old books nobody reads."

"Miss Vangarten," Tess said, "maybe it would be best if you waited in the front room."

"I'm not going anywhere." She thrust her fists on her hips and tried to look fierce. "Peter will be *furious* when he learns about this. It's an invasion of privacy. It's a violation of his rights!"

Tess was quite sure the girl wasn't faking it. Few models were that good at acting.

"Found something." This was one of the agents exploring the wall behind the bookshelves. He had removed handfuls of volumes from a shoulder-level shelf. "There's a seam in the paneling." His hand ran lower, behind other books. "Metal. A hinge."

Two other agents grabbed the shelves and pulled on them. Slowly a section of the wall and shelving rotated outward, revealing an older wall and a rather ordinary door.

Tess glanced at Elise. The girl had gone pale—well, paler than before.

Oh, my God, she mouthed, the words inaudible.

An agent carefully tested the doorknob. "Locked."

One of his associates produced a set of lockpicks and got to work.

"Kent and Garcia, you're first through the door," Michaelson said.

They nodded, weapons drawn.

It took less than a minute for the lock to be defeated. "Got it," the agent said, holding the doorknob so the latch would not automatically reengage.

Kent and Garcia flanked the door. Tess moved Elise back, out of the line of fire.

If Faust was in there, and if he was armed, things might get nasty.

The agents did a silent count, then flung open the door and charged in, sweeping the room.

"Clear!"

Michaelson and the others started to approach. Elise broke free of Tess and pushed past them onto the threshold, and then she was screaming.

"Oh, God, Peter, oh, God!"

Tess pulled her away. The girl collapsed on the floor, still screaming. One of the uniformed cops knelt by her. Tess turned and looked into the room.

She saw what had made Elise scream. In an open cabinet, row upon row of jars, each holding a human hand marked with the *wolfsangel.*

Across the room, the only other item of furniture. A mattress and headboard, and chained to the headboard—a girl. Naked, gagged, a leather strap twisted around her neck.

But alive.

She was kicking at the mattress, struggling against the manacles, her eyes wild.

Garcia fumbled with the gag, trying to remove it, while Kent applied a handcuff key to her shackles.

Then she was free. Instantly she clambered off the mattress, and her hands were tugging at the strap, work-

ing at the knot until it unraveled, then tearing the strap
loose and casting it into a far corner, as if it were a
snake that had nearly bitten her. That done, she
crouched down, hugging herself and shivering, her teeth
actually clacking as if with cold.

"We need a blanket," someone yelled. "She may be
going into shock."

Tess thought the girl might be less panicky in the presence of a woman. She approached her. "It's all right
now, Jennifer. It's all right."

She was sure the girl was Jennifer Gaitlin, though she
was scrawnier than her photo, and her hair was an un-
washed, matted pile.

The girl responded to her name. She looked up.

"Gonna kill me." Her voice was a raw croak.
"Said . . . couldn't wait any longer."

"It's all right," Tess said again.

"He left me. Left me for a long time. With that . . .
that *thing* 'round my neck . . ." Her fingers crawled over
the purplish blotches bruising her throat, and Tess saw
the seared insignia on the back of her left hand. "But
he came back. Couldn't wait any longer, he said." She
stared into space. "Had on pajamas . . . but he couldn't
sleep. . . ." She blinked rapidly. "Is it night? Is it the
middle of the night?"

"Yes, it is." Tess patted Jennifer's shoulder, but the
girl jerked away. Someone arrived with a blanket and
draped it over her.

"Where is he now?" Michaelson asked, his voice surprisingly gentle. "Jennifer, where did he go?"

"Don't know. Buzzing noise. Over there."

Tess saw a speaker in the wall, like an intercom panel,
but without a transmitter button. Faust had rigged up a
system so he could know when he had company.

"That was when we arrived," Michaelson said. "He
must have known something was up if he had company
at three A.M." He looked at the others. "It's obvious

he's running. Check with Hanson out front, make sure he's okay."

One of the agents left to comply.

Tess met Jennifer's gaze. "What did he do when he heard the buzzer?"

"Opened the door. Listened. Voices. I couldn't hear much. But I knew . . . I knew there was someone else. . . ."

"Someone else in the house?" Tess prompted.

"In the world. Someone else in the world . . . Tried to make noise so they could hear, but . . ." Her hands dropped in a gesture of defeat.

"And then he left?"

"First he went to the cabinet. Took something." A strong shudder racked her body. "Knife."

"A knife. But no gun? Did you see a gun?"

"Nuh-uh." She was watching the memory with horrified eyes. "Thought he was gonna cut me. Finish things. But it was like . . . like he forgot about me. He left and closed the door. He'll come back, though."

"No," Tess soothed.

The agent who'd checked with Hanson reported that everything was quiet in the front yard. "I told him to keep an eye on the gate. With the high perimeter fence around this complex, the gate is Faust's only way out."

"Then he's somewhere in the house or on the grounds," Michaelson said. "We need to pair up, fan out, conduct a search."

"We can use a K-Nine unit," a patrolman suggested, meaning a trained search dog. Tess wondered if he was just looking for a pretext not to search for Faust on his own.

"We may have to," Michaelson said. "But first we check the area ourselves. We do it now, before he finds an exit." He glanced at Jennifer, then at Garcia. "Have we called an RA?"

Garcia nodded. "They're on their way."

"We'll search the house and grounds. Not you, Tess. I want you back at the field office, coordinating activities from there."

She wasn't sure she'd heard correctly. She drew Michaelson aside. "Coordinating activities? This isn't even my turf."

"You'll have the authority you need to get the job done."

"Wouldn't it make more sense—"

"It will make sense to do what I say. I'm running this show."

She thought about arguing her case, then realized it was pointless. She knew his real intentions. Michaelson wanted her off the scene and out of the way, safely hidden in the field office, so that when Faust was caught and the media showed up, she wouldn't be around to capture the limelight. Really, she couldn't blame him. Her previous exploits in L.A. had made her a magnet for the local TV news cameras. The last thing the Nose wanted was someone stealing his glory.

"All right," she said. "But I need a vehicle."

Michaelson handed her a set of car keys. "Take mine."

Tess was about to leave when Garcia stopped her. "Let me radio Hanson and tell him you're coming out. We don't want to take him by surprise."

It was a good idea. With Faust on the loose, everybody was jumpy. Tess wasn't too keen on being taken out by friendly fire.

She waited until Garcia had given Hanson a heads-up. As she was leaving the rear hallway, she saw Elise staring at her with red-rimmed eyes.

"Don't let them hurt Peter," Elise said. "Okay?"

Tess stiffened. "You saw what he did to that girl."

"Yes . . . I saw . . ."

"And you *still* care what happens to him?"

"He's not a bad person."

Tess resisted the urge to grab her by her thin shoulders and shake her. "How can you say that? How can you *possibly* say it?"

"He has a problem, that's all. He just needs somebody who . . . who understands him. He needs help."

"Miss Vangarten, with all due respect, you're the one who needs help."

Tess walked away, not looking back. She didn't want to hate Elise, but somehow she couldn't help it.

As she descended the front steps, she saw the distant figure of Agent Hanson, a shadow among the eucalyptus trees edging the far end of the driveway. She waved to him, and he lifted an arm in reply.

Michaelson's sedan was first in the line of cars. She unlocked the door on the driver's side, still thinking of Elise and of women like her, women who wrote love letters to serial killers in prison, women who stayed married to men who beat them, women who offered themselves up as objects of abuse, even as objects of sacrifice. They all said the same thing—that they could change the guy, fix him, reform him by bestowing the loving kindness he needed. Some kind of rescue fantasy mixed up with a masochistic fascination with the dark side of human nature. They liked the bad boys, the villains. They all wanted to play Little Red Riding Hood to some brooding Big Bad Wolf.

The thought of the wolf lurking in the forest for Little Red made her think, unaccountably, of Hanson among the trees. She glanced in his direction again, but he was gone.

Must have changed his position. Where he'd been standing hadn't afforded him a very good view of the driveway or the gate. The trees screened most of the area from his sight. Of course, they had concealed him, as well. She had hardly seen him. If she hadn't known he was stationed here, she might have thought he was—

Faust.

It struck her like a slap—the simple, obvious truth of it. She hadn't seen Hanson at all. The dark figure who had returned her wave . . .

She grabbed for the SIG Sauer in her side pocket.

And a hand seized her wrist, steel at her throat, a breathy voice in her ear.

"Tess McCallum. How thoughtful of you to arrange my ride."

To Raven it remained a dream. She had been in the little hidden room so long that she could barely believe in a world outside. Even when the ambulance came and the paramedics were lifting her onto the stretcher, she still expected to blink and find herself shackled to the headboard with the strap squeezing her neck.

The man named Michaelson had stayed with her, awaiting the ambulance. As the attendants started to leave, he asked which hospital they were headed to.

"Cedars-Sinai," one of the pair said.

"I want one of my men to ride with her. She's not to be left unprotected until her assailant is caught."

"The guy's still at large?"

"We believe he's somewhere on the grounds."

"Better shut the front gate, then," the other paramedic said.

"Wait a minute. The gate is open?"

"How'd you think we got in?"

"I stationed a man out front. I assumed he opened up for you."

"We didn't see anybody."

"Shit." Michaelson was fumbling with the controls on his radio when another man in a suit entered the room. "Sir, we have a situation."

"I know. We need to make contact with Hanson."

"He just called in. Said he was coldcocked from behind. One of the Bureau cars is missing. Your car, he thinks, though he still sounds a little woozy."

"Where's McCallum?"

"He hasn't seen her. He got KO'd right after he was told to expect her."

"Send everybody to the front yard. I want an immediate grid search. You two stay here," he added, speaking to the paramedics. "I don't want you out there until we're sure the area is clear."

"Who the hell *is* this guy, anyway?" the first paramedic asked.

"He's Peter Faust," Michaelson said, leaving.

Raven had never heard the name. It meant nothing to her. She was almost disappointed that her captor's name was so ordinary. She would never have thought of him as Peter. Peter was a saint's name. Wasn't it?

She lay on the stretcher thinking of nothing. Outside there were shouts and footsteps and the distant crackle of radio static. After a long time, a cop in uniform came into the room to tell the paramedics it was safe to leave. They asked if the missing woman, McCallum, had been found.

"We didn't find anything. He's got her. He took her alive, probably. Though she may not be alive for long."

They carried the stretcher through the house. It was much larger and nicer than Raven had guessed. A mansion. She found it outrageously unfair that this man Peter Faust should live in a house like this.

As they brought her outdoors, she felt the breeze on her skin for the first time in days. She saw a few stars overhead, glittering feebly through the heavy urban air. She saw trees.

That was when she knew it wasn't a dream. Even in a dream she could not have imagined seeing stars and trees again.

Michaelson was consulting with the others, saying loudly, "How should I know? Hostage. Plaything. He met her once before. She assisted on the Roberta Kessler case. He may feel he has a score to settle. Who the hell—"

He saw her and stopped talking. He left the group

and walked alongside the stretcher as it was borne to the waiting ambulance.

"You'll be okay, Jennifer," he promised. "And you'll be protected the entire time."

"The woman he took," she said in the hoarse whisper that sounded nothing like her voice. "Was she the one who talked to me?"

"Yes."

"She's . . . she's nice."

"Agent McCallum is the reason we're here," he said quietly. "The reason we rescued you."

"So . . . who's going to rescue *her*?"

Michaelson had no answer.

46

Abby didn't know how long she stayed with Wyatt, holding his hand in silence. She only knew that at a certain point she couldn't be with him anymore. Couldn't be in the hospital. Couldn't deal with it, any of it.

Somehow she remembered the number of the parking space where the feds had left her car. She slipped behind the wheel, thinking that the last time she'd driven the Miata, Wyatt had been alive.

Was that how it was going to be from now on? Was every daily activity, no matter how routine, going to spark some painful memory? And how was she going to handle that? How would she keep herself from going insane?

Maybe she was insane already. Maybe she'd snapped when Wyatt was shot, or when she learned he was gone. It was possible. Only a crazy person would be having the thoughts that had been running through her head.

Thoughts of killing Tess.

She keyed the ignition and drove out of the garage, going nowhere, just needing to put distance between herself and the place where Wyatt had died.

She wouldn't really do it, of course. Go after Tess. Hunt her down and take her out. She didn't honestly want Tess dead.

Did she?

That was the thing. She wasn't sure. She could imagine herself doing it. She could see herself putting the gun to Tess's head, could feel the squeeze of her finger on the trigger, could hear the gunshot and the soft splash of brains.

One bullet. That was all it would take. A life for a life.

Tess had ignored her phone call. Tess had worked on Wyatt and coerced and manipulated him into arranging the rendezvous. Tess was responsible for the dead body under the sheet.

A few pounds of pressure—that's all it would take to pull the trigger.

Abby glanced at her face in the rearview mirror. Her eyes did not look crazy. Except that they didn't blink. Didn't blink at all.

She didn't know if she had lost her mind or not. She might be having a psychotic break.

Or maybe she had never been so sane. Had never seen things so clearly.

Ever since Tess had come into her life, things had gone wrong. She'd been arrested twice and could have gone away on a murder rap each time. Her anonymity had been compromised; the FBI had known all about her since the Medea case.

Now she'd lost Wyatt. She'd lost everything. Why shouldn't Tess lose, too? Why should she always be the hero, the savior cheered by the public, while Abby vanished into shadows? Tess coasted from triumph to triumph and left Abby with the broken pieces of a ruined life.

She ought to pay. She *had* to pay.

At the very least, she had to know that Wyatt was dead. Had to hear it, right now.

As she switched from the 210 Freeway to the 118, she removed her cell phone from her purse. She punched in the number of Tess's cell from memory. The phone rang three times. She began to worry she would be transferred to voice mail. That wasn't what she wanted. She wanted to speak to Tess. She wanted—

On the fourth ring, the call was answered.

"Yes?" a voice said. A man's voice, edged with a German accent.

She couldn't quite believe it, couldn't understand. *"Faust?"*

"Miss Sinclair. This is rather a surprise, though a welcome one, I hasten to add."

"What the hell are you doing with Tess's phone?"

She heard him chuckle. "You might more intelligently inquire what I am doing with Tess herself. Her phone is about to be destroyed, to ensure that its signal cannot be traced. The destruction of Agent McCallum will follow shortly thereafter."

Abby felt everything drop away—hatred, grief, confusion, all of it—and there was only a sudden stillness inside her. "What's going on, Faust?"

"It appears I am on the run. But I do have company. Regrettably, your friend cannot come to the phone. She is, may you pardon the expression, rather tied up at the moment."

"She's not my friend."

"I would have guessed otherwise. You believed she had recommended your services to me. And now you are calling her cell phone."

"It wasn't a friendly call."

"No matter. Whatever the particulars of your relationship, you will not have to concern yourself with it any longer. You will never see her alive again."

Which was what she'd wanted. Tess, dead. And it was better this way, with Faust as the killer. He would take his time with her, make her suffer. As Emily Wallace had suffered.

She thought of Emily, her mutilated body displayed in the photo section of Faust's memoirs.

Tess could end up like that. Cut apart.

It's what she deserves, a voice in her head whispered, cruelly jubilant.

But that was wrong. Tess didn't deserve this. No one did.

And she couldn't let it happen. Couldn't let Tess die. It wasn't an option. Had never been an option.

"Are you there?" Faust asked.

She realized she had been silent for a long moment. "What've you got against Tess, anyway?"

"She has exposed me. My secret career has been found out."

"What career?"

"Killing women. Do you remember my telling you that death is art? I would be a poor artist indeed were I satisfied with only one masterwork."

So there had been others. Other Emily Wallaces. "How many have you done?"

"Twelve in all. Tonight would have made thirteen. Still, Agent McCallum will substitute nicely. I only regret you cannot join us. I would like to arrange, how do you say, payback for your maltreatment of Elise."

"I didn't hurt her."

"You scared her. And she is a delicate thing."

"Okay, then. You're gunning for revenge? Just give me an address. I'll go mano a mano with you."

"It would be most enjoyable," he said in a wistful tone. "Sad to say, it is not to be. You would lead the authorities straight to me."

"No, I wouldn't, Faust. Right now I'd like a shot at you all by myself."

"Would you?"

"Damn straight. I'm in a nasty mood. A mood for . . . tasting blood."

He caught the reference. She almost heard him smile. "You know my book. How flattering. I might almost believe you. But, of course, you are a master deceiver, and I cannot take the chance. You have betrayed my trust once already."

"The police and the feds will be hunting you. They'll track you down without any help from me."

"I do not think so. I need lie low for only a short

time. Procedures have been set in motion to ensure my safe delivery from the arms of the law."

"What procedures?"

"You cannot possibly expect an answer to this question. Now I really must go. Tess grows restless, as do I."

She needed to keep him on the line. "It's no use, Faust. There's no place you can hide in this city."

"Then find me, Abby Sinclair. Find me if you can."

Click. The call was over. She redialed, frustrated, but there was no answer. Probably he'd destroyed the phone, as he'd promised.

From background noise and the varying quality of the transmission, she was sure he'd been on the move. Driving someplace—a hideaway where no one would seek him out, at least for the next few hours.

Café Eden? It would be closed for the night. He could sneak inside, hole up there.

Too obvious, maybe. He was a regular. But he might be counting on the police and feds not to know that. And maybe they didn't. Brody knew, but he'd been working solo, and he was dead. Hauser might know, but no one would be talking to him. And Elise . . . Elise would protect Faust. She would say nothing.

He could be inside the café. It was possible. An idea, anyway. A chance.

At least now she wasn't driving aimlessly anymore. And at this time of night, Hollywood would be only minutes away.

47

Faust kept driving even as he methodically smashed Tess McCallum's cell phone to pieces against the dashboard.

He had discovered the phone in her pocket after striking her unconscious with the haft of his knife. Then he had parked at a strip mall and placed a quick local call from a pay phone, using coins pilfered from the sedan's glove compartment. The mall shops were closed, and no one was around—a good thing, since his robe, silk pajamas, and bedroom slippers would draw stares even in Los Angeles.

The call was the first and most critical step in preserving his freedom. The use of a public telephone ensured that it could never be traced to him.

When he returned to the car, Tess McCallum was beginning to stir. He pulled off the belt of his robe and cut it in two. The longer piece was wound around her wrists in her lap, while the shorter piece, knotted at the back of her head, made a serviceable gag.

The phone started ringing only moments after he had resumed driving. He answered it, expecting to hear from someone from the FBI. Instead it was Abby Sinclair's voice on the line. He almost wished he could have arranged a meeting with her. What she had done to Elise was unforgivable. But he had more urgent priorities.

Beside him, Tess was now squirming in her seat. She had regained consciousness during the phone call and had been restless ever since.

"Quiet yourself," he said. "I would not want to render

you unconscious a second time. A repeat blow might pose a serious risk of cerebral hemorrhage."

She did not appear to appreciate his advice, but she did settle down a bit.

"Much better." He smiled. "It is good to know that you can be reasonable."

He guided the car through empty streets. The city was asleep, and only nocturnal creatures like himself were on the prowl.

"You cheated me of Raven," he said in a gentle conversational tone. "I had completed all my preparations. I had broken her spirit. That is what I do, you see. Anyone can kill the body. I kill the will to live. Or perhaps it is truer to say that I allow it to die of attrition over many days. The young typically have more of a will to live and thus pose more of a challenge. You are not so very young anymore, are you? Yet you do wish to live. You wish, no doubt, to add me to your own roster of victims, to place my name beside those of Mobius and the Rain Man and the long-forgotten drug dealer in Miami. You will not have the opportunity to do so."

He found the familiar street and pulled into a rear alley. The FBI car would be safely out of sight here. It might be spotted by a cruising patrol car, but this was a risk he had to accept. He would need the car soon. In less than an hour he would be on the move again.

But then he would be alone. Tess McCallum's ride— and her life—ended here.

He escorted her out of the car and down the alley to a rear door. He knew the combination to disarm the security system. And in the cabinet in his secret room he had kept a spare key set, which he had taken along with the knife. One of the keys on the ring opened the door.

"Inside," he said, switching on the pocket flashlight he had removed from her coat.

She entered, and he followed, closing the door behind him. It clicked shut, locking automatically. He could not rearm the alarm system, or their own movements would set off the motion detectors. But it was all right.

The Unblinking I would be perfectly safe while he was here. He was not going to steal anything. He was a partial owner of the art gallery, after all.

"You do not know this place," he said as he walked Tess McCallum to the front of the building, the flashlight's narrow funnel of light bobbing ahead of them. "I know it well. It is appropriate that I will kill you here."

He looked for a reaction from her. In the dim glow of the flashlight he could see no flicker of expression. Her eyes were wide and dull. Perhaps he had struck her harder than he had thought.

"Although I could not kill Raven," he said, "I did leave my mark on her." He arrived at the front desk in the foyer, where the master control switches were located. "And I will do the same to you." One set of switches for the track lighting, another for the minispots focused on the holograms. "In your case, as I lack a branding iron, I will carve the *wolfsangel* into your flesh."

Leaving the room lights off, he flipped the second set of switches. In the darkness a bevy of small, faint spotlights blinked on, and the holograms came to life, smudges of color glowing in the adjacent exhibit room and in more distant rooms beyond.

"Images of death," he said. "Your body will be found among them, Tess. Another work of art."

The blow to her head had left Tess spacey and uncoordinated for a while, but slowly her strength had returned. Getting out of the car and moving about had helped. She could focus her eyes again, and her fingers responded when she willed them to flex.

She tried not to let him see any change in her. He had to think she was helpless.

But she was never helpless. Never.

Faust was not experienced in physical confrontations.

He was an intellectual, whose victims had been chosen for their inability to fight back. Yes, her hands were tied in front of her, but she could still use them. All she needed was a weapon.

The telephone on the desk. A large, rectangular office model with multiple lines and a built-in answering machine and speaker.

She took a slow, sliding step closer to the desk. Faust, preoccupied by the switches, didn't notice. She lifted her hands, taking care to avert her body from the spill of the flashlight's beam.

Elsewhere in the building ceiling lights came on, and bright colors leaped out of the dark. She ignored them, staying focused on the phone.

He looked up, looked past her, said something about art and death.

She wasn't listening. It didn't matter what he said.

All that mattered was that he was within arm's reach, and distracted. Vulnerable.

Now.

She seized the phone and swung it up in a powerful arc, tearing out the cord. He turned, not fast enough, and the corner of the metal box caught him under the chin and whipped his head back. She heard the clack of his jaws and knew she'd hurt him. She stepped forward and delivered a smashing downswing, aiming for a knockout blow, but he jerked to one side, the sharp edge of the speaker raking his cheek.

Then the phone was in his hands. He wrested it away and threw it aside. Her flashlight was rolling on the desk where he'd dropped it. She grabbed for it, thinking that it, too, could be a weapon, but already he had her hands in his, and he was staring at her as blood trickled down his face.

He made a gasping noise, almost like a lover's sigh, and thrust her backward, slamming her into the wall, and then the knife was in his hand and its blade was arrowed at her face.

"Now *there* is the Tess McCallum I expected. I did not think you would remain passive. Nor did I want you to."

He pressed the knife closer, the needle-sharp tip almost touching her left eye. With one flick of his wrist he could insert the knifepoint in her eyeball.

"I could do it, Tess," he whispered. "Pop your eye like a grape."

But he didn't. The knife withdrew.

"I do not wish to have you blinded. I wish for you to *see* what I will do to you. To see the spectacle I will make of your bare body."

He seized her by the hair with one hand, the knife now teasing her neck, and hustled her through the partitioned rooms, past the glowing paintings—no, not paintings, but something else, some kind of luminous art, like sculptures in neon. He brought her to a corner, and together they slipped around the bend into a still darker room, where skulls floated in the dark.

Halfway inside the room, he threw her down on the floor. She stared up at him, at the knife, at the jack-o'-lantern faces around her.

It was a dream. She'd been right—he *was* a demon, and this was hell.

"You fear me, Tess McCallum. I sensed it in our meeting."

He was smiling. She wanted fiercely to remove that smile from his mouth.

"And you fear this, as well." He rotated the knife in his grip. The long blade flashed, catching the light of one of the minispots in the ceiling. "As you should. It is an authentic knife once used by an officer of the SS. See the finely detailed oak leaf on the handle. See the engraving in the stainless steel blade. *'Alles for Deutschland'*, it reads."

She thought of Hitler with his lashless blue eyes and hypnotizing gaze. Hitler in his bunker with Eva Braun, the two of them playing out the death dance of a suicide pact.

"This blade will do terrible things to you, Tess. The Chinese had a method of execution called the death of a thousand cuts. I may not have time for one thousand, but I believe I can manage one hundred cuts before the last of your lifeblood drains away. I wish to see you grow weak before me, weak from pain and loss of blood."

Like his victims, she thought. He was accelerating the process that normally dragged on for days of limited food and water.

"You will try to scream, but the gag has been knotted tight. Your voice will die in your throat. You will try to beg, but no words will reach me. And when I am done, I will peel the flesh from your face and leave you grinning, like these happy ones."

His circling arm took in the skulls, their teeth bared in ageless smiles.

"Now," he said, "let us begin."

He knelt by her. He pushed her back, prone on the floor, and took hold of her bound hands. She twisted her wrists, but the belt of the robe had been tied too expertly to work free. And suddenly she thought of Abby with her wrists restrained by flex-cuffs, facing a man who intended to make her suffer before she died. This was just like that, no different—except Abby hadn't been in a room full of floating skulls.

"I often said I was an artist. Now I will prove it. Of course, it was necessary for me to downplay the point, to make light of it, even to deny it. But that was merely for my own protection. I had secrets to keep. But you and I, Tess—we will have no secrets between us, will we?"

She didn't know what he was talking about. She thought perhaps he had lost what remained of his sanity.

"You are thinking I am crazy," he said, as if reading her mind. "Wrong. I am fulfilling my destiny."

The knife flashed. A hot wire of pain shot through the back of her left hand.

"I was born to hate. In my heaven there is no God, only power and the will to power."

Another sizzling arc of pain. He was slicing her hand. Cutting a zigzag pattern. The *wolfsangel.*

"Joy is the conquest of weakness. I am building a more joyful world, culling the herd, disposing of the feeble. You see, I do believe in something larger than myself."

A third cut. Her fingers going numb. Wetness on her skin. Blood.

"I believe in a world of men like me. And with every book I sell, every autograph I sign, I bring us that much closer to that world. It is nearly upon us, Tess. Sadly, you will not live to see it."

He leaned closer. The expression on his face was one she had never seen before on any human being: a look of feral enjoyment, the grin of a hyena on a carcass.

"And neither will Joshua Green."

The words pulled all the breath out of her. She felt herself deflate, go limp. She was dizzy. . . .

Another kiss of the blade on her hand. Pain brought her back from the edge of unconsciousness. She blinked, rallied.

"Oh, yes." There was humor in his voice. "I know about your secret paramour."

But he couldn't. It wasn't possible. Unless he really was the devil, really did possess occult powers . . .

She could almost believe it. She could almost believe that this man with his jackal smile in a gallery of skulls was something fiendish, inhuman.

Blood soaking the belt of his robe now, the belt that tied her wrists. But not enough blood, not for him. He cut again, digging deeper, drawing a groan from her as she shut her eyes against the pain.

"Hauser knew," he said calmly. "I was always interested in you, always pressing him for details and gossip in our phone conversations. He no doubt saw it as a harmless way to lead me on and gain my trust. Or perhaps he relished giving away your secrets for reasons of his own. I had the impression he disliked you most heartily."

Hauser. So that was all it was. Nothing supernatural or magical. Just a man with a grudge, who had dug up dirt on her and passed it around.

And Faust . . . he was no devil, only a sick man, a psychopath, a crazy son of a bitch who had issues with women, with power. . . .

And who had a knife. It worked its way down the back of her hand, slicing lightly this time, its touch almost a caress.

"He learned somehow of your illicit relationship with Mr. Green. He found it most unprofessional. Now you and Joshua will pay for your transgressions. You are paying now. Joshua will pay later."

She thought of Paul Voorhees, killed by Mobius. And now Josh . . .

It couldn't happen again. Couldn't happen twice.

She tried to say something, to communicate, but of course the gag made speech impossible. All that came through were muffled grunts, animal sounds.

He balanced the knifepoint on her hand and spun it like a compass. He was smiling.

"I want you to understand how thoroughly I will destroy your life, Tess. Not only will I murder you, but I will kill the one you love. I can bide my time. I can practice patience. A month from now, or a year . . ."

From outside the exhibit room, a noise like the crunch of safety glass.

Faust looked up, his breath held. He listened.

"No." His voice was very soft. "She could not be here. Could not possibly . . ."

Abby, he meant. Tess had heard his end of the phone conversation. But he was right. Abby couldn't be here.

Could she?

He stood. For the moment he had forgotten her, just as he had forgotten Raven when his own survival was at stake. He left the room without a sound.

She had to take off the gag. Had to shout a warning. But Faust had tied it tight, just as he'd said, and her left hand was numb, the fingers all but useless, slick with blood, drained of strength.

She struggled with the knot. If he had left the knife she could have cut herself free, but he had taken it, of course.

Taken it—and the gun.

Her gun.

48

Faust slipped along one wall of the gallery until he reached the nearest hologram, a large wall-mounted display, very bright in the surrounding darkness. The image projected two feet into space, and pinned behind it he was invisible, like his countryman the Red Baron diving out of the sun.

From this position of concealment he could scan the gallery with no risk of being seen.

The noise might have meant nothing, but he was too cautious to rely on assumptions. It was perhaps not out of the question that Sinclair had guessed where he would go. He could not imagine how. Although she had been to the gallery, she had no reason to connect it with him, and she could not know that he was an owner. He had kept that fact well hidden in a maze of dummy corporations and offshore accounts.

No, she could not—could *not*—be here.

Yet there she was.

He saw her enter this room, the last room before the skulls gallery. She moved slowly in the dark, her gun leading her.

Somehow she had divined his whereabouts. She was smart, this one. Intuitive. A worthy adversary.

He lifted Tess McCallum's gun. He was no marksman, but he had sufficient experience with firearms to know his limits and his capabilities. From this distance, aiming at a stationary target, he would not miss.

One round to the head. She would never even know
what happened.

He only needed her to come a little nearer. When she
passed the first hologram in the room, the glow would
illumine her face, and he would shoot.

Abby had been en route to Café Eden when a snatch
of her conversation with Faust had come back to her.

Do you remember my telling you that death is art?

Why use that metaphor again? It had seemed to come
out of nowhere. And statements that arose with seeming
irrelevance were often the most meaningful clues to the
speaker's state of mind.

She recalled what Elise had told her about the art
gallery. Faust, she'd said, was a part owner, but he kept
his ownership secret.

An owner would have a key. Would know the alarm
system code. And if his financial involvement with the
gallery was unknown, no one would look for him there.

Or maybe she was overthinking it, and the coffee shop
was still the better bet. She had hesitated, considering
both options, knowing that time was of the essence. Finally she went with her gut, which rarely failed her. Her
gut said the Unblinking I was the place to look.

And it had been right. She'd found an FBI sedan
stashed in the alley behind the gallery. Faust was in the
building. Tess must be with him, unless he'd disposed of
her already.

She doubted it. He would want to take his time.

Despite her aversion to authority, she was momen-
tarily tempted to call Michaelson and let his shock
troops handle the situation. It would make more sense.
Going in alone was the kind of boneheaded, reckless
stunt she was ordinarily smart enough to forgo.

Not tonight, though. Tonight Wyatt was dead, and she
wanted blood.

She spent less than a minute picking the lock on the
gallery's back door. She wasn't worried about the alarm

system. Faust couldn't move around inside if the motion sensors were on.

She eased open the door to face a tunnel of darkness. Faust had left the lights off. That was okay. She was nocturnal. She could hunt in the dark.

She entered, her .38 already drawn—the .38 that killed Brody.

Soon it would kill again.

Down a black hallway. Ahead, a glimmer of ambient light. She went toward it and found herself in the foyer, where a penlight, its beam slicing the darkness, lay on the front desk. She wondered why Faust had left it there. She picked up the flashlight, turned it off, and stuck it in her pocket.

Beyond the foyer were the exhibition rooms. She remembered the layout from her previous visit. The main body of the building was L-shaped, with most of the exhibit rooms occupying the long arm of the L, and the gallery of skulls taking up the base at the far end.

The ceiling spots had been turned on. Piers Hoagland's ghastly holograms hovered against walls and pylons.

She rounded the desk and moved forward. Something crunched under her foot. The noise seemed loud in the stillness. She retreated, ducking low, and could just make out a rectangular box on the floor—some sort of telephone console, it looked like. She'd stepped on it and broken the speaker.

What the hell it was doing there, she had no idea. Evidence of a struggle, presumably. The more important question was whether Faust had heard the noise.

She listened. She heard nothing. No movement, no footsteps.

Moving away from the desk, she crept along the wall into the first exhibit room. As she approached the first hologram, she averted her face and half shut her eyes. Didn't want to lose her night vision by staring into the light.

She reached a partition and crabbed along it to the

doorway to the next room. More holograms in there, some mounted on pedestals or displayed on pylons. The garbage dump with the flash image of a skeleton's hand. Roadkill. A nest of dead wasps. In a shoe box, the remains of a cat.

Death all around. And more death to come.

She passed through two more rooms. Faust must be in the back, with the skulls. She had one more room to cover before she got there.

She entered carefully, nearing the first of several holograms on the wall. It was beginning to look like this would be easy. She could burst in on Faust and take him out before he had a chance to return fire. She could—

"*Abby!*" Tess's shout, echoing in the dark. "He knows you're here!"

Instinct took over. She pushed herself away from the wall, and in the same instant the hologram where she had been standing shattered and winked out, and a gunshot rang in the stillness.

She looked up in time to see the muzzle flash. Then she was diving to the floor in a snap-roll that carried her behind one of the pylons. She snapped off two rounds in the shooter's direction, then plunged sideways, behind a second pylon, changing her position so Faust couldn't shoot back.

Her ears were chiming, her night vision compromised by the purplish afterimages of the muzzle flares. She could hardly hear or see, and in the blackness Faust could be anywhere.

Gun battle at close quarters in near total darkness. Not a good situation. She could hope that the handgun reports would attract the attention of passersby, who would summon the police—but at five A.M. there weren't likely to be any passersby, and police response time in West Hollywood had to be at least seven minutes.

She didn't have seven minutes. These things never lasted that long.

Two options, then. She could stay hidden and let Faust

wear himself out searching for her. There was a good chance he wouldn't find her. He might even flee.

Or she could take the offensive, go after him. A less intelligent strategy. In a shoot-out, the mobile and aggressive party was always more vulnerable.

But Tess altered the equation. Faust could retreat to the skull room and use her as a hostage or a human shield. Which meant sitting back and waiting wasn't a viable plan. She had to intercept him, if possible.

She scrambled out from behind the pylon and made her way to the closest wall, staying well clear of the holograms and their telltale glow.

The clamor in her ears was dying down. Her vision wasn't as badly impaired as before. She scanned the room, looking for movement. She saw only the holographic images of decay, each one shimmering with its sickly monochromatic glow. The minispotlights overhead glowed feebly like distant stars.

And then they were gone.

All the lights, out. The holograms, vanishing like ghosts.

Faust had reached the master controls and darkened the gallery. She didn't know where the controls were. She hadn't seen them on her prior visit. They could be anywhere, and so Faust could be anywhere, and now with the spotlights dark and the windows blacked out, there was no light at all.

She couldn't search for him in total darkness. She wouldn't know where he was, even if he was a foot away.

All she could do was crouch by a corner of the exhibit room, still her breath, and listen.

Creak of floorboards.

From where? She wasn't sure.

Faintly, a soft metallic whine. Hinges. A door, opening.

There were only two doors—the rear door by which she'd entered, and the front door in the foyer. Both too far away.

No, wrong, there was a third. The door to the basement.

A click—the door had shut.

He had retreated into the basement. She was almost certain of it.

Unless it was a ruse. He might want her to think he'd left this floor, so she would get careless and show herself.

She crawled along the wall to the nearest doorway. The bend in the L was close by, the room of skulls just beyond.

Could he be waiting for her to go in there? Hoping she would do the obvious thing and make the simple, fatal mistake?

Slowly she stood up. She held the gun in both hands as she pivoted at the hips, sweeping the darkness.

She heard nothing, sensed nothing.

The penlight was still in her pocket. She took it out and held it in her left hand, her arm extended well away from her body, and turned it on.

The pencil-thin beam cut the blackness. If Faust were here, he would fire at the beam, with any luck missing her main body mass.

But no shots were fired. She played the beam around the room and saw only blank walls and the mirrorlike glass panels of the holographic plates.

In one of the plates, movement. A figure, reflected, emerging from the back room.

Abby spun and almost fired, realizing only at the last moment that the figure was Tess.

She lowered the gun.

By now she was convinced Faust was gone. Had he been present he would never have passed up this opportunity to take down both of them at once.

"You okay?" Abby whispered.

Tess was holding one hand with the other. "Hanging in there. He tied me up. Took me a few minutes to get free." She smiled. "I thought you never wanted to see me again."

"I decided one more time wouldn't hurt." She looked closer and saw blood on Tess's left arm. "You're cut."

"It's nothing. Where's Faust?"

Abby heard a low tinkle of breaking glass. It came from below.

"The cellar," Abby said. "He's getting out."

Faust had not wanted to retreat from the field of combat, but he knew he could not best Sinclair in a gunfight. His only chance had been to shut off the overhead lights, then escape into the cellar.

Narrow windows lined the rear cellar wall, looking out on the alley. The windows were protected by the alarm system, but the system was off.

It was easy enough to find a monkey wrench among the janitor's tools, smash one of the windows, sweep away the shards. He hoisted himself up and climbed through.

Sinclair would be after him, of course. She would have heard the shatter of glass.

He thought of crouching in the alley and gunning her down when she emerged from the building, but somehow he knew she would anticipate this maneuver. He could not outwit her in this arena. He must flee. There was no shame in it. He would save himself, and live to fight under more opportune circumstances.

The FBI sedan was blocked in by Sinclair's Miata. That was all right. He smashed the sports car's window with his elbow, unlocked the door, and used his knife to pry open the nest of wires under the steering column. It took him only seconds to hear the motor rev.

When he looked up from behind the wheel, Sinclair was there, already in the alley, McCallum at her side.

He could get them both.

He stamped on the gas pedal and the Miata blew forward, tires screaming. Sinclair turned, saw him, but did not run. She stood with feet planted wide apart, the gun in both hands. He ducked low as the first bullet cracked the windshield, then the second.

He risked a look. She was yards away. Still not fleeing. McCallum still beside her.

He braced for the double thump of impact.

But McCallum was too quick. She grabbed Sinclair and pulled her back, the two of them sprawling onto the asphalt, the car missing them by mere inches.

He half considered throwing the Miata into reverse. The snap of a gunshot from behind made him think better of it.

He accelerated out of the alley, fishtailing onto the street, gunning the motor as he raced away.

They would live, it seemed.

For now.

"Damn," Abby said, lowering the gun. "I *really* wanted to nail that guy."

Tess got up slowly, holding her left hand high to reduce blood loss. "Not long ago you wanted to nail me."

Abby saw that she had wound some fabric around the hand, but it was already soaked through with red. "Who says I still don't? It's not like we're pals again. And by the way, Vic Wyatt is dead."

Tess lowered her head. "I'm sorry."

"Everybody keeps saying that like it's their fault. Oh, wait. In your case, it is."

"I never meant for anything like that to happen. And I want to thank you for coming here. With everything that's gone on, I never thought . . ." Tess looked away. "I just never thought you'd do that."

"Kind of took me by surprise, myself."

"You saved my life."

"I guess you returned the favor a few seconds ago. Would've been kinda ironic if I'd been run down by my own car. For a second there, I wasn't thinking too clearly. Just wanted to keep shooting until I hit him."

"Or until he hit you."

"Yeah, well, that was the downside of my strategy." She stared down the alley toward the street where the Miata had disappeared. "So what do we do now?"

Tess shrugged wearily. "He's gone, Abby."

"You're telling me he gets away? After all this, we just let him go?"

"Give me your phone and I'll call it in. Maybe the police can pick him up. There aren't too many vehicles on the street yet. But I think . . ."

"What?"

"He had some sort of escape plan in mind. Something he had already arranged. He seemed very confident about it."

"Meaning the cops won't catch him."

"Maybe not."

"Damn." Abby thrust her hands into her pockets. "We *have* to do something."

"There's nothing we *can* do."

"Yes, there is. There's always something. *Always*."

"Not this time," Tess said.

Abby didn't answer. She was staring into the night.

49

It was noon when Tess finally got out of the last debriefing at the federal building.

She had spent two hours at Cedars-Sinai Medical Center having the wounds on her left hand cleaned, sutured, and bandaged. Then another five hours in an interview room in the field office, telling and retelling the story of her captivity and escape. She might have taken some small comfort from the thought that Abby was being similarly detained—but before the feds had arrived at the art gallery in response to Tess's phone call, Abby had vanished into the night.

Tess had no idea where she had gone or how she had made tracks without her car. She wasn't at home, that was for sure; Michaelson had agents watching the Wilshire Royal. Not that Abby was in any sort of trouble, but she had to be interviewed, if only to satisfy the ruthless demands of Bureau procedure.

The media knew about the ongoing manhunt for Faust, though Tess's role in the case had not been publicized. A crowd of reporters occupied the lobby of the federal building. Not wanting them to see her, Tess requisitioned a Bureau car and took the elevator directly to the parking garage. A Protective Services employee raised the gate for her, and she drove out of the garage and onto the street.

What she needed was a shower, long and hot, followed by sleep, hours of it. She had been up for more than twenty-four hours, and she wasn't feeling her best. Not looking her best either, she assessed as she glanced at herself in the rearview mirror. Deep circles bruised her eyes, and her face was pale and drawn.

On the other hand, she looked a lot better than she would have if Faust's knife had continued its work on her. She had Abby to thank for saving her. If only she knew where the hell Abby was.

It occurred to her that Abby might have tried calling. Her smashed cell phone had been replaced by an identical unit, programmed with her existing phone number. She'd had the new phone turned off all morning. Any calls would have been shunted to voice mail.

She reviewed her messages as she headed west on Wilshire Boulevard toward the MiraMist Hotel in Santa Monica, her usual destination when in town. There were no calls from Abby, but three from Josh.

She wondered if he'd heard what happened. He wasn't supposed to know. Her abduction remained a closely held secret. Then again, Mark Brody's death had been kept secret too, but he had known about that.

She called his work number and reached him at his desk. She tried to sound casual. "Sorry I didn't get back to you sooner, but this Faust thing has been making us crazy."

"Yeah, I think I may have heard a little something about that." He chuckled. "So how come the big news only happens when you're in L.A.? We could use some of that media attention around here, you know. The Denver field office likes to make headlines, too."

It sounded as though he wasn't in the loop, after all. "There aren't as many crazies in Denver. Besides, I really didn't have much to do with this one."

"No, huh? So you just happened to be there when all this stuff went down?"

"I may have made a minor contribution. But I'm only a bit player this time."

"I noticed Michaelson didn't mention you in his news conference. He was in his element, though, really soaking it up. You sure he wasn't stealing your glory?"

"There's no glory to steal. It's his turf and his case. His people did everything that counts. They deserve the credit."

"Sure, I guess." Josh paused. "I mean, all *you* did was find the secret room where Faust was hiding his current victim . . . then get yourself kidnapped . . . then manage to escape. No big deal."

She shut her eyes. "Cary Palumbo?" she said, remembering his pal in the D.C. office.

"This year I need to send him something really nice for Christmas. So why were you holding out on me?"

"We're trying to keep my involvement low-profile."

"Whose idea was that?"

"Michaelson's."

"And you're letting him get away with it?"

"Yeah, I guess I am. He's been pretty reasonable about . . . well, about a lot of things."

"Am I hearing you right? Have you made peace with the Nose?"

"I wouldn't call it peace. More like a temporary cessation of hostilities."

His tone changed, his jocularity fading. "How bad was it, Tess?"

She glanced at her bandaged hand. Prescription painkillers, antibiotics, and a tetanus shot had minimized the aftereffects. Doctors did not believe there was any permanent damage to nerves or tendons, and did not expect any loss of motor control. There would be a scar, of course. A jagged shape like a lightning bolt—the beginnings of a *wolfsangel*.

"It could have been worse," she said.

"That's not exactly an answer."

"It was bad. Scary. But I'm all right now."

"I heard there was . . . torture."

"He inflicted a few cuts on my left hand. They're healing. That's all."

"I hope we find that cocksucker. I hope—" He pulled in a ragged breath. "Sorry. But I'd like to be alone with him—just for a few minutes."

Tess felt a chill. She knew there was a chance Josh's hope would come true, and not in the way he meant.

"How'd you get away?" he asked.

He didn't know about Abby, it seemed. That part of the story hadn't made its way through the grapevine. "It's complicated. I've related my exploits too many times already."

"Then I'll wait till you get back to hear the details."

"Okay."

He wouldn't hear *all* the details, though. She might or might not tell him about Abby—that was an open question at this point—but she would not tell him about Faust's threat. Not yet, anyway.

So far she had told no one. She had said not a word about it in any of her debriefings. She wasn't sure why she felt the need to remain silent. Perhaps because revealing the threat against Josh would inevitably reveal their relationship.

But there was more to it than that. She didn't want Josh to know that his association with her might have put him in danger. She didn't want to be Typhoid Mary, spreading fear and death to anyone she touched.

For the moment she could afford to stay quiet. Faust presently had higher priorities than going after Josh. With any luck he would be captured before too much time passed.

If not, she would have to speak up. She hoped it wouldn't come to that.

"When you do get back," Josh said, "we ought to do something to celebrate your safe return."

"Have anything specific in mind?"

"We could get married."

She had to tighten her grip on the wheel to avoid steering off the road. "What?"

"Us. Me and you. Husband and wife. To love, honor, and obey. Well, maybe not obey. They don't usually say that anymore."

"Are you making a joke?"

"No. I'm not."

"We can't get married. We can't even let anyone know we're dating. Remember?"

"Because of the wrath of the almighty Bureau?"

"Well . . . yes."

"But don't you get it? That's the whole point. They can't touch you now, Tess. You're the one who took down Peter Faust. You're golden."

"Nobody knows that."

"The Bureau knows it. D.C. knows it. That's all that matters."

She considered this. "Maybe . . ." she said slowly.

"No maybe about it. You've never known how to use your status. You never really capitalized on Mobius or the Rain Man or Medea."

"I never *wanted* to capitalize on any of that."

"I understand. But sometimes you have to play the game. And right now you can cop to any violation of policy, and they can't do a damn thing about it. Tell them you've been taking J. Edgar's skirts out of storage and wearing them to parties. What are they gonna do?"

"Hoover wasn't a cross-dresser. That's an urban legend."

"I think you're missing the bigger picture here." He hesitated. "Unless you're trying to change the subject. In which case I'll drop it. . . ."

"No. Don't drop it. I'm just a little . . . rattled, that's all. I never thought . . . It never occurred to me that the two of us could have a future. *This* kind of future. You know what I mean."

"We can have it. But the window of opportunity won't stay open long. A month from now the shine will start to wear off, and you won't be so golden anymore."

"It's now or never. Is that what you're saying?"

"Not that I'm trying to put you under any pressure."

Tess stopped at a red light. She let herself forget the traffic and the night with Faust and how tired she felt. She let herself just imagine it—no more sneaking around, no more lies, no more doubts. A life together. A real life.

"Tess? You still there?"

She smiled. "You know, when you ask for a lady's hand, it's customary to go down on one knee."

"I'm kneeling. Really."

"Now that's a bad sign."

"What is?"

"Starting off our marriage with an obvious lie."

"Did you say our marriage?"

"Yes, Josh. That's what I said."

Tess was pulling into the parking lot of the MiraMist when her cell phone chirped. Had to be Josh again. Their conversation had ended only moments ago.

"Think of a few more declarations of love you want to recite?" she teased.

"Gee, Tess"—Abby's voice—"I didn't know you cared."

Her mood switched instantly from elation to annoyance. Abby's phone calls had a way of doing that.

"Where the hell have you been?" she asked. "In case you don't know, there are a lot of important people who have questions for you."

"Those important people will get to ask their important questions eventually. Meanwhile, remember the Boiler Room?"

Tess wrinkled her nose. "That greasy spoon in Santa Monica?"

"The spoons aren't greasy, just naturally shiny. Can you meet me there?"

The place was only a few blocks from the hotel. Still, Tess was reluctant. "I was hoping to get some sleep."

"You can sleep when you're dead. Which you already would be, if not for me."

"Is that your subtle way of saying I owe you?"

"I didn't think it was subtle. Fifteen minutes?"

"Right," Tess said with a sigh. Her long, hot shower would have to wait.

50

Tess found Abby in a booth away from the windows. She slipped into the faux-leather bench seat on the opposite side of the table.

"You look like hell," Abby observed.

"You, too."

"We're both operating on zero sleep. Adrenaline can carry a girl only so far. Hungry?"

Tess realized she was. There had been some sort of tasteless breakfast pastries at the field office, but she'd hardly touched them, and she'd had no dinner last night. "As I recall, hamburgers are the house specialty."

"They are. And I already ordered some for both of us."

"Kind of presumptuous of you."

"Tess, by now surely you've learned how cocksure I am. Hey, I like that word—cocksure. Conjures up an interesting mental picture, doesn't it? How's the left paw?"

"Throbbing. I'm due for another dose of painkiller."

"Industrial-strength Tylenol?"

"Something stronger. The hand's okay. I can still move my fingers."

"But can you *give* somebody the finger?"

Tess tried it. The middle finger of her left hand saluted Abby. "Nothing personal," she said.

Abby grinned. "You sure about that?"

"I must say, you seem a lot less stressed than when I last saw you."

"It's a by-product of sleep deprivation. I'm so zoned out, I'm giddy."

The febrile gleam in her eyes seemed to confirm this. "Then I think," Tess said slowly, "you should get some sleep."

"Later. First we talk. Then we eat. Then we sleep."

"All right. Where have you been, anyway?"

"Wyatt's place."

Abby said it so casually that it took Tess a moment to hear, really hear, the words. "Wyatt . . . ?"

"I have a key. And he has—had—a computer with an Internet connection. I do, too, of course, but I figured if I went back to my condo, I'd end up in long, pointless conversations with boring men in suits."

Tess still couldn't get past the idea. "You were in Wyatt's apartment. . . ."

"Last place anyone would look, right?" Abby smiled again. There was something empty in that smile. "I can be a coldhearted bitch when I want to be. I needed a computer, and I got hold of one."

"What did you need it for?"

"Research. But before we get into that, how about giving me an update on the investigation? Dish me some of that inside dirt."

Tess nodded. "First of all, we found your Miata. It was abandoned at the corner of Santa Monica Boulevard and Centinela Avenue, not far from here, actually. It will be returned to you as soon as the crime scene guys are through with it."

Abby waved her hand as if the return of the car was immaterial.

"Faust left my gun in the car, for some reason. Apparently he didn't think he needed it anymore. Which is kind of worrisome, inasmuch as it suggests an awfully high degree of confidence that he won't be found."

"Confidence that so far has proven to be justified," Abby said.

"True. We have no idea where he's gone, but we're

showing his photo at all the major local airports, train and bus stations, rental car agencies, and so forth. He can't get out of town. We're also working the room where he kept his victims. It was a secret room in his house, soundproofed and hidden behind a false wall. He had a cabinet in there filled with mementos—a dozen human hands, each one branded with his insignia. Always the left hand."

Abby's glance flicked to Tess's bandages, then traveled away. "If they haven't deteriorated too badly, you can get fingerprints off them."

"He preserved them in formalin, which is basically a solution of formaldehyde in water. Yes, we can pull prints. In fact, we've identified one victim already. Roberta Kessler, a girl who went missing three years ago." She sighed. "The police knew he was good for that one. They just didn't know where to look. If they'd found the room . . ."

"Faust is smart, Tess. He knows how to play the game."

"Yes." She shook off her regrets. "We found something else in the cabinet. A scrapbook. He liked to keep clippings about missing girls. We expect to be able to match the girls in the news stories to the hands in the jars."

"What else was in the scrapbook?" Abby asked, her eyes narrowing.

Tess frowned. "What makes you think there was anything else?"

"The way you placed your right hand over your left when you mentioned it."

Tess looked down and saw that she had unconsciously covered her wounded hand. "You're good," she said with a smile. "Better than most Bureau interrogators. There *was* something else. There were clippings about me. He was . . . interested in me."

"I know all about that kind of interest. In my line of work, we call it obsession."

"That's what we call it, too. I have to admit, I don't like knowing he's still out there. Faust isn't your ordinary psycho. He's . . ."

"Not just evil," Abby said, finishing for her. "He's Evil with a capital *E*."

This was so close to Tess's way of thinking about Faust that she straightened in her seat. "I guess you could say that."

"I just did. Let's face it, we both have a major beef against this guy. He tried to shoot me and run me over. Not to mention he was kind of rude to me on the phone. Also, I'm not expecting to be paid for my work on his case, which is the kind of thing that really chills my grapefruit."

"They'll find him," Tess said, not quite convinced.

A waitress arrived with two plates piled high with hamburgers and macaroni salad. Two glasses of ice water accompanied the meal.

"Hope water's okay," Abby said. "They don't serve anything stronger, and soda rots your teeth."

"Water is fine."

Tess couldn't have cared less what she had to drink, just so long as she could satisfy the hunger that was now clawing at her insides. She took several greedy bites of the burger before continuing the conversation. "So what was it you wanted to talk about?"

Abby leaned forward in her seat. Her eyes had that feral glint again. "I've been thinking about skulls."

"Skulls?"

"Yeah."

"You *really* do need some rest, Abby."

Abby showed her a fierce stare. "No, I don't. I need to talk about skulls."

"I'm listening."

"Faust is part owner of the Unblinking I. Did you know that?"

"I assumed as much, from his access to the place. The

Bureau is running a check on the gallery's financial records."

"Faust kept his ownership a secret, supposedly because his reputation would be bad for business. But I'm thinking there's another explanation."

"Go on."

"Piers Hoagland, who hails from Faust's native country, has a deal with that gallery. Hoagland specializes in holograms. His artwork was on display last night. You saw it. He specializes in dead things. Rotting carcasses, bones. Skulls."

"Yes . . ."

"Faust's victims were all decapitated. Their skulls have never been found, right? You've got their hands in formalin, but not their heads. Right?"

"That's true."

"Okay. Now where did Hoagland get the skulls he uses in his art? Has anyone ever asked?"

"I don't know," Tess said quietly.

"Suppose he got them from Faust. A cozy little arrangement on their part. Hoagland gets the materials he needs for his work. Faust has the fun of displaying his victims in plain sight. He liked to say that murder was art. This was his chance to be the artist he always wanted to be."

Tess thought about it. "When he had me in the gallery, he told me that death is art. And he said he'd had to publicly downplay that philosophy in order to protect himself. I didn't know what he meant."

"To protect himself from being linked to Hoagland. I think that's the real reason he kept his participation in the gallery a secret. It wasn't about his reputation. It was that he couldn't afford to have anybody looking at Hoagland's skulls too closely."

Tess finished off her burger and wiped her mouth with a napkin. She was astonished at how quickly she'd consumed the meal. "Thanks, Abby. This is helpful. If it pans out, we can get hold of the holograms and identify the victims from dental records."

"What is this, *CSI*? I'm not interested in ID'ing the victims. I'm interested in getting Faust."

"Tell me how."

"If Hoagland was getting human skulls from a man like Faust, he had to know what was up. He's not just a dupe; he's an accomplice. An accessory. And if he was willing to look the other way on the skulls, how else might he have assisted Faust?"

"In his escape? That's what you're thinking?"

Abby nodded. "Hoagland has family money, lots of it. He owns a private jet. A Gulfstream. Transcontinental range."

"Does he?" This was interesting.

"You bet. Faust told me on the phone that he'd done twelve girls in all. They can't all have been local or he would have been caught by now. So I'm assuming he traveled."

"Yes."

"And he left no trail. No airline reservations, for instance."

"How did you know that?"

"Because if he'd left a trail of plane tickets that matched up with his victims' disappearances, you feebs would have arrested him months ago."

"Okay. You're right." Tess frowned. "Don't call us feebs."

"So he wasn't flying commercial. He could've driven, but a man with a busy schedule like his can't afford to be out of touch for extended periods. And he's well known enough that he could have been spotted anywhere along the way. Too risky. So I'm guessing he traveled a different way. He used Hoagland's plane."

"All right . . ."

"If he used it on other occasions, who's to say he didn't use it to get out of town last night? You said my car was ditched at Santa Monica Boulevard and Centinela. Someone else must have picked him up there. From that location it's a straight shot down Centinela to Santa Monica Municipal Airport. Which just happens to be where Hoagland's Gulfstream is stored."

Tess felt a tremor of excitement. "We can check the airport and find out if the plane left early this morning."

"Or you can take a leap of faith and assume I'm right."

"Suppose I do. I'll still have to obtain the flight plan to learn where Faust went."

"No, you won't. I already know."

"Do you?"

"Well, okay. I don't actually *know*. I mean, in the literal sense of being certain beyond any doubt. But I have a pretty strong hunch."

"And what does your hunch tell you?"

"Where does a person go when his whole world is falling apart? I'll tell you where. He goes home."

"Home," Tess echoed.

"Piers Hoagland lives in Manhattan. But he also keeps a small country villa in Paderborn, Germany. If Faust left before dawn, he's probably refueling at some private East Coast airfield right around now. Then it's another eight hours or so to the land of beer and bratwurst. He'll be there tonight."

Tess sat very still. Her hand was throbbing worse than before. "It's possible," she said finally.

"It's more than possible. Hoagland's villa is the perfect place for the world's most wanted fugitive to hide out. Isolated, remote, and it has no obvious link to Peter Faust. Unless someone made the connection between him and Hoagland, nobody would look for him there."

"I'll give the lead to Interpol. If you're right, they'll intercept him when he lands."

Abby pursed her lips. "That's one way to handle it."

"Is there another?"

She drummed her fingers on the table, a slow, staccato

rhythm. "Faust has already been a subject of the German legal system once. They put him in a mental hospital for a couple of years. When he came out, he was a celebrity."

"It'll be different this time. These murders were committed on U.S. soil. The U.S. has an extradition treaty with Germany. They'll hand him over to us."

"We can hope so."

"Are you saying they won't cooperate? In a case this high-profile?"

"The high profile is the problem. Our Mr. Faust has a lot of fans in Germany. And a lot of powerful friends. And you know we'll have to seek the death penalty."

"Yes," Tess said slowly.

"In a capital case, there can be extradition problems. The Europeans don't like giving us one of their citizens when there's a chance he's going to fry. They could keep him there indefinitely while the wheels of justice spin in the mud."

All of this was true, and discouraging. But Tess couldn't see the point of bringing it up. "Well, what choice do we have?" she asked.

"That's the question, Tess." Abby's gaze, hot and steady, drilled into her. "What choice *do* we have?"

"What are you suggesting?"

"I think you know."

And, of course, she did know. She supposed she had known from the moment Abby mentioned the villa in Germany.

"Question is," Abby went on, "are you willing to play it my way for once? And I mean my way, *all* the way."

Tess looked at her hand, scarred with the mark of the wolf, the Werewolf. She thought about Josh, who would be a possible target until Faust was stopped. She thought about Hitler with his lashless blue eyes. Hitler—and devils. Devils in human form.

"I'm in," she said quietly.

Abby reached into her purse and produced a leather

credentials case. She slid it across the table. Tess opened it and saw a passport with her own photo staring back at her, and the name Melissa Ruth Conroy.

When she looked up, Abby was smiling.

51

It took Abby seventeen hours to fly from Los Angeles to London, then from London to Bonn. She spent the flights trying not to think about Wyatt.

Later there would be time for memories. Now she was in the present. She was focused on the job at hand. And she was glad to be traveling, glad to be in motion, with an objective, a purpose. Glad, because she could see too clearly the shape of the days to come—the days and, worse, the nights. The loneliness and the helpless self-accusation and the useless anger. The ever-present grief. It was as if her future was drawn only in shades of gray. As if she'd died along with Vic, only they'd forgotten to bury her.

She met Tess at the baggage claim area for a Lufthansa flight from Frankfurt. They had agreed to take separate flights in order to minimize the chance of being seen together and remembered.

"We need a car," Tess said without preamble.

Abby flashed a set of keys. "Already got one."

The car she'd rented was an Opel Corsa hatchback. It proved surprisingly peppy on the autobahn, hitting 180 kilometers per hour without strain.

She and Tess said little during the drive. There was nothing to say.

Paderborn lay in the northeast corner of the province of Westphalia, on the threshold of a primeval forest dominated by Schloss Wewelsburg, a sixteenth-century castle perched on a limestone cliff. The hotel Abby had selected was in nearby Büren, overlooking a lake. At the front desk she asked if an express delivery package had arrived for her. It had. She accepted it with a smile, wondering what the desk clerk would think if he knew its contents.

They deposited their luggage in their adjoining rooms, along with the unopened package, then returned to the Opel and scouted Hoagland's villa. It occupied a remote spot in the forested hills, crouching at the foot of a slope that ascended to a tree-lined ridge. They did a quick drive-by, not daring to linger on the road.

The front door was shut, the windows closed. There was no vehicle parked outside, although there might have been one in the small detached garage.

"Think he's in there?" Tess asked when they'd passed the villa.

"No way to tell. But it's nice and isolated. Easy enough to do some B and E once it gets dark."

"Unless there's an alarm."

"Alarms can be defeated. Any security can be bypassed. There's always a work-around."

Tess shook her head. "You would know."

"Yes. I would. Hungry?"

"Not especially."

"Neither am I. Let's try out the hotel restaurant anyway. It's not a good idea to let our blood sugar get low."

Westphalia was pork country, as they discovered when they perused the menu. Abby wasn't ordinarily real big on pork, but when in Rome and all that. She ordered roast pork served on kebabs with diced potatoes and vegetables in a pleasing sauce. Tess ordered the same. Their waiter recommended a white wine, but they demurred, needing to keep their heads clear. They drank ice water instead. The waiter seemed miffed.

After dinner they returned to their rooms and changed into dark clothes. Abby opened the package and took out two 9mm semiautomatics with spare maga-

zines. The guns had been obtained from a black-market
supplier and could not be traced. It would have been
risky to put them in the checked baggage. Sometimes
those bags were X-rayed.

She let Tess select a weapon. Not surprisingly, she
picked the SIG Sauer, similar to her Bureau-issue model.
It was always a good idea to stick with a familiar
weapon. Abby took the other gun, a Ruger. She had no
preference. She could handle any firearm.

In silence they loaded the pistols. Then there was
nothing to do but wait for nightfall.

"So this is how it feels to be you," Tess said.

"Come again?"

"Working a mission under an assumed name, using an
untraceable gun. No legalities. No rules."

Abby smiled. "Pretty cool, huh?"

Tess didn't answer.

Her silence troubled Abby. "Hey. We're not having
second thoughts, are we?"

"Don't worry about me. I'm in for the duration."

"That's good. 'Cause there's no turning back now."

Tess wondered how many years it had been since
she'd prayed the rosary. She did it tonight, guiltily,
sneaking out the beads when she was alone in her room.
She prayed for forgiveness for what she was about to
do. She prayed that she was not endangering her immortal soul.

But even if she was, she would do it anyway.

When darkness fell, they donned coats against the
night's chill, then left the inn and drove into the forest.
Two miles from the villa, Abby killed the headlights and
steered by moonlight. After another mile she pulled into
a turnout and parked the car.

"On foot from here," she said.

Tess didn't argue. Abby was running this show. She
got out of the car and started toward the road.

"Not that way," Abby whispered. "Through the woods."

"You expect him to be watching the road?"

"No. But it's always what you *don't* expect that trips you up."

They navigated the forest, sometimes finding deer trails, other times simply pushing through the dense underbrush. Tall trees rose up around them, the branches interlaced to form a high, rustling canopy. A ground cover of mist began to curl around their ankles.

In the mist and moonlight, strange rock formations slid into view, an eruption of limestone shapes. Tess thought of Stonehenge. Of druids and spells. Witchcraft.

There was evil here. The thought came to her suddenly. A malignancy, a foulness in the creeping fog, the malformed rocks, the encroaching trees.

Abby seemed to read her thoughts—or more likely, her body language. "Not a great spot for a picnic," she said mildly.

"No. It really isn't. It feels like"—words failed her—"something bad," Tess finished lamely.

"Memories, maybe. If a place can hold memories. And I think some places can."

"Memories of what?"

"You didn't read up on the local history, did you? There was a labor camp in these woods during World War Two. Most of the prisoners were worked to death."

"I didn't know that," Tess said softly.

"It was Himmler's idea. He needed them to renovate the local castle, the one on the hill. It was going to be his Camelot. A spiritual retreat for his knights of the SS. They would come there for training and indoctrination. And for, you know, pagan rites."

Tess shivered. The forest, enticing by day, was a different world in the darkness. A place of pain and death, old secrets, unspoken crimes.

She knew people who had traveled to Sedona, Ari-

zona, convinced that the spot was a nexus of mystic ener-
gies. She doubted it. But this place, in the bone white
moonlight, might indeed be the meeting point of occult
forces, not the benevolent kind imagined by Gaia wor-
shipers, but something colder, grimmer, darker. Something that had drawn Himmler to this spot.

And not only Himmler . . .

"Faust is here," she said suddenly. "I know he is. It's
where he has to be."

Abby nodded. She knew it, too.

52

The only light in the study was a green-shaded banker's lamp, casting its pale glow over the clippings on the desk. Faust leaned forward, into the small circle of light, and pasted another article into the scrapbook.

This article had run in today's edition of the *Los Angeles Times*. He had found it on the Internet and printed it out, here in this study. Marvelous resource, the Internet. With it, he had been able to follow the news coverage of his escape from justice in satisfying detail.

The scrapbook was an empty one he had found in the house and appropriated, just as he had appropriated a set of clothes from the closet to replace his pajamas and robe. The outfit was tolerably comfortable, a bit loose at the waist and narrow at the shoulders, but it would serve. It would have to serve. He could hardly go shopping. Since his arrival, he had not set foot outside the house, and he did not plan to do so for some time.

Thus the scrapbook. He must keep himself occupied.

He could not complain. By all rights he ought to be in a prison cell in California, and he would have been, had he not placed a pay-telephone call to Piers Hoagland, waking him with an urgent demand for help. It had taken Hoagland only two hours to make the necessary preparations for his plane's unscheduled departure from Santa Monica. Hoagland himself had driven Faust to the airfield, after meeting him at the prearranged rendezvous point. Neither man could fly a plane, but Hoagland em-

ployed a pilot who was discreet and well paid, and who
had flown Faust around the western states, asking no
questions. All Hoagland had ever requested in return
were the skulls, defleshed in boiling water and ready to
be used in his art. The arrangement had been mutually
satisfactory. Hoagland obtained his models, and Faust
had the pleasure of putting his victims on public display.

Hoagland had not accompanied Faust on the flight. It
would have been suspicious if he had left town while his
exhibit at the art gallery was still in progress. The pilot
had flown Faust to a private airfield in Maryland, then
to another landing strip outside Büren. Hoagland kept a
car there. Faust had driven himself to the villa, following
directions he had memorized.

The large freezer was well stocked, and the shelves of
the study were lined with diverting books. He would not
perish either of starvation or of boredom. And he had
his scrapbook, of course.

The old one would be in the possession of the authorities now. He disliked the idea of some officious detective
thumbing through those well-loved pages. Worse was the
thought of his collection, his beauties—the graceful
hands in their formalin baths—reduced to the status of
evidence, labeled and stored away with the other detritus
of crime.

But he would start a new collection. It was difficult to
begin again in middle age, but he was strong. He would
do it.

Already he had filled ten pages of his new scrapbook.
There were articles on Raven, whose real name, he had
learned, was Jennifer Gaitlin. There were photos of
Elise, and photos of himself, and artists' conceptions of
how he might look under a variety of disguises. In actu-
ality he had not altered his appearance at all. There
would be a need for that later.

For the time being he must lie low. That was all right.
He liked this place. In the stillness of these woods at
night, he could almost believe he was a boy camping in

the Black Forest, when a wolf in the moonlight had shown him his destiny.

But he would not hide forever. The public's curiosity would inevitably prove short-lived. In days or weeks the news stories would fade away, and his photo would no longer shout for attention from every newspaper. Then he would reemerge. He would travel. He would reinvent himself.

Not in the United States, nor in Germany. He was far too well-known in both locales. He thought he would head east, into the Slavic countries of the former USSR. A man could do well in that region—a man with the proper qualities of ruthlessness and daring.

He would have a new identity, new papers. Money could buy him those things, and he knew people who could provide them. His money, protected from lawsuits in Swiss banks, was not altogether lost to him. Some accounts were undoubtedly compromised and frozen; even the Swiss must cooperate in an international manhunt. But there were others, less easily traced, that would remain intact.

With money, documentation, and a minor change of appearance, he would be a new man. He might not succeed in remaining at large forever. Even if he were eventually caught, he would have claimed more victims and extended his already considerable résumé.

The most intriguing question still to be decided was that of revenge. There were people in the United States whom he would like to visit. Two women in particular who deserved his vengeance. He would very much like to see them again.

And then he did.

The door to his study swung wide, and they were in the doorway, holding guns, trained on him.

He sat unmoving for a long moment before he raised his hands. He was cornered, unarmed. He had no illusions about fighting back.

"*Willkommen,*" he said with a slow smile. "You have

my congratulations. You have tracked the beast to his lair."

They did not answer. They stepped into the room, separating to cover him from different angles. He admired their efficiency, their stealth. He did not even bother to ask how they had gained entrance to the house, defeating Hoagland's expensive security system. Sinclair would have handled that. She had a burglar's skills.

"May I ask what has become of Elise? The news reports are unclear. I am concerned that she may be charged as my accomplice, which would be most unjust."

"She won't be charged." It was Tess who spoke. "She says she didn't know about the room, and I believe her."

"That is good. I had not wanted to think of her in prison. She never would have survived such an ordeal." He lifted his eyebrows in the equivalent of a shrug. "I do not know why I care about her. But I find that I do."

"Love's funny that way," Abby said. She was not smiling. Neither of them was smiling. Their faces were grim, aloof.

"I suppose it is. I honestly would not know." Faust pushed back his chair and prepared to rise. "You will arrest me now?"

Abby shook her head. "Not this time."

He looked at her, then at Tess. He saw how it was going to be.

"I see," he said softly.

Until this moment he had visualized handcuffs, extradition, a trial, a cell. Now he knew that there would be none of that.

He felt cold suddenly. It lasted only a second. Then he mastered himself. He would not quail in fear. He was the Werewolf. He was Peter Faust.

There was one last decision to make. He could die sitting down or on his feet. He chose to stand. His knees did not buckle, nor did his hands tremble as he lowered them to his sides.

"So you *are* a jungle cat," he told Abby Sinclair. "And you"—his gaze traveled to Tess McCallum—"you are a killer of killers, just as I thought."

Abby nodded, and Tess said, "That's right," her voice low and hard and without apology.

Faust smiled. "I knew I had not misjudged you."

He shut his eyes. He listened to the beat of his heart. He waited. But not for long.

The two women fired together, the gunshots blending as one, echoing in the dark German night.

Author's Note

Tess and Abby have previously teamed up in *Dangerous Games* and *Mortal Faults*. Tess appeared separately in *Next Victim*, and Abby was introduced in *The Shadow Hunter*.

Many thanks to all the people who made it possible for me to write *Final Sins*: my agent, Jane Dystel of Dystel & Goderich Literary Management; her partner at the agency, Miriam Goderich; Tracy Bernstein, executive editor at New American Library; my friend Rene in Holland, who told me about the real-life case of a Japanese serial killer who became a celebrity; and fellow Arizona novelist Margaret Falk, who was always there with moral support. The idea of Tess's obsession with Adolf Hitler's demonic aspects was prompted by James Hillman's fine book *The Soul's Code*—specifically the chapter titled "The Bad Seed."

Readers are invited to visit me at michaelprescott.net, where you'll find information on all nine of my books, as well as interviews, essays, and a link to my blog.

About the Author

Michael Prescott is the *New York Times* bestselling author of several novels. You can contact him at his Web site at www.michaelprescott.net

New York Times bestselling author
Michael Prescott

MORTAL FAULTS

A one-woman private operative, Abby Sinclair stalks the stalkers. Her new client is a U.S. congressman shadowed by a mystery woman believed to be a disgruntled ex-employee. He wants her stopped. What Abby doesn't know is that FBI agent Tess McCallum is already on the case. Now, despite vowing never to work together again, Abby and Tess have been partnered in a deadly game. And this is a case that takes one surprising turn after another—because there's more to the story than anyone knows.

0-451-41204-4

Available wherever books are sold or at
penguin.com